C000273706

ANNA SAYBURN LANE

Unlawful Things

Copyright © Anna Sayburn Lane, 2018

All rights reserved. No part of this publication may be reproduced, stored or transmitted in any form or by any means, electronic, mechanical, photocopying, recording, scanning, or otherwise without written permission from the publisher. It is illegal to copy this book, post it to a website, or distribute it by any other means without permission.

Anna Sayburn Lane asserts the moral right to be identified as the author of this work.

This novel is entirely a work of fiction. The names, characters and incidents portrayed within it are the work of the author's imagination. With the exception of characters and events in the historical record, any resemblance to actual persons or events is entirely coincidental.

First edition

ISBN: 978-1-9164208-0-9

This book was professionally typeset on Reedsy.
Find out more at reedsy.com

For Philip

Preface

At first, he thought he'd been punched. A dull thud, low in his back. He spun around as hands yanked at his jacket, scrabbled for the inside pocket. He'd hidden the book just in time. The man yelled in his face, demanded to know where it was.

He pushed back, fingers jabbing for his attacker's eyes. With tremendous effort, he broke free of the man's grasp, staggered towards the road and tried to shout for help, his voice ragged in his ears. But his legs felt heavy and unreliable, as if he were wading through water.

His assailant was gone, a shadow dissolved into the dark of the churchyard. He tried to get his breath. It was cold. His heart began to thump faster, a panicky, urgent rhythm that told him something was wrong. Really, properly wrong. He fumbled to loosen the tie that constricted his throat. He needed help. There were lights close by: a London pub. He stumbled to the door and pushed his way in. It smelled of warm beer. A handful of men looked up.

'Shit! You're bleeding, mate.' A man with wide eyes, staring at the floor beneath his feet.

His trousers were soaked through, he realised, sticking to the back of his thighs. He brought his hand round from the ache in his back, held it before his eyes; it was gloved in red. A million flies buzzed in his ears as he struggled to make sense of what he could see. The glare hurt after the dark churchyard.

The world lurched.

He fought to stay conscious as hands helped him into a chair. Voices were raised, calling for someone to ring a bloody ambulance, there's a bloke here's been stabbed. A woman emerged from the wall of bodies and pressed a cloth against his side. The buzzing was so loud now, he couldn't hear the words coming from her pale lips. She was trying to help. Surely someone would know what to do, someone could stop this. He looked down, saw a dark pool around the chair. *Oh, Christ.*

He didn't have much time. He needed to tell someone. He reached out, saw the woman recoil as he smeared crimson onto her white T-shirt.

'Cut,' he said. 'Cut is...' His chest heaved and his mouth filled. He leaned forward and spat. A string of bloody mucus hit the floor, splashed onto work boots and trainers. He looked up at the woman, apologetic. He searched her face for a sign of compassion. She was young and frightened. Tears started in his eyes.

He wiped his mouth on his sleeve. 'Cut is the branch,' he said. 'Tell her. Cut is the branch...'

He felt pressure building in his chest. If only he could get his breath. But he knew, now. His mind fixed for a second on another woman's face, troubled and uncertain, sweet. *Is this the face?* he thought, words swimming through his brain. *Was that the face?*

The smell of booze and sweat receded. A Deptford pub, he thought. How very appropriate. He wanted to laugh. The laugh became a cough, and then the blood came.

Chapter 1

Two weeks previously

H elen Oddfellow wanted a hot shower, a large gin and an early night. She'd spent the day tramping through London drizzle, trying to entertain the tourists who'd booked onto her historical walking tour, despite the miserable weather. On a good day, she had the best job in the world. This was not a good day.

Shopping bags cut into her wrists as she juggled with her keys outside the tall Victorian house at the corner of the street. With relief, she slammed the door and dumped the groceries in the hall.

'Oh, God.' Pinned to the wall, above the table where the house's residents left the mail, was a newspaper's double-page spread. Her photograph gazed back at her, blown up across three columns of text. The photographer had caught her mid-sentence, hair whipping across her earnest face, the river in the background. *They might have used one of me smiling*, she thought.

'Walking through Deptford's deadly past,' said the headline. She detached the pages from the wall, sat on the stairs and began to read.

The piece wasn't bad, she supposed. She'd been anxious when her boss at Capital Walks had asked her to take a local journalist along on a tour. The reporter had been cocky and flirtatious, a young lad with short, neat dreadlocks who seemed barely old enough to have left school. But he'd been full of questions, scribbling in his notebook as they walked the south Thames riverside, where a line of handsome Georgian buildings marked the former royal dockyard at Deptford.

She'd told him about the ship-building industry that had once animated the place, building the boats that saw off the Spanish Armada. It was on Deptford Strand that Queen Elizabeth I knighted Francis Drake, on board the Golden Hind. And a few years later, the notorious Elizabethan playwright Christopher Marlowe was stabbed to death along the same stretch of water.

The reporter had seized gleefully on the Marlowe story, relating in the article the gory details of the four-hundred-year-old murder. Marlowe was stabbed through the eye with his own dagger, supposedly turned back on him when he started a brawl after a boozy dinner. Helen had absolutely denied that his ghost had been seen haunting the place where he died. 'Go on,' the reporter had urged her. 'The readers love a ghost story.'

But she was deep in work for her doctorate on the play-wright and took Marlowe too seriously to make up stories. To her surprise, the article mentioned her PhD research: an attempt to establish the disputed chronology of Marlowe's plays through close textual analysis. 'Helen's dream is to discover a lost Marlowe play,' the article concluded. She frowned. She didn't remember saying that.

At the bottom of the stairs to the basement flat, a door creaked open. A bald head poked out, then a skinny neck adorned with a yellow silk cravat craned around the door. He looked like a tortoise coming out of its shell. A very dapper tortoise.

'Is that you, sweetheart? Come and have a drink to celebrate your celebrity. I got you a copy.'

Crispin Day was a retired actor. His career had never gone beyond touring with a repertory company and occasional spear-holding in the West End, but he was full of salacious gossip about thespian greats from the past. Helen suspected most of his stories were wishful thinking. But since she'd moved to the house two years ago, he'd become one of her best friends. He'd been kind to her, and she'd been much in need of kindness.

'Won't be a tick. Got to get the shopping in the fridge. But I'd love a G and T. Isn't the photo awful?'

'It's gorgeous, and you know it. Bring me a lemon, will you?'

She lugged her bags up the four flights of stairs to the attic. Helen loved her tiny apartment, up above the trees with an expansive view over Greenwich, but it had its drawbacks. As she reached the landing, she could hear her home phone ringing. She grabbed the receiver just before the answerphone clicked in.

'May I speak to Helen Oddfellow? The Marlowe researcher?' The man's voice was old-fashioned, courteous. The sort of voice, she thought, you heard on old British films, intoning 'Whitehall two-five-oh' into Bakelite telephones.

She wondered for a minute if this was one of her colleagues, winding her up. Several of them were actors, with a talent for mimicry.

'Who's calling?'

'My name is Richard Watson. I'm a historian at Kent University. I read about you in the newspaper and wondered if you could spare me some time?'

She frowned. The number given in the newspaper was for the Capital Walks office, not her home phone.

'How did you get my number?'

'Directory enquiries. It's an unusual name.'

Who still used directory enquiries? But she supposed it was true. Helen had endured thirty years of comments about her surname, exacerbated by the fact that she'd attended the school where her father taught. There was no pretending she wasn't related to the eccentric beanpole of a head teacher, especially when she turned twelve and started growing with startling speed, not stopping until she stood six foot tall. Neither experience had made school much fun.

'Right. How can I help you?' She didn't much like the idea of meeting a stranger who had looked her up after seeing her photo in the newspaper.

'It's rather complicated. I've come across a certain reference – more of a hint, really – in some trial papers from the early seventeenth century. A treason trial. I think the reference may be to Christopher Marlowe, or his work. But it's not clear, and I don't know the plays well enough. It could be important.' Helen let the pause stretch.

'I don't blame you for being suspicious. I should have gone through your office. I did try, but it was closed. Could I perhaps buy you a coffee, show you what I'm working on?

4

How about tomorrow?'

Helen was about to refuse – Saturday was always a busy working day – but she was intrigued by the mysterious trial papers.

'I'm doing a walk on the South Bank tomorrow,' she said. 'Shakespeare's London, with a sprinkling of Marlowe. It finishes at the Globe. Do you want to meet me afterwards?'

'Could I join you for the walk? It sounds great.'

Helen decanted the groceries in the tiny kitchen, wondering if she should have told him to get lost. But there was no reason why he shouldn't join her walk, so long as he coughed up a tenner. She pulled the blue-and-white checked curtains and selected a frozen pizza. She was too tired to think about cooking.

He'd sounded harmless enough: an elderly academic with a bee in his bonnet, no doubt. She'd met plenty of those. She headed back down the stairs. No doubt her mother would have warned her against meeting strange men, but then her mother had warned her against most things.

* * *

'You forgot the lemon.'

'Damn. Sorry, Crispin. Please don't make me go up those stairs again.' She flopped into a faded orange armchair while he fiddled with ice cubes. Opaline tropical fish flitted around the wall-mounted fish tank, while the television chuntered away in the background. Helen had never seen it switched off. She took her drink, ice melting rapidly in the stuffy room.

'What's up?'

'Hmm? Oh, nothing. Strange phone call from some bloke

who'd seen me in the paper. That's a very fine cravat.'

He smirked. 'A gift from an admirer, during a gruesome tour of the provinces with *Private Lives*. I used it to strangle the horrible woman playing Amanda.'

He passed her a copy of the newspaper. 'Here. I do like that red coat, darling. It makes you look like a guardsman.' Helen re-read the article while Crispin launched into wistful memories of nocturnal encounters with soldiers barracked opposite St James's Park.

She wondered what had attracted the attention of her caller. The reporter had said she was a 'Marlowe expert', which was pushing it a bit. She hoped her PhD supervisor wouldn't see it. He was a remote, cerebral man with an almost-international reputation, who informed Helen that most of her research would involve double-checking the work of previous scholars.

An outburst from Crispin caught her attention. He was glaring at the television.

'That man's a menace. They should deny him the oxygen of publicity. Better still, the oxygen of oxygen.'

On screen was a pleasant-looking man in his thirties, smiling at the glossy chat show host next to him on the sofa. She took a minute to place him. With his plump, pink-and-white face and curly brown hair, he looked like an overgrown schoolboy.

Father Francis Nash, she remembered: a Church of England vicar who seemed to be all over the media at the moment. He leaned forward, his face serious, as the host trotted out a string of statistics about falling church congregations and a marked drop in the numbers of people identifying themselves as Christian.

'There has indeed been a fall in people finding comfort in our church,' he agreed, his voice mild. 'And I find that very sad. Perhaps it is no surprise that we have also seen a rise in the numbers of people suffering from depression, anxiety and loneliness.'

Helen wondered. Her own Sunday school Christianity had fallen away as she grew up. She knew plenty about depression and loneliness, but she'd not been tempted to return to the church as a result.

'Statistics aren't everything. I could tell you plenty of stories of people who have found the church an invaluable refuge during dark times. Starting with myself,' he said.

The chat show audience burst into applause. The camera panned out, showing the other guests on the sofa – a grumpy scientist known for his atheist views, and a man in white Islamic robes.

'And that's why I feel so strongly that all children in this country should learn about our Christian heritage, the shared Christian values that shaped our nation. How can children understand the world without at least knowing about the beliefs that underlie our laws?' he asked.

The man in white broke in. 'And that's what I want for Muslim children – Islamic schools which teach them our heritage, our laws.'

Father Nash shook his head, sadly. 'I have the greatest respect for Islam,' he began. 'But must we really separate our children on religious grounds? Does this not risk creating suspicion? Even, although I know this is far from my friend's intention, dangerous radicalism?'

The imam looked outraged. 'But you want more Christian schools—' he began.

Father Nash held up his hand. 'I want all our schools to teach traditional British values, to all our children, from every type of background.'

Crispin changed the channel. Father Nash was replaced by a woman with sparkly eyeshadow belting out a pop song.

'Why don't you like him?' Helen asked. 'He seemed to make some decent points.'

Crispin shivered theatrically. He did most things theatrically. 'Traditional British values like hypocrisy. I don't trust people who are convinced they're right,' he said. 'Give me woolly-minded liberals any day. They don't bother the rest of us. He campaigned against gay marriage, you know. Says it undermines the sacred nature of the institution. A bit rich, coming from an institution that's been buggering choirboys for centuries.'

Helen swirled the remaining gin around her glass. 'Did you ever want to get married?' She realised she'd always thought of him as single, never imagined him as part of a couple, shopping for furniture or planning holidays together.

'It wasn't thought of in my day, dear. We rather looked down on you breeders, with your mortgages and wedding anniversaries. I've never wanted to be part of an institution, sacred or otherwise.' He waved the bottle in her direction. 'Top-up?'

Chapter 2

Borough High Street heaved with humanity. A river of people flowed up the steps from the tube station and across the road to the ancient marketplace. Traders had sold fruit and vegetables on the south side of London Bridge for centuries, but the market had been spruced up in recent years. Now tourists and foodies flooded the covered halls, prepared to pay high prices for artisan cheese and the finest Spanish ham.

Helen scanned the crowds for anyone who might be the historian Richard Watson. He was late. She already had nine people waiting, huddled into doorways to shelter from the vicious March wind. Buttoned into her scarlet coat, Helen was warm enough, but she worried for the elderly Texan couple in their lightweight matching anoraks. Three Swedish students looked prepared for anything, but she could already hear complaints from the two Californian kids, moaning to their parents that they were cold. She decided to get started and raised her voice to carry over the clatter of traffic.

'Right, everyone! Welcome to the Borough, one of the oldest and most disreputable parts of London.'

She smiled at the children, hoping to get them on side. They didn't smile back.

'We're going to travel five hundred years back in time to the London of Queen Elizabeth I. The market was already here, but instead of talking about celebrities or football, people would be gossiping about the new Shakespeare play they'd seen at the Globe Theatre, or the money they'd won betting at the bear pit. Borough was at the heart of the Elizabethan entertainment industry. And we're going to start with a great London tradition – the pub. Follow me, and please try to keep together.' She turned smartly to her right and walked straight into a man's chest.

This was unusual. Because of her height, Helen tended to trip over people rather than walk into them. Gasping an apology, she looked up from the woollen overcoat. He'd taken her arm to steady her. His face was long, with hollow cheeks shadowed by stubble. He looked mournful, until a smile crinkled the corners of his deep-set eyes.

'Helen? I'm Richard. We spoke on the phone. Sorry I'm late. Train trouble. Can I join you?'

'Oh, yes, of course.' Flustered, she checked the rest of the group was still with her. 'We've just started.'

She led them down the street and through a pair of tall wooden gates into an enclosed courtyard, the quiet enveloping them after the clamour of the road.

Counting heads, she took a proper look at the latecomer. He was younger than she'd expected, maybe in his forties. His height made him ungainly, a lean scarecrow of a man with swept-back dark hair, greying at the temples. Yet he was attractive, in a dishevelled sort of way. She noticed his coat was frayed around the cuffs, and his brogues were worn. He stooped a little, leaning in to hear her words as she addressed the group. She felt self-conscious, like a schoolgirl reading an essay to a teacher. Her usual audience was tourists, not professional historians. She did hope he wouldn't point out her mistakes.

'The George Inn is known as Shakespeare's local,' she told them, stretching the truth a little. It was perfectly feasible that the playwright had visited the venerable pub, although there was no hard proof. Helen had quickly learnt that his was the name that everyone wanted to hear on literary tours.

'There's been an inn here since at least the middle of the sixteenth century. The two great playhouses that showed Shakespeare's plays, the Rose and the Globe, were close by, so there's every chance the actors drank here,' she told them.

'Before the reign of Elizabeth, there were no purpose-built theatres. If you were a nobleman, you might see a play at court, by troupes of players summoned to entertain the royal household. But if you were a working man, your best chance of seeing theatre would have been somewhere like this – the courtyard of an inn.'

Helen gazed around the cobbled yard, overhung by wooden galleries. Empty of the city drinkers who thronged the place in the evening, it was easy to people it with the faces of the past.

'Imagine this place with horses stamping and snorting in the stables, carts rattling through the gates, porters rushing about. And then a troupe of travelling players, in bright costumes with clowns and musicians, setting up to perform right here, where we're standing. All the customers crowding around, guests coming out onto the galleries to watch. Throwing down flowers and money, or maybe rotten oranges if they didn't like the show.'

She had them now, she thought, seeing even the children

gaze up at the balustrades, as if expecting a rain of fruit. The elderly Texan lady took her husband's hand, eyes bright. The Californian woman was nodding, whispering to her husband that she'd studied this at college. Helen shot a glance at the historian. His eyes were fixed on her with a hint of appraisal that made her nervous.

From the George, it was a short walk to the courtyard of an even older inn, the Tabard in Talbot Yard. Sadly, nothing remained of the building but a blue memorial plaque, high on the wall of a boarded-up shop. Helen looked at the expectant faces.

'Byfel that in that sesoun on a day,

In Southwerk, at the Tabbard as I lay,

Redy to wenden on my pilgrimage

To Canterbury, with ful devout corage,' she recited.

The prologue to *The Canterbury Tales*, the first great poem written in the English language, by the medieval poet Geoffrey Chaucer.

'Does anyone recognise that?' she asked, then wished she hadn't. The Texan couple looked confused, and the Swedish students blank. The Californian mother frowned and chewed her lip. Then:

'Whan that Aprille with her shours swete

The droght of March hath perced to the root …'

The historian recited the prologue with ease. Helen gave herself over to the pleasure of hearing the words she loved spoken so fluently. Then she noticed the distinctly fed-up look on the face of the Californian woman.

'Thank you, sir. Quite right. It's by Geoffrey Chaucer, from *The Canterbury Tales*, written in the fourteenth century. And this is where the poem begins, as the pilgrims gather at the Tabard Inn before setting out to Canterbury together. The inn was demolished in the nineteenth century, but old photographs show it with upper galleries all the way around.'

Reaction was muted. Helen decided she'd drop this particular stop from the tour next time. Not enough to look at.

'Let's get on with our pilgrimage, then. We're going through Borough Market. The next stop is Southwark Cathedral, so if you do get separated, meet us by the entrance.'

The historian fell into step with her as they crossed the busy road and plunged into the crowds. 'They don't teach Chaucer in schools any more,' he told her. 'Did you know that? At the risk of sounding like a terrible old buffer, I think that's a shame.'

'Me too. I used to teach English, but Chaucer was considered too difficult, even at A-level. My dad would have been appalled,' she said. Her father had been the one to ignite her own love of literature, declaiming great swathes of poetry on country walks as Helen skipped to keep up.

'We should start a campaign. The middle classes for Middle English.' Laughing, he forged ahead, Helen following in the temporary path he had opened up. She wasn't sure what to make of him. Had he been showing off, reciting Chaucer? Or just coming to her rescue when none of the group responded? And now he was leading the way, taking her role. In most people, it would look like arrogance. But he clearly knew where he was going, and she rather liked not having to shove her way through the mass of people. *He wanted to consult me*, she reminded herself. She was the one in charge.

For centuries, she told the group, Southwark Cathedral was known as St Saviour's, the parish church for the mayhem that swirled around its walls. Its parishioners would have included prostitutes from the brothels of Rose Lane, actors, bear-keepers, ale-wives and breeders of fighting dogs. Shakespeare's brother was buried in the church and there was a memorial to the playwright in the nave. She waited in the garden as the tourists milled around inside. Richard Watson, the historian, was the first to exit.

'Are you booked up with history fans since the article in the paper?' he asked.

'No, not really. A few more calls to the office, so they're pleased. And a couple of local schools want to come.'

'I'm surprised you've not had more. It sounded so intriguing. And, of course, the photo …' She felt her cheeks flush to match her red coat. Was he flirting with her?

'You mentioned Marlowe?' She steered the conversation back to the impersonal. 'We're just around the corner from the site of the Rose Theatre. His plays were staged there often – *Doctor Faustus*, *The Jew of Malta*, *The Massacre at Paris*. I hope you'll find it interesting.'

His face grew serious at the playwright's name. 'Indeed. I'm sure I will. How did you first come to study Marlowe?'

Helen felt the rush of pleasure she always got from talking about her literary hero. 'I was in a production of *Edward the Second* at university. It was a tiny part, but I was hooked immediately. His work is just astonishing,' she said. 'He revolutionised English theatre. He was such a trailblazer. And to have done so much, in such a short career. It makes me feel a bit hopeless – he was younger than me when he died.'

'And you haven't revolutionised English theatre yet? You've been slacking.' His smile was teasing.

14

She laughed, ticking Marlowe's achievements off on her fingers. 'Seven plays, still performed four hundred years after his death, several of them as fine as anything Shakespeare wrote. Three major poems. The introduction of a new verse form, and the invention of the history play. If Shakespeare hadn't been born at the same time, Marlowe would be seen as our greatest playwright. I suppose I feel a bit sad that he gets overlooked.' She paused, realising she had been ranting. 'Sorry. I get carried away.'

'Not at all.' Richard's eyes were warm. 'I think I came to the right person. If you can't be passionate about your work, you're in the wrong job.'

Remembering that she was, indeed, in the middle of a job, Helen turned in time to see the group of tourists emerge from the cathedral. The Californian father rushed back from the market, cradling a bag of expensive donuts. 'I figured it would cheer the kids up,' he whispered to her, apologetically. Helen sympathised. It was always a challenge to keep children entertained on the literary walks. 'Try the Jack the Ripper tour next time,' she advised.

The two great Elizabethan playhouses were situated within a hundred yards of each other. 'You can imagine the rivalry between the two,' said Helen. 'The Rose was the first, built in 1587. Its greatest hits included the major plays of Christopher Marlowe, and Shakespeare's earliest work. But when the Globe was built ten years later, Shakespeare became its lead playwright. It was so successful that it forced the closure of the Rose.'

There was nothing to see at the site of the Globe, apart from a few explanatory noticeboards. But Helen beckoned them through an unpromising doorway into the riverside office block that had risen above the Rose.

They stood on a boardwalk above a pit. The place was cold and dank. A line of red lights on the floor marked the theatre's foundations, uncovered when the site was excavated. The riverside site was half-submerged in water, which reflected back the lights and created a weirdly echoing acoustic. Helen smiled at the Texan woman, who was peering uncertainly into the gloom.

'We're standing where it all began,' she said, her voice soft. 'The "wooden O" of the Elizabethan playhouse, encircling us with its magic, cramming battles and triumphs, love affairs and tragedies within this little space. Imagine coming here, leaving your everyday life outside, for the world premiere of a play by a daring new playwright. Standing in this place as Tamburlaine the Great vows to conquer the world, or Doctor Faustus summons up the devil.'

They stood in silence for a second. Helen felt a shiver run over her skin, as if one of those long-dead actors had passed right through her. 'I don't like it,' muttered one of the Californian children.

The group filed back outside.

'How do you know so much about the place? I mean, the plays that were staged and so on. What sort of records are there?' Richard's tone was casual, but this was a historian's question.

'The diary of the Rose's owner, Philip Henslowe. It still exists. He kept all sorts of accounts from the building of the Rose, right down to how much he paid for the nails. He records what played when and how much money each production took. It's a fascinating document.' Helen had spent many hours poring over Henslowe's scribbled notes, trying to make sense of his abbreviations and eccentric spelling.

He nodded. 'Good. That sounds like the sort of archive I need.'

The tour was coming to an end. Helen delivered the group to the gates of the modern reconstruction of Shakespeare's Globe, sitting on the riverside a hundred yards from the original site. Its white walls, massive oak beams and thatched roof lifted her heart. The place was an anachronism, a space capsule beamed down amid the shiny glass buildings of the modern city.

The Texan couple had tickets for the matinee performance of *Julius Caesar*. They took it in turns to shake her hand, the man pressing an additional ten-pound note on her. 'It was worth every penny,' said his wife. 'I'll appreciate the show all the more.'

The Californian kids were already dragging their mother away as their father handed over the money. The students waved their farewells, heading for more culture at the Tate Modern. Helen was left alone with the historian.

'So,' he said. 'Your dream is to discover a lost Marlowe play. I think I've found something that might interest you.'

Chapter 3

Nick Wilson, senior reporter on the *South London Courier*, ducked as another bottle went flying over his head and smashed against the wall behind him. This wasn't how the day was supposed to go.

He had been sent to cover the opening of a new mosque in East Greenwich, expecting a boring ribbon-cutting ceremony with interminable speeches from the mayor and various community leaders. But just before he left, he'd been tipped off about an unofficial anti-Islam demonstration. 'It could get lively,' said his informant, who had not given his name.

There had been disquiet in the predominantly white neighbourhood about the new mosque since the planning application first went in, much of it expressed in the comments section on the *Courier's* website. Some had been expressed in uglier fashion, through smashed windows and swastikas sprayed on the walls of the new building. The police had dismissed it as bored kids. Nick hadn't been so sure.

The police might have to think again. A mob of white guys whooped through the streets, engaged in running battles with a group of Asian men. A handful of panicky coppers, batons drawn, clustered around the mosque entrance.

'Come and fight on our side,' roared the mob to the police,

who came under a renewed hail of bottles. Nick saw a police car being rocked then overturned onto its roof. The crowd cheered and swarmed over it, on to the next target.

The violence seemed to have taken the authorities by surprise. When Nick had arrived at the mosque, there had been just a couple of community police officers outside. Some Asian men had been standing by the front door, under the optimistic mission statement: 'Respect for all, peace to all'. Nick knew the mosque's imam, having interviewed him about the swastika incident. He'd gone to say hello. Then a group of white men had arrived, positioned themselves across the road, and hoisted placards onto their shoulders.

He'd known they were trouble as soon as he saw the slogans. 'England First,' they read. 'No More Mosques.' One guy wore a T-shirt proclaiming 'Death to Islam'.

More men had arrived, ugly great blokes with shaven heads and thick necks. Some carried the red-and-white flag of Saint George to complement their England football shirts. One tall, skinny guy in combat trousers wore a balaclava. The chanting began.

Growing up half-black and half-Irish in Liverpool, Nick had learnt to avoid their sort or risk a beating. But he was in London now, and a reporter. He had no choice but to follow the story.

He took a deep breath and headed across the road. The crowd had started with monkey noises, hooting and cackling. A flush of anger propelled him up to them. He waved his press card. 'I'm from the *Courier*,' he called over the noise. 'Any of you lot want to tell me what's going on?'

'Give him a banana!' the guy in the balaclava yelled.

Nick swallowed his rage. 'That's what you want in the

paper, is it? A bunch of racists came out to shout at people, but no one knows why?' He never could leave trouble alone, as his brother was always telling him. But this time his bravado paid off.

'Shut it, you morons,' yelled a guy in sweatpants and a tight khaki T-shirt. The crowd quietened surprisingly fast and let him through to the front. 'Sorry about that,' he said. 'I organised the protest. What do you want to know?'

The man looked ex-army, with military-style tats of daggers on his muscle-bound forearms. Neat brown hair and hazel eyes: good-looking in a brutal kind of way. He looked too sane to be caught up in this sort of rubbish.

'What's this all about?' Nick asked again. 'What's with your racist mates?'

The man pushed his hands through his hair. 'This has nothing to do with race. The English Martyrs Brigade defend English communities. And we don't need another mosque.'

Nick snorted in disbelief. English martyrs. Another bunch of white guys feeling sorry for themselves.

'It's about extremism. You should cover that in your paper. We don't want those radical preachers, turning the local Muslim kids into terrorists. Bringing in Sharia law and all that.'

Nick gestured to the thugs behind them. 'Some of your friends don't seem to have got the message that it's not a racial thing,' he said. They were still making monkey gestures, seeming not to tire of the infantile insults. 'Are you not worried that you're stirring up trouble, antagonising the Muslim community like this?'

More Asian men were arriving all the time, lining up in front of the mosque. As if they'd heard him, a crowd of maybe twenty Asian guys walked straight up to the protesters, ignoring the barrage of abuse.

'Go home, please,' said one young Asian man, his face sombre. 'You've made your point. You are not welcome here.'

The man Nick had been talking to looked incredulous. 'This is my home,' he said, jabbing a finger. 'You don't get to decide where I'm welcome.'

The noise level had risen, shouts and accusations from both sides. Glancing across the road, Nick had seen the police finally rouse themselves. One officer had started to jog over towards them, hands raised. With perfect timing, the mayor's limousine had swept around the corner, the little flag on the front fluttering in the breeze. The mayor had disembarked to shake hands with the imam as the police bunched around the car.

A placard flew through the air, the wooden handle catching a Muslim teenager on the shoulder. The kid grabbed a protester by his camouflage jacket. A white fist crunched into a bearded jaw. And then the white guys pulled on balaclavas. The air was suddenly full of the sound of smashing glass, bottles pulled from backpacks and broken against the wall to use as weapons. They'd been prepared for this, Nick realised. The man supposedly in charge had disappeared, lost in the mass of bodies. Nick felt a gob of saliva land on his neck. A hand grabbed his shoulder. He yanked himself free, raced back across the road. He wanted to watch the action, not participate.

The police hustled the dignitaries into the mosque and formed a chain across the door. Nick counted. There were eight of them, far too few to control the situation, let alone break up the fighting. 'Tell them to get over here now, as many

21

vans as they have,' yelled one copper into his radio. 'And get some ambulances on standby.'

He saw the policeman stagger back across the road, clutching his cheek. Blood oozed between his fingers. Nick grabbed his mobile and started taking photos. The photographer, running late, had yet to arrive. He grinned, realising he'd have the front-page story and photo this week. No contest.

From a distance, he could see that someone was directing operations. The white guys attacked in waves, didn't let themselves get separated, moved as one. The Asian lads were taking a beating. Nick saw a bare-chested figure, head covered with a khaki T-shirt, standing on a wall, yelling and gesturing like a football manager on the sidelines. The guy he'd been talking to, he realised, was orchestrating the violence. He grabbed the arm of one of the younger white lads. 'Who's that? Up on the wall?'

The boy grinned through his balaclava. 'That's Paxton,' he said. 'He's the boss.' Then he was lost in the whirl.

Nick saw the young guy who'd confronted the protesters earlier punched to the ground. The crowd seethed around him as he fell.

He heard sirens and checked his watch. It had been more than fifteen minutes since the violence began. He'd have questions for the police tomorrow about their planning for the event. He wondered if they'd had the same tip-off that he'd had. It didn't look like it.

There were fewer men fighting now. He realised the guy on the wall – Paxton – was calling them off. They were separating, running down side streets and throwing their weapons away. Nick saw the Asian man who'd been surrounded lying horribly still on the ground. Three thugs lingered, aiming kicks at his head. *I can't watch this.*

He ran towards them. They scattered, laughing. Nick crouched down among shards of broken glass. The man's face was mashed, his eye swollen and bleeding. His lip was cut through. Nick tried to remember from TV programmes what you were meant to do. *Breathing*, he thought. He put a hand on the man's chest. Was he breathing?

Something smashed into the back of his head and he blacked out. When he opened his eyes, the tarmac was inches away. Someone was digging in his pocket.

'You won't need this,' hissed a voice. His phone, Nick realised, through the roaring in his head. The bastards had taken his phone.

Chapter 4

Helen raised her eyebrows at the historian, in the hope of conveying severity. 'You're not going to tell me Marlowe faked his own death and wrote all Shakespeare's plays, are you?' This story, known as the Marlovian theory, had been doing the rounds for decades, and she was heartily sick of it. 'Because I should tell you now that I've read all the so-called evidence and I don't believe it for a minute.'

Richard laughed, a burst of merriment that seemed at odds with his sober face. 'Absolutely not. And if I was, I wouldn't dare now.'

'Sorry. It's just that I get that a lot. As does anyone who works on Marlowe. My PhD supervisor goes puce at the mention of Shakespeare.'

They leaned together on the railing. Across the water, the pewter dome of St Paul's Cathedral gleamed in a shaft of afternoon sun, against a backcloth of leaden cloud.

'To be honest, I've never even heard that theory before. I don't know much about literary history.'

She wondered how true that was. 'You know Chaucer.'

'I know the prologue to *The Canterbury Tales*. But so did everyone when I went to school. I did O-levels, you know,' he said, in a stage whisper. 'That's how old I am.' Helen smiled, pulling her coat tighter around her. The day had grown increasingly chilly. He noticed.

'It's freezing, and I promised you coffee. Come on, let's find somewhere warm and I can fill you in on the background.' He offered her his arm, an intimate and old-fashioned gesture. Discomfited, Helen pretended not to notice.

'There's a cafe down this side street. I often use it. And I'd prefer tea.'

She led the way to a corner table. When their drinks arrived, she warmed her hands around her mug and stretched out her legs.

'Go on, then. Tell me all about it. I promise not to get stroppy.'

He steepled his fingers and gazed at the ceiling for a moment. His deep-set eyes were the exact same colour as the Thames, Helen thought – a greenish-grey that changed with the light. She wondered if he'd been hurt when she didn't take his arm.

'Let me tell you a bit about my involvement. As I said, I'm a historian. I go down to Canterbury a couple of times a week to lecture at the university. Ecclesiastical history and the Reformation is my specialism.

'Shortly before Christmas, I started doing some private work for a client who wants to write her family history. She comes from a very old Kentish family, the Brookes of Cobham. Do you know Cobham Hall?'

The Elizabethan mansion was renowned as one of the best-preserved in Britain. 'I've heard of it. Isn't it National Trust?'

'Nope.' He grinned. 'My client owns it. Lady Joan Brooke de Cobham, still chairman of Brooke Estates at the age

25

of seventy-nine. It's the biggest landowning, mining and financial company you've never heard of.'

Helen raised her eyebrows. 'She's rich, then?'

'Extremely. But not happy.'

Lady Joan, he explained, was the sole descendant of a family who had come to England with William the Conqueror in 1066 and set about garnering wealth and power. By Elizabethan times, they had amassed vast estates in Kent and an array of lucrative appointments. Cobham Hall was rebuilt to impress the Queen, who visited several times. Then, with the family at the peak of their influence and grandeur, Elizabeth died.

'Catastrophe. Henry, Lord Cobham, had been Elizabeth's favourite. But he was accused of being involved in a plot to oust Elizabeth's successor, James I. He was sent to the Tower of London and lucky not to lose his head. Worse still, in Lady Joan's eyes, the estates and the title were confiscated by the Crown, and the descendants disinherited. The Brookes were turfed out of Cobham Hall, which was given to one of James's Scottish mates. The family spent the next three centuries trying to get it back.'

'And they succeeded?' Helen was starting to wonder where this was going.

'Eventually. Lady Joan's great-grandfather made a fortune in the East India Company, then bought up half of the Midlands. His son bought back the hall. But the point is that Lady Joan is convinced her Elizabethan ancestor was framed. The last Lord Cobham was tried and convicted alongside Sir Walter Raleigh.'

Helen sat up, expectant. The links between the famous adventurer and the playwright Christopher Marlowe had intrigued historians for years. 'Ah. The Marlowe connection?'

'Maybe. Raleigh had loads of enemies at court, and the only evidence against him was Lord Cobham's testimony. He only testified because he'd been wrongly told that Raleigh had accused him first. There's a transcript of the trial in the National Archives. It sounds like a stitch-up.' Richard paused, as if waiting for her reaction.

She was thinking about dates. 'But Marlowe was dead long before Elizabeth I died. How can he have had anything to do with it?'

He reached into his inner jacket pocket and pulled out a black, leather-bound notebook. It was the expensive sort, with a band to keep it closed. His long fingers snapped back the elastic and extracted a folded sheet of paper that had been tucked into the cover.

'The family has a roomful of documents at Cobham Hall,' he said. 'Some of them were catalogued by Lady Joan's grandfather, Albert Brooke. He spent years investigating the family's history. I've been going through the papers, especially those relating to the period in question. I found this. It's a transcript, not the original, in Albert Brooke's writing. He says it's a letter from Raleigh to Henry Cobham, sent while they were both awaiting trial.' He handed it to her. 'Read it.'

The elegant fountain pen script flowed across the page. Helen read the text aloud.

'My Lord, be of good chere, for I doubt much they will procede against us. I pray you to be watchful and do not admit priests to your rooms, for they will press you to confess. Admit nothing, my Lord, and nothing can be shewn against us. The chief concern of the King is poor merlins Canterbury booke, which displeases him much. I praye you to see to it.'

Helen's heart began to beat faster. Merlin. Canterbury. And a letter from Raleigh, potentially a friend or patron of Marlowe.

'What do you think? Who is poor Merlin?' Richard's eyes were bright now, and he jiggled his knees like a schoolboy.

She read the lines over again. 'It's possible,' she admitted, trying to keep her voice steady. 'Marlowe was sometimes referred to as Merlin, as I'm sure you know. There were various versions of his surname – Marly, Marlin, Marlowe. Merlin, on occasion. It was a bit of an in-joke because of the magic in *Doctor Faustus*.'

'And the Canterbury book?'

'Marlowe was born and grew up in Canterbury, but I don't remember anything in his plays or poems that refers to the place.' A tremor of excitement was building within her. 'In Henslowe's diary, he calls play scripts "books". It could mean a Canterbury play.'

'You said you wanted to find a missing Marlowe play…'

She shook her head, laughing. This was all too much. 'No, I didn't. Don't believe everything you read in the papers.' She took a gulp of tea and realised it had gone cold. 'Let's not get carried away. This is all conjecture. We don't know the letter actually refers to Marlowe. You've not even seen the original, Richard. This might be a forgery, or a mis-transcription.'

She examined the paper again. It was neatly headed with the words 'Copy of a letter from Sir Walter Raleigh to Lord Cobham, October 1603, written at the Tower.' She imagined Raleigh the adventurer, confined to a bare stone cell, frantically writing letters to anyone he could think of to try to get him out of his predicament. A treason charge meant he would be writing for his life. She remembered seeing his

28

prison notebook on display in the British Library. If they could find the original of this letter, it should be possible to authenticate by handwriting analysis.

'The date fits,' said Richard. 'A month before the trial, so he was still trying to persuade Henry to recant his confession.'

1603. Ten years after Marlowe had met his grisly end – his mouth stopped, as one of his enemies had put it, forever. But could it be true – that Marlowe had written one more play, yet to be heard? A play set in his home town. A Canterbury play, a Canterbury book. Nothing in his established canon of work fitted that description.

'Another cup of tea? Or do you have to be somewhere?'

She hesitated. She had planned to spend the afternoon at her desk, painstakingly cross-referencing between the two texts of *Doctor Faustus*, as many scholars had done before. The work had absorbed her. Yet now it seemed pedestrian, stifling. The possibility of a new play, undiscovered and unexamined, was intoxicating.

'Let's go outside.' She jumped up, wanting to be out of the steamed-up cafe and in the fresh air, with the expanse of the river beside her. 'I can't think in here. It's too stuffy.'

* * *

She led the way to the riverside steps. Below, the silt of the river bed was exposed, gleaming wetly. Seagulls waded in the shallows, turning over discarded takeaway food and crying like babies. The stairs, fringed with emerald weed, were treacherous with slime.

'Shall we go down?'

Helen looked doubtfully from her hiking boots to his

brogues, but he was already picking his way down the steps. They walked in silence for a moment. She kicked over oyster shells and broken bottles, their edges worn smooth by the water. You could find anything down here, centuries of the city's detritus endlessly turning in the tide.

'Look.' Richard stooped to pick up a thin length of clay pipe, white against the grey-green silt. He rubbed it clean with his thumb, peered down its narrow bore. The river was littered with these fragments, relics of the clay pipes smoked by Thames ferrymen and dockers. 'Amazing how the pleasures of the city persist. Oysters, beer and tobacco.'

'"*All those that love not tobacco and boys are fools*",' said Helen. 'One of the more outrageous statements attributed to Marlowe. Probably after a few pints in the George.'

'Showing off to Raleigh and his mates, all of them puffing away on pipes stuffed with the latest craze from America,' added Richard. 'Tell me what you know about Marlowe's connection with Raleigh. They were both part of this School of Night business, weren't they?'

The School of Night was a name later given to the scholars, mathematicians, poets and natural philosophers who gathered around Walter Raleigh. Marlowe was rumoured to be among them, although the evidence was scant.

'The main source for that comes from the testimony of a government informer trying to have Marlowe executed. He said that Marlowe had read Raleigh and his friends a lecture on atheism, which of course was illegal. But there are other connections between the men. Raleigh wrote a reply to one of Marlowe's poems, which suggests they were very much aware of each other. And we know Marlowe wrote plays for Raleigh's friend, Lord Strange, who was definitely part of the School of Night. But there's nothing to show Marlowe regularly attended their meetings.'

They had reached the dank stone arches under Blackfriars Bridge. The tide had turned, flooding back into London against the river's flow. Dark water churned around the piers. As the gloom engulfed them, Helen felt her excitement about the letter dissipate. So little could be established firmly about Marlowe and his life. He was an elusive figure, fading in and out of the historical record. He had been variously a scholar, poet, playwright, counterfeiter and spy. On several occasions he had been arrested for street fighting. He had even spent months in prison on suspicion of murder. Would this rackety character really have been admitted into Raleigh's inner circle? Most of the members of the School of Night were noblemen, aristocrats with the leisure to pursue their scientific enquiries. Only one or two, like the brilliant mathematician Thomas Hariot, were commoners employed as in-house scientists and teachers.

'What about the Earl of Northumberland?' she said, struck by a sudden thought. The young aristocrat, a key member of the School of Night group, had been famed for his interest in the esoteric. 'They called him the Wizard Earl. What if Raleigh meant him, when he referred to Merlin?'

Richard was walking beside her, his shoulders hunched against the wind. 'Yes, I did think of that. But "poor Merlin"? He was the richest man in Britain.'

'He was imprisoned in the Tower too, wasn't he?' Helen mused.

'Not in 1603. That was after the Gunpowder Plot, 1605. Anyway, he has no connections to Canterbury. Marlowe does.'

She shook her head. 'He grew up there, of course. But he was in Cambridge or London for most of his adult life. He wrote about Greek myths, history, tragedies on an epic scale – things to excite the playhouses. I just don't see him writing about his provincial home town.'

'Well, that's why I wanted to talk to an expert. Just have a think about it. Anything that's mentioned in the records. Surely he visited his family from time to time?' He steered her back towards the Blackfriars steps.

Back on dry land, his face lit by the street lamps that had started to glow along the South Bank, he leaned again on the river walk balustrade.

'There's more. Lady Joan says there's a legend in the family that Henry was framed because he knew a dangerous secret. Her grandfather believed the secret was revealed in this Canterbury book. So if I'm right, it's a secret that Christopher Marlowe was privy to. One, perhaps, that could have led to his death?'

Helen laughed. 'It sounds to me like everyone's getting carried away. The last thing we need is another theory for why Marlowe was killed. What's the big secret, then?'

He shrugged. 'That's what I'd like to know. Wouldn't you like to help me find out?'

Chapter 5

A policewoman half his size hauled Nick to his feet, dizzy but intact. He didn't want to go in the ambulance at first, protesting that he was fine. Then he touched the lump on the back of his head and felt it sticky with blood.

The ambulance was busy. Two Asian lads, Nick and the injured policeman were loaded into one crowded vehicle. Behind them, paramedics tended to the man lying in the street. As they pulled away, Nick dug out his notebook and pen and started to question the police officer. No point missing an opportunity for an interview.

The man turned towards him and wordlessly held the dressing away from his face. A slice of his cheek went with it, exposing a raw wound, blood oozing into the dressing. The paramedic grabbed his hand and moved it gently back to his face. 'Hold it there, sir. Don't move your hand, and don't try to talk,' he said. He glared at Nick. 'And you can shut up, unless you want me to chuck you out now.'

* * *

It was chaos at the hospital. An A&E nurse yelled at the

33

paramedics, saying they had no room and should be taking their casualties elsewhere. Young men slumped on plastic chairs along the corridors, nursing wounds. Nick allowed himself to be led to a curtained cubicle, where the lump on his head was cursorily examined. As soon as the nurse was gone, he left. He found the young woman police officer who'd helped him earlier, standing outside a closed door.

'Hey, thanks for rescuing me. What's your name?' he asked.

'I'm PC Knight,' she said. She was a diminutive redhead with curly cropped hair. 'Are you OK now?'

He nodded, then wished he hadn't. Any movement of his head brought pain. 'What about the guy I was with? The one lying on the ground?'

She jerked her thumb towards the door. 'Unconscious, but breathing. Is he a friend?'

'I'm a reporter for the *Courier*. I was covering the mosque opening for the paper when it all kicked off.'

PC Knight looked annoyed and glanced quickly along the corridor. 'Don't quote me, please. I'll be in trouble for talking to you. You have to go through the press office.'

Nick turned on his most charming smile. 'Don't worry, I know the drill.' He loathed press officers, who never told you anything interesting and saw it as their job to keep news out of the newspapers. He wandered down the corridor, looking for a public phone. The editor would be going ape.

He called the office. 'Boss, it's me. My phone's been nicked. Yeah, I was there. I had some great photos, but they were on my phone. I'm at the hospital now. One of the Asian kids is still unconscious. A policeman had his face sliced open with a broken bottle.' He didn't bother telling the editor about his own injury. Instead, he flicked through his notebook to where he had started writing up his notes. As he was transferred to the office secretary, he composed his thoughts, putting the story together in his mind. He grinned to himself. This was proper, old-fashioned reporting. This was why he'd gone into journalism. The girl gave him the go-ahead and he started to dictate.

When he came off the phone, a stern-faced middle-aged woman in a neat navy suit was waiting.

'Sorry I took so long. Are you after the phone?' he asked.

'I'm after you, Mr Wilson of the *Courier*,' she said. 'I'm DCI Greenley of Greenwich Police, and I want a word.'

They sat on hard plastic chairs in the waiting room. The woman grilled him thoroughly about all he'd seen at the mosque. 'They said they were from the English Martyrs Brigade. D'you know anything about that lot?' he asked.

'You'll have to ask the press office,' the DCI said.

'Look, I'm telling you everything I know. Fair exchange?' he protested.

'Mr Wilson, one of my officers found you by the body of a man who'd been repeatedly kicked in the head. I'm the one who gets to ask the questions.'

He expelled a long sigh and sat back in his chair. His previous experience with police officers had taught him that innocence was no guarantee of being believed.

Chapter 6

Helen was getting exasperated. Maybe Richard was a crank after all, she thought, disappointed. Marlowe scholarship was awash with theories about why the playwright was murdered, if indeed he had been murdered at all. Historians and cranks alike were obsessed with his death, and it wasn't always possible to tell the two groups apart. She didn't want to get drawn into yet more conspiracy theories.

'It's getting dark. I should go home.' She tried to keep the annoyance out of her voice. She'd liked the man, and he'd seemed to be a serious historian. She really didn't want him to turn out to be a weirdo.

'Don't go. How about a drink? Something to eat?'

They were outside a riverside pub, its windows glowing warmly. Her stomach grumbled. It was a long time since the bacon roll she'd eaten at Borough Market before the tour. The sun had disappeared and the wind was chilly. As usual, she had no plans for Saturday night and was resigned to spending it reading or watching rubbish television. It had been some time since an attractive man had begged her to go for a drink with him.

'Oh, go on then,' she said, watching a smile spread across his face. 'Just one drink.'

He installed her at a table by the window and set off for the bar. It was quite nice to be looked after, she supposed. She was tired of having to push through crowds to try to attract the attention of a barman, and of eating alone. She usually brought sandwiches, eating them on park benches to keep her costs down. But in the winter, it was tempting to round off a walk somewhere warm, with hot food. She told herself sternly not to get used to the idea. Being looked after by a man had not served her well in the past.

She'd broken off her engagement after her father died, while still mired in grief. The shock of his death had stripped away all the little lies she'd been telling herself about her life. Her teaching job, which she'd pretended she loved when Monday mornings brought dread. The dreary new-build maisonette with its small windows. The man she lived with: a fellow teacher whose wit had soured into lazy cynicism.

From the outside, she knew, it looked fine. Her sister had been delighted when they announced wedding plans, pleased to see Helen settle into the same path she'd chosen herself. 'Don't wait too long to have kids,' she'd advised. 'Then they can play with mine.'

Her father had always been the one to question her choices. After university, when she enrolled on a teacher training course. When she'd accepted a job at a south London school, twenty miles from where she grew up. When she moved in with Simon, her first serious boyfriend. 'Really, Helen? There's a big world out there,' he'd reminded her. 'Why be in such a hurry to settle down?'

She'd shrunk from the challenge, settled for familiarity. Then she woke up the morning after his funeral and realised she was living a life that seemed to have been intended for someone else. Her father had lived until he was eighty-two. Could she really spend half a century living someone else's life? She'd packed a bag and left while Simon was out, unable to face the chore of explanation. He had not taken it well.

'Penny for them.' Richard set down a large glass of red wine, a Coke and the menu. 'You're looking very thoughtful.'

She smiled and raised the wine glass. 'This is enormous. It'll go straight to my head.' She took a gulp, trying to banish her ghosts. 'You've given me a lot to think about.'

'I have, rather, haven't I?' He looked concerned, as if he might be over-taxing her brain. 'And you've been very good. I'm sorry if I've presumed too much. It's so nice to talk to someone who knows the field.'

'I hope I've been of some use.'

'You certainly have. I could tell on the tour that I'd come to the right person. You do it so well. How did you get into the tour guide business?'

Before she knew it, Helen was telling him about how her teaching job had begun to stifle her. 'It's not teaching, most of the time. More like crowd control. I wasn't much good at it. I hate shouting and I was rubbish at dealing with the rowdy kids.' The only time she felt the children were learning, she explained, was when she managed to get them out of the classroom, to see a play at the theatre, or visit somewhere connected with the texts they were studying.

'We went to see a couple of plays at the Globe, and I'd take them round Bankside. Some of them just ran around making a nuisance of themselves, but some of them got it.' Then, one summer, she'd been asked by a friend in the local history society to take them on a tour of the area, and she'd loved it. 'It was so great to talk to people who actually wanted to learn something. And you can bring it to life so much more when you're standing there, where the events took place. I started to train and do tours in the school holidays.'

Richard was a good listener, prompting with gentle questions when she paused. She hesitated, on the brink of telling him how she'd handed in her notice after her father's death, the same week she'd walked out of her home. She remembered the heady release of it, throwing all the pieces of her life into the air, with no particular plan. Within the space of seven days, she'd become a homeless, jobless orphan.

Too many big changes, too quickly. She tried not to think much about the months that followed. She'd spiralled into a depression that had left blanks in her memory, a pervading numbness during which she lost touch with most of her friends, sitting aimlessly in a string of rented rooms, staring at the bare walls. It had been a traumatic time, but she'd fought her way through. A year later, she'd washed up in her Greenwich flat, with a small legacy from her father and his firm posthumous instruction to use it to do something she loved. Instinctively, she'd returned to Marlowe, her first literary love, to heal her wounds. Her tour guiding just about paid the bills. But she still felt precarious, as if the new life she had constructed would unravel if she tugged on a thread. She bit the words back, remembering that Richard was almost a stranger. She felt like she'd known him for ages.

'Anyway,' she said, 'tell me more about yourself. How long have you been at Kent University?'

He talked with enthusiasm, yet she got the feeling he too was holding something back. He was amusing about his students and colleagues, interesting about the religious upheaval of the Reformation and its profound effects on England. But he did not speak of his personal life, his home or his circumstances. Was he married? He wore no ring, although she knew that was no guarantee. Was he, like her, alone in the world? She supposed she'd been equally reticent. Two wary people, she thought. She lifted the glass of wine in her own ringless fingers and sipped, smiling at him over the rim. She couldn't remember when she'd enjoyed an evening more.

Chapter 7

The editor slapped a pristine copy of the newspaper down on the desk. 'Good lad,' he said, his hand on Nick's shoulder. Nick's chest swelled. Coming from the old man, there was no higher praise.

The banner headline stretched across the page, his photo byline prominent beneath it. 'Man in coma after mosque riot,' it read. The photo was a shot of the smashed-up car and the abandoned placards, taken by the *Courier*'s snapper when he finally turned up. Nick was still annoyed about losing his phone, with all his contacts and the photos of the violence in full swing.

But he'd been in demand. The local radio and TV news bulletins had interviewed him, as the only journalist on the spot when the trouble kicked off. He had hopes of landing a few freelance shifts on one of the national newspapers, most of which had picked up on his story. He'd been greeted like a hero when he got into the newsroom on Monday morning, especially when they saw the lump on the back of his head. People had made him tea all day, and the receptionist had given him a chocolate biscuit from her under-desk stash.

Now the editor wanted a follow-up about the group that had emerged from nowhere to stage the protest and disappeared when the riot police arrived. Nick was on the trail of the English Martyrs Brigade and the mysterious Paxton. It made a welcome change from sitting through tedious council meetings and re-writing press releases.

Online, the search had taken him quickly into a morass of far-right forums and message boards, full of anonymous commentators spewing out racist bile. Half-truths and outright lies about immigration, asylum-seekers and the European Union.

Nick waded through so-called jokes about new arrivals 'just off the boat', trying not to let it get to him. Both his parents had arrived in Liverpool by sea, his mother in the short hop across the Irish Sea from troubled 1970s Belfast, his father as a baby on a ship from Trinidad. Despite the odds, they'd made a good life for themselves and their sons.

'What are you up to?'

Meena Chaudhury, the only reporter in the office younger than him, was peering over his shoulder. She was tiny, fierce and wore jeans and gold trainers with a bright yellow headscarf. She'd spent the morning at the hospital with the family of Anjoy Uddin, the injured man, who had not recovered consciousness. Nick was still sore that the editor had handed that side of the story over to another reporter.

'They're family,' she'd said, rolling her eyes. 'Like every other Bangladeshi in south London. Anjoy's mother is some kind of cousin of my dad. It helps.'

'I'm trying to find out about the arseholes who kicked Anjoy's head in,' he told her now. 'The so-called English Martyrs Brigade. I can't find any contact details outside of the message boards. It looks like Saturday was planned, though.'

He showed her a string of messages referring cryptically

to an 'upcoming event in Greenwich to greet a new religious organisation'.

'What about that guy you interviewed? Any leads?'

'Paxton.' Nick shook his head. 'The name's mentioned a few times, but no contact details.' He opened another tab. 'Here. I think that's him.'

They looked at a photo of a dark-haired man in a tight T-shirt, caught with his mouth open yelling at the photographer. It was on the website of the anti-fascist newspaper *Lighthouse*. A couple of years old, the photo accompanied an article about a group called Crusade for Saint George, which had organised marches in Northern towns with big Asian populations. 'It sounds like the same bunch of charmers.'

'I've got a mate who works at *Lighthouse*,' said Meena. 'We were at journalism college together. I'll ping you his email.'

'Got a number?' Nick much preferred to do his investigations over the phone. Email exchanges gave people too long to think about what they wanted to tell you. Minutes later, he was talking to the news editor of the magazine, who was as pleased to hear from Nick as Nick was to talk to him.

'Yeah, we've been keeping an eye on this Paxton toerag for a while,' the man confirmed. 'First name's Gary. He's had a run of these poxy little Englander groups. Crusade for Saint George went tits-up a couple of years back. We've just started picking up on the English Martyrs Brigade. He lives down your way, incidentally, over in Eltham.'

'Right.' Nick knew Eltham as a mainly white, middle-class suburb, the sort of curtain-twitching place that he avoided if possible.

'The other name we have for him is Gary Street,' continued the man. 'He was using that when he came out of the army five years ago, after a tour of Afghanistan. When we last spoke, he was working as a security guard on a building site in Woolwich. Might be worth looking into that, if you want to find him. Give him our regards, won't you?'

Half an hour later, Nick had called six of the security companies listed with a south London phone number. None had any record of a Gary Paxton or a Gary Street. The seventh was more helpful.

'Yeah, Gary Street. He worked here for a couple of months, taking the dogs round the building sites and that. He's got his own business now. Secure Solutions. They've got a website.'

Nick looked them up and scribbled down the address. He pulled on his leather jacket and grabbed his motorbike helmet. Phone calls were good, but face-to-face was even better.

* * *

Gary Paxton was sweating hard. Stripped to the waist, he landed one swift blow after another on the punchbag suspended from the ceiling. He was feeling good. The ruckus in Greenwich at the weekend had made the local telly, and the front page of the *Courier*. The reporter had quoted him, although he'd also reported on the ragging he'd got from the lads. He'd given them a right bollocking about that. Keep focused on the religion angle, he'd told them. Islamic terrorism scares the shit out of people. Don't get distracted by race.

But it had gone well, and no one had been charged with anything so far. There had been a few knocks on the doors of the more well-known troublemakers. A couple of people had been arrested then bailed, but they'd covered their tracks well and there was no photographic evidence. Paxton was paranoid about photos and insisted all the lads left their mobiles behind before they went on an engagement. He had a couple of mates in the local nick who had told him in advance that the mosque CCTV was disconnected while they finished the painting and decorating. So there was no proof about who had started the ruck. All the neighbours knew was that the first day the mosque opened had resulted in a bloody great punch-up on their doorsteps. A few more of those and they'd be begging the council to shut it down. Job done.

What he was concerned about now was taking it to the next level. There was no shortage of volunteers, but they needed training, organising. He couldn't be everywhere at once. He'd decided to concentrate on London for now, his manor. Get a unit set up properly and show what it could do.

He'd been training the lads himself, dragging them out on Sunday mornings for circuit training in the park. They needed to be properly fit, battle-ready. He'd made staff sergeant in the army before they chucked him out. These were good lads, mostly, and they listened to him. He thought about all the apathetic kids around the country, sitting at home playing video games and smoking spliffs. They needed a leader, someone who could get them off their arses and give them a purpose. Since Brexit, he'd felt the atmosphere shift. People weren't scared any more. They'd had their say, and won. Now it was time to finish the job.

With a final volley of punches, he finished his workout and grabbed a towel. The secret was not to let yourself go. He'd seen how tempting that was, after he came back from Afghanistan that last time and Jackie told him she was leaving. He could've sat on the sofa for the rest of his life, feeling sorry for himself. But he had a kid, and he wasn't going to give Jackie a reason to deny contact.

He'd retrained, got himself a job, paid the child support, kept himself in shape. Then he'd set up his own business. Security was a good game to be in, what with all the building sites and the price of property in London. He ran the company out of a pre-fab unit on a light industrial estate, trained up some mates for when things got busy, had a couple of dogs in a yard out the back. They did security patrols, nightly checks on construction sites, occasional door work for the local pubs and clubs. All legit; they'd done the training and paid the taxes. It was good, steady work, but he wanted more.

He was getting into body-guarding and surveillance now, through a client from one of his previous jobs. He was learning a lot. Know your enemy, that was the key. Gather intelligence, file it away, know when to use it. Build up a picture of their habits, their weak points. Always be one step ahead. And it could turn into a lucrative contract; he'd been promised as much.

It wasn't money for its own sake, although he could always do with more of that. After Afghan, he'd sworn he'd do something about making this country fit for his kid to grow up in. He'd seen the way it worked there, the militias and the police working together. And that was in a godforsaken desert, seething with towel-heads expecting kick-backs for everything, then turning round and shooting you in the back. They called it resistance and they called the UK presence an invasion. Well, from his point of view, Britain was the place being invaded. And he was the man to organise some resistance. If he could support others using more conventional means, so much the better.

The doorbell rang. He pulled on a T-shirt and went through to the front desk. On the other side of the glass door, he could see a guy in motorbike gear. Probably a courier. He gestured for him to remove his helmet, then buzzed the door open.

'Remember me?' The guy took off his headgear, revealing dreadlocks and a face the colour of milky coffee. Shit. It was the kid from the newspaper. How had he tracked him here?

'I thought you could tell me a bit more about your mates, Gary. The ones who beat Anjoy Uddin into a coma then nicked my phone. Any comment?'

He had pulled out a notebook, was standing there like an idiot, pen poised. Paxton ran through his options. Outright denial was tempting, but if the kid identified him to the police, it could backfire. He didn't want the business linked to Saturday's ruck. Even with police supporters, it would be preferable not to be flagged as a person of interest. They could only watch his back so far.

Paxton flipped up the hatch. 'Come on through,' he said, beckoning the kid inside. 'Have a seat. Fancy a cuppa?'

* * *

Nick followed the man into the back office. His ears strained to hear whether anyone else was on the premises, but the only sound was a couple of dogs barking. The office smelled strongly of fresh sweat. There was a damp towel flung over the cheap sofa and a punchbag hanging in the doorway. He stayed standing while the guy filled a plastic kettle. He'd have put money on Paxton throwing him out. He was wary, half expecting a bunch of goons to storm into the room and rough

47

him up.

'I saw your story,' said the man, chucking teabags into stained mugs and sniffing a carton of milk. 'Front page. Very impressive.' He handed a mug of strong tea to Nick, then sat on the edge of the desk and gestured towards the sofa. Nick had learnt long ago that he was better suited to running than fighting. He really didn't want to sit down with Gary Paxton's muscular bulk looming over him. He perched on the sofa arm, balancing his notebook on his knee. He began to wish he'd told someone where he was going.

'So you'll know that there's a kid in a coma as a result of your protest. Do you know who did it? Will you be helping the police identify them?' He'd trained himself to keep his voice calm, no matter what the circumstances of the interview. Getting angry might make him feel better, but it rarely got answers.

'Yeah, it's a tragedy.' Paxton didn't sound particularly bothered. 'Wish I could help. But I left when the Asian guys started throwing punches.'

'It was your lot who started the violence.'

'Not from what I saw.' He held Nick's gaze without flinching.

'Come on, Gary. I saw you, up on the wall, telling people what to do.'

Paxton held his gaze, his expression bland. 'Not me, mate. I got the hell out when it kicked off. I don't do violence.'

'You were in the army. Afghanistan. How does that figure?'

A second of surprise, a flicker of disquiet in his eyes. Then he smiled. 'That's different. I was a professional soldier, fighting insurgents. Not having punch-ups in the street.' Paxton got to his feet, threw a battery of blows at the bag. The noise cracked in Nick's ears as he watched the man's muscles shift and bunch under his T-shirt. Shit, he could really do some damage. Nick put down his mug and checked the exits.

'Listen,' the man continued, wiping sweat from his forehead. His breathing was normal, Nick realised, as if he'd hardly been exerting himself at all. 'Some of the lads got a bit out of hand. Thing is, that's going to happen. They've lived in this area all their lives. They see all these people coming in, bringing these different cultures with them. They get worried about what might happen. They just want to protect their communities.'

'So what's your involvement?'

'I try to keep them in line. Give them a bit of organisation, a bit of structure. The sort of discipline I had in the army. Sometimes it works, sometimes it doesn't.'

'And that makes you what – a scoutmaster?' As soon as the words were out, Nick regretted them. He could never resist a sarky comment, even when he knew it would cost him a beating. He watched the man's brow lower and wondered if it was time to leg it. Then Paxton forced a smile.

'If you like. Listen, mate, keep in touch. I'll let you know what's really going on round here. I hear about stuff you won't get to know about. Get you a few more front pages?'

Nick nodded. 'OK. Give me your number.' The guy reached into his desk and brought out a pile of business cards, handed one over. Nick dug in his jacket pocket and found his own card. Before he realised what was happening, his hand was enclosed in Paxton's meaty fist. *That's the first time I've knowingly shaken hands with a racist*, he thought.

Chapter 8

Helen sat on the low sofa outside the headmaster's office, her long legs awkwardly folded. She'd been here many times, yet never managed to get comfortable. The situation brought an echo of her own school days, which had invariably ended with her sitting outside her father's office, waiting for him to finish his work and take her home. She remembered keeping her eyes down to avoid the stares of the other kids who ran past, whooping and laughing on their way to the gate.

The bell rang and she half-expected her father to emerge from behind the closed door. Instead, the corridor began to fill with well-behaved boys in blazers, bright voices cutting through the air. Richard, beside her, was reading a newspaper. He looked up with a smile. 'God, doesn't it take you back? Not that I went anywhere like this, of course.'

'This' was Dulwich College, a vast Victorian Gothic construction. One of the oldest and most expensive schools in the country, it had originally been established on a modest scale in the early seventeenth century by retired local actor Edward Alleyne, former star of the Rose Theatre.

The school, intended to educate the poor of Dulwich Village, was now crammed with the sons of the wealthy. The village had been engulfed by London, but the college retained its rural feel, surrounded by an expensive oasis of smooth green playing fields.

'Sorry to keep you, Helen. Good to see you again.' The keeper of the archive, a young, bookish man with a pleasant face, made his way through the schoolboys and held out a hand. Helen and Richard struggled to their feet.

'Thank you so much for fitting us in at short notice, John. This is Richard Watson from the University of Kent. Richard, John is the archivist here. He's been enormously helpful.'

'Not at all. I saw you in the paper, by the way. Nice photo.' The young man blushed as he led them through wood-panelled corridors and high-ceilinged halls hung with portraits of illustrious alumni.

They made their way to the handsome library and upstairs to the office. Richard and Helen set up their laptops on a big round table in front of the archivist's cluttered desk.

'It's Henslowe's diary and the Alleyne letters, isn't it? Let me fetch them out for you.' The man disappeared behind a heavy metal door.

If he was serious about looking for traces of a missing Marlowe play, Helen had told Richard, the first place to search would be the priceless collection of documents held at Dulwich. Edward Alleyne had been Philip Henslowe's son-in-law, as well as the chief actor in the company that performed at Henslowe's Rose Playhouse. Henslowe's diary and account book, along with Alleyne's correspondence, had been bequeathed to the college on the actor's death. By some miracle, the documents had survived and now represented the most complete record of any theatre from the time.

'I'll take the diary. Henslowe's handwriting is a nightmare,

51

but I'm used to it. You start with Alleyne's letters.'

Helen was a little on edge, uncertain about bringing Richard into her territory. She felt like a careful domestic cook, inviting a wildly successful and adventurous chef into her kitchen. Who knew what he'd make of it, or what sort of state he'd leave it in afterwards?

After their first meeting, Helen had looked him up. She'd been astonished to see page after page of citations for papers in prestigious academic journals. The man was a world authority on the history of the English Reformation, she realised. Yet he held a relatively lowly position as a part-time lecturer. She'd have expected someone with his publication record to have been well on his way to becoming a professor. Then she noticed something else. His publications were all dated more than eight years previously. And he'd held his current position for less than a year. Curious, she thought. What had happened to interrupt his career?

His hypothesis about Marlowe knowing a dangerous secret had turned Helen's own theories upside down. She'd often thought that Marlowe seemed to live a charmed life, constantly given surprising opportunities, getting into trouble then wriggling off the hook.

He'd been the son of a shoemaker, yet was picked at age fourteen to attend the prestigious King's School. At that age, most tradesmen's sons would be joining their fathers in business, not embarking on further education. He was then awarded a scholarship to Cambridge University, where he studied for about seven years. During this time, he was suspected of defection to the Catholic seminary in France, yet instead of expelling him, the university awarded his master's degree after receiving a letter from the Privy Council, stating that Marlowe had 'done her Majesty good service'. This was usually taken by historians as a tacit admission that he'd been spying on Catholics at the seminary.

In adulthood, Marlowe had been arrested no less than seven times, including once for his part in a brawl that resulted in the fatal stabbing of an inn-keeper, and once for inciting a metalsmith to forge coins. Either incident could have seen him hanged. Helen had often wondered who had been watching Marlowe's back. Now she began to ask herself – what did Marlowe know? Did he use this secret as some kind of 'get out of jail free' card, to be cashed in as needed?

Four heavy boxes thumped down on the table. 'Have you got everything you need? I'll be right here,' said the archivist. Helen knew that wasn't just a matter of courtesy. The archive's precious documents had been much molested in the past, with pieces of the diary cut away and whole pages missing. Now the college knew the documents' value, they were not let out of their keeper's sight.

She removed the lid of the first cardboard box and lifted out the big book with its heavy parchment pages. The close-written pages of the diary contained the names of hundreds of plays, only about a third of which had been matched to plays identifiable today. Worse, she warned Richard, Henslowe's spellings were eccentric and he re-named plays at will – so the play now known as *The Massacre at Paris* made its first appearance in the book as *'The tragedy of the guyes'* and was only later referred to as *'the masacer'*.

'So we're looking for anything that could be a play about Canterbury, or simply written in Canterbury ... and we don't even know if the play was actually performed. If it was so controversial, perhaps the theatre rejected it. Or it might have been censored,' she pointed out. The scale of the hunt made her dizzy.

Richard was already rifling through the buff folders of letters. 'Can we narrow the time period at all? These cover decades.'

'Marlowe was killed in May 1593. Any reference to his writing the play or being paid for it should be before that date. But any performance could be much later. Alleyne retired to Dulwich in 1607, so I wouldn't bother looking later than that.'

The archivist looked up. 'Helen, do you mind me asking what you're looking for? Is it a particular play?'

'It's probably nothing.' She realised she was embarrassed to admit to such a far-fetched quest. 'Richard came across a reference to a late sixteenth or early seventeenth-century play set in Canterbury, possibly by Marlowe. I thought I'd see if I could find any likely candidates.'

John opened his desk drawer and brought out a stack of paper. 'It's a hobby,' he admitted. 'I've been making a list of the play titles in my spare time. I've got up to one hundred and fifty. The ones with a tick next to them – about thirty – are clearly identified. The rest we don't know.'

'You absolute star, John.' Helen could have kissed him. The neatly typed pages included the dates the play had been performed and whether it was recorded in Henslowe's notebook as being a first performance. The list could save her days of trawling. 'I don't suppose you could make me a copy?'

'Take that one. I can print another.'

Helen began scanning through the titles. She glanced at Richard, who had been uncharacteristically quiet. 'How're you getting on?' she asked.

He frowned and shook his head. 'I can't make sense of these. There has to be one missing. Probably two or three.'

Helen looked over his shoulder. Richard was reading an exchange of letters written between Alleyne and his family while the acting company was on tour, through the spring and summer of 1593. The London theatres were closed because of the plague.

'How do you mean?'

'Look. There are one or two letters most months. We start with this one, sent May the second, 1593 from Chelmsford, Alleyne writing to his wife. Nothing in June. Then the next is from Henslowe to Alleyne, July 1593, lots of guff then "all other matters are well"'. He paused. 'But they weren't well, were they? Marlowe was dead.'

Helen stared at the box of letters. He was right. Marlowe had been killed at the end of May, after Alleyne's first letter home. Yet there was no June letter, and no reference to the death in the letters exchanged in July. She'd always read the letters on the alert for any mention of plays, texts, costumes. She'd noticed their affectionate nature, with Alleyne addressing his wife as his 'mouse', and asking for 'domestic news' of her life, his garden and the family's health. She'd shuddered to read Henslowe's descriptions later in the summer of the numbers of their neighbours who had died of the plague. But she had never before noticed this glaring omission.

'I mean, come on!' Richard leaned back in his chair. 'Marlowe was one of their most successful playwrights. He wrote the parts that Alleyne was renowned for playing. How likely is it that Henslowe would fail to mention Marlowe's murder?'

Or that Alleyne would fail to respond, or would not at least hear of it on the theatrical grapevine, Helen thought as she took up the next sheet. Yet there was his next letter, dated the end of July, arranging to have his orange stockings dyed black and asking them to plant spinach in his garden. Not a word about his friend and colleague's shocking death.

'Don't tell me no one's noticed this before,' said Richard, incredulous.

'There was a lot happening,' said Helen, her voice full of doubt. 'The plague – Henslowe says that hundreds were dying each week, including their friends and neighbours. One more death? Among all those?'

He shook his head vehemently. 'This was business, Helen. Even if they didn't care about the man, they'd have cared about the effect this would have on their repertoire. More important than Edward Alleyne's stockings, surely?'

They fell silent. Helen wondered how she had missed it. She'd rather avoided all the stuff about his death, she realised, with a scholarly distaste for all the speculation and conspiracy theories it gave rise to. She had focused closely on his work, and the texts that might have informed them. The intellectual tide had been against biographical readings of the plays.

'John?' she called. 'I don't suppose you know whether there are previous records of missing letters in the Alleyne correspondence?'

The young man looked up with a regretful smile. 'I'm sure there are letters missing. The whole archive was pillaged in the eighteenth century.'

Helen knew that early scholars had borrowed the documents for years on end. Richard had to be right. There would have been some mention of Marlowe's death. There had to be two letters, she thought – Henslowe to Alleyne, breaking the news, and Alleyne's response. She thought again of Henslowe's reassurance in July: 'all other matters are well'. Which matters was he referring to?

'Richard. What if the missing letters mentioned Marlowe's play? What if they discussed what they should do with it, whether it was too dangerous to perform? Maybe Alleyne advised him to hide it, or destroy it. And then Henslowe was letting him know in July that he'd done so. And that he'd destroyed the letters, too.'

He smiled. 'All conjecture. You're learning.' She frowned at his condescending tone, then saw he was teasing. She flushed, annoyed with herself for rising to it. 'Anything in the play lists?' he asked.

She shook her head. 'I already know them pretty well. I can't find anything that sounds appropriate.' She turned back to the faded pages of Henslowe's cramped scribble. 'If it was a new play, they'd need a licence before it was performed. I'll check through the payments.' Plays had to be licensed by the Master of Revels, Edmund Tylney, who seemed to have enjoyed a steady income from Henslowe and the companies of players. Tylney acted as the official censor, ordering cuts or changes to plays that were thought likely to lead to civic unrest. If the play was suppressed, it was possible that it would be on his orders.

Helen turned the pages, looking for payments close to the date of Marlowe's death. Unfortunately, they tended to be lumped together without listing the individual plays. She could check the accounts of the Revels Office, she supposed. She totted up the amounts paid in 1593, intending to check it against the numbers of plays listed as new. As she did so, she noticed an entry she'd previously assumed to be unconnected to the plays.

'Doctor Tho. Lawes at Canterbye, £6 for the archbishop,' it read. This was the only reference to Canterbury she knew of in the whole book. Six pounds was a fair bit of money, about what a playwright might get for a new play. Was Henslowe buying a play? She made a note to consult her edition of the diary to see what other historians had made of the entry. What did he mean by 'for the archbishop'? Was the payment to be given to the Archbishop of Canterbury? Or – a quiver of excitement – was that the name of a play? A Canterbury play, even? She noted it down, checked against the printed list. There was no mention of a play called *The Archbishop*.

A bell rang. The archive was open for only a few hours a couple of mornings a week.

'Sorry,' said John. 'That's the five-minute warning. Can I ask you to get packed away?'

Her mind was still turning on the payment as they walked down the stairs and through the library. She realised she'd left behind the list of play titles. 'Hang on,' she told Richard. 'I won't be a sec.'

As she ascended the stairs, she heard the young archivist's voice. He was speaking urgently into the telephone. 'I need to speak to the master,' he was saying. 'There have been enquiries. I tried to give her the approved list, but she's left it behind.'

Helen stopped, one pace from the doorway. John looked up and saw her. His face filled with confusion and guilt. She turned quickly and ran back down the stairs.

Chapter 9

The cab swung through the gates and up the long drive, through meadows dark with last year's grass. Helen craned forward from the back seat, watching for the first glimpse of the house. She tugged at the hem of her blue dress, which kept riding up over her knees. She rarely wore frocks but had decided her first trip to Cobham Hall deserved a bit of an effort.

'There it is!' As they crested the hill, she saw turrets rising from a long red-brick building that reminded her a little of Hampton Court. Chimney pots spiralled upwards, silhouetted against a pearl-grey sky. The hall had none of the symmetrical elegance of later Georgian palaces. It slunk low to the ground, brooding over its centuries, a dark presence in the countryside. She tried to imagine Queen Elizabeth I arriving when it was new, stepping down from a gleaming gilt coach.

'Pull up this side of the topiary garden,' Richard told the cab driver, turning his head to smile at Helen's excitement. His territory this time. He'd warned her that Lady Joan could be a little intimidating. She rather wished he hadn't; her nerves were getting the better of her. She was glad they were going together.

They crunched over the gravel to a forbidding stone porch. The black door sported a heavy brass knocker in the shape of a turbaned head. Instead of knocking, Richard pulled out his mobile phone. 'Hello, Charlotte. We're here.'

Moments later, a smart young woman in a tailored black suit opened the door. Her shiny dark hair was cut into an immaculate chin-length bob. Helen immediately felt like a scruffy student, worried about her too-short frock and whether her hair, plaited into a braid down her back, was coming loose.

Richard introduced the woman as Charlotte Elms, Lady Joan's private secretary. 'And this is Helen Oddfellow, a literary scholar who has kindly agreed to help me with some references.'

The woman's smile was professional but warm. 'Lady Joan is engaged with a visitor, Richard. She asked me to take you straight to the office and will send word when she's free.'

They followed the woman down stone corridors, her patent-leather heels tapping briskly. Helen shivered. It was freezing, even colder than outside. Draughts raced along the passageways as they passed through panelled halls. They passed rows of portraits, mostly yellowing oils of men in gloomy hats. One imposing portrait of a man in mutton-chop whiskers stared down from a grand stairway.

'James Brooke, Lady Joan's great-grandfather. The one who re-made the family fortune,' said Richard. 'He was a great friend of Prince Albert. Named his son Albert in the hope of currying more favour. It worked – Queen Victoria raised him to the peerage.'

Helen tried to smile, feeling a little oppressed. 'Happy ending,' she said.

Richard laughed. 'Not until I clear Henry Brooke's name. Look, there he is.'

A much older, smaller portrait showed a man in magnificent red-and-white silk, a wispy beard doing little to disguise a rather weak-looking chin. 'Very fancy,' said Helen.

Charlotte Elms smiled. 'They're his garter robes, to show he was a member of the Order of the Garter,' she said. 'Lady Joan bought the portrait herself. She's very proud of it. Some people think it's actually the Earl of Shrewsbury, but we don't mention that.'

Finally, she stopped and unlocked a door at the end of a passage.

'Don't worry. There's an electric fire in here,' she told Helen. 'It was the first thing I insisted on when I took the post.'

The room was an incongruous mixture. Modern office furniture – desks, computers, swivel chairs and filing cabinets – stood on an ornate yellow rug with a Chinese design. The walls were hung with hand-painted Chinese wallpaper, a riot of white peacocks and yellow lotus flowers on a turquoise ground. A crystal chandelier descended from the high ceiling. Outside, topiary figures of heraldic animals marched across the lawns.

'I'll get you some coffee. Milk and sugar?' She whisked away, leaving them to it.

'This place is amazing. Look at that wallpaper! It must be Georgian, don't you think?'

'It is. It should really be conserved and protected, but Lady Joan doesn't think anything is properly antique this side of seventeen hundred.' Richard unlocked the filing cabinet. 'It was all a complete muddle. But I've been bringing order to chaos. This drawer has all the household accounts.' He lifted out a pile of folders. 'These are the trial papers. Then there's this folio of Albert Brooke's family history research.'

Helen pointed to the folders. 'I want to know more about the trial. What exactly was it they were accused of doing?'

He flicked through until he came to a typewritten transcript. 'Here.' He set the paper before her, pulled up his chair and leaned across the desk. She was suddenly very conscious of his nearness, his unruly hair almost brushing her face. She looked down at his hands, his long fingers resting on the paper, and tried to focus on what he was saying.

'This is a translation I had made of the trial transcript. The original is in the National Archives, in Latin, of course. This section deals with Walter Raleigh defending himself. He tries to get them to bring Lord Cobham into the court, but they refuse. The charge was that the two of them were plotting with Spain. It was the second year of James's reign, so everyone was jumpy. Elizabeth hadn't named him as her heir until right at the end, and there were plenty of other candidates.'

He turned the page. 'Raleigh and Cobham were accused of encouraging a Spanish invasion. The plan, supposedly, was to depose James in favour of his cousin, Lady Arbella Stuart, and impose Catholic rule. Arbella had a fairly decent claim to the throne. At one point she was thought to be about to marry the Earl of Northumberland, who also had a distant claim. So she was involved in Cobham and Raleigh's circle in some way.'

'Wait.' Helen's brain was fully engaged now. 'Arbella Stuart. You know there's a potential Marlowe connection there?'

'Go on.' He let the papers drop.

'He may have been her tutor. It's not certain. Arbella's

guardian wrote that she had engaged a university man called Morley to teach her. It was quite common for students to take posts as private tutors in rich households, and several of Marlowe's friends did just that. A lot of people think Morley was actually Marlowe.'

'You star.' He grinned at her. 'I didn't know that.' He put his hand over hers.

The door opened and she jerked away. It was Charlotte Elms with the coffee. Richard jumped up to help her. Helen rummaged in the filing cabinet for a blank pad of paper.

'I'll write it down,' she said, her voice sounding too loud. 'It's far from a certainty, but it would fit with Marlowe's potential role in the secret service. It was quite likely that they'd have wanted someone watching Arbella, given her position and the interest that the English Catholics had shown in her.'

Richard passed her a tiny white-and-gold cup and saucer. 'OK, so that's an intriguing connection. Marlowe's student becomes the figurehead of a plot twenty years after his death. Could she have been in touch with Raleigh through Marlowe?'

They fell silent. There was so little chance of finding out these things, thought Helen, so many gaps in the record. She felt the familiar sense of disorientation that she often got when considering Marlowe's life. Just when you think you've got him, he wriggles away, leaving you grasping at air.

'Lady Joan has asked if you would join her in half an hour,' said Charlotte. 'She's in the library.' She closed the door softly behind her. Helen wondered if she'd seen Richard's hand on her own.

She took her coffee over to the fire. 'I need warming up,' she said, hoping that didn't sound too much like an invitation.

He smiled, an eyebrow raised. 'Careful with that cup. It's

eighteenth-century Wedgewood.'

She gazed at the delicate porcelain and set it carefully down on the mantelpiece. 'God. I don't think I'm made for places like this. My kitchen is full of chipped mugs.'

Richard took up a large folio bound in marbled card and tied with ribbon. 'Come and look at Albert Brooke's papers. There were loads of bits and bobs just folded up and stuffed inside. I've been cataloguing them and putting them in order. Here's the page where I found the Raleigh letter. What do you make of this?'

He sat on the corner of the desk. She read over his shoulder, recognising the same elegant hand that had written the transcript of Raleigh's letter. 'Wealth hidden from all eyes. Never Fail Never Talk Ever.' She looked at him in bewilderment. 'What does this mean?'

He shrugged. 'I hoped you might be able to tell me. You don't recognise it? Not a quote or something?'

She shook her head. 'It sounds more like a crossword clue. An anagram, perhaps?'

'It does, doesn't it? I don't suppose you're one of those people who does the *Times* cryptic while you wait for the kettle to boil?'

'Unfortunately not. I'm the sort who throws out the *Guardian*'s weekend crossword the following Friday with most of the squares still empty. You?'

'I'm more of a sudoku man.'

That figures, thought Helen, remembering his facility for seeing patterns in seemingly unconnected facts. Taking out her phone, she looked up the first line, wondering if it was a quotation from a play. No exact match was returned, and nothing seemed relevant. Another loose end. She sat at the desk and began a list.

'Let's go through the stuff we need to investigate. There's this one – wealth hidden from all eyes – on the page of the folio where you found the Raleigh transcript. Maybe a hiding place for the hidden treasure of the play?'

He perched on the desk next to her, his long jeans-clad legs distractingly close. 'That'd make sense. And the Raleigh transcript itself, referring to Merlin's Canterbury book. What else? The Arbella question. The missing letters in the Dulwich archive after Marlowe's death.'

'Yes. And the 1593 payment in the account book to Doctor Lawes of Canterbury. I looked him up.' She flicked back through her notebook. 'There was a Dr Thomas Lawes, who was a canon of Canterbury Cathedral and master of something called Eastbridge Hospital in 1593.'

'Eastbridge? That's interesting. It's still around. One of the oldest charitable foundations in England. It used to be a Canterbury pilgrim hostel, then became almshouses after the shrine was destroyed. We should visit sometime.'

'I'd like that. But there's also a connection between him and Marlowe. Dr Lawes was a fellow at Corpus Christi College in Cambridge. That's where Marlowe studied. I wondered if their paths might have crossed there.'

Richard raised his eyebrows. 'Marlowe was at Corpus Christi? Then he'd have known the Parker Library. Full of Anglo-Saxon manuscripts and early church documents, half of them looted from the monasteries when they were being dissolved. Amazing collection. I was always planning to go.'

'That's the one. Absolutely worth a visit,' she said. 'I've been there a few times. They've got a copy of the *Anglo-Saxon*

Chronicle that Marlowe might have used.'

She hesitated, wondering whether to pass on her suspicions about the Dulwich archivist. 'There is one other thing. It's probably not important.'

Richard grinned. 'Those are the best things. Go on.'

Quickly she explained about the conversation she'd over-heard. 'He said something like "I need to talk to the master. There have been enquiries, and I tried to give them the list." I suppose he might have been talking about something else, though.'

His smile had disappeared. 'It sounds pretty suspicious to me. He tried to give you the list of plays he had conveniently ready in his desk, didn't he? And we'd certainly made enquiries. Who do you think he means by the master?'

'I don't know. The head teacher of the college, I suppose. I think he's still called the master at Dulwich. Unless…' She began to wonder about Eastbridge. If it was still in existence, did it still have a master?

A little antique clock on the mantelpiece chimed prettily. 'Oops,' said Richard. 'It's time we went. Lady Joan doesn't like to be kept waiting.'

Chapter 10

As they passed through the entrance hall, a man walked towards them, dressed in black with a clerical collar, the light on his hazel curls forming a halo around his smooth face. With a jolt, Helen recognised him from the television programme she'd watched with Crispin. It was Francis Nash, the campaigning vicar. He was smiling broadly.

'Richard!' He advanced on them, holding out both hands. 'How wonderful to see you working again. Lady Joan has been telling me about your intriguing research. How is it going?'

Richard stuck his hands in his pockets. 'What are you doing here, Francis? I didn't know you knew Lady Joan.'

'She's a great supporter of the cause, bless her. Not to mention a parishioner. I'm vicar of Cobham Parish Church, you know. We've been discussing progress. Christianity in Crisis now has ninety thousand members, which is very exciting. We're planning to register as a political party and put candidates up at the local elections. And this is?' Nash turned his smile on Helen.

'Helen Oddfellow. Helen, this is Francis Nash. We met when I worked in the archive at Lambeth Palace.' Helen wondered why Richard was being so short with the man. It seemed at odds with his usual courtesy.

'I recognise you, Father Nash,' she said. 'I saw you on TV the other night.'

He beamed. 'Did you? It's marvellous to be able to reach so many people.'

'I liked some of what you said,' she added. 'About loneliness and about making sure children know their history.'

Richard snorted. 'Depends what you mean by history.'

Father Nash ignored him. 'History is so important, isn't it? You should join us, Helen. Here, let me give you a leaflet.' He reached into his briefcase and pulled out a stack of glossy paper, his smiling face emblazoned on the front. 'What brings you to Cobham Hall?'

She took the leaflet, a little embarrassed. She didn't like to tell him she didn't share his faith. 'Christopher Marlowe, I suppose. I'm trying to help Richard with his work,' she began. 'We've found an interesting letter that mentions Marlowe. Something about a lost Canterbury play—'

Richard jumped in. 'Helen has been very helpful. But we mustn't keep Lady Joan waiting. If you'll excuse us?' He put a hand on her shoulder and steered her down the corridor. His face was grim. Glancing behind her, Helen caught a glimpse of Nash watching, a thoughtful expression on his face.

Before she could ask Richard about his antipathy, they were through a door and into the library.

'Oh! What a lovely room,' Helen exclaimed. The red carpet and the leather-bound volumes on the shelves gave warmth to the high white-and-gilt ceiling. Tall windows onto the park filled the room with light.

At the centre of the room, four armchairs were grouped

around a white marble fireplace of elegant design. In the grate, a small fire softened the chill.

A white-haired woman was seated close to the fire, her posture rigidly upright. To Helen's surprise, Richard bent to kiss her cheek. She accepted his greeting without comment, then turned penetrating grey eyes on Helen. With her heavy eyebrows and prominent nose, she put Helen in mind of a bird of prey surveying her territory for mice.

'This is Helen Oddfellow, Lady Joan. She is an expert on the work of Christopher Marlowe. She has kindly agreed to help me with that aspect of our research.'

Helen felt her knees give an involuntary bob. 'Pleased to meet you, Lady Joan,' she offered. 'It's very exciting to visit Cobham Hall.' She stuck out her hand.

The woman flinched slightly, took her fingers for a second and dropped them. 'How d'you do? I won't get up,' she said. Her voice had the clarion confidence of the aristocracy, a little cracked with age. 'Please, sit.'

They perched in the delicate chintz-upholstered chairs. Helen tugged her frock down over her knees again and wished she'd worn trousers. Lady Joan wore a tweed skirt and pale blue twinset, a string of pearls the size of mint imperials fastened around her neck. Her hooded grey eyes were fixed on Richard.

'This connection, then, with Marlowe. You think it is valid?'

Richard leaned forward, his elbows on his knees. 'One thing first. What was Francis Nash doing here?'

She raised her considerable eyebrows. 'He is my parish priest.'

'He's a troublemaker. I don't trust him.'

The eyebrows lowered. 'He is a Church of England

clergyman, Richard. And a much-needed defender of the faith of this nation. I am a supporter of his work.'

Richard sighed and flung himself back in his chair. 'That's a pity.'

Helen saw Lady Joan flush a mottled red. 'I would be happy to discuss your attitude to religion another time. However, you are here to inform me about your progress with the investigation I am employing you to pursue. May we return to the subject at hand?'

He raised his eyes to the ceiling, his fingertips pressed together and his jaw clamped shut. Helen wondered if she should break the silence.

'It does sound interesting,' she ventured. 'The letter certainly could be about Marlowe, perhaps even a missing Marlowe play. We know he moved in those circles. And we found another link this morning.'

Lady Joan was looking at her as if she were a dog that had suddenly stood up on its hind legs. She faltered and stopped. Richard was biting his thumb, tearing at the skin around his nail.

'The thing is,' he said, 'I don't want Nash to know about this. He was always badgering me at Lambeth, trying to find out what I was working on. When I agreed to work with you, Lady Joan, the question was your ancestor's innocence. The letter we've found suggests that there was more to the trial than the plot with Raleigh. It could be important.'

He leaned forward and put his hand on the woman's arm. 'I truly think we are getting somewhere, Lady Joan. Like Helen said, we've made another connection, just this morning, between Marlowe and Arbella Stuart. It seems to give further credence to the Marlowe theory. But I don't trust Francis

Nash.'

Chapter 11

Meena's usual bounce was missing as she came through the swing door and slumped against the wall. Anjoy Uddin was still unconscious, his family keeping vigil by his bedside.

'Alright?' Nick had come along at her suggestion to be introduced to the family.

She shrugged. 'He's not getting any better. It doesn't look good. I don't think he's going to make it.'

'Really?' That would make it a murder case. At least the police might get off their backsides if that happened. As far as Nick knew, they'd made no progress in their investigation, which seemed mad when the crime had happened in front of half a dozen coppers, the local press and the mayor of Greenwich. There had been no arrests, and his contacts at the mosque said the community was getting angry.

'The family won't have it. They're still praying he's going to pull through. His mum hasn't slept since it happened, I don't think. She's in there singing to him, holding his hand, telling him to wake up.'

Meena rubbed her face. 'He was doing business studies at college. His mum says he's been offered a job in marketing when he graduates. His dad doesn't say anything at all. Just stands and stares out of the window.'

Nick tried to peek through the grilled glass in the door. He could see nothing but another corridor. 'Should we go in?'

'No. Wait here. His brother wants to talk to you.'

Five minutes later, the door opened and out came a teenage boy in jeans and a cheap leather jacket, his hair cropped short. He was trying to grow a goatee beard, but it was sparse.

'Amir, bruv. You OK?' Meena touched his arm. He shook off her hand.

'You,' he said to Nick. 'You were there, weren't you? You saw them kick my brother's head in.'

'Yeah. I'm sorry. I tried to help.'

'We want to talk to you. The police are bullshit. We're going to sort this out ourselves.'

'OK.' Nick was cautious. 'Who's "we"?'

The guy checked his phone. 'Come and find out.'

Nick and Amir walked out of the hospital, through the car park and down the high street. It seemed too bright, too loud after the dim hush of the hospital. Amir took a pair of fold-up sunglasses from his jacket pocket and strode through the crowd like he couldn't see anyone else. Nick had to force his pace to keep up.

They went through the shopping precinct into a fried-chicken shop. A group of young Asian men sat around a table littered with cans of Lilt and cardboard boxes of chicken bones. They rose to their feet as Amir approached the table, offering solemn handshakes.

A big black man, older than the others, turned to Nick with a grin. 'It's been too long, man.'

Surprised, Nick fist-bumped him. 'Steve. How's it going?'

He shook his head, a shy smile on his face. 'It's Mohammed

now. I converted last year. Best thing I ever did.'

Nick shuffled onto the hard plastic chair and took his notebook from his jacket pocket. He'd briefly shared a flat with the man when he first moved down from Liverpool. Last time he'd seen him, he was on the fringes of one of the less scary south London gangs, dealing a little skunk, smoking a lot and heading nowhere. Since then he'd grown a beard and was the only one of the group to wear white robes rather than jeans.

'No notebook,' said Amir. 'We want to ask you some questions.'

Nick put down his pen. 'That's not the way it usually works.'

'Shut up,' said Steve.

Nick ignored him, kept his eyes on Amir. He was the younger brother, Meena had said, the one their mother used to worry about. He was seventeen, too impatient for school, keen to join his uncle in business. Not like his studious, level-headed brother, whose attempts to defuse the situation at the mosque had landed him in hospital.

'We saw you talking to them. Writing stuff down in your little book,' he said. 'Who were they? Where do they live?'

'They didn't give their names,' said Nick. Much as he sympathised, he wasn't going to hand Gary Paxton's business card to a lynch mob.

'But you know who they are,' said Steve, grabbing Nick's wrist across the table.

'Only what I've put in the paper. A bunch of racists calling themselves the English Martyrs Brigade.' Steve's grip tightened. *Any minute now he'll start giving me Chinese burns*, thought Nick.

'We know that,' said Amir. 'We think you know more.' *Why?*

wondered Nick, uneasy. Surely Meena wouldn't have told them about his investigations? *Family*, he remembered her saying. *It helps.*

The men were pressing in on him, eight guys with solemn faces. Nick flicked his eyes to the shop counter. It was unattended. He saw the owner standing outside, his back to the glass door, smoking. *This is an ambush. And I bet Meena knew this was coming.*

'Alright. We're on the same side here, guys,' he said. 'Let go, Steve. I'm not going to help if you break my arm.'

'Mohammed,' said the man.

'Sorry. Mohammed, please let go of my arm.'

He let go.

'I can give you one name. The guy on the wall. Paxton. That's what one of them told me.' He'd passed that much onto the police, although he'd seen no sign that they'd followed it up. He doubted this lot would have the contacts or resources to track him down.

'Write it down,' said Amir. 'And anything else you know.'

Nick sighed. 'Look, you were there. You saw as much as I did. A bunch of big, ugly white blokes with tea-cosies over their heads. I've told you what I can.'

'Paxton,' repeated Amir, pocketing the bit of paper. 'If he's from round here, we'll find him.'

Bet you don't, thought Nick. 'And then what?'

The men shifted in their seats. A few covert smiles broke out.

'We'll go and have a chat,' said Steve. *Mohammed.*

Nick sincerely hoped that wouldn't happen. He remembered the dogs, Paxton laying into the punchbag, his command of his group of thugs.

'Well, be careful.' He rose to his feet.

'Like Anjoy?' spat Amir. 'Worked well for him.'

Nick took in the earnest young faces and sighed. They were going to get pulped. 'Listen, I'm not kidding. You saw the way they fought on Saturday. Paxton had military tattoos. He's trained, and he's training them. You're going up against a little army.'

'I'm trained,' said Mohammed. 'Last year. I went out east. Learnt a lot. I'm Amir's big brother now. Don't worry about us.'

Nick did worry, all the way back to the office. *What sort of training? Where was "out east"? And what trouble was he going to get Amir into now?*

Chapter 12

Helen and Richard walked from the train station into the centre of Cambridge, past ancient colleges bathed in early spring sunshine. The day was unusually warm and Richard had discarded his heavy overcoat in favour of a tweed jacket and jeans, like all the other academics thronging the university town. He fits right in, thought Helen, with his purposeful stride and abstracted air. She wondered again why he wasn't already a professor here or at Oxford, with a coterie of adoring students and a steadily growing pile of books to his name.

Helen always felt a bit of a fraud in Cambridge, even when she was visiting for her PhD research. In her heart of hearts, she wished she'd worked harder at school and tried for a place to study there. But she'd always hated standing out, the headmaster's daughter ever-wary of the taunt of being teacher's pet. She'd learnt to keep her head down, earned middle grades and put a rein on her imagination. She'd bored her teachers with stolid, reliable progress. No one except her father had suggested she might be Oxbridge material.

She watched with envy as confident young men and women from all over the world flew past on their bicycles, college scarves looped around their necks. She'd enjoyed her time at her middle-ranking university, but it had never taught her the carefree exuberance that these students seemed to exhibit. She wondered how Marlowe had felt, arriving as an undergraduate in 1580 after his long journey from Kent. She imagined him cocksure, keen to impress the university with his sharp wit. But perhaps defensive, a bit chippy about his social status. As the son of a tradesman with a modest scholarship that had to cover all his expenses, university would matter to him in ways it didn't matter to his richer peers. Their lives were already settled, while his was all to be determined. Cambridge was his one big chance.

From the street, Corpus Christi presented a grand frontage of tall turrets and gothic arches, a glimpse of pristine green lawn visible through the gatehouse. The sun gilded the warm stone walls.

'This is it.' Helen stopped before the gatehouse, rummaging for the letter her PhD supervisor had written months ago, which explained that she needed to visit the Parker Library for her doctorate research.

'Very impressive.' Richard gazed up at the towers. 'But it's not very old, is it?'

She shook her head. 'No, New Court was built by the Victorians. The Old Court still survives, though. I'll show you later.'

They bounded up the twisting staircase to the Parker Library, where they presented their credentials. The long room was lined with elegant wooden bookcases filled with leather-bound books. Tall windows illuminated the high, vaulted ceiling. Display cases showed some of the library's most precious artefacts – a Caxton edition of Chaucer, one of the earliest manuscripts of the *Anglo-Saxon Chronicles* and a sixth-century book of the gospels, believed to have been brought to England by Saint Augustine. Richard lingered over it, longingly.

'Incredible,' he sighed. 'You'd never guess it was already a thousand years old when Cambridge got their hands on it.' Helen looked over his shoulder. The little volume was open to show an illustration of Saint Luke, swathed in drapery and sitting on a marble throne. Above his head was a winged ox, Luke's mythological symbol, spreading its magnificent feathers. The text was clear, the image fresh and the colours bright. She marvelled at how modern it looked, compared to the cramped and tattered Elizabethan documents she was used to working with.

'It's beautiful.' The scene was recognisably Italian, framed in tendrils of vines and classical architecture. It gave her a sudden longing for hot summer holidays, carafes of rosé wine and long lunches outside under the trees.

'It was originally kept in Saint Augustine's monastery, just outside Canterbury's city gates,' he said. 'Parker carried it off during the Reformation. It was supposedly given to Saint Augustine by the Pope, when he set off to spread Christianity in England. I think it's the oldest book in the country.'

'Come on,' she said. 'Work to do.' They'd come to the library to consult the college archives. Helen wanted to see whether the mysterious Thomas Lawes, master of Eastbridge Hospital and fellow of Corpus Christi, had been at the college with the young Christopher Marlowe. The archivist met them in the back of the library, where long leather-topped tables were available to scholars with appointments. Helen had searched online for references to Dr Lawes and ordered any papers that might be relevant in advance.

The woman set out three cardboard boxes. One contained the chapter book, which noted the date of Thomas Lawes' election as fellow of the college in 1558. Too early, then, Helen realised with disappointment, to have had anything to do with Marlowe, who wouldn't arrive for another twenty years. Thomas Lawes must have been much older than him.

They turned to the other two boxes, which contained documents relating to the scholarships offered at Corpus Christi from the sixteenth century. One set outlined the foundations of the scholarship, while the other contained letters of recommendations for students.

'Marlowe was one of the Parker scholars,' Helen told Richard. 'As well as donating the library, Matthew Parker endowed a number of scholarships for bright Canterbury boys without the money to attend university. They were usually expected to become priests. Marlowe didn't seem to fancy the religious life.'

She lifted the lid from the box of letters and began to sift through them. She quickly found a letter relating to Thomas Lawes in his role as master of Eastbridge. He seemed to have been one of the people who nominated boys for scholarships to Corpus. He had recommended a John Boys from Canterbury, but his authority had been challenged by the college. The next letter, a rather testy missive from the Dean of Canterbury Cathedral, confirmed that he consented to Lawes' nomination and had 'little interest in this affair'.

The correspondence was dated 1587, towards the end of Marlowe's time at the university town. Presumably Lawes was no longer at Corpus but installed in Canterbury at the mysterious Eastbridge Hospital. Why would that give him the right to make recommendations for scholarships? With a thrill, Helen found Marlowe's own letter of recommendation, which had come from the Dean and Chapter of Canterbury Cathedral. Again, the Master of Corpus had noted on it: 'This letter ys of no force because the schollership belongeth to the nomination of my Lord his Grace Of Canterbury.'

Helen rocked back in her chair and bit the end of her pencil. Interesting. There seemed to have been some in-fighting around who was allowed to make the nominations for scholarships. She imagined that the Elizabethan archbishops of Canterbury, caught in a firestorm between recusant Catholics on the one hand and emergent Puritans on the other, would have been more than happy to leave such a minor matter to their underlings. But why Thomas Lawes?

She turned to Richard. 'I don't see why Lawes was making nominations. The boys came from the King's School, within the boundaries of the cathedral. Surely it would make more sense for the school to make the recommendations, or the dean of the cathedral?'

Richard looked up from the box he was excavating, eyes bright. 'Not necessarily,' he said, lifting out a charter. 'Look here.' The charter marked the establishment of two scholarships, 'founded out of the revenues of the Eastbridge Hospital', to be nominated by the dean of the cathedral and the master of Eastbridge. They should be natives of Kent and have attended the Eastbridge school, it said.

'Eastbridge was a school, too, from the time of the Reformation. Parker had a hand in setting it up. They taught boys in the former chapel of the hospital, as well as housing the poor,' said Richard. 'The school was still running until well into the nineteenth century.'

He turned to the next document. In 1585, the scholarship

charter had been amended by Geoffrey Whitgift, then Archbishop of Canterbury, stating that the archbishop's consent was now needed for all scholarships.

They stared at each other. 'Someone had been making scholarship recommendations that Whitgift didn't like?' he suggested.

She laughed. 'Like that of Christopher Marlowe, perhaps? His first play, *Dido Queen of Carthage*, was first performed in 1584, while he was still a student. It's tremendously sexy and provocative. It was probably not the sort of thing Whitgift wanted to see from scholarship boys intended for the priesthood. Perhaps he insisted that the archbishop should approve all scholarships as a reaction to that.'

He grinned. 'I think that's a reasonable theory. You should write it up, submit it for publication.' Helen glowed. If only her PhD supervisor was as encouraging, she thought. For a moment, she allowed herself to imagine a life like this – the two of them working together, making joint discoveries. Encouraging each other, each bringing fresh insights and illuminations into their respective fields. She blushed, feeling the presumption of her imagination.

'What is it?'

'Nothing. But wait a minute. Marlowe was at the King's School, not at Eastbridge. He was a Parker scholar.'

Richard shrugged. 'Maybe he'd been to both schools.'

That was a good point. Christopher Marlowe had been a late arrival at the King's School, joining at the age of fifteen. He must have had his earlier education somewhere. Perhaps that somewhere was Eastbridge. Helen took a pen and reckoned up the dates. Thomas Lawes had been master of Eastbridge from 1570. Marlowe was born in 1564, so if he spent ten years at the Eastbridge school from the age of five or six, Doctor Lawes would have been the master throughout his early education.

'Was the master of Eastbridge the school teacher?' she asked, antennae twitching. To identify Marlowe's earliest teacher would be an enormous coup.

Richard shrugged. 'I don't know enough about it. It's possible. Although if Lawes was also a canon of the cathedral, maybe he wouldn't have taught full-time as well. We can find out.'

'If Lawes was his teacher...' Helen's mind raced ahead. 'And if Marlowe did know some kind of secret to do with Canterbury...'

'Maybe he found out from Thomas Lawes.' Richard finished her sentence. 'He was a canon of the cathedral, a friend of Archbishop Parker. And maybe Lawes recommended Marlowe for the King's School, and then Cambridge, as a reward for Marlowe keeping his mouth shut.'

'Maybe.' Helen turned back through the pages of her notebook. 'Although that'd be a bad bet. Marlowe seemed incapable of keeping his mouth shut about anything. And it doesn't explain why Henslowe was paying Lawes money in the year Marlowe died.' She frowned. A bribe, perhaps? But why would the owner of the Rose Theatre be trying to bribe Marlowe's old schoolteacher?

Richard sighed and swung back in his chair. 'We need to know what Marlowe's play was about. He'd have told someone, wouldn't he? Think, Helen. What interested him at that period in his life? Where was he going, intellectually?'

Helen wished she could answer. The play last performed before his death was a history play, *The Massacre at Paris*.

It was a bloodthirsty, cynical piece that played on English anti-Catholicism and anti-French sentiment. And yet his last piece of work, unfinished at the time of his death, was a classical love poem, based on the myth of the doomed lovers Hero and Leander. It had more in common with his earliest work. The man was an enigma.

They lapsed into silence, finishing their notes and replacing the documents in the boxes. Helen's mind kept shooting off in different directions, all the potential avenues of research beckoning her away from her PhD thesis. She would get back to it sometime, she promised herself.

* * *

'Come on. I want to show you the Old Court.' Helen led the way back down the narrow staircase, past the entrance to the grand Victorian chapel. She ducked through a doorway and into a covered passage. They emerged into a smaller court, a square of low, grey buildings with steeply raked tiled roofs. The windows were small, the arched doorways modest. Sunshine warmed one corner, while the bigger, newer buildings threw the rest of the court into shadow. The place was quiet, only a faint hum of traffic audible from the street. Then someone threw open a casement window on the upper floor and called to a couple of students walking through from the chapel. They waved and hurried to join him.

'This is where Marlowe lived,' said Helen, walking around the lawn to stand in the sun. 'It's the only home he had that's still standing. The Canterbury house he was supposed to have lived in as a child was bombed during the Second World

War. Nothing survives of the Elizabethan buildings where he lodged in Shoreditch. Even Scadbury Manor, where he was staying at the end of his life, has been demolished. But this survives.' She laid a hand on the grey stone. Richard mirrored her gesture, his hand alongside hers, and looked into her face, his eyes soft.

'You really feel it, don't you?' he said. 'History, I mean. It's not just a puzzle to solve.'

She felt herself blush. 'I think because the building is still serving the same purpose. Students still lodge here, masters still give tutorials. It's not a museum.' If she stopped talking, she thought, he looked as if he might kiss her. She felt a squeak of panic. She liked him enormously. But she also liked their working relationship, the way they sparked ideas off each other. This would complicate everything. She kept talking.

'This side of the college is linked to the church behind it. St Bene't's, which is also pretty ancient. There's a corridor linking the two buildings. You can see the door from inside the church.' She led him around the court and to a side garden, where an ancient tree spread its branches. Small daffodils pierced the grass, their delicate heads nodding in the breeze. 'I think this is my favourite place,' she said. 'It's a mulberry tree. I don't know how long they live, but I kind of like to imagine Marlowe and his friends here, eating mulberries and lounging on the grass.'

He laughed. 'What an idyll. You're a romantic, Helen Oddfellow, and should be drummed out of academia. Come on. Let's get some lunch. There was a decent-looking pizza place on the way from the station.'

Chapter 13

'Sorry I've not dropped by for a while. I brought you some bits and pieces.' Helen handed over a bag of fresh lemons with their glossy leaves attached, a box of Italian almond biscuits and the *Sunday Times*.

'Ooh, you shouldn't have. Lovely. Time for a coffee?' Crispin was still in his dressing gown at eleven o'clock on Sunday morning, a silk paisley number with a shawl collar. Helen leaned on the kitchen counter as he measured coffee beans into a grinder and poured water into the top of what must have been the oldest coffee machine still in operation.

'The lovely boys who owned Bar Italia in Soho gave it to me when they were buying new ones,' he said, heating milk in a little jug. 'It makes the best coffee in London.' Five minutes later, true to his promise, he produced the most delicious cappuccino Helen had ever tasted. They sat on high stools and dipped biscotti into the creamy foam.

'God, this is bliss. You're a man of hidden talents,' she told him.

'And you're a girl of hidden something. Come on, what have you been up to? Your eyes are sparkling. Are you in love?'

She laughed. 'Not me. I'm on the trail of something, though.

It's exciting.' She filled him in on the research, the missing Marlowe play, her trips to Cambridge and to Cobham Hall and her encounter with Lady Joan.

'It's the most amazing place, Crispin. And she lives there practically on her own, in this vast hall. I thought she was going to chuck us out when Richard was having a pop at Father Nash. But he talked her round. She's even invited us to dinner on Friday. I say invited – it was more of a summons, really.'

He turned the paper over to the back page and picked up a pen. 'Yes, I believe she's a bit of a dragon. Nothing like her sweet brother.'

'You know Lady Joan? I didn't think she had a brother.' Helen looked at him with suspicion. Crispin had a tendency to claim close friendship with the aristocratic and famous, even if they'd only passed him in the street.

'He died. It must be forty years ago now. More. But everyone in Soho knew John Brooke back in the sixties. In the biblical sense, mostly. Gorgeous, rich and titled – he cut a swathe through us poor chorus boys.' Crispin looked up from the crossword. 'Like the sun, he shone on rich and poor alike. He shone my way once or twice.' He smirked.

'Wow.' Helen scrutinised her friend, trying to see past the frail old man he'd become to the handsome young boy he'd once been, cruising Old Compton Street with hope in his heart.

'He killed a man, you know,' said Crispin. 'Appalling scandal.'

'What? Who did?'

'John Brooke. Ghastly business. A dreadful little rent boy called Kenneth Lloyd. He had it coming, really.' Crispin was feigning indifference, a sure sign he was dying to spill the beans.

'Good God. What happened?'

He sighed dramatically. 'Are you sure you want to know all this ancient history? It's rather grim.' There was nothing Crispin liked better than relating old gossip, the more salacious the better. She decided to indulge him.

'Alright, then.' He drew himself up, the better to project what Helen thought of as his ac-*tor* voice. 'It was a different world, Helen. Buggery was still illegal, remember? It was one thing for thespians like me to get a louche reputation. But John was heir to the title and expected to take over as chairman of Brooke Estates. His father was a tyrant, and terribly proper. John should have been more careful.'

It was a sordid story. Rich, handsome John Brooke fell for one of Soho's most notorious denizens, who supplemented his usual income with petty theft and blackmail.

'Ken was pure poison, but lovely to look at,' said Crispin. 'Welsh, you know, all dark brooding looks and lilting voice. We got on quite well, until he nicked my rent money. Don't look like that. Money to pay the rent. I kept it in a jar in the kitchen.'

For a year, he said, Lloyd swanned around Soho in bespoke suits, flaunting presents from John Brooke. Eventually he went too far, stole and pawned John's watch. 'It was a twenty-first birthday present from his father. Cartier, inscribed with his name and the family motto. Dangerous. John went mad and chucked him,' he continued.

Lloyd began to blackmail and to turn up uninvited at Cobham Hall, joining weekend parties and balls, seducing debutantes, lifting a few bottles of whisky and the occasional pearl necklace. John had to pretend he was a university friend, while Lloyd rampaged through the aristocracy, looking for a rich bride to pick up his bills.

'Respectable young women burst into tears when his name was mentioned, and their brothers went pale. It was terribly exciting. Like Dorian Gray, but without the portrait. We were all desperate to know how it would end.'

Helen thought of Lady Joan, her stiff propriety and fierceness. This man might have danced with her, maybe even stolen her jewels. How much had she known about her brother's life?

'Then John left for Argentina, supposedly on business. Six weeks later, the girls in the knocking shop below Ken's flat started to complain about the smell. They thought it was drains. The landlord found the body. The back of his head had been blown off.'

'God!' Helen gasped. 'How horrible.'

'As you say. They found a gun under the sink. A shotgun from Cobham Hall. So then it all came out – poor John's secret life, as they called it. All over the newspapers, reporters camped outside Cobham Hall. John didn't come back from Argentina. About a year later, he died of an overdose in his hotel room. Possibly deliberate. No one really knows.'

'You're not having me on, Crispin?' Helen was seized with sudden suspicion.

'I am mortally offended. You can look it up. I was even interviewed, as an acquaintance of both parties. *Daily Express*, I think. I told them it was completely out of character. John wouldn't hurt a fly. He was a truly gentle man. Something appalling must've happened to make him do it.'

He turned back to his crossword. Impressed, Helen saw

he'd already filled in half the clues. Her mind flew to the lines they'd found in Albert Brooke's book at Cobham Hall.

'Wait here!' she said. 'I've had an idea.' She ran up to her desk, heedless for once of the four flights of stairs. She grabbed her notebook and clattered back down. Crispin hadn't moved an inch.

'I don't know where you thought I was going,' he began.

'You never told me you were such a whizz at crosswords,' she said, her tone accusatory.

'You never asked. I spent a lot of time waiting around backstage before going on to deliver one line. *The envoys from Rome are come, my Lord.* Crosswords are an actor's best friend.'

'Here. Forget the *Sunday Times* and help me with this.' She opened her notebook to the lines she'd copied down in Cobham Hall. *Wealth hidden from all eyes. Never Fail Never Talk Ever.* 'We think it refers to a hiding place, maybe even for the missing Marlowe play. I thought it looked like a crossword clue or something. What do you reckon?'

He narrowed his eyes and picked up a pen. On the facing page, he scribbled down jumbles of letters, looking for anagrams. Then he listed the initial letters of the second line, placing them in single file down the page.

N

F

N

T

E.

Suddenly he laughed. 'Very good. Can you see it now?'

Helen stared at the letters. 'Do they stand for something else?'

'Look again. What's missing?'

She shook her head, feeling dense.

'Hidden from all eyes? Really, I thought you were the intellectual one.' Picking up the pen again, he added the letter 'i' three times.

'Infinite!'

'Exactly. Does that help?'

Wealth hidden from all eyes, infinite. Infinite wealth hidden from all ... She had it. Marlowe again. Hopping down from her stool, she raced back up the stairs and grabbed her copy of Marlowe's complete plays. Back in Crispin's kitchen, she flipped through to the opening scene of *The Jew of Malta*. Triumphantly, she read the lines aloud:

"'And thus methinks should men of judgement frame

Their means of traffic from the vulgar trade,

And as their wealth increaseth, so enclose,

Infinite riches in a little room."

That must be it, Crispin. Infinite riches in a little room.'

Crispin's eyes were bright. 'How exciting, darling. Does that solve your mystery?'

Helen scribbled the lines into her notebook. 'It solves something. I'm not quite sure what, though.' Infinite riches in a little room. Something about the line nagged at her.

'What's the context?'

'In the play? Barabas the miser is counting his money, waiting for his ships to come in. He complains about how tiresome it is to count silver coins when you have a lot of money. He says it's best for rich men to hold their wealth in jewels, which are of such value that you can hide a treasury of wealth in a small room.'

Something infinitely precious, she thought, kept hidden in

a small space. The play? It would certainly represent infinite riches to her, something of incalculable value.

'Isn't there a Shakespeare connection?' asked Crispin, shuffling towards his bookshelves. 'That line. Something about a little room. I know it from somewhere.'

That was it, Helen thought with excitement. That's what had been niggling at her. 'Yes! Of course it is.' She closed her eyes, trawled her memory. 'And the line is about Marlowe. A great reckoning in a little room. *As You Like It*, I think.'

His head cocked sideways, Crispin rifled through his collection of play scripts before locating his copy of the Shakespeare play, dog-eared with turned-back pages and underlinings. 'I remember that. It was my line. I played Touchstone the jester. Nottingham Playhouse, 1967.' He flicked through the pages. 'Here we are. Touchstone wooing Audrey with poetry.'

Helen read over his shoulder.

'"When a man's verses cannot be understood, nor a man's good wit seconded with the forward child, understanding, it strikes a man more dead than a great reckoning in a little room."'

The words always made her shiver. The line had long been understood by scholars as a reference to Marlowe's death, when the lack of understanding of his verses had him murdered in a little room in Deptford. The story for the coroner was that Marlowe started a fight over the bill, or reckoning, for the meal.

Infinite riches. A great reckoning. What tied the two together? She tried to think as Richard thought, stitching ideas together like a spider spinning webs. Somehow, she thought, they came together in Marlowe's death. His coffin?

Was that his final little room? Could it be that the missing play, his last work, was buried with him?

'I should call Richard,' she said. She reached into her pocket for her mobile.

'Ho-hum. I'm not in love, oh no?'

Helen blushed. 'We're just working together. And he's much older than me.' But the quickening in her heart as she called his mobile was not entirely down to her recent racing up and down of stairs.

'Good morning, Helen.' His voice was a little creaky, as if he'd not spoken to anyone yet that day.

'I've worked out Albert Brooke's clue.' She saw Crispin arch an eyebrow. 'Well, I've had help. My neighbour, who's very good at crosswords. But listen, it's Marlowe again. Another link. Infinite riches in a little room. And there's more.' She gabbled her explanation.

'Genius.' His voice warmed her down the phone line. 'That would have taken me ages to put together. D'you fancy a trip to Deptford this afternoon? Let's check out Marlowe's graveyard.'

After lunch, Helen dragged a brush through her hair and plaited a long braid down her back. She brushed her teeth and put on mascara. Buttoning up her scarlet coat, she remembered Crispin's mocking question. She didn't want to think about what Richard was starting to mean to her. She only knew how glad she was to be on her way to see him again.

Chapter 14

He was there before her, leaning against the red-brick wall of the charnel house, coat collar turned up against the wind. The weather was cold again. Above his head, a pair of carved stone skulls glowered down from the gate, guarding the entrance to the churchyard. He was reading, his eyes fixed on a paperback. Her mind full of *As You Like It*, Helen saw him as the melancholy Jacques, his wit too quick for his companions. He looked lonely and cold. She called his name.

He looked up and broke into one of the smiles that transformed his face. 'Hello! I've been mugging up.' He showed her his book, the same Penguin Classics edition of Marlowe's complete plays that she owned herself. 'I like the descriptions of the jewels. Heaps of pearls like pebble stones. Did you see Lady Joan's string of pearls?'

'I did. I suppose they're real?'

'Can't say I've bitten them to check, but I'd guess so.' He closed the book and slipped it into the leather satchel he carried over his shoulder. 'Where's Marlowe's grave, then? Is he buried in the church?'

'Ah.' She realised she should have explained on the phone. 'No one knows. But almost certainly not in the church. He was murdered in dodgy circumstances and had been accused of atheism. I'm a little surprised he got a Christian burial at all.'

They walked through the churchyard. 'There's an entry in the parish register that records his burial, but not the spot. There's a rumour that he's buried near the tower, but that might be unfounded.'

Richard shrugged. 'No grave-robbing today, then.' She wasn't altogether sure if he was joking. 'Let's take a look around.'

They circled the church, an architectural mish-mash with baroque brick walls, elegant arched windows and a stone bell tower. They stood a moment below the twelfth-century tower, square and uncompromising. There was nothing to see.

'Let's go in,' said Helen. She'd begun to regret her impulse.

Inside, the church was cold and gloomy. At the altar, candles stood unlit on the plain white cloth. Lent, she remembered. It was two weeks until Easter, when the church would be full of spring flowers and decked with celebratory green and gold. She showed him the memorial stone on the wall dedicated to Marlowe. 'You know, it's possible Shakespeare may have attended his funeral. Certainly some of his friends and colleagues were here.' It must have been a melancholy, nervous gathering. The printer, Edward Blount, had written to Marlowe's patron, Walsingham, of how they 'brought the breathless body to the earth' and took their last farewells.

The church door clanked shut, making her jump. She looked to see if someone had come in, but the entrance was empty. Richard had crossed to a side chapel and stood before an array of candles. As she watched, he lit a spill and carefully transferred the flame to two little tea lights, set them glowing red in their glass holders. He stood, head bowed, his hand on the altar rail. A muscle twitched in his cheek. Quietly, she withdrew to the porch. There was no one outside. Perhaps the wind had blown the door shut.

A moment later, he followed her out. She saw sorrow etched around his eyes, but he rubbed his hands together, feigning enthusiasm. 'Right. What else?'

Helen led him around the church, through the drab garden. Bare earth borders yielded spiky, municipal shrubs. The lawns were still the reluctant sludge-green of winter, pierced by pale daffodil spears. A sad patch of crocus had wilted. She showed him a modern marble plaque set in the red-brick wall that circled the church yard.

He read the lines aloud. 'Near this spot lie the mortal remains of Christopher Marlowe, who met his untimely death in Deptford on May 30, 1593.' He traced his fingers over the chiselled quotation from Marlowe's best-known play, *Doctor Faustus*, which ran beneath. '"Cut is the branch that might have grown full straight." Very apt. Poor Marlowe.'

'There's nothing here, is there?' Helen felt foolish. The greyness of the day and the melancholy of the graveyard oppressed her spirits. 'I'm sorry. I should have thought about it more.'

He put his hand on her shoulder. 'It was my idea, remember? I dragged you out here. I'm glad we came. It seems appropriate, paying our respects to Marlowe. Don't you think?'

They parted by the skull-topped gates. Helen watched him go, loping along the busy road, heading west towards the city.

She didn't know where he lived, she realised. She thought of his face as he lit the candles. There was so much she didn't know about him. She wondered who else he'd been paying his respects to.

* * *

Paxton watched as the woman finally turned and walked away. Then he was running lightly on the balls of his feet, weaving through the pedestrians after the man's receding back. Richard Watson had something he wanted. That was not good news for Watson.

As soon as he was comfortably in range, he slowed to a jog-trot and assessed the situation. On the road, the traffic was flowing freely, headlights coming on now in the gloomy afternoon. The pavement was damp and slippery beneath his trainers. There were few people on this side of the road and none between him and Watson. At the bus stop on the other side, four people waited with their shopping bags. If he was quick, no one would get a decent look at him or be tempted to intervene. Ahead of him, the man walked fast, hands in his pockets and his coat collar turned up, head down into the wind. His leather bag was slung casually over his shoulder.

Paxton pulled up the hood of his tracksuit. He was right behind him now. Watson was tall, taller than he was but rangy, with none of his own stocky heft. He reckoned he could take him, no problem.

He was wrong. Watson whipped around as Paxton yanked at the bag's strap. It slipped off his shoulder, but he clung on, let out a tremendous roar and shoved Paxton hard in the chest. He staggered backwards.

'Get off me!' Watson yelled, shoving him again. Paxton stepped back, absorbing the blow so that Watson was off balance. He threw a punch, catching him neatly on the mouth. Blood sprayed from his lip. That was better. Watson's eyes registered shock – a man unused to violence. Paxton felt liberated, joy pulsing through his veins. He followed up with a blow to the solar plexus that doubled the man over. Still he clung to his bag, clutching it to his chest as he crashed to his knees on the pavement. Paxton prised it from his grip, the two men sweating and panting, eyeball to eyeball.

'Just take my money,' Watson said, eyes desperate. Paxton wrenched the bag away and jumped to his feet. Cars had started to slow down, people staring at them from the windows. There was a woman looking his way and talking urgently into a mobile. A man at the bus stop across the road shouted something, barrelled his way through the traffic towards them. *Time to get out of here.*

He dodged past Watson, running up the road against the traffic. Headlights poured past as he accelerated, feet pounding the broken pavement. He snatched a look over his shoulder. The man was still on the ground. None of the people now clustered around him seemed keen to give chase.

He took the first turning, then immediately doubled back parallel to the main road. He glanced behind him, saw nothing. He turned again, then zipped through an alley between two big blocks of flats. He was on the Pepys Estate, a wasteland of high-rise council housing leading down to the river. He listened and heard sirens in the distance. You'd hear that at any time round this way, but you couldn't dismiss it. If there were police in the area with nothing else to do, they might cruise through the Pepys looking for a mugger.

He slowed his pace to a steady jog. In his tracksuit and trainers, he might look like someone out for an afternoon run. Except for the satchel, the leather bag awkwardly looped round his arm. He stopped, breathing hard, sheltered behind a line of big steel bins.

He opened the bag, tipped out the contents. A mobile phone, a wallet. A paperback book. A nice-looking fountain pen. He flipped through the wallet. It contained cards for the British Library and National Archives, about twenty quid in cash, an identity card with his name and mugshot on it: resident, St Christopher's Hostel, Bermondsey. There was a photograph, flimsy with handling, of a dark-haired woman and a little kid.

Paxton stuck the book into the waistband of his jogging bottoms and tucked his T-shirt over the top. The rest went back into the leather bag, which he dropped into the bins, rearranging the plastic bags of rubbish so they covered it.

He chucked his hoodie in another bin, enjoying the cold air against his sweat-soaked T-shirt, and pulled out a couple of bulging black plastic bags from the rubbish. He saw lights. Sure enough, the white van had police insignia. It glided by slowly as Paxton made a show of dumping the rubbish back in the bins, then walked to the nearest tower block, keeping his pace casual. He fiddled with the entry code pad.

'You alright, mate?' He jumped. 'Forgot the code? Always happening to me.' A dopey-looking kid sitting on the ground by the door grinned at him, showing teeth that were green at the gums. The state people got themselves into. The teenager was skinny, his black T-shirt flapping loose, showing track marks up his bare arms. Paxton forced himself to grin back, swallowing his disgust. If there was one thing he hated, it was a junkie.

The kid jumped up and pressed a button. 'Mum? Can I come in now?' The door buzzed and he held it open.

The reek of urine from the stairwell caught the back of Paxton's throat. The kid loped up the stairs. 'Lift's still broke,' he called. 'Fifth floor and all.'

Paxton sat on the concrete stairs, rubbing his arms for warmth. The fluorescent light illuminated graffiti, fag ends, crisp packets and grime. He'd give it half an hour. The police would soon have better things to do in Deptford on a Sunday night. He pulled the book from his waistband and took a closer look.

It was a paperback copy of *The Complete Plays* of Christopher Marlowe. On the cover, a line drawing of a man in a fur coat, standing in a circle of symbols, holding a book in one hand. Paxton flipped through. The corner of one page was turned back, one section underlined, notes scribbled in the margin. He grinned. *Thank you very much*, he thought, reading it through. He examined the rest of the book but could see no markers of any sort. He tore out the page with the underlined text and folded it into his pocket, satisfied.

Chapter 15

'Helen, it's me. Richard. Can I come in?' His voice over the intercom was ragged with distress. She almost fell down the stairs in her haste to open the door.

He stood with one hand on the door jamb, steadying himself. His face was livid, dark dried blood crusted around his mouth. His jeans were ripped at the knees.

'Dear God. Come in. What happened?' She helped him into the hall. His hands were icy.

'Give me a second.' He sat on the stairs, getting his breath back. 'Someone stole my bag. And wanted it enough to fight me for it.'

'You poor thing. Have you called the police?'

He nodded. 'Yeah. They took the details. But they didn't sound hopeful. Just another mugging, I suppose.'

'Come on in. I'll make some tea and you can clean up. Is it very painful?'

She did a quick sweep of the living room as they entered the little flat. Sections of her Sunday newspaper were scattered across the floor, along with a couple of empty mugs, but it was otherwise respectable. Excusing herself, she bundled her drying bras and knickers off the airer in the bathroom and into the cupboard. Few people visited her flat; even fewer of them unexpectedly. While he washed his face, she filled the teapot with boiling water, piled chocolate biscuits onto a plate and carried them through.

'It's just how I imagined it.' His eyes flickered around the dark red walls punctuated by framed antique maps of London and heaving bookshelves. More books were piled on the Turkish rug on the floor. She set the tray down and perched on a tapestry ottoman. He drifted down to the red leather armchair and dabbed a folded handkerchief to his mouth, checking for blood.

'Do you need to go to hospital?'

He shook his head. 'I'm fine. It's stopped bleeding.' He leaned back, took a shaky breath. 'Sorry to burst in on you like this. The police offered to drop me back home, but I wanted some company.'

He told her briefly what had happened. 'I'm so fed up. The bag had everything in it – my wallet, my phone, the Marlowe book.' He rubbed his eyes. 'A photograph that can't be replaced.' His glance was full of misery. She poured the tea and added sugar, handed him a mug of the hot, sweet liquid.

'Who of?' She thought of the two candles he'd lit in the church, his sorrowful expression as he stood in the side chapel.

He blew on the tea, sipped it. 'Thanks, that's what I needed.' He set his mug down. 'My wife and our daughter. They died, eight years ago.'

His simple words froze her heart. Eight years. She remembered how she'd puzzled over his career, the abrupt end to his publications.

'I'm so sorry. It must be...' She trailed off, overcome with the inadequacy of words. Impulsively, she took his hand.

'They said it was an accident.' His voice was dull. She listened in horror as he told the story, forcing the words out as if compelled. He had married a research student, Ruth, while teaching at the University of Kent. They had worked together, co-authoring several of Richard's earliest publications as he began to make a name for himself. When he was offered a prestigious post at Lambeth Palace, working in the archives on the history of the church in England, they moved to London. Soon afterwards, Ruth gave birth to their child.

'We had a little girl. Madeleine.' His voice caught on her name and he stopped, steadied himself. When she was four years old, Ruth walked her home from nursery school along a narrow pavement. A lorry had taken a corner too fast. It ploughed straight into them, crushing them against a wall.

'They died together, and immediately. That was some comfort.' Helen could hear no comfort at all in his bleak tone. She realised she was weeping, fat tears rolling from the corners of her eyes. She pushed them away, seeing through the blur that Richard was dry-eyed, as if all his tears had been spent years ago.

'People were kind. But I couldn't bear it. I drank a lot. It was horrible, but it muffled things, obliterated them if I drank enough. I was so angry, Helen. I didn't know what to do with that anger. I wasn't a nice person to be around. I lost my job, the house, most of my friends. I spent time on the streets. It was a long way back.'

Rain had begun to patter on the roof. Sitting at his feet, Helen held his hand in both of hers, hoping in some way to transmit comfort through the warmth of her skin. She remembered him in the pub, ordering wine for her and drinking cola himself. The words of the priest, Father Nash, when they met at Cobham – 'how wonderful to see you working again.' This man had been tested almost beyond endurance, she thought. Yet, somehow, he had endured.

'But you made it.'

He nodded. 'Sort of. It's better than it was. Charles, my old boss at Lambeth Palace, helped a lot. He got me a place at a church hostel for recovering alcoholics. That's where I live. He helped me find work, when I was ready. It's good to have a distraction. Keeps me busy.' He gave her a twisted grin, pushing back the hair that had flopped over his forehead.

Unthinkingly, Helen raised his hand to her lips. He stroked her cheek for a moment, met her eyes. 'You're so sweet.' He kissed her, his mouth cold and his kiss clumsy, as if he had not kissed anyone for a long time and had rather forgotten how.

'Ouch.' He pulled away, laughing.

'Oh, God. Your poor lip.' She laughed too, winded by her sudden upwelling of desire.

He rose to his feet, pulled her close, held her for a long minute. 'I'll call you tomorrow. Thank you for everything.'

'Wait.' She rummaged in her purse, pulled out a tenner and a handful of coins. 'For the bus. And to tide you over.'

She listened to his footsteps descending to the hall, then heard the front door bang. She collapsed into the armchair, still warm from his body. Life had just got a whole lot more complicated.

Chapter 16

The ring of her mobile telephone jolted Helen from sleep. She'd lain awake half the night, thinking about Richard's terrible story of loss and about his kiss. Had it just been a reflex, reaching out for comfort? Or did he really feel something for her, as she had begun to feel for him?

She sat up, fighting off the ragged remnants of an unhappy dream, fumbled for the handset and checked the bedside clock. It was almost eight thirty. Damn. She'd forgotten to set the alarm.

'Sorry, did I wake you?' Helen's heart crashed at the sound of his voice.

'No, not at all,' she lied. 'What's up?'

'Strange thing happened. The police just came by, with my bag.'

'Great!'

'Yeah, good news. They said some bin men handed it in. It had been abandoned not far from where I got mugged. And the odd thing was, there was hardly anything missing. Not even the cash in my wallet.'

'Your photograph?' She thought of his misery the previous night, when he spoke of the picture that could not be replaced.

'Even that.' She could tell from his voice he was smiling. 'My wallet, my phone. Everything.'

'That's weird. Maybe the thief was worried about being caught and just dumped the lot?'

'Yeah, that's what the police said. But it seemed strange, when he fought so hard to take it. Then I realised there was something.'

She could hear suppressed excitement in his voice, the same tone he got when they made a discovery, another link in the chain. He seemed to have forgotten about their kiss, or had decided not to mention it.

'After they left, I realised the Marlowe book was missing.'

Helen kicked off the bedclothes and swung her pyjama-clad legs to the floor. She needed coffee before she could process any more revelations. Shivering in the chill morning air, she pushed her feet into slippers.

'Odd.' She headed for the kitchen and put the kettle on.

'So, either my mugger had a profound interest in the works of Christopher Marlowe and was so moved by them he didn't bother to nick my money…'

'Seems unlikely.'

'Indeed. Or the mugging was something to do with our research. Which is worrying, to put it mildly.'

Sipping coffee, Helen tried to keep up with his thinking. He explained how he'd underlined the words in the Marlowe play, turned back the corner to mark the place. He'd written the words from Albert Brooke's clue in the margin.

'And then I remembered what you said about the archivist at Dulwich.' Helen was remembering something else. The door slamming behind them in the church at Deptford. She'd forgotten about it, with Richard's mugging and all that had happened since.

'Someone's interested in what we're working on, Helen. It's started to remind me of something. When I was at Canterbury, before I moved to Lambeth.'

'Uh-huh?' Helen clutched the phone between shoulder and ear while attempting to extract burning bread from the toaster. God, she was going to be so late.

'I was using the cathedral library a lot. And the books and manuscripts I wanted started to be unavailable. At first, I didn't think anything of it. There's always a lot of conservation work going on. But it was only ever when I was looking into one particular question. Eventually I complained. Then I was told the cathedral was reviewing its access procedures and some passes might be revoked. I took that as a threat. I kicked up a fuss, as you can imagine. I was planning to get the vice chancellor involved, then Charles offered me the job at Lambeth. I let it drop, but I always wondered what was behind it.'

Helen swallowed a mouthful of dry toast. 'What were you researching?'

'Thomas Becket. I was trying to find out what happened to his body.'

Now Helen really was lost. 'You mean Saint Thomas Becket? The murder in the cathedral? Isn't he buried in Canterbury Cathedral?'

She heard a long sigh on the other end of the phone. 'Not any more. Blame Henry VIII. Anyway, it's a long story. I'll tell you some other time. It's just that all this business with archivists and stolen books got me thinking about it.'

'Hmm.' Helen was sceptical. But the missing book was a strange thing. 'Look, I know this sounds daft, but are you

107

absolutely sure you didn't drop the book somewhere? Put it in your jacket pocket or something?'

She heard him expel air in irritation. 'Of course not.'

'So what do you think this means?'

He sighed. 'Like I said, I think someone wants to know what we're doing. Someone follows me from Deptford, from Marlowe's grave, and goes to great trouble to steal one book, which just happens to contain the best clue we've found yet.'

She went to her desk and picked up her own copy of Marlowe's plays. She flicked through the pages and read the lines over. 'Except there was nothing at the church in Deptford.'

'We read it wrong. We'll have to think again. But we have to think quicker than whoever mugged me yesterday.'

Helen had a full day of walks ahead, so not much time for thinking. She pulled on jeans and a warm jumper, dragged a brush through her tangled hair and tied it back in a ponytail. She slung Marlowe's plays in her bag on her way out of the door.

Across the road, she joined a bored-looking lad dressed in labourer's boots and sweatpants at the bus stop. She asked how long he'd been waiting.

''Bout ten minutes,' he said, looking at his phone. He seemed embarrassed, as if she'd crossed some boundary by speaking to him. He waited for her to board first when the bus arrived. At least he's got manners, she thought, heading upstairs for a better view as the bus sped through Deptford towards London Bridge.

* * *

She made it just in time. The walk went well: an attentive and knowledgeable group of German teachers who all seemed thrilled to be in the neighbourhood where Shakespeare and Marlowe first dazzled the theatrical world. They had booked onto the Globe tour afterwards and asked her to join them. She opted for an early lunch instead, at the coffee shop where she and Richard had talked that first day. She had half an hour before the next walk began. The cafe, between the sites of the original Globe and Rose Theatres, seemed a good place to think.

Sipping coffee, she pulled Marlowe's plays from her bag. She realised she'd made the jump from Marlowe's lines to Shakespeare's referencing of them, prompted purely by Crispin's suggestion. And then the jump to the churchyard, because she'd been thinking about Marlowe's death. Maybe she'd tried to be too clever. She went back to the words from *The Jew of Malta*. 'And as their wealth increaseth, so enclose, Infinite riches in a little room.' She thought of Albert Brooke, the Victorian scholar, tucked away in his ancestral home. The wealth of his family piling up, pouring in from his father's investments. Where did they enclose their riches?

She read on. 'Bags of fiery opals, sapphires, amethysts, jacinths, hard topaz, grass-green emeralds, beauteous rubies, sparkling diamonds.' She remembered how Richard had remarked on the 'pearls like pebble stones' and Lady Joan's enormous pearls. Helen thought of a chancer like John Brooke's lover, Kenneth, stealing a necklace at a weekend party. She imagined Lady Joan unhooking those pearls and putting them… where?

Where did a rich family keep their jewels? A jewel safe, she thought with excitement. They must have a safe for the family jewels, a little room enclosing their infinite riches. Where better to hide a valuable, secret document? The hidden play, if that was what Albert Brooke had found, would be in the Cobham family's jewel safe. And yet... Would Lady Joan not know the contents of the safe? If she used it, she would surely have investigated any piles of papers in there. Or was there another, secret safe she didn't know about? So many questions.

'We need to know what Marlowe's play was about,' Richard had insisted in Cambridge. A secret, connected with Canterbury. She thought of Richard's words that morning, about his thwarted research into Becket's grave. Pulling out her phone, she looked up the story. She knew the basics – Archbishop Becket fell out with King Henry II, fled abroad into exile, came back and was cut down by knights in his own cathedral. 'Will no one rid me of this turbulent priest?' as Henry had supposedly said.

She delved into the background. The quarrel seemed incredibly arcane: a battle between the Catholic Church and the English throne about who had jurisdiction over priests who broke the law. Becket had been Henry's boyhood friend, then his loyal chancellor. Finally, he'd been made archbishop, despite not even being a priest at the time, because Henry wanted a yes-man in the job. Becket, to his dismay, had been anything but a yes-man. It had truly been a turbulent life.

After his death, the whole Catholic Church had been outraged by his murder and blamed Henry. The Pope had made Becket a saint; miracles had been recorded at the place of his murder. The monks set up a thriving industry in Becket memorabilia, and pilgrims had visited his shrine from all over Europe. At the time of the Reformation, as Richard had said, the shrine was destroyed. Helen could find no mention of what happened to Becket's remains.

It was almost time for her next walk. She glanced out the window to check the weather. Across the street, a young lad in work boots stood in a doorway, fiddling with his phone. She recognised the boy from the bus stop. He looked up and saw her. For a moment, his face flashed confusion and guilt, reminding her powerfully of John, the Dulwich College archivist. Then he turned away, and she wondered if she'd imagined his expression.

Chapter 17

S he was jumpy for the rest of the day. Had the boy been following her? Had he been watching her flat, even, waiting for her to emerge that morning? Perhaps it was simply a coincidence. She didn't see him again, although she couldn't quite shake the sensation that someone was watching her. She spun around quickly once or twice, startling her tour group but seeing nothing suspicious.

It was a relief when the last tour finished and she was alone with her thoughts. She turned down Park Street, heading away from the Bankside crowds towards Borough High Street. As she passed the site of the Rose Playhouse, she saw the doors were open. A notice outside advertised a performance about to begin, of Marlowe's bloodthirsty history play *The Massacre at Paris*. The piece was rarely staged nowadays, having been dismissed by critics as a flawed text with little characterisation, and she had never seen it performed. It was first staged by Henslowe at the Rose mere months before Marlowe's death. What had he been thinking about? What was he interested in at the time? Richard had asked her. Here was one way to find out. She bought a ticket.

If Marlowe's ghost walked anywhere, she thought, he'd be here. Not in Deptford, where he died, but here, where he lived, and his characters still breathed. Had he been in the audience for the first performance in 1592, sitting with the toffs or standing with the commoners, waiting for the reaction to this, his most contemporary piece of theatre? Perhaps he was backstage, irritating the actors with last-minute instructions. Helen imagined him drifting in through the doors, sitting down beside her on the wooden bench, eager to see if he'd written another hit.

The play began. The cast made the best of the narrow stage, which had been built out over the excavations. The production was quick and lively, using contemporary references and pop culture imagery to play up the cartoonish nature of the violence. Marlowe had spared the audience little in his depiction of the horrors of the Saint Bartholomew's Day massacre of Protestants, which had occurred a mere twenty years before the play was written. His anti-hero, the manipulative Duke of Guise, was depicted as a preening sadist, leading a band of merciless thugs. His speeches were electrifying in the small space, the actor spitting the words straight into the audience's faces.

Helen felt the familiar rhythms of Marlowe's verse lift and carry her into the heart of the play. He loved a villain, she thought, contrasting the verbal dexterity of the Duke of Guise with the supposed hero's tedious speeches. The play was unashamedly populist, with gory murders heaping one on another and an outrageously pro-English finale. It had been a wild success, and Henslowe often staged it at the Rose. Its potent mix of anti-Catholicism, patriotism and violence had found great favour with Elizabethan audiences.

Helen joined the enthusiastic applause at the end of the play as the bodies piled on the stage jumped nimbly to their feet.

If only Marlowe could be resurrected as easily. What would she ask him, if his ghost did join the line of actors to take a bow?

No point asking about his murder, she thought. He probably knew no more than they did. The killer was known; it was the motive that was unclear, and the difficulty was too many possibilities, not too few. Two weeks ago, she'd have asked him prissy academic questions about his source material for *Doctor Faustus*. Now, she wanted to ask about Canterbury, about his childhood and the secrets he may have learnt there. And about the missing play, the Canterbury play.

Outside the theatre, the dull evening had turned to drizzle. Helen pulled her coat tight and hurried down the back streets, cutting into the alleyways around Borough Market. It was deserted.

Helen's head was full of Marlowe, his themes of ambition and daring. His characters, whose most dangerous weapon was their eloquence. The over-reachers, daring God out of heaven, summoning demons from hell and unseating kings with the power of their words. Watching a performance, seeing the audience held rapt with attention by the words you had written – that, thought Helen, could make a man feel untouchable, drunk on power. After the success of the Paris massacre, where could Marlowe go next?

If you took the question literally, he'd gone to Canterbury. He'd returned there in autumn 1592, perhaps while the London theatres were shut by the plague. Was it a triumphant return, dazzling his former schoolfriends with his London success? Or had he been beating a retreat, trying to keep his head down while damaging rumours swirled about his atheism, his blasphemy? Whatever the intent, it had ended badly, with arrest and an assault charge for attacking a man in the street. Marlowe seemed to have been utterly incapable of staying out of trouble.

Like Canterbury's most famous victim of knife crime, thought Helen. Thomas Becket, the man who became England's most powerful politician, then its highest churchman. A Marlovian over-reacher if ever there was one. Like Marlowe, Becket had seemed to seek out trouble, alienating both the church and the court, missing no opportunity to defy the King. If Marlowe wrote about Canterbury, surely he wrote about Thomas Becket, the boy who grew up to champion the Pope above the King and died for his audacity.

She stopped abruptly, taking in the implications. At a time when the state was actively hunting for Catholic plotters, when Elizabeth herself had been excommunicated by the Pope, this would be an extraordinarily dangerous undertaking. With Marlowe's increasingly murky reputation, it would have been well-nigh suicidal. And yet she was sure of it. The Canterbury play must have been the archbishop's tale.

She heard footsteps behind her and whipped around. This time she caught him – a glimpse of grey sweatpants and hooded top vanishing behind a line of bins.

'Hey!' she shouted, her voice sounding uncertain even to her own ears. She took a step towards the bins, then thought again. Her footsteps echoed in the empty market. There was no one else in shouting distance. *Get out of here*, her brain was urging. Yet she hated being spooked. 'Stop following me. Leave me alone,' she called. There was no reply. Helen realised she was shaking, hard. She turned on her heel and sprinted towards the street.

Chapter 18

'I'll be honest with you. We are worried,' said the old man. He opened his hands, placing them palm upwards on his knees.

Nick wasn't surprised. The mosque was under pressure from all sides. The imam had invited him in to discuss whether the *Courier* would run a feature on the new building, their plans and hopes for the ways it could serve the community.

He sympathised, but knew it wouldn't go down well with the readers. Things had deteriorated to the point that they had to close mosque stories to comments. The readers emailed and posted on their social media accounts instead, accusing the paper of pro-Muslim bias. The editor had assigned Nick to all reports on the mosque, after Meena's byline attracted a wave of hate-filled abuse.

Since the violence that had attended their grand opening, the imam said, they'd noticed an increase in hostility. Racist graffiti had appeared on the walls nearby. One morning, worshippers had arrived to find packets of bacon strewn across the threshold.

'Bacon!' said the man, laughter creasing his face for a moment. 'As if we will drop dead at the sight of it!' He shrugged. 'It doesn't hurt us. But it is upsetting to know that people want us to be hurt.'

And then there was the problem of Amir and his friends. The elders were concerned at their talk of revenge, of seeking out the men who attacked the mosque and who put Anjoy in hospital.

'We tell them to leave this to the police and to Allah. But they say they have no faith in the police.' He sighed. 'I ask if they have no faith in Allah. They say Allah will help those who help themselves.'

The police's lack of progress was becoming a problem, Nick knew. He'd been onto the local nick daily for news updates, until the editor got a formal complaint from the DCI in charge of the investigation, claiming he was wasting her officers' time. He'd repeatedly asked if they'd had Gary Paxton in for questioning, but the press office stonewalled him, and his usual contacts said they didn't know.

He put down his teacup. 'The police won't tell me anything, either,' he admitted. 'There is a name, one man I think they should talk to …'

'This Paxton person. Yes. I wish you hadn't told Amir that,' said the imam. 'He says he knows who he is, where he lives. His friend – you know the man? Mohammed. He began worshipping here only last year.'

Nick nodded. Steve. Did they really know where Paxton lived? Nick had only found his business address after some serious detective work.

'I worry about his influence. He boasts about having been in Syria, about military training. I don't know if it is true. But Amir and his friends, they believe everything he says. I worry about what they have planned.'

117

'But we should get back to our interview,' said the imam after a moment. 'Look to the future. Let me show you the upstairs rooms. We want to make them into classrooms to hold English lessons for the women and to teach the children about Islam. Teach them properly, so they don't grow up seeing enemies everywhere.'

Nick followed him up the stairs to the bright and airy upper rooms, well-equipped with desks and chairs, audiovisual equipment and whiteboards. The imam talked of their hopes to open a free school in the area, specialising in languages and STEM topics.

'Islam has a proud scientific tradition,' he said. 'We want our sons to be doctors, engineers, scientists.'

'And your daughters?' asked Nick, thinking of Meena.

'Our daughters too.' The man smiled. 'You must not think we are so old-fashioned that we don't want the best for all our children.'

Nick couldn't see it happening. There was already a lobby for a Church of England free school close by, with a vocal minority of parents hoping that 'the Muslims' would send their children elsewhere. If only the two religious organisations could put in a joint application instead of each treating the other as the enemy. They'd have a much better chance, and the kids might actually get to know each other. With separate schools, they'd be growing up in almost-separate communities.

Enemies everywhere. He hoped that the imam's words were not prophetic.

Chapter 19

Helen sat in the light and airy cafe of Southwark Cathedral, reading. The cathedral bookshop had furnished her with a recent biography of Thomas Becket, which outlined the twists in his mixed fortunes.

She was following up on her hunch that Marlowe's missing play might have been about Becket. She had arranged to meet Richard in half an hour to talk him through her theory. They'd not seen each other since Sunday night, three whole days during which she'd managed to convince herself that the kiss had come about entirely through her own doing, and that he was probably just being polite and had rushed off afterwards out of embarrassment. *This is why you should never get involved with colleagues*, she told herself, severely. *You always end up making an idiot of yourself.*

As ever, she took refuge in work. If she was to make a coherent case, she needed to know more about the troublesome archbishop. As she read, her conviction grew that the man's story would have been irresistible to Marlowe. Like the playwright, Becket had been of relatively modest background, the son of a London merchant on Cheapside. Like Marlowe, he seemed to have chafed against that modesty and seized the opportunities that came his way. He had been fond of ostentatious clothing and show, at least in his early life. Helen smiled and turned over her copy of Marlowe's complete plays, which showed a portrait of a dashing young man thought to be the playwright, posing in black and orange silks, brass buttons shining.

But Becket was successful beyond Marlowe's imaginings. After training as a clerk, he rose rapidly in the household of Anselm, Archbishop of Canterbury at the time, then was taken into the royal court. He swiftly became Henry II's chancellor – a dizzying rise to power. He brought up Henry's son in his own household and seemed to have been a close companion of the King.

Helen paused. Had it stopped there, perhaps the story would have had a happy ending. And yet she wondered. Marlowe would understand the temptation, she thought, the feeling that if your wit makes you the equal of a man, you should be seen as such, no matter the difference in status. From everything she'd read that morning, Becket, like Marlowe, had shown himself ready to make enemies to get what he wanted.

A familiar voice caught her ear. She looked towards the cafeteria queue and saw Father Nash, joking with the cashier. He picked up his tray and surveyed the room, smiled in recognition and raised a hand.

'How nice to see a friendly face. May I join you?'

Apart from the vicar's collar, he was in casual tweeds. He sat down heavily in front of a plate of lasagne.

'Are you here for a service?' she asked.

He'd spent a frustrating morning discussing the church's education policy, he explained, at a meeting held in Southwark's diocesan offices.

'I hear time and again from members of Christianity in Crisis how much they want to send their children to our schools. Church schools have the best results in the country, you know, and every one is oversubscribed. With the free school programme, there's never been a better time to open new schools. Yet my colleagues are cautious.'

He looked around the cafeteria and leaned towards her, mock-conspiratorial. 'They're a bunch of old women, between you and me. My parish is crying out for good primary schools, in Chatham, Strood and Rochester. The recent wave of immigration means our schools are over-full already. If we are truly to integrate these new arrivals, where better to do it than in Church of England schools? And if we don't... Well, there are others who will seize the opportunity.'

He took up his knife and fork and tucked in.

'I used to teach, myself,' Helen volunteered. 'But I struggled with keeping discipline. It was such hard work.'

He finished his mouthful and nodded vigorously. 'That's the thing. Church-run schools are so good at establishing a disciplined culture. It shouldn't be left to the individual teachers. It needs to run right through the school ethos. That's why I want our members on the governing bodies of schools, setting up free schools, being elected onto the local authorities' education committees. This trendy multiculturalism has done so much damage already.'

Helen started to gather her work materials together. His eyes fell on the book by her elbow.

'Saint Thomas Becket? I didn't know you were interested in that period of history, Helen.'

She smiled. 'It's just a theory. I know nothing about Becket, really. Do you remember I was working with Richard on some Marlowe research?'

He nodded. 'A Canterbury play, you said.'

'Marlowe's from Canterbury, of course. And we're trying to work out what he might have been writing about. I had a thought – just a hunch, really – that he might have written about Thomas Becket. I mean, it's such an amazing story. And he's a typical Marlovian character.'

'How very intriguing. Tell me more.'

'There isn't really much more to say.' Helen began to feel uncomfortable, remembering how Richard had told Lady Joan that he didn't want the priest to know about their research. 'Like I said, it's just a theory. I thought I should find out more about him.'

Father Nash laid his fingers on the cover of her book. 'Saint Thomas Becket has always been an inspirational figure to me. His stand in defence of the church against the tyranny of the state, even when he knew his life was at stake.'

His colour was heightened; his eyes had taken on a shine she had not seen before, even when he discussed his campaign. 'I would be so privileged if you would let me know about the progress of your investigations, Helen. Will you do me that favour?'

She laughed, a little awkwardly. 'I doubt it will come to anything. But of course, I'll let you know if I get anywhere.'

'Bless you for that,' he said. 'Now, I should be getting back to my parish. A priest's work is never done.' He picked up his tray and cleared it conscientiously away.

Helen checked her watch. Almost time to meet Richard outside the cathedral. She felt another tug of guilt. But she'd not told Father Nash anything of their research. It had just been a hunch, like she said. She pulled out a pocket mirror from her rucksack and checked her teeth for signs of spinach soup. Furtively, she unearthed a lipstick and painted it on. *Daft*, she told herself. *Like he's going to notice what you look like.*

Chapter 20

He was sitting on the wall with his notebook balanced on his knee, writing. Helen stopped and watched for a second. His concentration was total; he frowned slightly as he wrote and pushed the hair back from his forehead in a gesture of irritation. She felt as nervous as a teenager on a first date. *Get a grip*, she told herself, and tried to fix a confident smile on her face.

She was standing right in front of him before he looked up. 'Sorry, I was miles away.' He jumped to his feet, smiling. Awkwardly, they negotiated a tentative kiss on the cheek.

'You look nice. I just saw that creep Francis Nash. Luckily he didn't notice me.'

Helen flushed and tried to keep her tone neutral. 'Yes, I saw him in the cafe. He came to say hello.' They made their way out through the garden into the narrow street, crowded even on a weekday. 'Why don't you like him?'

He shoved his hands in his pockets, his shoulders hunched. 'Oh, I don't know. All that jolly bonhomie strikes me as a bit false. And I don't think much of his brand of Christianity. There's nothing in the Bible that I've seen about cracking down on immigration.'

Helen was silent. She too had been surprised by the politics in the leaflet he'd given her. They seemed at odds with his pleasant demeanour. But she supposed anyone who counted Lady Joan as their close ally would have to be pretty right of centre.

'Never mind him, anyway. Where are we going? You sounded very mysterious on the phone.'

'Round the corner.' She led the way through the uneven streets, past the replica of Sir Francis Drake's Golden Hind ship, to where a lone stone gable stood, the remains of a magnificent rose window outlined against the sky. Beneath the window stood the foundations of an ancient building.

'The old Bishop's Palace. What brings us here?' he asked.

'Thomas Becket,' she said, leaning on the railings that surrounded the site. 'I've been reading about him. He stayed here for a night, after his return from exile, with the Bishop of Winchester. I wanted to have another look.' Tourists milled past them. She marshalled her thoughts, taking courage from the history in the stones that surrounded her.

'He wanted to see the King's son, but was refused entry at the city gates. So, the next day, he returned to Canterbury. And was murdered, as you know, in the cathedral.'

'I do know,' he said, gravely.

She rolled her eyes. 'Well, yes. I'm just trying to think like Marlowe might have done. He'd have seen the remains of the palace, of course, every time he walked from the Rose Playhouse down to Southwark.'

'On his way to the George to meet Shakespeare for a pot of ale,' supplied Richard.

'Stop taking the mickey. What I mean is, if he knew the story – and I bet he did – then he'd have had a constant reminder of the archbishop's last journey. Becket must have travelled

125

on the same roads that Marlowe would have taken, between Southwark and Canterbury. He probably knew the route well, and up until a few years before Marlowe's birth, it was the pilgrim route.'

He nodded. 'True enough. What's your theory, then?'

She took a deep breath. 'You asked me where Marlowe was going, what he was thinking about, at the end of his life. He'd just seen *The Massacre at Paris*, his most contemporary play, go down a storm at the Rose. There was an appetite for history plays, especially those that touched on the religious divides of the time and that people could connect to.

'Just after the *Massacre* opened, he went to Canterbury for the last time in his life. We don't know why he went, or what he did there – except that he got into trouble, again, for fighting.'

She gazed at her hands. 'It's just a hunch. But perhaps he went back to Canterbury to talk to someone, ask questions, gather material for his next play. Becket was exactly the sort of character Marlowe liked. Humble origins, took on the world, defied kings – and finally died in a blaze of glory, his memory living on in sainthood.'

'Wow.' Richard leaned alongside her, steepling his fingers. 'So you think the Canterbury play was about Thomas Becket?'

'To be honest, I can't imagine what else he'd have written about in a play set in Canterbury. And this business about a secret. The secret that was in the play, that Lady Joan thinks her ancestor was framed to keep quiet? What about the work you were doing, trying to find out what happened to Becket's body?'

There was a long pause. Helen heard a helicopter overhead, chatter from a group of Japanese teenagers, a burst of laughter.

126

He doesn't buy it, she thought. *He thinks I'm stupid.*

'Bloody hell,' said Richard. 'Of course.' He turned and took her hands in his. 'There's even a folder of papers in Albert Brooke's folio all about Becket's tomb. I read them, just to see if he'd found out anything I hadn't, but it didn't occur to me that this was linked to the family history.' He squeezed her hands tight, his eyes shining. 'You're a genius.'

'Perhaps.' She grinned, absurdly pleased. 'So what did you find out when you were researching Becket's tomb?'

Three hundred years after Becket's murder, he said, Henry VIII had ordered the destruction of the Canterbury shrine, declaring that the archbishop had been a traitor, not a saint. The golden canopy was removed and the jewels that studded it were wrenched out. The King wore one magnificent ruby in a ring on his thumb, and the rest enriched his treasury. However, no one knew what had happened to the body of the dispossessed saint.

'It's a total mystery. I spent years trying to find out,' Richard told her. 'There are various accounts of what happened, but no eye-witness records from good sources. The most likely story seemed to be the one that reached the Pope – that the bones were destroyed, probably burned. But there have been persistent rumours that they were moved, perhaps hidden or buried elsewhere within the cathedral.'

The secret would have been religious dynamite, he explained. Becket was the embodiment of the power of the Roman Catholic Church, set against the English state. Henry VIII was determined that the saint's cult should be suppressed. The continued existence of Becket's relics, with their reputed miraculous powers, could be a dangerous rallying point for England's rebellious Catholics. With the religious turmoil of the following century, as England swung sharply from Protestantism to Catholicism and back, whoever held that secret could threaten the existence of the state.

Helen could see the importance of the bones in the Elizabethan period. The struggle between the two sects raged, with threats of invasion from Spain to re-establish Catholicism, and a papal bull of excommunication against Elizabeth. The secret service worked overtime to uncover and neuter Catholic plots against the Queen.

And the destruction of the shrine was not a long-distant event, she thought. It had taken place just twenty-six years before Christopher Marlowe's birth. 'That's within living memory. People who saw it happen would still have been living in Canterbury while Marlowe was growing up,' she said.

They were hunched over the railing, keeping their voices low as if a passing tourist might report them to the authorities. This was how conspiracy theories started, Helen supposed: a game of what if, lacing together supposition and rumour. Instinctively, she went back to the facts and began to list what was known.

'We know that he attended the King's School, and possibly Eastbridge. The King's School was – still is – next to the cathedral. I suppose that was close enough for gossip to pass around. Who do you think hid the bones?'

He shrugged. 'I'm guessing the monks. The same order of monks had guarded his body from the very night of the murder. Becket's shrine brought them enormous fortune over the centuries. From everything I have read, religious orders across the country were deeply distressed by the destruction of England's saints during the Reformation. There's evidence that the Durham monks planned to hide Saint Cuthbert's bones from Henry's commissioners.'

'But the monastery at Canterbury was dissolved, wasn't it? What happened to the monks afterwards?' she asked.

'A good question. There was a shortage of priests in the town. A shortage of people in the town, actually, because of the plague. Some of the vacant posts in the parish churches were probably filled with former monks. Some of the younger ones might have been released from holy orders and gone into another trade. Some might have become masters at the King's School, don't you think? Or Eastbridge, for that matter.

'So, what have we got?' He drew out his notebook and began to write. 'A hidden body. Marlowe, as a child, learning the secret. And he was a spy, yes?'

She nodded. 'Almost certainly an intelligence agent of some sort, dating from his time at Cambridge. Most likely reporting on Catholic sympathisers.'

'Good. Right. So perhaps inveigling himself into Raleigh's circle, listening out for Catholic gossip. Marlowe lets something slip about Becket's bones, perhaps trying to draw them out about their own sympathies. And he writes a play, hinting at the location of the bones. Word gets out to the authorities, leading to Marlowe's death. But Raleigh, or maybe Cobham, keeps a copy. Then ten years later, long after Marlowe's death, it's discovered. They are thrown in the Tower and accused of treason. Only one question left – what happened to the play?'

'Indeed.' She threw him a dry look. Only one question. A week ago, she'd have thought him a fantasist, but now she understood better how his mind worked. The high-wire act was dazzling to watch, as he swung from one barely established fact to another. But she knew he was also prepared to put in the work to prove his theories.

She told him of her idea that Albert Brooke's 'infinite wealth' clue might indicate a safe or safety deposit box. 'It makes more sense. I mean, where else would he have hidden something precious?'

This time, Richard was less convinced. 'I see what you mean, but surely it would have come to light by now? Anyway, we can ask Lady Joan on Friday.'

Friday. Helen was dreading dinner at Cobham Hall. She had no idea what to wear, for a start. She thought of Charlotte's black suit, Lady Joan's twinset. She owned nothing similar. Distracted for a minute, it took her a while to realise what Richard was saying.

'Do you want to go further with this, though?' he asked. His voice was quiet. 'I've been working on this problem, one way or another, for the best part of twenty years. This is the first breakthrough I've had in all that time. It's wonderful to have your help. But ...' He broke off, looked down into the palace foundations below them.

'It might be dangerous. I'm not being dramatic. This secret has been kept for a long time. Last time I worked on this, I was blocked at every turn. There are people who want this to remain a mystery.'

Helen thought of the man she'd seen following her, and of Richard's mugging.

'I believe you,' she said. 'And I want to work with you. The thing is...' She broke off. 'I can see why this was a hot topic in Elizabethan times. I just can't see why anyone would be so worried about it today.'

Chapter 21

Richard offered Helen his arm as they followed Charlotte Elms down the corridors of Cobham Hall. Struggling to keep up in her unfamiliar spike-heeled shoes, she took it with gratitude. She'd spent ages trying on frocks down in Crispin's flat until they decided on the slim-fitting red silk dress she'd bought for her sister's wedding, seven years ago. He'd piled her hair up into a French twist, secured by a million hairpins and half a can of spray. Crimson lipstick completed her transformation.

'He'll be putty in your hands,' Crispin had said, satisfied with his work. 'Lucky man. Now, remember to stand properly. You're not on parade; you're a princess.'

Richard looked almost elegant this evening, in a dark grey double-breasted suit. She suspected by the old-fashioned cut that he too had had it for some years. It was the first time they'd seen each other in formal clothes and she felt self-conscious. Richard, on the other hand, seemed entirely at ease.

He'd phoned Lady Joan to ask if they could arrive early before dinner, hinting that they'd made a breakthrough. She'd agreed, telling him mysteriously that she had a surprise for him, too. 'I don't know if Lady Joan's surprises are my idea of fun,' he'd warned Helen. 'I'm not sure we share the same sense of humour. If indeed she has one at all.'

The hall was seriously spooky by night. The passages were even colder, the echoes more pronounced and the shadows fell more deeply. She was glad when they reached the library with its welcoming fire. Lady Joan, however, was about as welcoming as a nightclub bouncer, in a black crêpe frock adorned with a large brooch of sparkling diamonds. It looked like an enormous dew-drenched spider, thought Helen, perched on her shoulder to be unleashed onto her enemies when the time was right. She stood before the fire, hands clasped behind her back, and nodded to her guests as they entered.

'Now, Richard. No more of this nonsense. Tell me what you have discovered.' *Before I set the spider on you,* thought Helen, suppressing a nervous giggle.

'It's been a joint effort,' he said firmly. 'In fact, Helen has done most of the work. Perhaps she should be the one to tell you?' He looked at her enquiringly. She gave him a tight little smile of panic. *No way,* she thought, trying to signal her alarm with her eyes.

Richard took the lead, telling Lady Joan about the cryptic lines Albert Brooke had written, just at the point in his folio where he had tucked the transcript of the letter from Raleigh to Lord Cobham. 'They made no sense to me. But Helen deciphered them and came up with a line from a Marlowe play. We think the line could point to a safe, or jewel box, and that Albert might have hidden something there.'

Helen saw scepticism on Lady Joan's face. 'Infinite riches, Lady Joan. The play talks about piles of priceless jewels and enclosing infinite riches in a little room. What would that have meant to your grandfather?' she asked.

'Interesting.' She touched a hand to her brooch, as if reassuring herself it was still there. 'There is a jewel safe in my bedroom. But that was installed during the 1960s, more than ten years after my grandfather died. I only use it for day-to-day pieces. Anything of real value is kept at our bank.'

A bank vault, Helen thought, exchanging a glance with Richard. Was that not more likely, after all? A proper little room.

'Have you had the same family bank vault since Albert's time? Or even before?' he asked. Helen pictured a room heaped with gold bars, sacks of jewels spilling their dazzling contents onto the floor. But she supposed it would mostly be piles of dusty documents, share certificates and bonds, paper indicators of wealth.

'We have. It's in Switzerland.' Helen saw Richard's face fall. He'd hoped to follow the clue tonight, she knew, not to have to arrange a trip overseas.

'Young woman.' Helen jumped. 'Would you kindly repeat the lines from the play?' She did so, trying not to stare at Lady Joan's spider as she spoke of beauteous rubies and sparkling diamonds.

'Infinite riches in a little room.' Something close to a smile broke on the woman's face. 'My grandfather was a man of wit and culture,' she said. 'I think you are being too literal.'

She walked along the wall of books, scanning the shelves. 'He was responsible for restoring the library. He collected many of the books. He had one particular favourite, which we read together. He used to tell me it held treasure from all over the world.'

She prepared to climb a set of mahogany library steps.

'Please, let me,' said Richard. 'You'll hurt yourself.'

'Up you go, then. You see the two volumes in tan leather with the gold chasing? Just to the right of your head.'

He turned his head to see the title on the spine, then laughed. He fetched them down and set them on a small rosewood desk, brushing dust from the covers. 'I don't think I've seen an original before. May I?'

Helen craned to see. Richard turned to the title page. *The Book of Days: a miscellany of popular antiquities*, she read. *Edited by R. Chambers, 1864.*

He grinned at her. 'Chambers' *Book of Days* was a classic Victorian text. It's a compendium of improving essays touching on just about everything, organised by the day they happened. There are birthdays of famous people, saints' days, historical events, popular mythologies and seasonal traditions. Enquire within upon everything.'

'My grandfather valued knowledge above all else, including mere wealth,' said Lady Joan, with the disdain of the very rich. 'To him, infinite riches would never be encompassed by jewels in a safe. Knowledge in a book, yes.'

'And Chambers – a chamber, a little room.' Helen had it now. Much cleverer than her own too-literal reading. No doubt Lady Joan thought her irredeemably vulgar. She turned her attention back to the book. 'But this isn't a hiding place. It's not hollow or something?'

'Certainly not.' Lady Joan frowned. 'My grandfather would not countenance the destruction of a book.'

Richard began turning the pages of the first volume. 'Yet if you are correct, he intended this to help you find the lost Marlowe play. There must be something here. Helen, when did Marlowe die? What date?'

'The thirtieth of May.'

He turned the pages. Chambers had not thought the event of sufficient significance to include, instead choosing essays on King Arthur, Alexander Pope and Joan of Arc. There was nothing, no marker to indicate that Albert Brooke had found the date significant in any way.

'Saints' days,' said Helen. 'Try Thomas Becket.'

The old woman's head swivelled towards her. 'Becket? Why Becket?' Her tone was sharp.

'It's just a hunch,' said Helen. 'We were wondering what Marlowe might have written about in a Canterbury play. I thought perhaps he'd have written about Thomas Becket, as he'd have known the story so well, growing up in Canterbury.'

'I see.' The woman hesitated, as if considering telling them more. Then she waved at Richard, gesturing for him to continue.

'And then there's the question of Becket's remains,' he said, eagerly. 'I know your grandfather was interested in that, Lady Joan. We wondered if they were somehow connected. If the play might actually tell us where the bones were finally buried.'

Charlotte Elms entered the room, elegant in a simple green dress, and gave a polite cough. 'Lady Joan, Mr Fairfax.' A small, neat man of middle age stood in the doorway. His dark suit was immaculate, his shoes shining like polished jet. He wore his grey hair closely clipped. His eyes were hard to see behind thick, round spectacles that reflected the light. He wore a tentative smile, as if uncertain of his reception.

'Charles!' Richard broke off from his perusal of the books' index. 'How marvellous. Lady Joan didn't tell me you were coming. How are you?' The two men shook hands, Richard pumping the man's arm until Helen feared it would come off. Eventually Mr Fairfax freed his hand and greeted his hostess.

'How d'you do, Lady Joan? It was most kind of you to include me in this gathering.' His pale face had flushed, Helen saw, and there were drops of sweat at his temples.

'Helen Oddfellow, Charles Fairfax.' Richard performed the introductions. 'Helen is a literary scholar, an expert on the work of Christopher Marlowe. Charles is my former colleague, the chief archivist at Lambeth Palace. He's a true friend.' She looked at the man with renewed interest. This was the boss who had stuck by him, then, helped him find his hostel place and another job after his dive into alcoholism. She smiled warmly. 'I've heard a lot about you,' she said.

He nodded, a little stiffly. 'And how do you know Richard?' he asked. She wondered if she'd imagined hostility in his tone.

'We're working together on Lady Joan's research,' she said. She still didn't know whether Richard thought of her as more than a colleague. The man's gaze flickered between them, as if he was wondering the same thing. She felt her cheeks warm and hoped she wasn't blushing too badly.

'In fact, you join us at a critical moment, Charles. We seem to be on the verge of a discovery. Would you mind if we press on for a moment?'

'Of course. What are you working on?' A pinch of anxiety had appeared between the man's eyebrows. He was so stiff, thought Helen, so tightly wound. She found it hard to imagine what he and Richard, with his impulsive and demonstrative nature, had in common.

Richard explained, pacing the room as if too keyed up to

keep still. Watching him speak, Helen found herself assailed by doubt. It was all so tentative. They had no hard facts, no evidence to bolster the theory. Just one letter, which wasn't even an original, and one cryptic clue. The rest was conjecture, circumstantial evidence linking a Cambridge college, a Canterbury hospital, a playwright, a churchman, a saint and an adventurer. She glanced at Lady Joan, wondering what she made of all this. To her surprise, the woman was watching Richard with what appeared to be a tolerant expression, almost indulgence.

'It all sounds most unlikely,' said Charles. His tone was dismissive. 'I think you're wasting your time, Richard. And the time of this young woman.' He placed his hand on the volumes, proprietorial. The challenge was unmistakable.

Richard looked hurt, like a small boy receiving a reprimand where he had expected praise. When he spoke, his voice was light and level. 'Let's see, shall we? No harm in looking.' Quickly, he flipped the second volume over and began leafing through from the back. Footnotes, then 31 December, 30 December. Becket had died just after celebrating the Mass of Christmas, Helen remembered. Richard turned the page to 29 December.

Chapter 22

Pressed between the pages was a scrap of paper, dirty and worn at the edges. It had a cross-hatching of creases, as if it had been folded into a small square. Richard looked up, his face shining with triumph. He breathed out, a long exhalation, and Helen realised she too had been holding her breath.

Lady Joan stood at one elbow, hawk eyes fixed on the page. Charles was on the other side, his expression closed. Richard locked eyes with Helen.

'Here.' He carefully turned the book around, without moving the paper, so she could read the text. 'You cracked the clue.'

She bent over the paper. In the top left-hand corner was a sketch of a crescent moon with three wavy lines beneath. The writing was in italic script, which could date it to the Elizabethan period. Italic was easier to read than the Gothic secretary hand, which made so many business documents of the time difficult to decipher. She began to read. Quickly, she realised the words were familiar.

My Lord, be of good chere...

She raised her eyes to Richard. 'It's the original. The Raleigh letter to Lord Cobham while they were in the Tower.' She concentrated on the script, trying to remember the examples of Raleigh's handwriting she had seen in the British Library. Would this match? Was it authentic? Lady Joan was by her side now, utilising sharp elbows to get close to the document.

'What's that?' she asked. 'That little drawing?'

Richard peered across the table. 'Isn't it a crescent moon? An Islamic symbol?'

Helen shook her head. 'I've seen it somewhere before. Something to do with a portrait.' She trawled her memory. 'The crescent moon – I think it's about Elizabeth I. A symbol of her purity, or something like that.'

'Mr Fairfax, are you alright?' Charlotte had stepped discreetly forward and taken the man's arm. He looked terrible, Helen saw, his face bloodless and his lips white. He swayed, one hand pinching the bridge of his nose. Quickly, Richard was with him, supporting him into an armchair. He lowered his head into his hands. Charlotte brought a glass of water.

'Do you need a doctor, Mr Fairfax?' Lady Joan's voice was impatient.

'No, I'm fine.' He took a sip of water. 'My apologies. I felt a little dizzy for a moment. Perhaps too close to the fire…' He gestured at the feeble flames.

Helen realised Lady Joan had taken advantage of the distraction to position herself firmly in front of the letter. She had taken a large magnifying glass from the mantelpiece and was squinting at the faint letters. 'Read it to me,' she told Helen.

She read the words aloud, Raleigh's plea to Lord Cobham not to make further confessions, but to deal with 'poor merlin's Canterbury booke'. Out of the corner of her eye, she saw Charles take off his spectacles and polish them fiercely with his big white handkerchief. Something about the discovery of the letter had upset him greatly.

'And what does that say?' Lady Joan pointed an arthritic, ring-laden finger to the bottom of the paper. Puzzled, Helen saw an additional string of letters set below Raleigh's flamboyantly loopy signature.

'I don't know. It wasn't in the transcript,' she said, her voice low.

An electronic buzzer sounded from the corridor outside. Charlotte excused herself and left the room.

'That will be our remaining guest,' said Lady Joan. Helen heard a note of triumph, or perhaps just excitement, in her voice.

'Richard, do you have a pen and paper?' Helen tried to keep her voice matter-of-fact. She didn't want to draw attention to the additional line. She cursed the tiny handbag that Crispin had insisted she carry, barely big enough for her keys and lipstick. She usually hefted around books, notepads and a handful of ballpoints in a practical rucksack.

He reached into his inside jacket pocket and extracted the black leather notebook and his fountain pen.

Carefully, she copied the string of letters across into the book, trying not to make blots with the ink pen. They didn't have any obvious meaning that she could think of. She looked at the note again. What else was different from the transcript? She began to copy the little picture of the moon and Raleigh's signature.

'Lady Joan, Father Nash.' Charlotte ushered the man into the room. He was beaming, dressed in a soft black suit and immaculate white collar.

'How wonderful, Lady Joan. Quite a reunion!' He took both

her hands in his own. 'You look marvellous.'

Helen saw Richard gesture towards his notebook, his eyes urgent. She placed the Chambers book on top and began turning the pages back from the Raleigh document, as if browsing.

The priest shook hands with the two men. Charles Fairfax, like Richard, was unsmiling. Helen felt a prickle of irritation at their hostility. Father Nash made his way to her side.

'Hello, Helen. You look very elegant. What is this that you're poring over? It looks interesting.' He leaned over to look.

'It belonged to Lady Joan's grandfather. They used to read it together. It's a sort of Victorian compendium of general knowledge. We were looking things up,' Helen gabbled. She felt embarrassed, not wanting to lie but aware of Richard's dislike of the priest. She found herself hoping Father Nash would not mention their discussion in Southwark Cathedral.

'We are making progress with my historical research,' said Lady Joan, firmly. 'We have discovered a letter from Walter Raleigh to my ancestor Lord Cobham, which was hidden in the book.' Helen bit her lip. Lady Joan opened it to show him.

'How fascinating. Let me see if I can decipher it,' he said.

'Lady Joan, please don't tell everyone.' Richard was on his feet and around the desk. He quickly pocketed his notebook.

Lady Joan looked outraged. 'Father Nash is not *everyone*. Richard, I know you historians like to keep your discoveries to yourselves until you can publish with a great huzzah. But you are working for me.'

He turned away and leaned against the mantelpiece. Helen saw a muscle twitch in his cheek. His long fingers gripped the marble ledge until they were as white as it was.

'You are my guest, as well as my employee.' Helen flinched. Did she have to humiliate him in this way? 'I invited you here tonight to hear more about your progress with my family history research. If I choose to invite others and share that information with them, that is what I shall do.'

Richard straightened his back and turned to face them. His face was flushed, but to her surprise, he was smiling. 'Of course, Lady Joan. Forgive me for my rudeness. But as Charles was saying, we're at a very early stage. You know what it's like. Until you're sure of your theory, you don't want to start shouting about it.'

Father Nash held up his hands. 'Richard, the last thing I want is to distress you in any way. I'm simply delighted that you are making progress. I won't pry, of course. But as you know, I have a great interest in Saint Thomas Becket. How does this relate to your previous work?'

Richard stared at him. 'Who said anything about Becket?'

Helen's stomach lurched. She knew she should have told Richard about her conversation with Father Nash. She tried to form the words, to admit that it had been her.

'That was the page you were looking at,' said Father Nash, nodding to the *Book of Days* with a smile. 'And you told me before that you were looking for a missing Marlowe play. Marlowe was from Canterbury, so it's not such a jump to think he might have written about Becket.'

Helen breathed again. She didn't dare to look at the priest. He'd somehow realised her dilemma and come to her rescue.

Charles Fairfax rose quietly to his feet. His colour had returned. He replaced his polished spectacles and gave a little cough. 'If I may, Lady Joan?'

The woman inclined her head. For someone Richard

described as a true friend, Helen thought, he didn't seem very friendly.

'As I understand it, the link to Thomas Becket is purely speculative. The letter you have found is certainly interesting, Lady Joan. It will require authentication, of course, and verification. We can help with that, at the archive, with our specialist equipment. I'm very happy to put our extensive services at your disposal.'

He was so stuffy, thought Helen. His pompous tones, his careful speech.

'With all respect to your grandfather, the Victorian era was awash with tricksters forging historical documents for one reason or another. Until the letter is authenticated, there seems little point in speculating on its putative meaning.'

Lady Joan's nostrils flared, but she said nothing.

The man's expression was cold as he addressed Father Nash. 'Francis, there is nothing in this work to concern you at present. Everyone knows of your interest in Thomas Becket. Rest assured that if anything more comes of this, you will hear about it.'

He turned to Richard. 'Perhaps it would be best if I took the letter with me tonight. I will see that it is correctly stored until work can begin.'

'No!' Richard placed a hand on the book. 'Not until I have had time to study it properly.'

'Enough,' said Lady Joan. Her voice, with its expectation of absolute obedience, cut through the room. She removed Richard's hand as if it was an empty glove and picked up the letter. Her gaze raked the men. She held the paper in both hands, a faint smile around her mouth. Helen saw she was enjoying the power, the knowledge that they all wanted what she had.

'Miss Elms.' The woman stepped forward. 'Please take this letter and put it in my safe.' She glanced at Helen. 'Perhaps that's a more suitable place for it, after all.'

The men watched the young woman's retreating back as she carefully carried the precious letter away.

Chapter 23

'Now,' said Lady Joan, beaming with satisfaction, 'let us go through to dinner.'

The meal was an ordeal. The six of them were spaced around a huge mahogany dining table, gleaming with silver and candles. The room was cold, and the company not much warmer. Helen's bare arms froze into goosebumps as she sipped claret from a tiny wine glass and chomped her way through tough lamb cutlets. She sensed that she was missing some of the cross-currents that swirled below the stilted conversation.

Lady Joan barely spoke, content to watch the effect of her machinations from the head of the table. Richard was uncharacteristically reticent, answering questions in monosyllables. Charles Fairfax avoided meeting Richard's eye; Lady Joan seemed oblivious to his reproachful glances.

Father Nash appeared to have recovered best from the scene in the library, producing a stream of light-hearted anecdotes about the television shows he'd appeared on. Helen warmed to him again. At least someone was trying to behave normally. She joined Charlotte Elms in attempting to keep his conversational sallies airborne.

'After all these chat shows, I hope to persuade the BBC to

let me do something serious. A documentary about Thomas Becket,' he said. 'He is such a fascinating figure. And then there's the mystery of what happened to his sacred remains. I know Richard has a particular interest in that?'

Richard looked up sharply, but said nothing. Helen gave a weak smile. 'I don't know much about it,' she said.

To her relief, Charlotte took up the baton. 'He's certainly an interesting figure. Cobham Village used to be on the pilgrim route, you know, from London to Canterbury. Chaucer's pilgrims might have walked past the hall, maybe stopped for a meal or shelter along the way.'

'The holy blissful martyr for to seek,' said Richard, catching Helen's eye with a smile.

'It's hard to imagine now, isn't it?' said Father Nash. 'Someone prepared to risk everything, even his life, to defend the church against the state.'

'I suppose there are still people who do that, though,' Helen mused, hoping to move the conversation away from Becket. 'Not necessarily in this country, and not just to defend Christianity. But there are lots of parts of the world where religion can get you killed.'

Father Nash eagerly agreed, pointing to the Christian communities in the Middle East that had been persecuted in recent times, by extremist Islamic groups.

'I don't think Islam has the monopoly on religious persecution,' said Charles Fairfax, diving into the conversation for the first time. Before long, the two men were deep in a theological discussion about whether Islam was an aggressive religion by nature. Helen saw Richard look up, as if intending to interject, then refrain. Finally, he launched himself into the argument, berating Nash for his lack of historical awareness.

'Just look at the Reformation!' he shouted. 'People all over Europe were beheaded, burned at the stake, for minor doctrinal differences between different branches of Christianity. It's all about power, not intrinsic to any one religion.'

Helen glanced anxiously at Lady Joan, wondering how she would take this outbreak of religious argument at her dinner table. Surely it was against all rules of polite social engagement? But the woman seemed to be enjoying it enormously, turning her head to watch the exchanges as if she was in the Royal Box at Wimbledon.

'Islam was one of the more tolerant religions in the late Middle Ages,' Helen ventured. 'And there was lots of trade going on between Europe and the Ottoman Empire in Elizabethan times. Plenty of merchants travelled to Constantinople, and to Morocco too. Some of them converted to Islam. There are portraits of them in Turkish robes and turbans.'

Richard smiled at her. 'Turning Turk. Isn't that what they called it?'

Helen nodded. 'There was lots of interest in the Islamic world too – you can see it in the plays. Marlowe and Shakespeare both wrote about Moors and Turks, and Marlowe's Tamburlaine was probably the first Muslim hero seen on the London stage.'

'He was also a cruel warlord,' said Charles Fairfax, frowning. 'I don't think you can use him as an example of peaceful Islam.'

'Perhaps not.' She was surprised that he knew anything about the play, which was rarely performed these days, not least because of the difficulty for modern productions posed by the defiant Tamburlaine burning a copy of the Quran on stage. She finished her wine and wondered if there was any chance of a top-up.

Discreetly, she took a glance at her wristwatch, dismayed to see it was only a little past eight o'clock. It looked like being a very long night. The meal and the discussion ground on, some kind of blancmange followed by a cheese course, then finally she saw Lady Joan rise to her feet.

'Ladies?' Helen realised with horror that they were expected to retire to the drawing room to make polite conversation, leaving the men to their politics. The argument had reached such a pitch that she almost wondered if it was safe to leave them alone. They barely seemed to notice the women's departure. Charlotte shot her a reassuring smile. 'They'll be fine. I do like your frock, Helen.'

* * *

At least the temperature in the small sitting room was a few degrees above the rest of the house. The three women drank coffee from the Wedgewood cups while Helen parried excruciating questions from Lady Joan about her family background, her academic credentials and her relationship with Richard. As there was nothing of interest to say about the first two, and she was in the dark about the third, they did not get far.

In desperation, Helen rose to her feet to examine a rather fine oil painting over the mantelpiece. A man with an intelligent face, hair swept back from his high forehead, wearing what seemed to be a white silk turban and red tunic. His level grey eyes crinkled a little at the corners, as if he was trying not to laugh at his unorthodox costume. Something about him made her think of Richard.

'This is nice. Who is it?'

'My grandfather, Albert Brooke,' said Lady Joan, to her surprise. 'He served in India for a time before his father died. He had this done when he returned. Like your Elizabethan gentlemen in their Turkish costumes.'

Helen looked with renewed interest. This, then, was the man who had hidden Raleigh's letter and devised a cryptic clue to its whereabouts. A man of wit and culture, Lady Joan had said. She could see it in his face. She scrutinised him for an echo of Lady Joan, with her hawkish eyes and prominent nose. Perhaps, she thought, if the expression was softer, there was something.

She turned to the older woman with a smile. 'I think I see the family resemblance.' Lady Joan made a dismissive gesture, but Helen thought she was pleased.

After what seemed like an age, Father Nash joined them. The priest made a beeline for Helen.

'They're just arranging taxis. Now, while I have you to myself, I wanted to ask more about Marlowe's work. I do find *Doctor Faustus* fascinating, from a theological point of view. Such a terrifying example of a man setting his face against salvation.'

Finally, a topic she could discuss till the cows came home without worrying about making social faux pas. He expressed real interest, asked intelligent questions. He wanted to hear all about the production of *The Massacre at Paris*, and before long she found herself explaining how that had led to her theory about the Canterbury play. Still, she reasoned, he already knew about her hunch and the letter they'd found. She explained about the transcript of the letter, and how she had deciphered the clue.

'Goodness, that's very clever. Infinite riches in a little room.

I'm not sure I'd have got from that to the Chambers book. Tell me, how does this link in with Richard's previous work about Saint Thomas? It was something we used to discuss when he worked at Lambeth with Charles. He was so sure that the relics had been preserved.'

Helen hesitated. 'I think it might just be a coincidence,' she said. 'I suppose there could be something in the Marlowe play, but we won't know unless we find it. And we've still got a long way to go.'

Richard and Charles entered the room, looking ill at ease. Richard didn't seem pleased to find her tête à tête with Francis Nash. *Well, too bad*, thought Helen. *You bring me to this freezing place, subject me to horrible Lady Joan and then leave me alone with her to be interrogated.* She threw him what she hoped was a carefree smile.

'We should get going,' he said, a hand on her shoulder. 'The cab will be here in five minutes. Charles will share with us. We're heading the same way.'

Great. She'd half-hoped that a long taxi journey through the dark night might have settled the question of Richard's feelings towards her. Now they'd have the uptight archivist sitting alongside, spreading caution and gloom.

* * *

'Sorry. It was a bit of a rough evening,' Richard admitted. 'Was Lady Joan very terrible?'

'Foul.' The car was warm and she started to relax now that the ordeal was over. 'Did the two of you beat poor Father Nash into a pulp?'

Richard laughed. 'He seems to have made a remarkable

recovery. What was he talking to you about? You were getting on very well.'

Helen noted the edge in his voice. Was he jealous?

'We were discussing *Doctor Faustus*. From a theological perspective. You're not the only one who can talk religion,' she told him, her voice mock-severe.

'Listen to me.' She jumped at Fairfax's voice, a hiss of urgency. 'You are playing a dangerous game. Both of you. It's not funny. I know you, Richard. The way you chase after a topic, never thinking for a moment about the consequences.'

'Charles, don't worry...' His voice was conciliatory.

'I do worry. I worry a lot. I think you are leading this young woman into dangerous territory.'

Helen was fed up. She didn't like being told off by a middle-aged bloke, and she didn't like his patronising references to her age. *You're Richard's former boss*, she thought, *not mine*.

'We're academics, Mr Fairfax. We are working together on an historical investigation. It's not a game, and we're not children. If you don't mind me saying so, it's none of your business what I choose to research.'

'I...' She could see him pinching his nose, turning to face the window. 'I apologise. Perhaps these are things I should explain to Richard alone.'

'Really? Am I too young to understand?' She was properly annoyed now. 'Or do you want to scare him off or offer him a more lucrative job, like you did at Lambeth Palace?' The words seemed to jump out of her mouth. Yet she had wondered about that, about Richard's story of how he abandoned his research at Canterbury Cathedral only when the Lambeth job arose.

'Helen, please stop.' Richard squeezed her hand, hard.

'That's not what happened. Come on, both of you. You're my friends. Let's drop it.'

They rode on in silence to Helen's flat. Richard released her hand, and she didn't have the nerve to reach for his again. She felt wretched, cursing herself for her outburst. She'd messed up the whole evening, antagonised Richard's friend and probably put Richard off forever. She scrambled out, worrying about whether she should offer to pay for the cab.

He followed her, running his hand though his hair in exasperation, and waited on the doorstep as she found her keys.

'I should see him home, Helen. I think we need to talk about whatever's bugging him.' She nodded, throat tight, unable to speak. *Don't cry*, she told herself. *Keep it together*.

He checked his watch. 'It's not that late.' He took her hand. 'Could I come back to see you later?' She looked down, tears spilling over her lower lids, and saw their fingers intertwine. He pulled her closer, dipped his head. And they were kissing again, softly at first, then with growing desire. Finally, he released her, held her at arm's length.

'Till later, Helen Oddfellow. Don't go anywhere.'

She closed the door and leaned against it, touching her fingers to her lips.

Chapter 24

Upstairs in her flat, Helen tried to calm herself with work. She'd neglected her PhD for weeks, the two texts of *Doctor Faustus* piled untouched in a corner of her desk. She picked up the text considered now to be closest to Marlowe's original work. She thought about her conversation with Francis Nash and turned to the powerful last scene of the play, where the magician Faustus counts down his final hour before Mephistopheles arrives to claim his bartered soul. The monologue had always fascinated her with its ability to convey Faustus's growing terror, his repeated, thwarted attempts to repent, the agony of the relentlessly passing minutes.

Yet tonight the minutes passed all too slowly. She kicked off her tight shoes, then jumped up to put the heating on so the flat would be warm when he arrived. She checked her face. Her eyes were big, lashes still dark with mascara. Her lipstick was long gone. She considered refreshing it, then decided against. She planned on doing a lot more kissing tonight. She smiled at herself in the mirror, saw a knowing look that she'd not seen for some time. Hastily, she returned to her desk.

She read the Faustus speech aloud, its luminous, chilling

poetry. Her breath caught over the final lines, where Faustus makes a desperate promise to repudiate learning and burn his books. Glancing around the little room, she saw her books as a protective shell, shielding her from the outside world as she absorbed what she wanted through reading. She remembered Richard's look of triumph as he'd lifted Chambers' *Book of Days* down from the library shelves. And she imagined Marlowe, scribbling away in his chamber, his elbows propped on copies of Ovid and Machiavelli. All three of them seeking something from books, some knowledge or advancement. Remembering Charles's warnings, she wondered what price they might have to pay for their curiosity.

She thought again of the mysterious final line of the letter. It must be a code, some Elizabethan cipher. She reached for a history of the Elizabethan secret service, which she'd read to understand Marlowe's role. He must have been fluent in codes and secret writing as he carried messages and intelligence to and fro. She flipped through the book, looking for examples of the ciphers in use at the time. The most famous was that used by Mary Queen of Scots, which was used to entrap her into treason.

The Raleigh letter was a major find in its own right, she realised. A prison letter from Sir Walter to his fellow accused, with a new example of an Elizabethan code, would keep historians busy for years. It should be in the British Library, really, or the National Archives. Charles was right, she supposed. It had to be dated and authenticated as Raleigh's handwriting. In the meantime, there was the puzzle of solving the code. She felt impatient to get started, to see the letters she'd copied into Richard's notebook.

She checked her watch. Half past eleven; almost three

quarters of an hour had passed since he left her. Her phone buzzed from her handbag and she grabbed it. *Please don't say you've gone home*, she thought.

'Walking back from Deptford,' the text message read. 'With you shortly.' The walk should take ten, maybe fifteen, minutes. Anticipation fluttered in her stomach. He'd be here soon.

She went to the window, looked down the street for his familiar, loping stride. Traffic had thinned as the night wore on, but a few headlights still pulsed through the dark. It never got properly quiet on the London to Dover road. She opened the window and leaned out into the chilly air, looking as far up the road as she could. She tasted traffic fumes, metallic on her tongue. The wind was getting up, tugging at her carefully constructed hair-do. She reached up and pulled her hair loose, scattering hairpins.

There were sirens in the distance. There were always sirens; the flat was between a fire station and a police station, and she heard them all day long. Did she want him to see her hanging out of the attic window, hair blowing in the breeze like Mr Rochester's mad wife? She withdrew her head and looked at her phone. Should she send a text back? Call to see where he was?

The phone rang for a long time then switched to voicemail. Perhaps it was on silent. Perhaps he was still with Charles and didn't want to answer. She left a quick message, letting him know she was still awake. She tossed the phone onto the bed, then picked it up immediately, waiting for it to ring. Ten minutes later, she called again. The call went straight to voicemail this time. She began to worry. He should be here by now.

* * *

By midnight, she could bear the waiting no longer. She pulled on knee-high boots, tied back her hair and buttoned her coat. She left him another message, telling him she would walk down towards Deptford to meet him. It felt better to be out in the night air, on the move.

As she neared the corner by St Nicholas Church, she saw flashing blue lights. A police car and an ambulance were parked on the pavement outside a pub. Blue-and-white tape fluttered in the wind. She stumbled forward into a run.

She'd made it under the tape and to the pub door before a policeman caught her shoulder.

'No, you don't. Outside the taped-off area, please.' He placed himself between her and the door, wielding a clipboard like a shield.

'Please – what's happened? I'm trying to find a friend. He's gone missing.'

'There's been an incident. I need you back outside the taped-off area.' Looking at his stolid face, Helen realised she would get nothing further from him. She turned to the crowd of onlookers. The pub was an old-fashioned boozer with a clientele to match. The men milling around the pavement had clearly just been turfed out, some still clutching their pint glasses. She scanned the faces, looking in vain for Richard. A woman police officer was taking down details. A man, bulky in his jacket and stab vest, was extending the line of tape across the road to the churchyard, beneath the sightless gaze of St Nicholas's skull-topped gates. Helen saw dark patches on the ground, gleaming.

'What's happened?' She grabbed the arm of one of the exiled

drinkers, an old bloke in a tatty anorak. He turned and grinned, showing broken teeth. 'Hello, sweetheart.'

'Do you know what's going on?'

'Sorry, love. My hearing's not what it was.' Just as she was about to scream with frustration, someone called her name.

'Helen! What are you doing here? I didn't have you down as a regular at the Three Anchors.' It was the kid from the newspaper, the one who'd interviewed her about the guided walk. *He'll know*, she thought with relief.

'I'm trying to find a friend. What's this all about?'

'Some bloke's been stabbed. I've only just got here.' He had a motorbike helmet under one arm. 'Got a call from a mate at the ambulance station. I'd better crack on. I want to get some decent quotes before everyone disappears.'

Stabbed. There was absolutely no reason, Helen told herself, why this should be connected with Richard. Why would he have been in the pub? Her eyes were drawn back to the dark patches on the pavement outside the church. What if he'd been attacked outside? Would he not have headed for the first place he could get help? He'd have walked past here to get from Deptford to her house. She felt in her pocket for her phone. *Bloody hell, Richard*, she thought, furious. *Just ring, can't you?* She tried his number again. No reply.

She tagged after the reporter, who was interviewing a group of drinkers. They pointed across the pavement to a young woman standing under a lamp post, the sodium light illuminating streaks of blue in her dyed blonde hair. She was wearing faded tight jeans and smoking a cigarette as if her life depended on it. 'Ask Natalya,' one advised. 'She's the barmaid. She was brilliant.'

Helen followed as he went over to talk to the woman.

'Natalya? My name's Nick Wilson. I'm a reporter from the *South London Courier*. The guys over there said you tried to save the man's life. Can you tell me what happened?'

The woman's white T-shirt was smeared with blood, Helen saw with shock. She was shaking, despite the blanket draped around her shoulders.

'He died,' she told Nick. Her accent was strong, Eastern European of some sort. She turned her tear-filled eyes up to the reporter. 'I was trying to stop the blood from his side. But it come out of his mouth, and then he died.'

'What did he look like?' Helen asked.

'Tall. White, wearing a jacket and tie. A bit old.' She shrugged. *Oh, God*, thought Helen, starting to feel dizzy.

'And he was attacked outside?' asked Nick. 'It wasn't a fight in the pub?'

She shook her head vigorously. 'No fights. This is a nice place. He came inside, and we tried to help him.' She dropped her cigarette and ground it out with her shoe. Immediately, she reached for another. He held the lighter for her.

'He said something, before he died. I don't know … my English isn't so good.'

'It's brilliant,' he said. 'Much better than my Polish. What did he say?'

She shrugged. 'Don't make much sense. "Cut off the branch." Something like that. "Tell her, cut off the branch." That was the last thing he said.'

Helen's legs gave way beneath her. Nick grabbed her under the arms as she sank to the ground. 'No,' she whispered. 'No, no.' *Cut is the branch. Cut is the branch that might have grown full straight.* The words she'd just been reading, from the epilogue to *Doctor Faustus* – the words on Marlowe's memorial in the church. It had to be Richard. It *couldn't* be Richard – but who else would have said those words? Before the blood came out of his mouth and he died. She gazed into the gutter at the black churn of mud and diesel, the gape of a drainage grate. She retched, feeling sweat break over her face.

'Helen. What is it? Do you know who it is?' Nick was beside her, a notebook balanced on his knee.

'I… I hope not.' She met his eyes. 'Help me find out. Please.'

'I'll try. Give me the name and I'll ask the police. They probably won't issue an ID until tomorrow, though… later if they can't reach next of kin.'

The Polish girl sat on the kerb beside her and offered Helen a cigarette. She took it without thinking, felt the unfamiliar smoke burn down her throat.

'You know the guy?' the girl asked.

Helen closed her eyes. 'I think so.'

'Your boyfriend?'

She thought of the kiss they had shared less than two hours ago. 'Yes.'

'I'm sorry.' The girl took her hand. 'I did my best.'

Chapter 25

'I've got a potential ID of the victim for you.' Nick liked to make it clear that he was doing the police a favour rather than asking them for help. Too late, he recognised the dark-suited woman who turned to talk to him. It was the DCI who'd given him the third degree at the hospital, and complained to the editor about him, after the mosque protest. She didn't look delighted to see him.

'Mr Wilson. Wherever there's trouble, there you are.'

'It's my job. And I could say the same for you.'

She rubbed her eyes. She looked tired. 'I won't be making any statement tonight. But if you have any information – genuine information – then please let me have it.'

He handed over a page torn from his reporter's notebook. 'This might be your victim. I know you can't tell me. But his girlfriend is sitting over there by the lamp post. She's pretty upset. Any chance you can put her mind at rest if it's not him?'

She took the piece of paper, impassive, and read the name. She looked over at Helen, sitting on the pavement, oblivious to the muck she was getting on her coat.

'Alright. I'll take her details.'

Nick watched her crouch down beside Helen, help her up

and lead her to a police car. If it was the man Helen thought it was, he reflected, he'd got a decent chance of an interview with her. And they already had some great photos of her on file from the local history feature. He wished he'd taken a photo of her sitting on the kerb. As usual, the newspaper's photographer was yet to arrive, so he was grabbing his own snaps with his mobile phone.

The drinkers said the man had staggered into the pub after last orders, bleeding from a wound in his side. They didn't know him. He'd been barely able to speak. Odd, Nick thought. He'd managed to say something, those strange words about branches that clearly meant something to Helen. So why hadn't he said what had happened? He kept one eye on the police car as he continued with his work, nabbing a paramedic as he emerged from the pub. The man refused to give any details, but didn't deny it when Nick asked if the victim had died. That much was evident; they'd been there almost an hour now. If the man had survived, the paramedics would have transferred him to the ambulance and whisked him off to hospital.

Helen got out of the car. He hurried over to her. Her face was white, but her voice was steady again.

'They won't tell me. But if it wasn't him, if they didn't think it was him, they'd say, wouldn't they? I mean, if the description was completely wrong or something.'

'I'm sorry. Helen, can you tell me a bit about him? How did you know him?'

She walked away from the pub towards the road. It was surprisingly quiet. It took Nick a minute to realise the police had closed it off. Officers were diverting cars, taping around the churchyard, closing down the scene. Too late. Whoever stabbed the man was well away by now.

'I need to get into the pub,' she said, as if it was the most reasonable thing in the world. 'If they won't tell me, I'll have to find out.'

He stared at her, realised she was serious. 'They won't let you in, Helen. Look, I'll help you all I can, but …'

'Help me get in. I'll tell you all about Richard, once I know it's him.'

He stared up at the pub for a minute. He'd love a look inside, himself. He knew the place slightly; he'd been to a birthday party in the upstairs function room a while back. There was no way the police would let him through, and if he snuck in there would be repercussions. *Never upset the police too much*, his editor had advised him on many occasions. *They're one of our biggest sources of stories.*

If he could get Helen in, though, she could tell him what she saw. He supposed it was worth a go. He racked his brains, trying to remember the layout of the place. Suddenly he grinned.

'Got it. Follow me round the back. Not too close. When we get to the second corner, hold on and wait for a second.' He told her his idea. 'You'll have to be quiet, though. And if they ask, don't mention my name.'

He strolled around the taped-off area, down a side street and towards the yard at the back of the pub. As expected, there was a police officer stationed at the back door, holding a clipboard. A young copper with acne still fresh on his chin.

'Hello, mate, how's it going? Don't worry, I know you can't tell me anything. What do you reckon, though? Is it going to be an all-nighter?'

The man shrugged. 'I'm on shift till seven. Makes no odds

to me.'

Nick peered past him down the corridor. 'That's where it happened, then, is it? In the bar? Can I get a quick look? Photo for the paper?' He craned his neck, raised his mobile phone and tried to dodge past the man.

'Oi! Get back here.' The man swung around and grabbed him by the arm. 'No one goes in there. They haven't taken him out yet.'

Nick threw up his hands. 'Sorry, sorry.'

'Give us your phone. No pictures. It's not respectful.'

Nick showed him his photos. 'I haven't taken any in here. Don't worry.' The copper squinted at the pictures on the little screen.

'I should have you arrested,' he said, although on what grounds Nick couldn't imagine.

'Look, I'm just doing my job, like you're doing yours. Honest. I'll get out of your hair. Sorry to have bothered you.'

He retreated, hands raised, as if pacifying a dangerous animal. The copper was glaring at him. As he reached the end of the yard, Nick risked a glance up to the fire escape. He saw a flash of red: Helen's bright coat vanishing through the open door into the pub's private function room.

* * *

She felt unreal, as if all this was happening to someone else. She thought of Richard, his mercurial intellect and the warmth of his kiss. It was not possible that he could be lying still and cold inside this building. She was simply doing this to confirm that she'd been mistaken, as she'd been wrong before.

The barmaid had probably misheard the victim's words, and there were plenty of tall, thin men in London. She had an image of Richard standing outside her front door, right now, ringing and wondering why she didn't answer. Checking his phone, perhaps, and seeing it had been switched off, or the battery had gone dead. Well, she'd better get this over with so she could go back and let him in.

She walked through the dark room, stumbling over tables and bar stools, down the corridor, past piled-up steel barrels and the door to the gents, smelling strongly of ammonia and disinfectant. She was at the top of a narrow, twisting stairway. Quietly, slowly, she stepped down into a room bathed in white light that hurt her eyes.

Three tripod lamps were arranged around the room, spot-lighting a figure sprawled on the floor. An upturned chair lay next to him, in a dark pool that reflected the light. She moved silently around the bar. The smell of sour beer was overwhelmed by the metallic taint of blood. His face was turned towards her, the familiar dark hair fallen across his eyes. Dried blood around his mouth, his lips slightly parted. His eyes were still open. His face wore an expression of great sadness.

Helen dropped to her knees next to his body. She was aware of people around her speaking urgently, their hands reaching. She couldn't hear what they said. The white light seemed to be filling her head, blocking out noise. She reached for Richard's hand. It was not quite cold.

Then they got her, pulled her back from his body. The policewoman she'd spoken to before, her face agitated. Words started to come through, half-sentences, questions, exclamations, orders. They wanted her out of here. She gazed at his face, and the pain reached her heart. She gasped with the shock of it, like a sudden plunge into icy water. There were people either side of her, pulling her up by her arms. She'd forgotten how to breathe. Her chest shuddered, painful gulps of air forcing their way into her body. Richard dead. Her legs wouldn't carry her; the men dragged her from the room, her feet useless on the floor beneath her. She kept her eyes fixed on his body until the door closed.

'Give her a chair,' said a brisk female voice. She sat, wrapped her arms around herself, eyes shut. A hand pressed on the back of her neck, easing her head forward.

'Deep breaths, Helen. I'm sorry you saw that. We'll take you home as soon as you're ready.'

I'll never be ready, thought Helen, hunched over the pain in her chest. *I'll never be ready again.*

Chapter 26

Gary Paxton was struggling against the current in a small rowing boat, pulling on the oars until his arms ached. It hadn't looked far – maybe two hundred metres across the river from Deptford to the Isle of Dogs on the north bank of the Thames. But he'd reckoned without the ebbing tide that was pulling him downstream, away from the dock he'd been heading for.

A blast of pop music made him jump. It came from one of the big party boats that cruised up and down the Thames from Greenwich. He rowed harder, sweating to put distance between himself and the boat with its cargo of laughing drunks. The boat spun one way, then the other. If he stopped rowing for a moment, it would whirl off downstream like a dry leaf. He had no time to stop and think until he made the bank. Then he could take stock of what had happened. It was hard work, but he could swear he was getting closer to the river wall.

Soon he could smell the rotting weed and mud towering above his head. But the current was still pulling him downstream, the wall rushing past with its metal rings and ladders, much too fast for him to catch hold of. He tried wedging an oar into one of the ladders. The blade broke, splintering with an almighty crack. *Now what?* He couldn't row the Thames with one oar.

He snatched a glance over his left shoulder. There was the Cutty Sark tea clipper, floodlit in its dry dock at Greenwich. He checked the other side. If that was Greenwich, then – yes! He saw an inlet with a slipway beneath an overhanging building and used the remaining oar as a rudder to steer the boat inside. The current spun it around. Too late, he realised he was going to hit the wall – fast. He wielded the oar in an attempt to break the impact.

It shattered, thumping into his chest. He fell backwards into the bottom of the boat. *God, that hurt.* He lay still for a second, panting. Mercifully, the boat seemed to have stopped. He raised his head and saw it was wedged in place, grounded against the concrete slipway. His back was wet. Water was pouring in through a bloody great hole at the front. He scrambled to his knees and struggled out of the boat. He waded into the river and pushed the holed boat back into the current. It drifted away, shipping water, joining the mad dance of flotsam on its way to Gravesend, taking the knife and his gloves with it.

He lay on his back on the slipway, his lungs burning with effort. Above him, the sky was a sulphurous brown, heavy cloud reflecting the artificial light of the city. That had been close. He was annoyed with himself for not thinking through the risks of the boat properly before taking the chance. But it had made sense – to get across the river immediately. The police would be flooding Deptford, checking out train stations, tunnels and bridges. He had a march on them. He hunkered into the corner where the river wall met the doors of the rowing club boat house and began to think.

The mini-cab thing had gone fine at first. He'd worried that Watson would recognise him, but no one really looks at a cab driver. He'd taken them back into London, as planned. After they dropped the girl off, the two men had begun arguing, both angry. Then Watson had suggested they stop, take a walk. They both needed some air, he said. That had thrown him for a minute. He'd thought that Watson would be the last one in the cab, that he could take him somewhere quiet and do what needed to be done. The two men got out along Evelyn Street, headed through the estate to the river. It had taken him a couple of minutes to find a place to park the borrowed car, then another few minutes to find them. As he watched from the shadow of a wall, Watson had stormed off.

Paxton had moved silently in pursuit. Watson had walked fast, making it to the main road before Paxton could catch him. He'd been careful, keeping well back, baseball cap shading his face and anorak zipped close around his neck. Watson was heading back to the girl's flat, he realised, cursing. He wanted this finished tonight. He hurried to close the gap between them.

Then, just past the Three Anchors pub, Watson had swerved off the main road. When he arrived at the junction, Paxton couldn't see him. He'd run through Deptford Green to the river before realising Watson must have gone into the churchyard. He went in through the back gate. The man was standing by a plaque set into the wall, touching it. He turned, saw Paxton, and ran. He caught him just by the gates.

Paxton had killed before, of course. The army had trained them for long-distance warfare, taught them to operate mortars and RPGs. Then, in Afghan, all the training had been turned on its head. The danger was buried in the dust you walked on or inside the explosive-packed car that pulled up outside the barracks. It came from the man selling vegetables in the market or the police recruit you'd just handed a gun. They'd learnt to fight at close range, an arm around the windpipe, a knife in the guts. Something about it had stayed with him, a desire to do it again. The intimacy, the feeling of resistance as knife met skin. The way it gave for a moment like a rubber sheet before the knife slid home. The stink of fear in your nostrils as they collapsed in your arms. The rush of it, like landing a punch and fucking a girl and scoring a goal, all rolled into one.

Watson had fought hard. You wouldn't have thought he'd have it in him, but he seemed driven by rage. Even after the knife went in, he'd tried to stop Paxton getting to his inside pocket. But there'd been nothing there; the notebook had gone. He'd yelled at him, demanding to know where it was. Then the bastard had gone for his eyes and struggled free. Watson had reached the road, shouting for help.

Paxton had taken to his heels, back out the far end of the churchyard and down to the river. He'd found the sailing club, yanked aside the corrugated iron and slipped into the scruffy yard, piled with old sailing dinghies, knackered canoes and rowing boats.

So here he was. Watson was dead, or dying. He was sure of that. He didn't have the notebook. Either it was in the car, or Watson had dumped it somewhere. He could check the car later. He'd like to look around that churchyard, but it would be crawling with police right now.

There was another possibility, he realised. Paxton could have given the notebook to the girl, either in the car or when they kissed outside her door. And the girl knew the background. He thought quickly. One of his boys was in a Transit van outside her flat. Should they go in now, grab her and search the place? Once he moved against her, there was no chance of getting information from her any other way. But without the notebook, they had nothing. She was unpredictable. Her burst of temper in the cab had proved that. If she had it, she might give it to anyone. The police, even. The safest thing was to get her under control, and fast. He couldn't do it himself. He picked up his mobile phone.

'She left the flat about ten minutes ago.' The boy in the van was agitated. 'I didn't know whether to follow her. I tried to call, but you didn't answer.'

'Shit. Yeah, OK. Stay there. Wait for her to come back.' Where had she gone? Maybe Watson had called her – although he didn't think he'd have had time. 'Which way was she headed?'

'West. Up towards Deptford. Gary, is something kicking off? About a million police cars headed up that way too. And an ambulance.'

'Not that I know of.' No sense worrying the kid. 'Listen, you stay put. I'm going to send someone over. Ring me as soon as she's back.' He hung up, thought through his options. He scrolled down his numbers until he found the one he was looking for. They'd done the training, knew the drill. Time for his elite unit to go into action.

Chapter 27

Helen lay on her bed, staring at the shadows that moved across the ceiling with the passing traffic. She hadn't undressed or even taken her coat off. No matter what was before her eyes, all she could see was Richard's face, his eyes filmed with death.

The deep sadness in his expression, the regret for a life incomplete. Those eyes would not crinkle at the corners again; he would never break into the transforming smile that swept away the gravity from his face. A grave face, she thought, her tired brain making puns, doodling to itself. 'Ask for me tomorrow,' said Shakespeare's Mercutio as he expired from stab wounds, 'and you will find me a grave man.' The quicksilver, hot-tempered Mercutio in *Romeo and Juliet*, Helen had often thought, could have been Shakespeare's portrait of his great rival, Christopher Marlowe. Back to Marlowe – again.

The words from the Faustus epilogue marched through her brain. *Cut is the branch. Faustus is gone.* The phrases tolled one after the other. Who had stabbed Richard? She refused to believe this was a random robbery gone wrong, especially less than a week after Richard had had his bag stolen in almost the same place. She'd told the police about the mugging and about the evening at Cobham Hall, how she had last seen Richard driving away in the cab with Charles Fairfax.

Fairfax. Much as she disliked him, she struggled to believe this uptight little man had actually knifed Richard. Was it possible that his determination to block their research would stretch to violence? She remembered the passion in his voice, his anger. But surely he wasn't physically capable of it, everything else aside. Richard would have overwhelmed him in seconds. The policewoman had quizzed her about their argument, but she'd explained it as a disagreement between academics. Nevertheless, the police would be knocking on his door. The last person known to have seen him alive.

Then Cobham, she supposed: interviews with Lady Joan and Charlotte, Father Nash. She wished for a moment she could talk to the priest, demand that his God make sense of what had happened. He had been kind and easy to talk to, and he'd given her his card. She checked her bedside alarm clock. It was almost half past one. Should she ring? It was horribly late, but given the circumstances she thought he'd understand. She remembered their discussion about Faustus, who had found himself unable to pray as death approached. And Richard, with his last breath, gasping out the lines from the play's epilogue. His words, she felt sure, had been directed at her. 'Tell her: cut is the branch.'

Cut is the branch that might have grown full straight. Why had he wanted her to think of those lines? What was he telling her? Her tired mind refused to help. *Cut is the branch. Richard is gone.* The lines ran in tandem with the sweep of the cars on the street below, a rhythmic roaring and falling away, like the sea. It was soothing. Her eyes started to close.

Then she heard a different noise: one she recognised.

Scraping, rattling. Someone was trying to open the front door from the street, three floors below. The door was old and the lock stiff. You had to give it a good shove to get it to open. She heard a distant crunch as the door swung inward and hit the bottom of the bannisters.

It was very late for the house's inhabitants. Crispin rarely went out at all after dark. Rachel, on the ground floor, was usually home by midnight. And anyway, Helen remembered, she was away visiting family in France. Unless she'd arrived home from a late flight? A prickle of fear penetrated her exhaustion. She began to listen harder.

One, no, *two* sets of footsteps were coming slowly up the stairs. Not Rachel, then. No voices. The tread was light. But it was almost impossible to walk silently up the creaky old staircase. It could be the students who lived in the first-floor flat – but no, they had gone home for the Easter holidays.

She had always felt safe in her attic flat, knowing that any intruder would have to get through the heavy front door, then past all the neighbours before reaching her. It had been her refuge, her eyrie up away from the world. She listened uneasily to the progress of the steps. Where were they going? The flat beneath Helen's had been empty for months.

They reached the landing below and stopped. She listened for keys going into the downstairs flat's door. Nothing. The footsteps started again, slower this time. There were ten steps to her attic flat. She counted the first five, huddled on the bed. This wasn't happening. She was having a bad dream.

By the sixth step, she could hear their breathing, heavy from the climb. She swung herself upright. This was real. Police? More questions about Richard? *No*, her brain urged. *Danger*.

There was no knock. Instead, a tinny noise of metal on

173

metal. They were picking her lock, she realised with horror. They – whoever *they* were, whoever killed Richard – were coming for her. She looked around for a place to hide. Under the bed? In the wardrobe? Hopeless, they'd find her in seconds. Outside. The roof.

She pushed up the bedroom window and clambered through the gap into the narrow gutter that ran around the flat, feeling the shock of the cold night air as the world opened up, traffic noise and wind rushing around her. She crouched precariously, bare feet on the cold slate, working the sash down from the outside, then inched her way around the parapet. One dizzying look over the low wall was enough to keep her focused on her feet and hands, this side of the sheer drop to the street. She made her way to the next house along the terrace.

In the gutter between two pitched roofs, she moved quietly to the rear of the building and looked back, pressing her body flat against the tiles. At first, she could see nothing. Then a white figure passed across her kitchen window. She frowned. Odd. He looked like one of the policemen she'd seen in the pub, covered head-to-toe in a white paper suit. She caught another glimpse of a figure in white. She stared in confusion. What were the police doing, breaking into her flat? She struggled to make sense of what she was seeing. Only one thing was clear: whoever was in her flat, she didn't want them to find her. Moving away from the windows, she resumed her traverse of the rooftops.

At the end of the terrace, she hunched down in the back corner, sweating despite the cold. Now what? Wait until they'd gone? She turned up the collar of her coat. What were they doing in there? Would they notice the gap at the bottom of the bedroom window?

She jumped as her phone buzzed in her coat pocket. For one mad second, she hoped it was Richard. She fished it out and answered, her voice low.

'Helen? It's Nick, from the *Courier*. We didn't get a chance to talk before the police took you. Are you OK? Can you talk?'

It was the journalist. She almost laughed. 'I'm on the roof,' she said, idiotically.

'You're what?'

'There are men in my flat. They broke in. I'm on the roof.'

'Men in your flat? Are you OK? Do you want me to call the police?'

She hesitated. Were the men in the flat from the police? 'I don't think so. Can you get here?' She gave him her address.

'No problem.'

She dropped the phone back in her pocket. God knows what he could do, but the thought that someone was on his way was comforting. She wondered if they were still there. Cautiously, she crawled forward.

Her breath caught in her chest. Silhouetted against the dark tiles, she saw a white figure. He moved away, towards the front of the building. He was searching methodically, roof by roof. She huddled back into her corner. She was at the end of the row, with nowhere to go but down.

Down. Could she? Helen eyed the cast-iron drainpipe at the corner of the building. She reached over and gave it a tug, looked down the face of the house, swallowing fear. There was a window ledge about six feet below the parapet, next to the pipe. Then below that another window, and then a wall that joined the corner of the house, enclosing the garden. *No way*, screamed her brain. Yet the whole night had been full of the unthinkable. The usual rules no longer applied. She could wait to be found, hunched in her corner. Or she could try to escape.

Gripped by a growing feeling of unreality, she sat on the parapet and grabbed the pipe with sweating hands. She lowered herself over the side.

Her arm muscles contracted with the shock of her weight, and she whimpered, pressing her face against the rough brick, feeling around for a toe-hold. Her ankle glanced against the smooth stone of the window ledge below. Thankfully, she transferred the weight back to her feet. Perhaps she could stay here, wait till they'd gone. But she'd never be able to climb up again. The only way was down.

Hitching up her frock, she wrapped her knees around the pipe and gripped it with her toes, remembering long-distant PE lessons climbing ropes in the gym. She inched her way down the pipe, her progress agonisingly slow. Her muscles started to shake, threatening to unpeel her fingers. Her sweaty hands slipped on the enamel paint and she gasped, scraping her knuckles on the brick.

Something whizzed past her head and smashed. She almost fell, then caught her knee on the second window ledge and cowered into the window's recess. Something dark, perhaps a roof slate, lay shattered on the pavement. In disbelief, she turned her eyes upwards to where a white figure was outlined against the sky, holding something.

She flinched as a second slate thudded against her shoulder. It rebounded and fell, inside the wall this time, into the garden below. He was aiming at her, she realised, trying to make her fall. Her arm felt numb, heavy where the blow had landed.

She imagined the slate slicing into her neck, her face, the shock of it throwing her backwards, landing with her neck broken and skull crushed. *They'd say I killed myself*, she thought. *That I was so distraught about Richard I threw myself off the roof.* The thought filled her with anger. She would get down alive.

She contemplated dropping the ten foot or so remaining into the dark garden. She couldn't see what was below her, whether it would be a soft landing on grass or something worse. Some of the houses had concrete areas behind them or steps leading down to the basement. Also, she would be trapped in the walled garden, a sitting target. Not good.

She swung out onto the drainpipe again, hearing the seam of her dress rip. She took a deep breath and let herself slide down the pipe until her feet reached the wall, crouched on it for a moment then jumped, landing hard on her hands and knees. Another slate crashed next to her head, shards hitting her face.

She pulled herself up, ignoring the blood trickling from her cut knees. Her legs felt like lead as she staggered to the road. *Get away from the parapet, get out of range*, she told herself. She swung around the corner of the house. A man grabbed her shoulders. She screamed.

Chapter 28

'Woah! Steady there.' Nick took a step back. 'Helen, it's me.' He'd barely been able to believe his eyes when he roared up the road towards the house and saw her clinging to the drainpipe like a frightened monkey. He'd skidded to a halt, but she was already on the ground.

'Get me out of here,' she said. 'They're trying to kill me.' Her eyes were wild, her dress ripped and dirty. He didn't waste time asking questions. He handed her his spare bike helmet and she pulled it on. 'Do you have any shoes? OK, then keep your feet on the pegs, stay clear of the exhaust and hang on tight. We'll be five minutes.'

Then they were off, flying up and over Blackheath, the dome of the sky arching high overhead. Down the hill into Lewisham, slowing as he weaved his way through the leafy side streets. He pulled the bike into the scruffy front garden of the terraced house he shared with his brother.

'Are you OK?' It was a ridiculous question, he realised, ushering her into the kitchen. She limped, and a cut to her face was oozing blood. He sat her down, brought warm water and towels for her to bathe her hands and feet. She sat quietly and let him tend her wounds, hissing slightly as the disinfectant stung her grazed knees, filling the kitchen with the smell of childhood disasters. He made tea, strong and sweet. He pulled the bedspread off his brother's bed and wrapped it around her. She was still shaking, hunched over the mug of tea and warming herself in the steam.

Nick grabbed his phone and found the record feature. He didn't want to take notes: too unnatural and it might scare her off. Also, if it came out well he could use it on the website. The editor was very keen on multimedia.

'Helen, you said someone was trying to kill you. What did you mean?'

She looked up, eyes steady. 'What I said. They broke into my flat. I got out, onto the roof. They came looking for me. When I climbed down, they started throwing roof tiles at me.' She pulled her dress off her shoulder, showed an ugly red mark. 'See?'

He swallowed. He wished his brother was home. Colin was a junior doctor at the local hospital, working late shifts in the accident and emergency department. He'd know what to do. Nick felt a bit out of his depth. He supposed he should call the police. But he wanted this interview in the bag first.

'Who was it? Do you know?'

She shook her head. 'But it's got to be the same people who murdered Richard. I mean, who else? He was mugged, a week ago. And I think someone was following me, the other day in Bankside. The research – Richard said it could be dangerous.' Her voice rose.

'Tell me more about Richard.' He leaned forward, hoping to goodness the recording device was working. He wondered if he should get his notebook, just in case. 'How did you know him? Was he your boyfriend?'

179

She pressed her hands into her face. When she looked at him, her eyes were wet. 'Everyone asks that,' she said, her voice strained. 'What does it matter?' She pushed the tears away and lifted her chin.

'Richard was a historian. A very good one, a world expert in his field. You make sure you put that in your article.' She looked at him, accusingly. 'That's what you're asking for, isn't it? Why aren't you taking notes?'

He grabbed his pen, thankful for the permission. A historian. That was good, a nice peg for the piece. World-renowned historian Richard Watson, the greatest living expert in something-or-other … He started to write the intro in his head.

'Great. Where did he work?' He scribbled down the details: church history, Henry VIII and all that. They could run a background article with a profile of the dead man.

'We were working together on a research project. He read your article about my walk,' she said, smiling for a second, sun breaking through the clouds. 'That's how he got in touch with me. He needed someone who knew about Christopher Marlowe.'

'Marlowe.' Nick chewed his pen, thinking. 'The one who was bumped off on Deptford Strand? In a tavern?' He liked this murder more and more. Literary parallels, brilliant historians, madly photogenic women climbing down drainpipes. Another front-page splash with his name on it.

'That's him.' She frowned, as if it had just occurred to her. 'He's buried in the churchyard next to the pub.'

'So he is. You showed me the plaque on the wall when we did the walk.' *Excellent*. He could use the information from the history article. It would give the piece a spooky resonance.

'Oh! The plaque.' She pressed her hand to her mouth. Tears started in her eyes again. Nick searched the kitchen for tissues, then settled for a piece of kitchen roll.

'Here. What is it?'

She blew her nose. 'What he said. Do you remember? The woman, the barmaid from the pub. She told us what he'd said before he died.'

Nick had the woman's words in his notebook. He flipped back the pages. 'Cut off the branch. And then you fainted.'

'Cut is the branch. Cut is the branch that might have grown full straight.' She sat upright, gazing at Nick as if he should know the significance of the words. 'Marlowe again. Those are the words on the plaque in the churchyard. I'd almost forgotten.'

She pulled herself out of her chair. 'I should go back. He must have wanted me to go there. We visited the church together to look for … for something. Maybe he was there, before he died. Those words – he meant there was something to find, after all.'

'Helen, the churchyard will be full of police right now. You won't get in. And you won't see anything in the dark. Why not wait till the morning? I'll take you. We can look together.' He felt an inappropriate stab of lust at the thought of Helen climbing back on the bike behind him, wrapping her arms around his waist.

He heard the front door open and shut. Oh, great timing, he thought, as his brother put his head around the door. 'I'm off to bed. What the hell?'

'This is Helen,' said Nick, resigned. 'Helen, this is my brother, Colin. We share the house.'

'My house,' said Colin, firmly. He sat on the kitchen table

in his green scrubs and looked her over, taking in the torn dress and bruises and the patchwork bedspread around her shoulders. 'And that's my quilt. Nick, what's going on?'

'It's a work thing,' said Nick, hoping that would cover it. 'Helen's – she's sort of locked out of her flat. And she's hurt her arm. Sorry about your bedspread. Mine was a bit grubby.'

'That looks painful. Helen, I'm a doctor. May I see?' He took her arm, handling it with care. 'Well, it's not broken, but it'll be sore for a while. Might be best to strap it up, stop it from swelling. What happened?'

'Someone threw something at me. A stone,' she said. A quick glance at Nick, asking him not to complicate matters with the full story. 'Nick helped me get away.' He felt a flush of pride. *Take that, Dr Colin. I can rescue people too.*

'Did he?' Colin refused to be impressed. 'Well, I'd get some rest if I were you. Do you need a cab home?'

Her eyes flashed fear, looking from one brother to the other.

'Stay here tonight,' said Nick. 'It's late. You can have my room.' He saw Colin's look of incredulity. 'Actually, scrap that. My room is a bit of a pit. You'd be better off on the sofa. I'll find some blankets.'

To his relief, she nodded acceptance. *You're my story, Helen Oddfellow. You're not going anywhere without me.*

* * *

Helen awoke, her neck cricked by the sofa arm. For a moment she was confused, as if waking from a nightmare. Dull light came through a dingy red curtain into an unfamiliar living room. It looked like a student house, unwashed mugs teetering on piles of newspapers and books.

The fact of Richard's death landed like a lump of concrete on her chest. She struggled to sit up, saw the scrapes and bruises on her hands. One fingernail, ripped almost to the quick. Not a bad dream, then. The events of the night flashed into her consciousness, each more unthinkable than the next. Richard's body, lying in his own blood on the grubby floor of a south London pub.

'Can I come in?' The request was quickly followed by the action. Nick, bright-eyed despite having worked half the night, was already dressed in jeans and sweatshirt. 'Sorry to wake you. I need my laptop. Are you OK?'

She pulled the blanket around her. OK didn't begin to cover it. Everything hurt. Richard's death most of all.

'I've made some toast.' He set it down on the coffee table with a mug of tea. She looked at the triangles, smeared with margarine, and her mouth dried. She took a sip of tea.

Nick was sitting on the arm of an easy chair, balancing his laptop on his knees. 'Let me fire this thing up. I need to get a first draft of the story emailed over to the office. Then we can go back to the churchyard, if you like. Have a look at that plaque. And you should report the break-in, Helen. I need to go to the police station anyway, see if they'll give a statement.'

She sighed. The thought of getting up and going anywhere made her feel terribly tired. She wanted her own bed. She wondered if it was safe to go back to the flat. What if the men were still there, waiting for her?

'Here.' He passed her the laptop. 'Is that the quote from the Marlowe play?'

She read the familiar words of the *Doctor Faustus* epilogue:

'Cut is the branch that might have grown full straight

And burned is Apollo's laurel bough

That sometime grew within this learned man.
Faustus is gone. Regard his hellish fall,
Whose fiendful fortune may exhort the wise
Only to wonder at unlawful things,
Whose deepness doth entice such forward wits
To practice more than heavenly power permits.'

Last night, she'd been certain that Richard wanted her to
return to the plaque. Now, reading the whole verse, she
wondered. Was it a warning? Was he telling her to keep
away from the mystery, to take his own fate as a sign? Only to
wonder at unlawful things, not to pursue them? She thought
of Charles, hissing that they were playing a dangerous game.
A quick flash of memory: Richard tracing the letters carved
into the plaque with his long fingers, the same fingers that
later traced the curves of her face. She had an urge to touch
the letters herself, feel the cool stone against her skin.

'I don't like it much,' said Nick, cheerfully. 'It's basically
telling people to mind their own business. Not to poke their
noses into things that don't concern them. I wouldn't have a
job if I didn't do that.'

She smiled. 'You're right. Let's go uncover some unlawful
things.' She pulled her coat on over her torn dress, suddenly
desperate to be doing something. Maybe Richard was still
with her, still helping her look for the lost Marlowe play. The
thought warmed her as they stepped outside the house into
the chilly March sunshine.

* * *

Nick watched her run into the churchyard, tugging off her

184

bike helmet and shaking free her ponytail. She was wearing his old motorbike boots, which looked tough and punky with her red dress and coat. She wasn't his type – too tall and too brainy, too old, altogether too much trouble. He liked his girls short and sweet. But he admired her grit. He couldn't think of many women who'd shin down a four-storey house by the drainpipe. Meena, perhaps. She had grit to spare.

The churchyard was damp and gloomy with high walls. They entered from the rear, keeping well clear of the splashes of blood by the front gates, guarded by two gurning skulls and one yawning policeman. That half of the churchyard was taped off, the blue and white fluttering in the breeze.

Helen's coat was a splash of colour against dark ivy. She stood close to a pale stone monument set into the wall, touching the letters with her fingertips. He started forward to talk to her, then saw the rawness of grief on her face. He decided to give her a minute.

He checked his phone. A message from Amir. *Shit.* He'd been supposed to call him. He and his friends were organising a protest outside the police station, demanding to know why there had been no arrests for his brother's assault. Well, if he went to the police station later, he could catch up with them there.

Helen crouched down and started to scrabble through the dried leaves underneath the plaque.

'Can I help? What are you looking for?'

'Don't know. There must be something, though.' She pushed aside strands of ivy, revealing the bare brick below.

'I'll take a look around.' He walked over the lawns among the few remaining graves and checked the headstones for references to Faustus, Marlowe, branches or unlawful things.

185

He peered through the cobwebbed window of a brick building opposite the entrance to the church.

'What's this?' he called.

'The charnel house. Where they kept the bones.' She joined him and tried the door handle. It was locked. He checked the windowsills and nearby plant pots for a key. Nothing.

'Let's look by the bell tower. Marlowe is supposed to be buried over there.' Nick followed. As they rounded the church, he caught a glimpse of a man in tracksuit bottoms and a hoodie, jogging through the gates.

'Wait.'

He grabbed Helen's arm, pulled her close to the building. He peered around the corner. The man had started checking waste bins, looking under benches and bushes, as if he'd lost something. He glanced up. It was Gary Paxton. What the hell was he doing here?

Chapter 29

'He's seen me. Wait here. Trust me, you don't want to meet this man.' Nick strolled around the corner of the church towards a heavy-set man in a tracksuit. Helen crouched behind a laurel bush and peered through the branches. She frowned. There was something familiar about the set of his shoulders. Had she seen him before?

The man didn't look particularly pleased to see Nick. Helen strained to hear their conversation. She admired the way Nick could breeze through any encounter with chutzpah alone. She supposed that was what made him good at his job, able to talk his way into places he shouldn't be and get people to trust him. They were discussing the murder. Nick was acting dumb, pretending he'd just heard about it and had come down to see what he could find out. The man was anxious, his eyes constantly sliding away from Nick as if he needed to keep a general lookout.

'Have you lost something? Anything I can help with?' asked Nick, cheerful.

The man scowled. 'Nah, it's nothing. I was just having a look around.' He stood his ground, obviously waiting for Nick to clear off and leave him to it. What exactly was he looking for? Helen felt a prickle of fear. If Richard had left something for her in the churchyard, would whoever attacked him also be looking for it here? She stared at the man. Those times when she'd felt she'd been followed. Had it been him?

'It's an interesting place.' Nick launched into the history of the church, repeating back the facts she'd imparted on their first visit. He had a good memory. The man jiggled on his feet, impatient but trying not to show it. When Nick got to the bit about Marlowe being buried in the churchyard, his impatience faded.

'Where would that be, then?' Nick waved generally in the direction of the bell tower, and Helen shrank back. The man began walking over. Nick tried to distract him, to no avail. Should she walk casually around the corner? Nick's warning was loud in her head. She looked around, saw a fenced-off area with a couple of recycling bins and a compost heap. Quickly she ran to it, crouched behind one of the bins. She had barely reached it when the two men rounded the corner of the church.

Helen was now too far away to hear their conversation. She sat back on her heels and surveyed her surroundings. Old flower arrangements from the church rotted on top of a heap of grass clippings. She smelled wood smoke. Someone had made a bonfire to dispose of the trimmings from the shrubs and laurel bushes around the churchyard. A small square of cardboard, a memorial card from a funeral wreath, was half-buried in the ash. The atmosphere was heavy with decay. Helen's spirits, buoyed by the excitement of doing something, the feeling that she was following Richard's wishes, slumped. Somewhere, buried beneath this clay, lay all that was left of the brilliant young playwright Christopher Marlowe. And soon, she supposed, Richard's body would be disposed of too, his brilliance snuffed out. His warmth and humanity, cold. Ashes to ashes, she thought, staring at the remains of the bonfire.

And then she realised. Cut branches. Burned laurel boughs. *Cut is the branch that might have grown full straight, and burned is Apollo's laurel bough.* She bent over the bonfire and took the memorial card in her fingers. Beneath it was the corner of a black, leather-bound book. She almost laughed aloud. Carefully, she lifted it out, brushing damp ash from the cover. Richard's precious notebook. She hugged it to her chest.

In his last moments, fearing for his life, he'd hidden the book. Then, while his lifeblood drained away, he'd passed on the message. *He wanted me to have this*, she thought. *He wanted me to continue, to take his work on; he trusted me to unravel the final clue.* She turned the pages, curled with damp, found her own handwriting, with the line of code and the little drawing of the moon. It was barely twelve hours since she'd written those lines. At the time, sitting in Lady Joan's library, they had been an intriguing puzzle to solve. Now they had become her last link with Richard. And, she supposed, a possible explanation for his death.

She jumped at the crunch of gravel. Nick rounded the little fence. 'I wondered where you'd got to. I finally got rid of him. I don't think he was keen on talking to the policeman at the gate.' He looked pleased with himself.

She stood, held up the notebook. 'I found it. Richard left this for me.'

'Wow.' She realised from his expression of surprise that he hadn't expected to find anything in the churchyard. 'What is it?'

'Richard's notebook. All the key points of our research

189

were in here. Nick, who was that guy? Do you think he was looking for this too?'

Nick shook his head. 'Seems unlikely. He's a trouble-maker. Runs a far-right mob, stirs up trouble with the local Muslims.'

'But he was looking for something. Searching in the bins.'

'I know. It's strange. We should probably tell the police he was hanging around.'

The police. Helen remembered the policewoman who had taken her home, her brisk kindness. She stroked the book. Would they expect her to hand it over, bag it up as evidence and take it away? She wiped the ash from the cover and put it under her coat.

'Don't tell them about this, Nick. The book. I want to keep it.'

He shrugged. 'Your call.' He looked at her more closely. 'Helen, what is all this about? You know, don't you? You said that it was dangerous, the work you and Richard were doing. What is it you're trying to find out?'

Helen caught the gleam in Nick's eyes. He would splash this all over the papers, she thought. It would be irresistible. The quest for Becket's bones, the missing Marlowe play. It would be taken away; other academics would persuade Lady Joan to hand over the Raleigh letter. Other people would solve the mystery. It would no longer belong to her and Richard. She had allowed herself to imagine it: how they would find the missing Canterbury play. How she would read it, the first person to do so in four hundred years. She wasn't ready to give up on that just yet.

'We're not really sure. Richard was working for a woman from an old aristocratic family at Cobham Hall in Kent. Lady Joan Brooke. He was researching her family history and found a letter that may include a mention of Christopher Marlowe. That's why he called me.' She gestured towards the gate. 'Shall we go?'

Chapter 30

The policewoman was polite, but Helen wasn't entirely sure she believed her story.

'You climbed down the drainpipe? You could have been killed. Why on earth didn't you call us when you heard people breaking in?'

She shook her head. 'I don't know.' She remembered how she'd lain on the bed, listening to them coming up the stairs, still stunned by Richard's death. 'I wasn't thinking straight. And then when I saw their white suits … I wondered if they were police.'

The woman's level brown eyes were ringed with tiredness. 'I think we can rule that out.' She picked up the telephone on the desk and asked for a beat officer to check out Helen's flat.

'Listen, Helen. I have a briefing with the team in half an hour. We're doing everything we can to find whoever stabbed Richard. What else should we know? Why do you think you and Richard are being targeted?'

Helen felt a surge of guilt. She hadn't mentioned Richard's notebook, tucked away in her coat pocket. How much could she tell the woman without laying bare the whole mystery?

'This might sound odd. I think it could be to do with the research we were doing. Charles Fairfax – he warned us it was dangerous. I don't know why. He said we were playing a dangerous game.'

The woman massaged her temples. 'We're having a word with Mr Fairfax. Tell me about this research.'

If they spoke to Fairfax, Helen realised, he would tell them about the letter. Or Lady Joan would, or Father Nash. But the police weren't the newspapers; they wouldn't care about the story.

'We found a letter at Cobham Hall. Richard was working for Lady Joan Brooke, helping with her family history research. The letter suggests that one of her ancestors had a copy of a lost play by Christopher Marlowe. Marlowe is my specialist subject, which is how I got involved.'

'And why would a lost play be dangerous?'

'There's a theory that it includes a secret,' said Helen, reluctantly. 'The hiding place of the bones of a dead saint.'

The policewoman yawned, making no attempt to cover her mouth. She pushed back her chair and got up.

'Helen, I don't want to be rude, and this is all very interesting. But this is a live investigation, and we're still in that crucial twenty-four hours when we have a decent chance of finding the killer. What makes you think that research into a missing play and a dead saint could have caused Richard's death?'

Helen flushed. She knew the woman thought she was wasting her time. But the mugging, the break-in and the murder all pointed to the same thing. Before she could answer, the phone on the desk rang.

'Yes? Oh, Lord. Is the ambulance there? Right. And have you checked out the flat? OK, understood. Where are they taking him? Fine. Go in the ambulance, stay with him until I arrange for a relief officer. OK?'

She replaced the receiver and sat back down. 'Right. Your flat has definitely been broken into, Helen. We'll take you over later today to check whether anything has been taken.' *Good*, thought Helen. She could get out of this ridiculous dress and into her jeans.

'I'm afraid that's not all. An elderly man was found at the bottom of the stairs in the hallway. He has a bad head injury.'

'No!' Helen pressed her hands to her mouth. 'Is it Crispin? My neighbour, he lives in the basement flat.'

'I don't know the identity. But he was wearing pyjamas, so it sounds like a neighbour. He may have interrupted the burglary.'

'Oh, God.' Helen thought with horror of the hours he must have spent lying in the cold on the hall floor. 'Is he going to be OK?'

'Too early to say.' The woman took up her pen. 'They'll call me from the hospital and give me an update. Can you give me his full name? Any next of kin you know of?'

'I want to see him. He's a good friend.' She'd abandoned him, she thought, escaped the flat herself without thinking about the danger to her friend. Then all the time she was at Nick's house, sleeping on the sofa, then in the churchyard – all that time, poor Crispin on the floor, getting colder and colder. It was unbearable.

The woman looked at her thoughtfully for a moment. 'Alright. I have to give this briefing now. But I'll be sending an officer over after that. He'll be under police guard as a potential witness. If we confirm his identity, you can go over and sit with him. Are you OK to wait outside?'

* * *

The waiting area was cold, the metal seats chilly. Every time someone walked past, the automatic doors slid open, the wind bringing in a freight of litter from the street. She wrapped her coat close around her legs. Outside, she could hear ragged chanting from a small group of men holding placards. She let her brain tune into the words. No justice, no peace.

No peace. Crispin, badly injured. Her flat, her little sanctuary against the world, invaded. And Richard, dead. She felt as if everything she cared about had been smashed.

Nick breezed in through the doors.

'Two stories for the price of one,' he said. 'Did you hear about the attack on the mosque in Plumstead? Organised by that bloke we saw at the churchyard. One kid got beaten up so badly he's still in a coma. His brother's outside, demanding to know why they haven't arrested anyone.'

Helen raised her head, looked out at the angry, defiant faces.

'Which one is the brother?' she asked. Nick pointed him out; a boy really, the determined set of his jaw touching in his barely formed face. Impulsively, she rose and walked through the doors, straight up to the young man.

'I'm very sorry for what's happened to your brother,' she said. 'I hope they get someone soon.'

The boy eyed her suspiciously. 'Are you police?' he asked.

She shook her head. 'No. I – I lost someone yesterday. He was stabbed.' She nodded to the placard he was holding. 'I know what you mean. No peace without justice.' She held out her hand.

A big black guy in white Islamic robes moved in front of her, folded his arms. 'Time you went, lady.'

The boy blushed, ducked his head. 'Yeah,' he said. 'Thanks, though.'

She turned and went back inside. Nick was still waiting, pacing and fiddling with his phone.

'They're doing a press briefing,' he said. 'I should hang on for that. Make sure they don't tell all the other reporters everything.' He grinned. 'How did you get on with DCI Greenley? Did she waterboard you?'

She flopped down on the bench, exhausted. 'Not really.' She put her head in her hands. No peace. No justice and no peace, for any of them.

'Hey, now.' He sat next to her, surprised her with an arm around her shoulders. It was like being comforted by a younger brother. 'Don't be like that. You found the notebook, remember? That's progress, isn't it?'

The notebook. She pulled it from her pocket and opened it at the front page. 'Oh …' A message was scrawled across the inside cover, Richard's usually neat script hasty, the ink smudged.

'Helen, someone's following me. This is for you. I'm sorry. With love, Richard.'

With love. She touched the words, her heart full. It took a moment for the rest of the message to sink in. He was being followed. He must have written this after he'd sent her the text message, she thought, while he was walking back to her flat. Fearing he would be mugged again, perhaps, and lose the notebook. Surely he had not thought to be murdered, stabbed just moments later at the church gate? Yet he had kept his head, found a clever hiding place and managed to get his message to her. She was once more overcome with the quickness of his mind. Right to the very last, he was forging connections, making links. Her mind flashed back on his final look of sadness, the regret on his face. *I'm sorry.* What had he been sorry for?

Chapter 31

Helen sat beside her old friend and listened to his laboured breathing. She'd waited for hours at the police station, worried that they'd forget about her if she went home. Eventually word had come through that Crispin was conscious and had asked for her. By the time she arrived, he'd fallen asleep again.

One hand lay on the white sheet, a cannula feeding saline into his struggling veins. Brown liver spots marked his pale skin, translucent as antique lace. A clumsy wodge of dressing was taped to his forehead, half-obscuring one eye. She held his other hand, feeling the faint but persistent beat of his pulse through his fragile wrist. It seemed impossible he had survived the attack and the hours lying on the cold floor afterwards. Some tenacity in his spirit had clung on, refusing to be beaten.

But it had been a close thing. The PC who'd been sent to check out Helen's flat had been on her way out when she'd heard a faint mewing sound, like a trapped kitten. The doctor said he'd lost a lot of blood through the head wound and was hypothermic when he arrived at the hospital. He'd spent most of the morning in the high dependency unit. Now he was in a private room, a policeman sitting outside the door. Helen had been warned not to ask him about the attack for fear of confusing him.

The figure on the bed gave a croak. Looking up, Helen saw his bright blue eyes staring at her in surprise.

'Hello. How are you feeling?'

'Head hurts.' He licked his lips. 'Some water,' he muttered.

She held the plastic cup as he sipped for a moment then sagged back against the pillows.

'That's better.' He squeezed her hand. 'You forgot the lemon. And the gin.'

She laughed, then started to cry. 'I was so worried about you. It was my fault; they broke into my flat. And I ran away and let them whack you over the head.'

'Don't be silly, darling. So long as you're alright.' He closed his eyes again and slept.

He didn't look himself, with white stubble on his chin and his hair all mussed up. Without his teeth, his mouth had fallen in and his cheeks were deeply sunken. She'd go back to the house later, she thought, collect his false teeth and shaving kit, his natty silk dressing gown and a cravat. And get out of these stupid clothes and into her jeans. Back to normal.

But there wasn't any normal now. She could tidy her flat, spruce up Crispin and put on her usual clothes. But she couldn't undo Richard's murder or the grief that sat undigested in her chest. She clutched his notebook, re-read his final words to her. He'd saved this book, maybe at the expense of saving his own life. He'd wanted her to have it, wanted her to carry on with the work they had begun together. 'I'm sorry,' he'd written. Sorry for what? She wondered what they'd talked about, him and Charles, after dropping her off. Had Charles been more explicit about his warnings, even threatened Richard? She'd very much like to talk to the man, although she suspected the feeling would not be mutual.

She turned the pages to their latest discovery, the long line of letters she'd transcribed from the bottom of the Cobham note. D G B E X Z B T Z G J B H R E H W T M F V P V T Z K I F W P I D W O T N R I M W S T M G A L U A K V M E H M M A K V J E B K O E. They seemed completely random.

She remembered reading about Elizabethan spies communicating in code and how rudimentary ciphers could be cracked using letter analysis. The most commonly used letter in English was E, followed by S. Or something like that. You worked out how many times each letter appeared in the coded message, then tried the most common letters until you started to see the pattern emerge. Searching for a pen, she found a stump of pencil tied by string to the chart at the end of the bed. She detached it and began to count letters.

'What are you doing? Did you bring the newspaper?' Crispin's voice was more distinct now, his eyes brighter. He shuffled upright on his pillows and looked at her more closely. 'Lordy, Helen. What's happened to you? You look terrible.'

'I know. It's a long story. And not a very happy one. Let's not talk about it.' Wanting to distract him, she turned again to the notebook in her lap. 'Here. I'm afraid I don't have a crossword, but you can help me with this puzzle. It doesn't make any sense to me. I think it's some kind of code.'

He squinted to read the letters. 'What do you think I am, Bletchley Park? I need my specs. I don't suppose anyone brought them? And my teeth. I hate people seeing me without my teeth.'

'I'll bring them. Later today, when I've been home and had a shower.' Helen had a sudden longing to be standing under jets of hot water, pouring over her battered body. 'Were you at Bletchley, then? Or can't you tell me?'

He snorted. 'I was nine when the war broke out, young lady. It might have been an eccentric setup, but I don't think they recruited from the school room.' He took the pencil and completed the job she'd started, counting letters and putting them in order. After five minutes he threw down the notebook.

'No good. I think it's polyalphabetic, probably a Vigenère square. You won't get it without the key.'

'A what?'

'A Vigenère square cipher. You can't crack it by letter analysis because it uses twenty-six versions of the alphabet and each letter can be coded for as many times as there are letters in the key.' Animated now, he seized the pencil again and started writing out the alphabet across the top of the next empty page.

'Like this. You write the alphabet twenty-six times, each starting with a sequential letter. The first one starts with A and ends with Z, as normal. Then the second starts with B and ends with A, and so on. You use the key to work out which alphabet sequence to use for which letter. So the first letter of the message to be deciphered takes you to the relevant letter in the sequence starting with the first letter of the key. The second letter takes you to the sequence starting with the second letter of the key.'

'And if you don't have the key?'

'It's practically unbreakable because there are something like four billion possible combinations.'

Helen was impressed. 'You bloody well should have been at Bletchley. Even when you were nine.'

He grinned, forgetting about his teeth. 'They could have put me in the infantry.'

Helen groaned. She took out her phone and looked up the Vigenère square cipher. To her excitement, it was in use during the Elizabethan era, when it was considered unbreakable. Indeed, the famous mathematician and magician John Dee had a copy of an early work on the subject. And John Dee's young disciple, Thomas Hariot, worked for Walter Raleigh. *Bingo.* Hariot had lectured the School of Night group – including Raleigh and his friend Lord Cobham – on many mathematical subjects. Perhaps he had included a lecture on the use of the Vigenère cipher.

As she read on, her heart began to sink. The Vigenère cipher had been dubbed *le chiffre indechifferable* – the undecipherable cipher. It had not been decrypted until Charles Babbage cracked it in the nineteenth century. The instructions for solving the cipher when you had the key were difficult enough. How would she work it out without the key?

'Sweetheart, do share. Given that I've solved another clue for you.' His voice was wheedling.

'Hah! No, you haven't. You've just told me that my clue is unsolvable.' She relented. 'We found a letter from Walter Raleigh to Lord Cobham. Thanks to you working out the last clue about the infinite riches. It had this line of code written at the end of it. Trouble is, I have no idea about the key. And you say it's unbreakable without it.'

They stared at the letters in silence for a moment.

'Practically unbreakable. But you might need one of those machines they built to crack the Enigma code. I think you'd better find the key.'

Helen stared at the notebook. 'There's this.' She pointed to the little drawing of a crescent moon on its back with wavy lines beneath it. 'It was drawn at the top of the letter, in the corner. Like a little doodle.'

He leaned over to look. 'Is it the moon? We could try it, I suppose. But it's a bit short for a code word.'

She shook her head. 'There's more to it. I'm trying to remember – there was something in the news a few years ago about a painting with a crescent moon. A portrait of Elizabeth I, I think. They were full of symbolism, Elizabethan portraits. Messages about loyalty, or religious devotion, purity and so on. Courtiers were expected to wear miniatures, jewels with the Queen's image. Raleigh would certainly have had one.'

She tapped search terms into her phone. The results threw up a welter of imagery associated with the Virgin Queen. Pearls, sieves, white roses, pelicans, the crescent moon. All were allegories of purity or sacrifice. Later portraits, she read, emphasised empire and majesty.

She scoured her memory for the news story. 'The story was about a portrait with a little sketch of the moon that had been painted over. They found it when they were restoring the painting.'

Crispin was scribbling in the book, trying out different keys on the encoded text. 'Let's try Elizabeth. It's long enough to work.' She watched him mark up the alphabet sequences to use and quickly run through the text. But the exercise produced still more gobbledegook. 'Sorry. Doesn't look like that's it.'

'Never mind.' Helen yawned, realising again how tired she was. A nurse came in and checked the bedside monitors.

'You should be resting,' she told Crispin. She shot Helen a disapproving look. 'He shouldn't talk. I think it would be best if you let him be. We only said you could come in because he'd been worrying himself about you.' She folded her arms. Helen saw her noticing her ripped dress and tangled hair.

'I'm sorry. Crispin, I'll come back tonight with your stuff. Go back to sleep. I'll see you later.' She kissed his cheek, slipped the notebook into her coat pocket and walked through the long corridors.

She realised she was not just tired, but hungry. She considered the hospital cafe, a hot cup of tea and a piece of cake for comfort. Then she remembered: no money. No bus pass either. Damn. It was a long walk home, and Nick's motorbike boots were rubbing a blister against her bare heel. She took her phone from her pocket. It had one bar of battery left. Maybe she'd call Nick, ask him to pick her up and take her to the flat.

She sheltered under the canopy outside the accident and emergency department and rang the reporter's number. It went to voicemail. She sighed, left a message and began the long walk home. As she crossed the car park, a blue Transit van pulled up alongside her.

''Scuse me, love.' A guy was leaning out the window, grey sweatshirt, hood up over his head. 'Got any change for the parking machine?'

She stared. Even with the hoodie, she recognised the man from the churchyard. The one Nick had spoken to, who'd been looking through the bins. He didn't know she'd recognised him, she realised. But this was surely no coincidence.

'Sorry,' she muttered, picking up her pace. She kept her head down, walked faster. The van driver overtook, pulled the vehicle to a halt in front of her, blocking the path. She began to run, but he was out of the cab and took hold of her arm. She started to scream.

His arm slammed across her windpipe, cutting off the air. She panicked, unable to breathe. She began to feel dizzy. He opened the van door and threw her inside, slammed the door shut. In the darkness, she scrambled to her knees and beat her fists against the door. The van revved and drove off. She was flung to the floor.

Chapter 32

Paxton was sweating. That had been an insane risk. But he'd had little choice. He was deeply disappointed in his boys. They'd let him down badly. Abducting a sleeping girl from a near-empty house should have been a straightforward operation. It had taken him most of the day to recover the ground lost by their stupidity, and who knew what damage the girl had done in that time? He'd been trailing her since his contact at the local nick tipped him off that she'd walked in mid-morning, along with that idiot reporter. What was their connection? He couldn't make it out. It had been bad luck, running into the reporter at the churchyard. He should have guessed the press would be all over the place the morning after the murder. But he hadn't expected it to be someone he knew.

He swung the van through the south London streets. There was a chance someone had seen him grab the girl, or that they'd see it on the CCTV from the car park. He needed to get the van off the road and the prisoner under control, fast. That meant the only real option was the lock-up he rented under the railway arches. It was a bit close to home, around the corner from the office on the industrial estate. But he could drive straight in, and the neighbouring businesses knew to keep themselves to themselves. It would do for the short term.

He ran through his list of operational objectives. Firstly, secure the girl and hide the vehicle. Then he could go back to the client with a sitrep. At least he had something positive to report this time. Their last conversation had been a disaster. He'd had to admit that he'd not only failed to acquire the intelligence, but his men had alerted the target to their presence, then caused significant collateral damage that would attract unwanted attention from the police.

He still had trouble believing their version of events. How the hell had they managed to let her escape from a fourth-floor flat? They'd turned her flat over pretty comprehensively, they said. If she had the notebook, she either took it with her or gave it to the police. He'd found nothing in the churchyard – not that he'd been able to look properly, what with the kid from the paper turning up and wanting to chat.

The girl and the kid. He frowned. Something odd about that. He could see why the reporter would want to talk to the girl. He'd want her story, as the victim's girlfriend. But why would she give him the time of day even? His informant at the police station had been adamant that they'd arrived together on the kid's motorbike. So it hadn't been a coincidence.

Paxton thumped the steering wheel. They must have both been at the churchyard. Either they met there or they'd gone there together. The kid had come to talk to him, distracted him, while ... while what? While the girl looked for the notebook. That was the only explanation. And then they'd gone straight to the police station. He swore aloud. He supposed they'd have handed over whatever they found. And – a cold prickle of fear down his neck – the reporter might have mentioned that they'd seen Paxton hanging around. Which would put him right where he didn't want to be: in the vicinity of Watson's murder.

He punched the horn, impatient to push his way through the traffic and get off the road. If the police had his name, they might be looking for him. His insiders would keep him low on the priority list for a while, but not forever. The van wasn't his; it was a knackered old thing that belonged to one of his team. The man had been told to report it stolen, but it was another link back to Paxton that he could do without.

This was getting messy. He ran his hands through his hair, felt the sweat cooling in his armpits and down his back. The girl was making a din. He'd had no time to restrain her; she was banging the doors and walls. It wouldn't be noticed in the noise of moving traffic, but was a risk every time he had to stop at a junction. Every siren, every blue light, triggered another shot of adrenalin. He saw a gap in the clogged traffic and went for it, plunging through with his hand on the horn. Under enemy fire, making for the base. His heart pounded as fast as it had ever done in Afghan, as he weaved through the potholes on the crap dust roads, praying he wouldn't hit an IED before he made it back to the compound with his unit in one piece.

* * *

Nick was in the office, uploading photos from his phone directly onto the newspaper's website. They looked bloody brilliant. The editor was leaning on his shoulder, a big grin on his ugly mug. They usually had a skeleton team working weekends, but the lure of the big story had drawn them all in. A couple of reporters watched in envy as Nick opened a second window and started updating his story.

'Jammy bastard,' said Meena as he pulled up a cracking photo of Helen and attached it to the text. 'I've written millions of those local history articles. All I get is emails telling me I've got it wrong and the shop on the corner was the greengrocer not the bakery.'

'Never contradict the local history society.' Nick grinned. 'Get us a cup of coffee, Meena. I'm dangerously low on caffeine.'

'Get it yourself.' She stalked off.

He checked his mobile and saw he'd missed a call from Helen. He supposed he should ring her back; she'd been waiting to hear about her neighbour, the old man who'd been knocked about by the burglars. She could give him the latest.

'Hey, Helen. How's it going?'

At first, he couldn't make anything out. There was a lot of traffic noise and the line wasn't great. She sounded upset. He stuck a finger in his other ear, blocking out the sound of ringing telephones, gossiping reporters and fingers bashing keyboards.

'Can't hear you. What's up?'

'I've been kidnapped.' She shrieked the words, her voice breaking up so that he wondered if he'd heard her right.

'You what? Where are you?'

'I don't know!' she screamed. 'I'm in a van. The man…' The phone was interrupted by a burst of interference.

'Say that again. What sort of van?'

'Blue Transit van. The man from the churchyard…' The phone bleeped and cut out.

'Shit!' he yelled and rang the number again from his desk

209

phone. It went straight to voicemail.

'Problems?' The editor raised his eyebrows. He ran an old-school news desk; expletives and yelling were nothing out of the ordinary.

'That was Helen. She said she'd been kidnapped.'

'Then ring the police, lad!'

Nick did as he was told while the other journalists gathered around. Meena put a mug of instant coffee on his desk. He came off the phone to the police.

'They'll try to trace the location of her mobile.' He turned to Meena. 'Get your mate back on the phone. The one from *Lighthouse*. I think Helen meant she'd been picked up by Gary Paxton. Let's see what we can find out about him, shall we?'

She vaulted over the desks to get to her computer. Within minutes, all four journalists were hitting the phones or trawling through the archives. If Paxton had featured anywhere in the *Courier*'s back history, or knew any of their contacts, they'd find him. Nick saw the editor look up from his battered old contacts book, phone cradled beneath his chin, and gaze at his motley group of poorly paid journos. Just for a minute, they weren't rival reporters. They were a team.

Chapter 33

Helen crashed into the side of the van as it swung sharply around a corner. She was awash with nausea. Exhaust fumes, oil and hot metal mixed queasily in her nostrils. The van lurched again. She retched and swallowed hard, tried to control her breathing. Sweat washed over her face, then her mouth was full of sour saliva and her stomach convulsed.

She vomited onto the floor of the van, crouched on her hands and knees. Disgusted, she backed away from the puddle of sick, groped around for something to wipe her mouth. She found a handful of old rags, stinking of petrol, greasy against her lips. She'd not been sick for years, and the humiliation of it squeezed tears from her eyes. She shuffled up against the van wall, braced herself and closed her eyes, willing the van to stop moving. She tried to breathe normally, to pull herself back to a place where she could think.

They'd got her. Whoever they were, the men who came to her flat, the men who killed Richard, they had found her. What did they want from her? She clutched her arms, started to tremble. The shock of the struggle, the panic when he'd cut off her breathing. He'd known what he was doing. She had no chance of fighting him off. She checked her phone

one last time, but the battery was well and truly dead. She'd managed to speak to Nick, at least. That was one shred of comfort. He'd get onto the police; he'd know what to do. And he knew the man who'd kidnapped her.

She tried to remember what the reporter had said about the man. A local thug, a troublemaker. But he'd been searching the bins in the churchyard, which meant he too had been searching for Richard's notebook. She felt its outline in her coat pocket, hard against her chest. That meant, she supposed, he might have killed Richard for the book, then discovered he no longer had it. Or maybe killed him because he didn't have the book. In terror, she realised she was clutching the very thing that Richard had died trying to protect. And now she was helpless to protect it herself.

Could she hide it as he had done? The van was no good; she couldn't see around it, never mind find a hiding place that would be invisible in daylight. She could see cracks of light along the bottom of the van doors. Should she simply dump the book, squeeze it out through the gap and onto the streets? But she couldn't bear that, after Richard had worked so hard to get it to her. It was bulky, too thick and rigid to hide under her clothes. Except ... which page was the most important? The code. If she tore out just that page, she could at least keep the coded message secret. She shuffled down to the back of the van, where she could just make out the writing on the pages by the light around the doors. She traced again his final message, her throat squeezed tight. This notebook was all that was left of him now. She could hardly bear to damage it. Carefully, she tore out the page where she'd written the line of code, folded it small and tucked it into her bra. It was the best she could do.

The van slowed. It felt like they were off the main road now, jerking over rough ground and potholes. She strained her ears but could hear only the noisy engine. Was there a chance here?

She braced her feet against the doors and pushed, hard. They gave a little. She kicked harder. The noise exploded around the van, but the doors stayed in place. She tried again, was rewarded with a further glimpse of daylight. *One more time*, she thought.

The van jerked to a halt. She heard the driver's door clunk open, then a creak of metal doors. They drove forward again, then stopped. She readied herself, propped up on her elbows. The key turned in the lock. Now.

There was a burst of artificial light. Helen kicked wildly at the dark figure outlined in the doorway. Her boot connected, satisfyingly hard, with his face. He yelled, reeling backwards. Behind him, Helen glimpsed a metal garage door. Before she could get out, his fist crashed into her nose, then another blow threw her jaw sideways. She fell back into the van, blood running into her eyes and mouth. The pain from her nose was extraordinary, bringing an involuntary stream of hot tears.

Blood poured from her nose, tasting salty, flooding her mouth. She rolled away, propped herself up against the wall. He was on his hands and knees in the van, a balaclava pulled over his head. She could just see his eyes, dark with fury.

He grabbed her chin, fingers digging into her flesh, and put his own face so close to hers that she could smell his sour breath.

'You get one thing straight, bitch. You are my prisoner. You are nothing. I can do anything to you. Anything I want. If I tell you to beg, you beg. If I tell you to sit up and bark like a dog, that's what you do. And if you try to be clever again, I will break your fucking neck.'

Chapter 34

Nick rattled the letterbox and buzzed the door again. The only sound was furious barking, which had erupted from the yard as soon as he pulled up. He walked round to the back of Paxton's office building. One of the two dogs he'd seen before was in the cage. It was an ugly beast: a squat creature with over-developed muscles that looked like a fighting dog. He wouldn't like to be in the vicinity when the cage was opened.

He didn't trust the police to find Helen, even with the information he'd given them. DCI Greenley had promised they'd track Paxton down. But Nick was taking no chances.

His mobile rang. He'd set it to loud, not wanting to miss another call. He felt guilty that he'd missed Helen when she'd rung to ask for a lift from Lewisham Hospital. If he'd answered, maybe she'd have waited somewhere safe until he got there.

'Yeah?'

It was Meena in the newsroom. 'You wanted Paxton's home address? He's not on the electoral register, but I checked with Companies House and got the records of Secure Solutions. They have his address as a director of the company.' She sounded pleased with herself.

'Good going.' Nick scribbled it down. 'Anything else?'

'That policewoman rang. DCI Greenley? She wants you to go down to the station.'

'Too busy. Tell her you couldn't get hold of me.'

'I'm not your bloody PA. I gave her your mobile number. Are you going over to Paxton's house?'

'Yeah, there's no one here. I'll do a bit of door-knocking. If the police had any sense, that's what they'd be doing instead of harassing me.' He rung off and sat on his bike, looking up the address on his sat nav. The afternoon was gloomy and the light starting to fade. He checked his watch, saw with surprise that it had gone five o'clock. His phone rang again. He groaned, expecting DCI Greenley to give him a bollocking.

'Nick? It's Ollie from *Lighthouse*. Sorry, I just picked up your call. Run me through what's happened?'

He did his best to summarise. The man drew in his breath sharply when he recounted Helen's call and disappearance.

'Shit, that's not good. Listen, there's something we were investigating about Paxton, but we never got it firmed up enough to print it. There were some nasty rumours about him in Afghanistan. Mistreatment of prisoners.'

'Go on.'

'Remember years ago, around 2006, 2007? A bunch of soldiers got into trouble for taking photographs of naked prisoners all piled up in a pyramid? Standing around laughing at them?'

He remembered. He'd still been at school, had watched the news reports from Afghanistan and Iraq on the news, wanting to be one of those flak-jacketed reporters dodging gunfire and looking glamorous.

'I thought that was Iraq?'

'It was. They'd been in Afghanistan, though, on a previous tour of duty. Paxton was a sergeant in Helmand at the time. We heard he took an enthusiastic approach to interrogation of prisoners. Hooding, beatings, threats of sexual assault. Urinating on prisoners, cigarette burns. It seems like his attitude spread. He left the army in irregular circumstances. It's not clear why. He was never charged with anything.'

Nick remembered the flicker of anxiety he'd caught on Paxton's face when he'd questioned him about his time in Afghanistan. He thought of Helen, her courage and gutsiness, and felt sick. What was happening to her? 'OK. We need to find her, then.'

'You do,' agreed Ollie. 'Soon.'

He was in a gloomy mood when he swung the bike around the corner into the street where Paxton lived. These suburbs made him uncomfortable, gave him an itchy feeling on the back of his neck. Twenty-five years ago, the place had been notorious for the murder of a young black man by a gang of white racists, stabbed to death for nothing but the colour of his skin. People said things had changed, but it felt like hostile territory all the same.

Then he grinned. Sitting on the wall outside the row of maisonettes, cheerful in her bright yellow headscarf, was Meena.

'The boss thought you could use some moral support,' she explained. 'Oi! Let go.' He swung her off the wall and set her down.

'Excellent idea.'

Together they marched up to the house. It was surprisingly neat, a pot of flowers by the white-painted front door. The downstairs windows were shrouded in grey metal grills, rather spoiling the domestic atmosphere.

'It's divided into two flats. Paxton's is downstairs,' said Meena, checking the numbers. They rang the bell and waited. She put her nose against the grill and shielded her eyes. 'Can't see any lights. I don't think he's at home.'

Nick stepped back and looked up at the top windows. A net curtain dropped, just allowing him a glimpse of a face watching them. 'Let's try the neighbours.' He rang the upstairs bell. No reply. He tried again, holding the bell longer this time, then called through the letterbox. Whoever lived upstairs had decided not to get involved.

The two reporters split, taking the maisonettes either side and working their way out. Nick got one suspicious woman who threatened to call the police and a stroppy teenager who said he didn't know any of the neighbours and didn't want to. He was about to cross over to the other side of the road when he heard Meena's voice.

'Get off me, you arsehole!' He swung around to see her struggling with two white men. He sprinted towards them. One held her from behind, pinning her arms to her side and lifting her off the ground while she kicked ineffectually at his legs. The other yanked off her headscarf, pulling it from its tightly pinned moorings to expose a coil of thick hair, black and glistening like tar. Her face was a ball of fury, spitting insults into his face.

'Let go of her,' he yelled. He wasn't built for this. They were bigger than him, and there were two of them.

The man closest to him spun around, waving Meena's yellow scarf like a flag. He grinned. 'What, you want some too?'

Nick tried to think through the fear and rage that clouded his brain. Fired up as he was, he was never going to beat them physically.

He stopped, waved his mobile phone. 'Police are on their way,' he shouted. 'You really want to be up for racially aggravated assault?'

The other guy loosened his grip on Meena. 'We were just having a laugh,' he said. He was very young, maybe still at school. She wriggled free, advanced on his mate.

'Give me that back.' She looked different without her headscarf: younger and more vulnerable. She also looked bloody angry.

The first guy, a mean-looking thug in his twenties with close-cropped hair and bad teeth, balled up the swathe of cloth and threw it on the ground. 'Don't come round our manor asking stupid questions,' he said. 'We don't like Pakis.'

'And I don't like filthy racist scum,' she spat.

The man swung a punch at her, and missed. Nick grabbed her arm and pulled her away. 'Just run,' he yelled.

He wanted to get back to his bike, but it was at the other end of the street. They ran to the end of the road. He turned left at random, pulling her along.

'Keep going,' she puffed. 'Down through that next alley.'

He wasn't sure that back alleys were their friend right now, but let her lead. He heard a yell behind them, looked over his shoulder and saw the first guy coming around the corner.

'Shit,' he muttered.

'Keep going. Next turn,' said Meena. She seemed to know where she was going. 'Fam,' she explained, breathless. Of course.

Halfway down the next alleyway, a back gate swung open.

'In here,' said a woman's voice. He screeched to a halt and followed Meena through the wooden gate. An elderly Asian woman hurried them into the house and locked the kitchen door behind them. Nick bent double, trying to catch his breath. His heart jumped in his chest, kabooming like a sound system with an over-heavy bass.

Meena seemed to be in better shape than him.

'Hello, Auntie Begum,' she said, hugging the old lady.

The woman pulled out a kitchen chair and motioned Nick to it. 'Sit down!' she commanded. He sat.

Meena broke into some Indian language that he didn't understand. The woman tutted and shook her head, making noises of disapproval as she put on the kettle then found a headscarf and helped Meena fold and tuck it around her hair.

'We shouldn't stay long,' Meena told him. 'We don't want to get Mrs Chaudhury into trouble. I don't think those men saw us come in, but someone might have done. I rang Auntie before I left the office, said I'd come around for a cup of tea. Always helps to have family in the neighbourhood.'

A creak from the stairs made Nick jump. A young man came into the kitchen, nodded at Meena and took a can of Coke from the fridge. Nick narrowed his eyes. Wasn't he one of the guys he'd met with Amir at the chicken shop?

'Alright, Meena?' He gave Nick a cool look. 'You found him, then? This Paxton bloke. I thought you were going to let us know?'

'We've just tracked down his home address,' said Nick. The old lady handed him a mug of tea. He took a gulp; it was sweet and milky. Just what he needed. He realised his hands were shaking.

'Yeah, well. We were ahead of you, anyways.' The man

picked up his phone. 'Sources. We're planning on paying him a visit.'

'OK.' Nick was cautious. 'Have you seen him recently? He's wanted by the police. Not just for the attack on Anjoy. We think he's kidnapped someone. A woman, a friend of mine.' He took out his phone and showed him a photograph. 'Helen.'

The man raised his eyebrows. 'Yeah? So now that he's attacked a white woman, you're interested? Rather than when it's just some Bangladeshi kid lying in hospital.'

'Bruv, it's not like that,' said Meena. 'We've been doing all we can to track this arsehole down. And you know I've been in and out of hospital with Anjoy's parents.'

The woman put her hand over Meena's and scolded the young man in her quick tongue. He rolled his eyes, then eventually grinned at Nick.

'Ma says I'm not to give you a hard time. She says you saved Meena from Paxton's gang. So, what's going on? You two want to be careful, asking questions about Paxton round here. Might get more than you bargain for.'

Nick could well believe it. 'Helen rang me. She said she'd been kidnapped and was in a blue Transit van. Have the police been round? They should be looking for him.'

The young man laughed and unlocked the back door. 'You're joking me? Look at this. See if you think the police will help.'

The side of the house was covered in racist graffiti. Much of the wall had been painted over, then sprayed again and painted over again.

'I don't paint it over any more,' said Mrs Chaudhury. 'They put dog mess through the door. They throw bricks through the windows. One day they're going to set the place on fire,

221

with us inside.'

Nick was shocked. 'Who does this?'

'My neighbours. Friends of your Gary Paxton.' She closed the door, locked it carefully. 'I call the police. They do nothing. Tell us about this girl who's gone missing.'

Nick explained. They listened with concentration.

'I've not seen him today. Dunno about a blue Transit. He usually drives a white van with a cage in the back for the dogs. You know about his security firm?' asked the young man. They nodded.

'Some of the kids round here work for Paxton, casual shifts and that,' he said. 'I've got a contact.' He looked embarrassed.

'He's got a girlfriend,' said his mother, disapprovingly.

'Whatever.' He fingered his phone. 'Her brother works for Paxton. That's how we found out where he lives.' He curled his lip. 'She says he's going round flashing his cash about. Says they've got a big job and Paxton's taking him on full-time. Surveillance and that. Said he wasn't meant to talk about it. But he's a twat, can't keep his mouth shut.'

A surveillance job. Nick remembered Helen telling him that she'd feared she'd been followed before Richard's murder. Had Paxton's gang been stalking her as part of a security job? If so, that might make sense of his involvement. He struggled to understand what Paxton and his friends could possibly have against Helen and Richard, a couple of historians. But maybe they were just hired muscle.

'Can you give me her number? I'd like to talk to her.'

The man shook his head. 'Sorry. If her brother found out, there'd be trouble. Real trouble. He doesn't even know we see each other.'

'Just tell us what street she lives in. We're doing door to

door anyway, so we could do the whole street. The brother wouldn't know you'd said anything,' said Meena.

Nick couldn't believe that she was still up for door-knocking in this neighbourhood.

'Not a good idea. Specially not for you, Meena.'

Her smile turned icy. 'I'll take my chances.'

'No, you won't. We're getting out of here as soon as we can,' said Nick. 'I'm not rescuing you from Paxton's mafia again.' He turned to the young guy. 'You couldn't give her a call, could you? Ask if she's seen or heard anything?'

He sighed, fiddled with his phone for a moment, then shouted, 'Denise! You can come down now.' Another creak on the stairs. A white girl in a pink tracksuit, with a blonde ponytail, came sheepishly into the kitchen.

The older woman looked at her in astonishment. She unleashed a tirade of scolding towards her son, reverting to her first language. Nick could get the gist, though. He'd had the same talking-to from his own mother plenty of times. The girl looked embarrassed, started edging towards the door. Any minute now she'd make a run for it.

'Alright, Auntie!' Meena put a hand on the woman's arm. 'You can tell them all that later. But this is important, yeah?'

She crossed the room to the girl. 'I'm Meena. This is Nick. We're not going to get you into trouble, alright? But we really need your help. Paxton's kidnapped a woman, and we need to find her. Can you help?'

She shrugged. 'Don't know nothing about it. My bruv was up in Greenwich all day yesterday. Sitting outside someone's house in a van. Said it was well boring.'

'What van? Who did it belong to?' asked Nick. He remembered the break-in at Helen's flat the previous night.

Had this kid been involved? Was it the same van she'd been dragged into?

'How should I know? Paxton's, I suppose. Or maybe he hired it.'

'Did your brother say where he took it back to?' Meena jumped in.

'Didn't get home till the early hours. I dunno, maybe four o'clock? I heard him come in. He was on foot, though.' She frowned. 'I suppose he must have driven to the lock-up, then walked back from there.'

'You mean the office on the trading estate? I've been round there already, nothing doing.'

She shook her head. 'Paxton's got one of those places under the railway arches. My brother says he keeps all sorts there. Might be worth a look.'

Chapter 35

They went by bike, Meena clinging on as Nick scythed his way through the darkening streets. He pulled up at the end of the arches, where a muddy unmade road linked a row of shuttered workshops. There were no street lamps. They picked their way down the path, trying to keep out of the puddles. Halfway along, a radio played drum and bass over the clanging of metal. A couple of black guys had the bonnet off a knackered-looking car and were taking the engine to pieces.

'Alright?' Nick called. They looked up and nodded.

'I'm looking for a bloke called Paxton. Drives a blue van. Got a place down here somewhere.' The kid nearest to him shrugged and got back to his work. The older guy stared for a minute, then walked over, looking the two of them up and down.

'You don't look like one of his boys.'

'I'm not.' Nick swallowed, feeling the hostility of the man's gaze. 'Nor do you,' he added, taking a gamble.

The man snorted. 'Police?'

'Nope.' He pulled out his press card. 'Local paper. I want to talk to him about a story.'

The man inspected the card for a moment, then looked at

Meena. 'You might want to keep her out of it.' Nick felt her bristle. 'It's the end one. Don't say I sent you. Blue van drove down there this afternoon. Not seen it coming back.'

A roll-down metal garage door was padlocked to the ground. By the light of Meena's phone, they could see wide tyre tracks going right into the lock-up. He banged on the door, heard it reverberate around the echoing space. No answer. He got to his hands and knees and turned his head sideways, trying to squint under the door. He could see nothing. Was Helen inside, he wondered, tied up in the dark? He felt ridiculous, scrambling around in the mud. Maybe he could borrow some tools from the guys working on the car, bolt cutters or something for the padlock.

'Helen!' he yelled. 'Are you in there?' No response, just the echo of his own voice. 'Listen, I'm going to get help,' he shouted. 'If you can hear me, hang on in there. I'll be back.'

He jumped to his feet.

'We should call the police,' said Meena. She was looking edgy, as if the warnings had started to get to her. Reluctantly, he realised she was right. Door-knocking Paxton's neighbours was one thing. Breaking into his lock-up was another.

A set of headlights swung into the path, dazzling them as the vehicle bumped its way down the potholes, heading straight for them.

'Shit.' He pulled Meena to one side. The car drew up with inches to spare. The headlights were on full beam, pinning them to the wall. He prayed this wasn't Paxton, or some of his mates, come to find out who'd been asking questions. He didn't fancy their chances if it was.

The driver's door opened and the occupant strode into the light. Nick exhaled.

'Not you again,' said DCI Greenley. She walked up to the garage door, gave it a thump, then kicked it with her shiny black lace-ups. *Where do plods get their footwear?* Nick found himself wondering. *There must be a special shop.*

'We've tried that,' said Meena, brightly.

A young copper in uniform came around from the boot of the car, carrying a tool kit. 'We should have a warrant,' he said.

The woman turned to him with disdain. 'Immediate risk of danger to life and limb. Get on with it.'

While the policeman worked on the padlock, DCI Greenley quizzed Nick about everything they'd discovered. When he described the graffiti on Mrs Chaudhury's wall, and her complaint that the police did nothing, she looked even more annoyed than normal. She wrote it down, though, her lips pressed together as she made a note of the woman's name and address.

'Anything else I should know?'

Nick remembered the notebook Helen had found in the churchyard. She'd asked him not to mention it, had said she wanted to keep it and feared the police would take it from her. But Paxton had been nosing around the churchyard that morning, and quite possibly had been stalking both Helen and the murdered historian. The book could be important.

'Helen found a notebook. This morning, when we were in St Nicholas' churchyard. She said Richard Watson had left it there for her. She didn't want me to tell you because she wanted to keep it. But now she's missing...'

'Oh, for heaven's sake.' The policewoman rubbed her eyes. 'Time and again I tell people we need to know everything. She had the book on her when she was kidnapped, I suppose?'

227

Nick acknowledged that she probably did.

'Right. So, the notebook that Watson was quite possibly murdered for is now in the possession of the woman who has supposedly been kidnapped, probably by the murderer. Marvellous.'

She stalked over to the young policeman. 'Have you finished yet?'

He nodded, releasing the padlock.

'Right. Stand back. You two' – she gestured to the reporters – 'get out of the way. I don't want inconvenient casualties.'

Nick and Meena crouched behind the car as the woman pulled up the door. In the headlights, Nick could see a blue Transit van, back doors facing the exit. *Yes*, he thought. *We've got her.* He held his breath as the policewoman yelled into the lock-up, telling anyone inside to put their hands on their heads and come out.

There was no answer. The woman pulled on plastic gloves from her pocket and opened the van doors.

The inside of the van was spattered with blood, sprayed across the walls. It reeked of vomit. But it was empty.

Chapter 36

Helen could hear nothing but her own breathing. No traffic, no people. When she listened hard, the rasping caw of rooks. And the dog, growling a few feet from her head.

She didn't know where she was. In the garage, the man had pulled a sack over her head, stripped off her borrowed motorbike boots and secured her wrists and ankles with cable ties, which cut into her flesh. She'd been shoved into what felt like a car boot, cramped and uncomfortable. He'd thrown something over her, a blanket or rug. Then had come the dog, snuffling and growling. She could smell its meaty breath, inches from her face, during the long journey that followed. She'd kept as still as possible, barely daring to breathe.

They'd driven a long way: first, a stop-start journey through streets, then a long stretch on a smooth, straight road. She had no way of keeping track of the time; she couldn't even see whether it was still daylight. Finally, the vehicle had slowed, taken a few turnings and bumped over rough ground before coming to a halt. He'd pulled her out, her joints cramped and painful, and carried her into a building, where he dropped her on a hard floor.

He'd soon found Richard's notebook in her coat pocket, as

she'd known he would. Still, it broke her heart to think of this thug pawing through Richard's careful, neat pages. What use could he possibly make of it? But clearly this was what he'd wanted. He'd taken it away, gone outside. She heard a padlock securing the door.

She struggled against the ties around her ankles and wrists, rubbing her skin raw until she couldn't tell whether it was blood or sweat that soaked the palms of her hands. The dog growled again, close by, a full-throated gurgle of sound that built up into a volley of barks, reverberating around the room. Was it tethered, or could it reach her? She struggled to a sitting position, shuffled backwards until she could feel a wall behind her. She closed her eyes and focused her mind inward. *Think of something else*, she told herself.

She still had the page from the book with the line of code hidden in her bra. She tried to remember the sequence of letters. Crispin had said she needed a key to decipher it. Not too short or it wouldn't work. Longer keys were more secure, he'd said, but time-consuming to decode. Somewhere between five and ten letters was best. Crispin had tried the names Elizabeth and Marlowe. Neither had worked. Both, Helen thought, were too obvious. She thought with some fellow-feeling of Raleigh, imprisoned in the Tower, knowing he was doomed unless he could persuade Lord Cobham to retract his accusation. What did the two men have in common? What ties of loyalty bound them together?

Both men had risen high under Queen Elizabeth, only to lose everything when James I came to the throne. Both had become fascinated with the new knowledge of the Elizabethan age, with the mathematical, scientific and astronomical discoveries that had pushed out the boundaries of her realm and founded her empire. Their supposed atheism reflected their eagerness to discover more of the world, to look for answers beyond the scriptures. Like Doctor Faustus, making his pact with Mephistopheles, the School of Night had ventured into unlawful areas of study.

Helen tried to imagine them, a candlelit circle of the best minds of the time, quizzing men of science, summoning wits and poets to Raleigh's Durham House headquarters on the Thames. Thomas Hariot, the mathematician who studied with magician John Dee, with his interest in codes and ciphers. Christopher Marlowe, the brightest star of the London stage, with his outrageous opinions and provocative arguments. The atheist lecture he'd supposedly given the group, daring them to think that religion was merely a 'bugbear' to scare children. And perhaps more, perhaps the intelligence service gossip he'd heard, or even the dangerous secret he'd learnt at Canterbury. And finally, his last play, maybe vouchsafed to Cobham or Raleigh, handed over when he began to feel the noose tightening around his neck.

Somewhere, she thought. Somewhere in that shared history was the key to the cipher, the clue that would lead her to the missing play. But first, she had to find a way out of her own imprisonment.

* * *

Paxton sat on the steps of the building, lit a cigarette and looked up to the cloudy night sky. It was months since he'd last had a smoke; he'd given up at New Year. Been quite proud of himself, but the last twenty-four hours had been too much. He inhaled and the nicotine rushed to his head. The night

231

was damp and quiet, the trees muffling traffic noise from the road. You could see for bloody miles up here in the daytime.

He'd called the client and made his report. The woman was secure and he had the notebook. He'd swapped the Transit for the dog van, which was well-concealed in the woodland. The client was coming to the remote building to collect the book.

In the meantime, Paxton could rest. He felt the tender spot on his cheekbone where the girl's surprisingly tough boot had connected. Stuck-up bitch. He didn't think she'd try that again. He took fierce pleasure in having the woman entirely at his mercy. Knowing he could do what he liked with her, seeing the dread in her eyes. They all feared rape, of course. As if that was all that soldiers thought about, as if he couldn't get a willing woman when he wanted one. But let them think that, let them wet their pants thinking that's what was coming.

All the women who'd sneered at him, who thought they were better than he was. The miserable Afghan girl who'd made the complaint, snivelling to the interpreter. The posh bitch from the military police who'd threatened him with court martial. His ex, Jackie, slamming the door in his face when he got home, turning his little lad against him. Lawyers and social workers, debating whether he was good enough to see his own kid, doling out a couple of measly hours a week in access. All of them, when it came down to it, scared shitless about what he could do to them, if he decided to bother.

He flexed his arms above his head, stretching out the ache in his muscles. His shoulders were tight with the exertion of the previous night, the struggle of his row across the river. But it was a good ache, the sort you get from hard work. He dropped to the ground and pushed out twenty press-ups, arms pumping. He couldn't afford to get soft now. It was vital to keep your fitness up during an operation.

He would do the interrogation himself. He had a knack for it, he'd told the client. It was all about keeping your cool, letting the prisoner know there was no other way. It might take time, but they'd see the inevitability of giving you what you wanted in the end. He had a reputation in the army for getting results, even if some of the by-the-book types didn't like his methods. They liked it when he got them intelligence, though, liked it that he'd rooted out the plan to infiltrate the camp through kitchen deliveries, averting a massacre of resting troops. You had to fight fire with fire, play a bit rough in a situation like that. He'd learnt a lot about what made someone work with you in Afghanistan.

He took another cigarette from the pack, held it between his fingers for a moment, then replaced it. One was enough. Besides, he might need them. The dog was barking again. He wondered if the woman had worked out where she was. He listened carefully, heard nothing more from inside the building. But now he could hear the purr of a car engine, travelling slowly down the unmade path from the road. The engine was quiet, smooth. The headlights had been turned off. A few seconds later it stopped. Paxton waited to hear the door thunk closed. He stood in the shadow of the building, letting the man come to him. He picked his way across the leaf mould and mud, trying to keep his shoes clean.

'Gary,' said the man. 'All well?'

'Yeah, everything's fine, boss. I said I'd sort it, and I have.'

Chapter 37

He was back. She could smell cigarette smoke as his footsteps came nearer. The dog was whining, giving little excited barks. She heard the clink of a chain. A second later, she could feel its hot breath on her neck. She tried to wriggle away, but the animal followed. It was snarling, a throaty rumble of menace.

'You think you've been clever, don't you?' His voice was close to her ear. He must be crouching down, holding the animal. She said nothing. She'd promised herself not to speak to the man.

'But you haven't. You've just pissed me off that bit more than I was already. One chance, Helen. I'm going to take this hood off, and you're going to tell me what you've done with the page you tore out of the notebook.'

She screwed up her eyes as he pulled the sack from her head. He was holding a flashlight, shining it straight at her. As her eyes adjusted to the light, she saw for the first time the jaws of the dog, cruel teeth bared, inches from her face. The man was holding on by its collar as it strained towards her. She pressed her lips together, shook her head.

The man let the dog closer. Spittle flew into her face as it unleashed a torrent of barking. Helen saw its eyes, bloodshot pits of fury. She swallowed hard, pressed back against the wall. Any closer and the beast would tear her face off. Would he really let it do that? The noise was deafening, panic-inducing. She closed her eyes. A scream was building inside her chest.

Above the barking, she heard the man snigger. It was a surprisingly high-pitched sound, almost a giggle, cruel as a small boy with an injured bird. The sound took her back to her teaching days, the way that the classroom noise would rise in pitch as well as volume when the bullies found a victim to round on.

With an effort, she forced her breathing back under control, as she had once struggled to exert authority over her classes. She would not give this bully pleasure, add to his feeling of power. She reached deep within herself, began mentally reciting poems to block out the sound. Fragments of stuff she remembered from school, things she'd read aloud with her father.

He pulled the animal away.

'That was your chance, Helen.' He wasn't laughing now; he had the petulant tone of the bully whose tactics had failed. She opened her eyes, saw him tie the dog up at the far side of the small room. Her eyes widened as she took in her extraordinary surroundings, the flashlight glancing off the walls.

The room was circular and domed. The walls were a honeycomb of recesses, pale stone stained with green slime. The rectangular openings were dark. The ground beneath her was stone too, puddled with dirty water and overgrown with moss. Behind the man she could see a heavy wooden door, studded and barred. Opposite stood a stone table with a small fanlight above.

235

Helen looked again at the dark openings in the walls. She thought she knew what those were. She remembered photographs from the catacombs below Paris, vaults below churches and cathedrals. The openings were unsealed. She hoped that meant they were empty. She was being held prisoner in a mausoleum, a burial chamber for the dead.

The man lit a cigarette and stood over her. 'Take that off,' he said, gesturing to her coat. Wordless, she held up her wrists, cut and bloodied from the cable ties that bound them. He crouched before her and held his cigarette to the plastic until it melted and fell to the floor.

'You try anything and I'll let the dog have you. Now. Take it off.'

She struggled out of the coat, cramped muscles screaming in pain. She dropped it to the floor and he kicked it away.

'Now the dress.'

'No!' The word was out before she could stop herself from speaking. He grinned, knowing he'd forced her to break her rule.

'Yes.' He crouched beside her again, turned the cigarette in his fingers and blew on the tip. Without warning, he placed it against the skin of her bare neck.

She screamed as the pain seared into her flesh. She tried to squirm away, but his grasp on her shoulder was strong. He pressed harder.

'You will do as I say. You had your chance. Things will get worse.'

'Stop it! Please, just stop!'

He removed the cigarette. She heard the hiss as he drew on it again. The pain was urgent, pushing all other considerations from her mind.

236

'The dress.'

She reached her hands up to the zip at the back of her neck and fumbled with it. It stuck.

'Get on with it.'

'I'm trying.' She screamed again as he touched the burning cigarette to her collar bone. Sobbing, she pulled the zip down, dragged the dirty fabric over her shoulders. She shuffled out of the ruined silk, remembering with misery how excited she'd been as she put it on, hopeful that Richard might be the one to undo that zip after their Cobham Hall dinner. Now it was this disgusting thug, Richard's murderer, who saw her sitting on the ground in her best lace underwear. For a moment, nothing else seemed to matter. Richard was dead. She could not bring him back, could not fight his murderer. She stopped caring what happened to her. *I'm dead already.*

'And the rest.' She looked up. He was staring at her breasts. *Let him look*, she thought, tiredly. *Let him take what he wants. I'm not here any more.* Then she realised. He wasn't looking at her; he was looking at the paper folded inside her bra.

Chapter 38

Nick was knackered, but he wasn't giving up. He was down to his last lead. Helen had told him she and Richard had been working for a rich aristocrat out in the countryside – a Lady Joan Brooke of Cobham Hall. They'd been working on her family history, and there was some link to Christopher Marlowe. He'd checked the address and was back on the bike, having deposited Meena at the office to update the paper's website. DCI Greenley was busy co-ordinating forensic teams and had put out a call for Paxton's arrest. The *Courier* had it first, but there would be a media alert about Helen's kidnap, with Paxton's face on every news bulletin.

The blood in the van had made this very real. Nick couldn't shake the memory of Paxton laying into his punchbag, the solid muscle shifting as he unleashed a barrage of violence. What the hell had happened to Helen in the van, and what was happening to her now?

Deep in thought, he almost missed the turning off the busy A2 that took him into Cobham. He slowed as the streetlights thinned, hedges flashing past and the streets narrowing. A ghostly white war memorial marked the crossroads. Wrought-iron gates, slightly askew, stood at the top of the Cobham Hall drive. He manoeuvred the bike through.

The avenue to Cobham Hall ran through meadows and past clumps of ancient trees, their trunks thick and menacing in the dark. He slowed to avoid potholes in the uneven surface. The drive ran straight down to the hollow where the big house sprawled. Few lights showed, but enough that he could guess the extent of the place.

It was huge. There was a grand front with columns and high windows. Two wings sprouted gothic towers, and chimney pots punctuated the skyline. It looked like Hogwarts, he thought, half expecting to see a bunch of kids on broomsticks come riding over the rooftops.

He pulled up in a spurt of gravel outside an imposing gatehouse. It was a gloomy affair, three storeys high and topped with lions and coats of arms. He usually enjoyed door-knocking, but this was outside his comfort zone and then some. It was one thing charming himself into the council flats or suburban semis that made up his usual beat. He knew where he was there, could tell as soon as he saw the place whether he'd get the door slammed in his face or be asked in for a cup of tea. Looking at the turrets, he doubted that a black guy on a motorbike would be welcomed with open arms. *Whatever*, he thought. He was used to a rough reception, and there was more at stake than a news story. He hammered on an enormous iron door knocker in the shape of a man's head.

There was no reply. He waited for a couple of minutes, reasoning that it'd take you a while to reach the door if you were at the other end of the hall. He gave it another try. Then he walked around the building, stumbling over shrubbery.

He passed through a gap in a tall hedge and found himself surrounded by dark bushes cut into weird shapes: looming monsters lit by a sliver of moonlight. They gave him the creeps. He pushed on. There were a few lights showing, but none of the ground-floor rooms seemed to be in use. Finally, he came to a green wooden door, standing ajar. The light was on inside and one of the panes of glass in the door frame was broken. Cautiously, he pushed the door open.

'Stop right there.' An old woman was pointing a gun straight at his chest. He raised his hands.

'Sorry, sorry! I was looking for Lady Cobham.' He took in the fierce-looking granny. She was wearing a jumper and a tweed skirt with wellington boots. A silk scarf was tied around her head. The gun was long, with a polished wooden stock. He had a feeling he'd found her.

'The police are on their way. Sit over there with your hands on your head.' She gestured at a wooden bench. Nick sat. He'd anticipated being thrown out by the butler, not being held at gunpoint by the lady of the house. He glanced around. He seemed to be in a storage room for wellington boots and long-disused riding equipment. It smelled musty, of ancient socks and posh sweat.

'I'm a journalist, Lady Cobham. I wanted to talk to you about a story.'

She snorted with disgust. 'No, you're not. You're a common thief. Are you looking for your accomplice? I can tell you now, he'll be unable to sell that brooch for anything approaching its true value.'

Nick looked to the broken window pane. *Shit.* Had he just walked into the middle of a burglary? No wonder the old woman was so pissed off.

'I promise. I've got a press card in my wallet, if you'll let me get it out? I wanted to ask you about Richard Watson. He was killed on my patch. I'm investigating. I understand he was working for you.'

The woman frowned, eyebrows lowering. Those were quite some eyebrows, he thought in admiration. They put him in mind of his Belfast grandfather, whose white tufts and fierce temper had terrified him as a child.

'You'll wait here until the police come. I don't care who you say you are. We didn't catch the first one, and I'm not letting you after him.'

It looked like being a long evening. Nick's arms started to ache as he wondered how long it would take the police to arrive. Then there'd be the rigmarole of establishing that he was who he said he was, and then he'd probably get chucked out anyway. He'd better make the most of the time.

'Lady Cobham...'

'It's Lady Joan, boy. You might at least get my title right before you relieve me of my jewels.'

'Sorry. Lady Joan, I think the work that Richard Watson was doing for you might have got him killed.'

She took a pace towards him, aimed the gun right into his face. 'You don't know what you're talking about.' Her eyes were like grey marbles, glazed with fury. 'You don't know Richard.'

God, he thought. She might just shoot.

'Please. Don't do that with the gun,' he gabbled. 'I'm not going anywhere, Lady Joan. I seem to have come at a bad time, and I'm sorry about that. But it's important. I'm trying to help. To find out what happened to Richard. His colleague has been kidnapped. I don't know if you've seen it on the

241

news?'

Her eyes cleared as if awakening from a trance. For a moment she looked bewildered. 'The girl?'

'Helen Oddfellow. Do you know her? She's an expert on Christopher Marlowe. She told me that's why she was working with Richard, on a letter he'd found here. She was kidnapped this afternoon, after she found his notebook.'

Slowly, the woman lowered the gun. 'How do you know all this?' Her voice was sharp. The suspicion in her expression began to give way to something else more calculating. Almost greedy.

'I interviewed Helen for an article about local history a while back. She says that's why Richard got in touch with her. People broke into her flat last night, and I helped her get away. We were working together,' he said, elaborating slightly. He looked again at the broken window.

'Lady Joan, what was taken in your burglary? Was it just jewellery? Richard hid his notebook before he was murdered. Helen found it. Now she's been kidnapped, with the book. Is this about the work he was doing on your family history? Because it's starting to look like it to me.'

She sat down suddenly, as if her legs could no longer support her weight. 'The letter. I told Miss Elms to put it in the safe. It's gone.'

The woman let the gun drop to the floor. Nick breathed again, wondering if he dared move it away from her. Best not, he thought. Something told him that a jury would be lenient to an old white woman who'd shot a young black man who tried to take her gun off her. He cursed himself for not taking a proper look at Richard's notebook when Helen showed it to him. Whatever was in that book was the key to Richard's murder.

'What letter? What were they working on, Lady Joan? It can't just be family history if it's causing all this trouble now.'

The woman looked up, as if surprised to see he was still there. She picked up the gun, broke it over her knee and shook out the cartridges. She'd meant it, then. She stowed the gun in a gleaming mahogany case behind his head.

'Come,' she said, leading the way into the house. 'I need a brandy.'

Chapter 39

Helen sat near-naked on the stone floor, shivering hard. The man had gone. He'd told her she had two hours to come up with the key to the cipher before he returned. Her ankles were still tied, her feet now so numb that she could barely feel them. The burns around her neck and on her breasts hurt fiercely, as if he was still pressing the glowing embers to them. She'd begged, wept and pleaded with him, all thought of resistance abandoned. Finally, he'd stopped the torture, perhaps realising that she would have told him the key if she'd known it. She did not ask what would happen if she had no answers when he returned. Unless she could find one, she had less than two hours to live. And yet her weariness was such that all she wanted to do was sleep. Her shell-shocked brain was refusing to think any more.

She fixed her eyes on the only source of light in the macabre building. A thin sliver of moon showed through the fanlight above the altar, like a talisman of hope. She dragged her mind again to Raleigh in his cell in the Tower of London, writing his desperate letter to Lord Cobham. The threat of execution hanging over him as he tried frantically to put together a case in his defence, knowing the trial was designed from the start to convict him. He had written a heartbreaking letter to his wife, thinking it would be his last, apologising for being unable to settle her future and telling her to seek for comfort in God. She remembered Richard's last message to her, his hastily scribbled lines. 'Sorry. With love.' Like Raleigh, he'd been resolute and quick-witted under the shadow of death. Why could she not summon the energy to be the same?

She thought of Christopher Marlowe, her passion and her life's work, and wondered how he'd faced his death. Had it been a sudden shock or a gradual, growing realisation that he would not leave the little room alive? The understanding that he had walked into a trap and the men he'd thought of as his friends were to be his executioners. All of them, Raleigh and Richard and Marlowe, knowing that their wits were the only thing now standing between them and death. Raleigh had managed a stay of execution; Richard and Marlowe had not.

The moon. She focused on the crescent, thinking of the little drawing Raleigh had made on the letter. Perhaps he'd been able to see the moon from his cell, had been inspired by the sight. It had to be part of the message, part of the coded warning or instruction he was sending to Cobham. She tried again to remember the story about the painted-over moon in the portrait. Something to do with Queen Elizabeth, a tribute from her mercurial courtier and sea-faring explorer.

Suddenly she had it. The emblem had been uncovered in a portrait of Raleigh himself, not of the Queen. It had been intended to show his devotion to her. The moon symbolised Elizabeth, and the wavy lines beneath represented the sea, its tides controlled by the moon. Raleigh the sailor was the sea, his fate determined by his queen. And here he was, using the same emblem years after her death while imprisoned by her successor, James I. What had he intended to convey by its use? Perhaps he wanted to recall to Cobham their glory days, as favourites in the Elizabethan court. Or their former friendship, their studies together in the School of Night. A faint memory jangled in the back of Helen's mind. She stopped, tried to listen and let it come. The moon and the sea. Raleigh's prison notebook on display in the British Library, open to his handwritten poem. His poem.

The Ocean to Cynthia. He'd copied it into his notebook, a poem written to Elizabeth, his former Queen, while imprisoned in the Tower by her successor.

Raleigh had written the epic poem after Elizabeth discovered his secret marriage to one of her ladies-in-waiting. She'd been furious about the marriage, and his poem was an attempt to regain her favour. Elizabeth was Cynthia, the cold-hearted and beautiful goddess of the moon. Raleigh was the ocean, bemoaning her rejection and swearing eternal devotion. Did the emblem of the moon and the sea in the Cobham letter refer to the poem? In which case, was the key word Cynthia?

Her heart began to beat faster. She felt herself coming alive again. Seven letters, a little short for a cipher key, but it could be right. She longed for Richard's notebook to try it out. The man had taken the book and the page with the message. She wanted to solve this herself. Five minutes ago, she'd been trying to find the key to save her life. Now, the thought of handing over the answer to her torturer was impossible. Yet she knew she'd be unable to keep silent when he began his interrogation again. She had to get out of this prison before he returned. Her fighting spirit, crushed by the humiliation of her treatment, awoke. She had the key. Now she had to escape.

* * *

The pain bit deep, but she was almost there. Helen had scooted over to the altar table on her backside and sawed away at the cable tie around her ankles with the rough edge of the stone. She breathed her way through the pain, feeling the skin shred and the blood flow. She was sweating, despite the cold. She would survive this; she would not let Richard's killers have the secret.

She still had no idea who they were, who was behind the sadistic thug who'd kidnapped her. He had killed Richard, she knew it. He'd not admitted it, but when she threw the accusation in his face, she'd seen his guilt. He'd looked proud, almost, as if he'd done something clever. But he didn't know enough to be acting alone.

Questions ran through her mind as she pushed herself beyond pain. Who had blocked Richard's research at Canterbury? Who had paid the boy who followed her around Bankside, or the man who mugged Richard? Who had needed to be informed about the enquiries they made at Dulwich College?

Hovering at the corners of her mind was Charles Fairfax. She remembered his cold eyes, half-obscured behind his thick spectacles. You could believe he was capable of it, she thought. Not of carrying out the dirty work himself, of course. He wouldn't want to scuff his shiny shoes or rumple his suit. But she could well imagine him controlling a network of enforcers, men who relished the rough stuff. Like Francis Walsingham, deploying his intelligence men within Catholic families then handing suspects over to the rack-master to finish the job.

She shuddered, and the plastic tie finally snapped. Her frozen feet fell to the floor, wet with blood. She hunched over, trying to rub life back into them. They were like dead things, clumsy appendages. She tried to stand, stumbled and fell. How long did she have? She had no way of knowing how much of the two hours had expired. On her knees, she shuffled to the door. It was locked fast, and she'd heard him fix the padlock from the outside. Nothing doing there.

She found the heap of her clothes piled by the door. Gratefully, she pulled on the coat, leaving the rags of her dress on the floor. The fabric was rough against her skin, but she felt better, less vulnerable. She looked around her cell, saw the fanlight above the altar. The moon was no longer visible; it had risen higher in the sky as the night advanced. But she could still see the outline of the window, now that her eyes were adjusted to the dark. She pulled herself up by the table, sat on the cold stone and pummelled her feet back to life, whimpering with pain. The window was small, but she could just about reach it. And if she could reach it, she could break it.

She thought she knew where she was now. The unsealed slots for coffins and the dilapidated state of repair suggested she was back at Cobham, in the great unused mausoleum in the grounds. Richard had described the place, although she had never seen it. It had been built for the later lords of the hall, an eighteenth-century folly in the classical style with room for all the family's descendants. Yet it had never been consecrated. The lords continued to be buried in Cobham Church, and the place had been left to decay. It was, apparently, one of the finest classical structures in England. None of which was particularly helpful in finding a way out.

As soon as her feet would bear her, she stood on the table and reached for the window. With enormous relief, she felt the breeze on her face. The glass was already broken. Yet it would be a tight squeeze past the jagged edges. Cautiously, she began to wiggle the pieces loose from the window frame, chucking them down to shatter on the floor behind her.

She heard a dog bark.

Peering through the window, she saw a man emerge from dark woodland with a dog on a chain. She shrank back. It could only be him. Would she have time to get out the window while he unfastened the padlock? Already she knew the answer. She'd be caught on the broken glass. He'd capture her like a bird in a trap.

Chapter 40

The dog barked. Paxton stopped, listened hard. Something was wrong. He hurried along the path. Had someone found her? The animal growled, a low, menacing rumble. He couldn't hear anything else. Perhaps it had smelled a fox, or a rabbit.

It had been a risk to leave her, but he'd needed a break to think about what had to be done. He'd come to the conclusion that the girl really didn't know the code word. She'd gone well past the point of breaking. Anything she knew, he knew. He felt almost tender towards her. She was his prisoner; she'd given him everything she had.

The thought of it made his chest tight. He'd taken the folded paper from her bra, slipping the shoulder straps down so her breasts hung like heavy fruit. Then he'd begun, taking pleasure in burning them, marking them, making them his own.

Finally, the screams stopped. She quietened, then she'd told him everything she knew. But she didn't know the key to decipher the coded message. He'd wanted to take her in his arms, tell her it wasn't her fault. Everyone breaks. That's just the way it is. She'd been braver than many. If she'd been a man, he might have shaken her hand before returning the prisoner to his cell.

But there was no nice, quiet prison to keep her in. Now that he had everything he wanted from her, she had served her purpose. It was just a question of how to dispose of the evidence.

He'd had disturbing news from his unit on the ground. The reporter had been sniffing around with a Muslim girl. They'd been sent packing, but a neighbour had seen them coming out of the Asian family's house two streets over.

Worse, they'd gone to the lock-up where he'd dumped the van. Then the police arrived. That was seriously bad news. He'd anticipated having time to clean up the van and torch it somewhere quiet. He'd sent a couple of guarded texts to his men inside the Met. Most had been ignored. One cryptic message came back: 'Your name's come up'. Nothing more. Paxton had more sense than to push it. Whatever their sympathies, the boys who knew him would be keeping their heads right down at the moment.

It was imperative that he get rid of the girl as quickly as possible. He'd called the client, who had been reluctant. He still hoped to use her. But it was impossible. The girl could identify him. Even though he'd kept his balaclava on, he knew she would never forget his voice, or his eyes. She could send him down for life. A life for a life. He took the risks; it was for him to decide when to close them down.

He didn't want more blood. You always got spattered, and it attracted attention. He had considered simply leaving her there, tied up in the locked chamber. The chances were no one would go that way for weeks – months, even. She'd be long dead by the time anyone found her. For a moment, it had seemed like a good option. Yet there was the risk she'd be found alive. He imagined the next few days, waiting to hear if some walker or local busybody had reported the abandoned van or heard shouting. Then there was the client, who might decide to interfere.

It wasn't just fear of discovery. Leaving her to die of thirst or hunger revolted him. He would not prolong her suffering. It was kindest to do it quickly – tonight. He felt a surge of sentimentality. After all they'd been through together, it was right for him to finish things properly.

He would do it himself. Wrap his hands around her throat, press until she stopped moving. Watching the panic in her eyes, the struggle for oxygen, until the lights went out. It would be an intimate end. He thought of himself holding her limp body, gently laying her down to the floor, smoothing her tangled hair. He swallowed. It would be a deliberate, almost sacrificial act. He felt an ache of longing in his groin.

He tied the dog to the railings outside the mausoleum. He didn't want any noise. He switched on his flashlight and unfastened the padlock. Gently, he opened the door and swung the light around. Where was she?

She wasn't there. Her coat was gone. The flashlight caught shards of broken glass on the floor. No, he thought, surely she couldn't have got out of that tiny window? He ran to the table and clambered onto it. She was tall; she'd have been able to reach. But could she really have made it through the jagged glass?

'Fucking bitch!' he howled, thumping his fist against the wall.

* * *

Helen trembled, hearing his rage. She lay in the lowest tier of coffin shelves, damp stone above and below her. She'd crawled back as far as the space would allow. Even so, if he ran his flashlight more carefully around the room, if he bent down a little, he would see her. If he brought the dog in, it would find her in seconds. And she'd be unable to fight back, held completely helpless in her stone sarcophagus. She shuddered, wondering whether she had just climbed into her own grave.

He jumped down from the table. She heard him cross the floor. He stopped right by her head. From her low vantage point, she could see only his legs. He stood like a boxer, wary and on his toes, shifting his weight. She could have reached out and touched him.

'Where are you, Helen?' His voice was low, softening his rough accent. 'I'm going to find you.' He called to the dog. She pressed her eyes closed, biting her lips to stop her teeth from chattering.

His footsteps passed out of the door and up the steps. She heard him untie the animal, muttering threats and expletives.

'Come on, boy. Let's find the bitch,' he said. It growled in response. She waited, not allowing herself to breathe. Any second now, the beast would be slavering over her, its stinking breath in her face. She gripped her arms tight, braced herself for discovery.

The footsteps receded. She waited. She could hear nothing: no footsteps, no noise from the dog or the man. She opened her eyes, peered from the stone opening. The room was empty, and the door was still open.

She began to inch her way forward on her elbows, hardly daring to believe it was true. Perhaps it was a trap and he was waiting outside the door? She heard the dog begin to bark again – but at a distance. The sound stopped.

If they were searching for her, they'd start with the woodlands closest to the mausoleum. The dog would smell her, would bark the second she emerged from the building. Yet if she waited too long, he might realise that she had been hiding in the building, might come back and find her. Despite her fear, Helen thought she would prefer to be caught in open country, where there was some chance of escape, than in this torture chamber. She wriggled free from the coffin shelf, crouched on the ground beside the door and peered out.

The arched doorway gave onto pale stone steps, leading up to railings and a gate. Beyond, she could see the dark silhouette of woodland. High above her, the moon was just visible through the clouds. Slowly, she hauled herself to her feet and stepped over the threshold.

She paused at the gate and listened hard for the dog's bark. Nothing. The mausoleum stood on top of a small hill, surrounded by trees. Below her, perhaps a mile or two away, she could see the bulk of Cobham Hall. Away to her left were lights from houses and streets. Cobham Village, she supposed. She could just trace the track of the road they'd driven along, leading towards the lights. Which way? She imagined for a moment Lady Joan's reaction if she turned up on the doorstep like this, covered in filth. Maybe the village would be better. She thought of walking into a pub, asking for help, the horrified stares of the drinkers. But did it matter? She'd be safe. Out here in the woodland with her abductor searching for her was anything but. Then she caught a glimpse of a light bobbing through the woodland. Paxton's flashlight, heading towards the road to the village.

That was decided, then. She walked down the slope and into the woods, heading for the hall.

A figure stood by the track, hidden among the trees, and watched as she set off. He waited five minutes, then retreated to his car and purred away.

Chapter 41

Helen forced herself on, determined to reach safety. Everything hurt. Her bare feet and legs were shredded by brambles. Every now and then she looked up and located the sliver of moon, high in its sweep across the sky. Cynthia, the goddess of the moon, became her guide, leading her through the dark paths. At the hall was the letter, with the coded message, safely tucked up with Lady Joan's jewels. Later – when she'd had a bath, and something to eat, and the police had caught the bastard who'd tortured her – later, she would sit in the library with the letter and the key and decipher the message from Walter Raleigh. She held the image in her mind. Her wounds tended, clean and warm, wrapped in a dressing gown and sitting by the fire. The leather books surrounding her, a cup of tea by her side. Richard, leaning over the page and watching her work.

A long spray of thorns caught around her calf, tearing her skin. She gasped, and the image faded. *No matter*, she told herself. *Keep on.*

Finally, she broke through the undergrowth and out of the trees. There was soft grass underfoot and open ground. Hollows and flat lawns surrounded her. Was this the Cobham park? She stopped, bewildered, then realised. She was on the golf course. Ahead was a clear view of the hall; to one side, lights blazed from the clubhouse with its half-full car park. She supposed she would be conspicuous on the open ground, easier for the man to spot. But she felt safer here, with people around. She was nearly there. She strode on, the smoothness of the lawns blissful after the rough woodland paths.

'Hey! What are you doing?'

She turned quickly at the shout. A flashlight shone across the green from the direction of the clubhouse. Her first thought was of the man with the dog, but it wasn't his voice.

'I'm... I need to get to the hall,' she said. Her jaw was rigid with cold, making it hard to speak.

'This is private land,' he began, then saw her bare legs and feet. 'What's going on? Are you alright?'

'Nothing,' she said, unable to face the task of explanation. 'I'm fine. I'm going.' She kept walking, one foot in front of another. *Bastard golfers.*

He ran to her, shone the light in her face. It hurt her eyes and she flinched away.

'You don't look fine. You must be freezing, without any shoes on. Here.' He pulled off his waxed jacket and draped it around her shoulders. The warmth enveloped her. She began to shudder.

'Come on, now. Come into the clubhouse. Let's get you sorted out.' His voice was officious, but kind. He put his hand under her elbow. She had no strength left to resist.

The building was noisy with music and shouted laughter. To her relief, he bypassed the bar and took her to a small office. As her eyes adjusted to the light, she took in a paunchy, middle-aged man with thinning hair, dressed in a white shirt and black trousers. He plugged in a small electric fire and turned on the kettle.

'I'm Geoff, the bar manager. One of our regulars said he thought he saw someone trespassing on the green. Lucky for you that he did, I reckon.'

Helen let him talk, allowing life to seep back into her, eyes closed. She'd begun to shiver hard. The feeling started to return to her hands, her fingertips hurting as the blood coursed through them. In a moment, when she could talk properly, she'd ask him to call the police. The man was still out there. But for now, she had strength for nothing more than to sit before the fire and drink the mug of hot, sweet tea the manager pressed into her clumsy hands. She knew there were things she had to do. The moon. Cynthia. The letter. She sipped, feeling the liquid warm her from the inside. She could not yet believe that she was safe.

'Oh, your poor feet!' he exclaimed.

She couldn't feel them. She looked down. They were bloody and covered in dirt. Deep, raw circles ringed her ankles. Her legs were striped with weals.

'You don't have to tell me what's happened. But do you want me to call an ambulance? You don't look well.' The concern in his voice was breaking her heart. She weighed up the choices. Police first, she supposed. Until they'd caught the man, she wasn't truly safe anywhere. There was a tap on the door, and she jumped.

'Everything alright, Geoff?'

Her head snapped up. She knew that voice. *Thank goodness.* He would arrange everything. He would take care of her. He would understand.

'Is that you, Father Nash?'

The priest put his head around the door. 'Helen, my dear!

What on earth has happened?'

She saw the shock in his eyes as he took in the state of her. God, what did she look like? He stared as if he'd never seen her before. She realised he was looking at the burns on her neck. They hurt more than anything, a fierce burrowing pain that didn't let up.

'Do you know this young lady, Father Nash?'

'I certainly do.' He pulled out a chair and sat beside her, took her hand. 'Helen, we've all been so worried about you. It was on the news, you know, that you'd gone missing. I'm so thankful to see you safe.'

He pulled his wallet from his jacket pocket and extracted a card. 'Telephone my doctor, Geoff. Ask him to come straight here. Let's get you seen by a medic, Helen, then you can tell me about it.'

She nodded. Someone was taking charge. That was good. She couldn't think any more. She felt a sudden wave of exhaustion. There was still so much to do. The police, and the coded message. Richard. But she was so tired. Tears gathered and spilled over her eyelids. Soon she was sobbing, the tears soaking her hands as she shuddered and gasped. Father Nash passed her an enormous, snowy-white handkerchief and patted her shoulder.

'It's alright,' he told her. 'Everything's going to be alright. You're safe now.'

'He hurt me.' She turned to look at his reassuring face. 'I tried to be strong, but he burned me with his cigarette. Look.' She pulled aside the coat and showed him the wounds. He looked quickly away, pulled the coat around her again.

'Who did this, Helen?'

'The man... I don't know his name.' She was still shaking

hard. 'But I've seen him before. Nick knows who he is.'

'I'll call the police. But I think you should see the doctor first. He'll give you some painkillers, make you more comfortable.'

'It was the man who killed Richard,' she said.

'What did you say?' Father Nash's voice was sharp.

'Richard,' she said. His name brought a fresh wave of tears. 'He's dead.'

'Indeed, the police told me. I'm so sorry, Helen. What a dreadful thing to happen. He is in my prayers.' He patted her shoulder again.

'He took Richard's notebook,' she said. 'We need to call the police.'

'Of course,' he said. 'I'll do it as soon as the doctor is here. I don't want to leave you alone like this.'

'I can't bear it that he's dead,' she said. Her eyes hurt too much to cry more. She saw streaks of dirt and blood on the sodden handkerchief twisted in her hands.

He laid a hand over hers. 'It seems very dark, doesn't it? But I promise you, God has a plan for each of us. Perhaps Richard had fulfilled the purpose God had for him. In the bleakest of times, I find great comfort in trusting to God's infinite wisdom.'

She pulled her hand away. 'He hadn't fulfilled his purpose. He had the rest of his life to live. There were things… we had things to do. If there is a God, He doesn't seem very wise to me.'

'We can't know what God intended. Richard lost his family, you know? His wife and little child. Perhaps God thought they had been apart long enough.'

Father Nash's words came like a blow to the stomach, winding her. She'd almost forgotten how Richard had already faced a much worse loss than this. The idea that he might have embraced death, might have longed for it even, left her feeling more bereft than ever. *He didn't really want me. He just wanted to get back what he'd lost.*

Father Nash was still speaking, his soothing voice an undercurrent to her despairing thoughts.

'The important thing now is for you to find your purpose. God brought you and Richard together, for a while. Perhaps there was something you needed to learn? I think He wanted to show you where your work should be.' He passed her a clean handkerchief. 'Here. I have lots. A vicar never knows when he will need one.'

A respectful tap on the door, and Geoff was back with the doctor, a smooth-looking man in middle age, in a dark suit with a briefcase.

'This is your patient, Dr Simpson,' said Father Nash. 'Poor Helen has been through a very traumatic experience. She's distressed and in pain.' He turned to her with a compassionate smile. 'I'll leave you in Dr Simpson's capable hands,' he said. 'And I will telephone the police.'

Chapter 42

Nick always knew he'd got his story when he was sitting around the kitchen table drinking tea with the family, going through their photos of the deceased. This, he supposed, was the aristocratic equivalent. He sat in a fancy armchair beside an open fire, a heavy glass of brandy by his elbow. On the little table before them was an enormous leather-bound Bible, open to show a family tree stretching back for more generations than he could count. It was a bit more impressive than a Facebook page.

He struggled to keep up as Lady Joan gave him a potted history of the family, from Norman times to the reign of Queen Elizabeth I. She seemed very keen that he should appreciate the significance of the family having come over with William the Conqueror in 1066.

'Ha. So your lot are immigrants too, then?' he'd said, chancing it. She'd stared at him with her cold grey eyes for a long moment, then barked a laugh that was almost scarier than her frown.

'Very good. A few more generations back than your family, I imagine?'

He told her about his dad, who visited Trinidad every year and made his annual threat not to return. 'But my mum's a redhead, so she burns after five minutes in the sun. He can't stand Belfast, so they're stuck with Liverpool.'

'How interesting,' she said, in a voice that implied her interest had come to an end. 'Now, this is the important bit. It's always the younger sons who cause trouble in our family. Pirates, rebels, womanisers and spendthrifts. Do you have brothers?'

'One older. He's a doctor,' said Nick, thinking how cool it would be to include a pirate among your ancestors.

'So you're the troublesome younger brother.' She glowered at him over the book. He shrugged. She was probably right. Colin would certainly agree.

'This is where it all went wrong,' she said, sounding as cross as if the downfall had happened yesterday. 'Five centuries of inheritance, snatched away.' She indicated a name halfway down the second page.

Attainted, said the script, under the name Henry, Lord Cobham, 1558 to 1603.

'Attainted as a traitor, stripped of lands and titles in perpetuity.' Lady Joan's voice held real anger. She walked to the window. 'Betrayed. Entrapped and wrongly convicted, our lands stolen from us.'

'That's very sad—' he began.

'It was a miscarriage of justice.'

Hardly Hillsborough, thought Nick, but he listened attentively as she explained the various plots that the Cobham brothers had been caught up in after the death of Elizabeth. 'George, the younger son, was a fool and a coward. He was taken to the Tower after colluding with a couple of priests who intended to kidnap the King. He then implicated Henry, Lord Cobham, his elder brother, in a second plot. Trying to save his own neck, you see. I'm glad to say it didn't work; he was executed.'

Blimey. Not much sympathy there.

'Henry was accused with his friend Walter Raleigh. Well, the court had been out to get Raleigh for years, so that was marvellous news for them. Of course, it was completely untrue. The two men were framed.'

She turned back to the book and the last Lord Cobham. 'Henry was one of nine children. No more sons, so the line passed to a cousin. The title died with him, but the family did not.' Nick watched as her finger moved downward, sideways, down again. What must it be like, he wondered, to have that knowledge of your ancestors? Finally, she paused.

'Albert Brooke, my grandfather.' Her voice softened. 'He was a great scholar. The family historian. That's his portrait, over the mantel.' She indicated a man who seemed to be in fancy dress, with a turban and curled moustaches.

'That's your grandfather? Was he an actor or something?'

Lady Joan snorted. 'Don't be ridiculous. He'd been out in India. Lots of Victorian gentlemen had their portraits painted in native costume.'

Nick sighed. He'd never understand the upper classes.

'It was his work that began to uncover the truth about our great betrayal. This is what I hope to complete.'

She lowered her heavy eyebrows as if daring him to contradict her. She closed the Bible with finality. 'And that's what I had employed Richard Watson to prove.'

He took a mouthful of brandy, seeing she had almost finished hers, and choked. Bloody hell. No wonder the aristocracy seemed off their rockers half the time if they knocked that stuff back every night.

'OK. But why would all that bother anyone today?'

She smiled, her eyes crafty. He saw that trace of greed again, as if she took delight in knowing things that he didn't.

'Thomas Becket. Did they teach you about him at school? Or is history-teaching as poor as I read in the newspapers?'

God, she was a mardy cow. 'I think they mentioned him in passing. When they weren't getting us to dress up and re-enact the Peasants' Revolt.'

'Splendid.' If she knew it was a joke, she wasn't about to acknowledge it. She went on to explain about the desecration of the saint's tomb in the time of Henry VIII, and a theory that the sacred relics were hidden to save them from destruction.

'There has long been a tradition in the family that Henry and Raleigh knew a secret: one that would have been dangerous for the King if it had been known. Richard believed that the play written by Christopher Marlowe, who was known to Raleigh, contained this secret. That's where the Oddfellow woman came in. They had uncovered evidence that the play contained the resting place of Thomas Becket. That evidence was contained in Richard's notebook, which you tell me she has. And yet she too has vanished. That is most inconvenient.'

Nick felt like he'd tried to absorb about a year's worth of history lessons in one go. He was struggling to piece it all together into a coherent narrative, much less to understand how these historical events could get a man killed and a woman kidnapped centuries later.

'I can see why Helen would want to find a missing Marlowe play. But what does it matter to you? And why would anyone want to kill Richard for it?'

Lady Joan rose to her feet and walked to the windows. 'I want to know because it would add weight to my theory

265

that Lord Cobham was framed – that he was silenced to stop him from uncovering the secret, not because he had colluded against the King.' She turned to look at him, and he was surprised to see a shine of tears in her eyes. 'Why anyone would want to kill Richard because of this, I have no idea. I suppose someone must have wanted to stop the truth from getting out.'

He considered this. Who might want to suppress the hiding place of the relics of Thomas Becket? The Church of England? It seemed unlikely that the mild-mannered established church would go to such extremes. He well understood the power of religious factions and their symbols – no one who knew Northern Ireland could be under any illusions about that. His mother had ensured her boys grew up with due reverence for the Catholic faith, its saints and rituals. It wasn't a part of his life he thought about much, but it was there in his bones. And he knew too that anti-Catholic prejudice ran deep in English life. Deep enough to commit murder to prevent the discovery of a saint's relics? In Northern Ireland, it might just about make sense. But in England?

'Now. Tell me all that Helen had told you,' she commanded. 'I need to know about this notebook. She wrote down the code from the bottom of the letter. It's the only copy we have.'

Shortly after he'd arrived, the Kent Constabulary had made an entrance: two overexcited coppers in a wheezy old Vauxhall Astra. They'd gone off with Lady Joan's secretary, who'd discovered the burglary, promising to call in the forensic team to take fingerprints. They'd been so stunned by Lady Joan's casual estimate that her missing diamond brooch was probably worth half a million pounds that they'd barely bothered to take note of the missing historical letter. Yet,

Nick realised, that was the link with Richard's murder and Helen's kidnap. He should probably ring DCI Greenley and tip her off. He told Lady Joan the little he knew about Helen's discovery of the notebook in the graveyard.

The secretary slipped silently into the room. 'The police have gone, Lady Joan. They say the forensic officers will be here in the morning to take fingerprints. They've requested that you don't use your dressing room tonight. I hope that's not too inconvenient.'

'It's extremely inconvenient,' snapped the old woman. 'Why can't they do it tonight? I shall telephone the chief constable.'

The secretary came across to the fire. 'There is something else, Lady Joan.' She flicked her eyes at Nick. The message was clear. She wanted him out of the way. He gave her what he hoped was a charming smile.

'Don't mind me. I'll go and look out the window.' He crossed the room, praying she'd accept that. He positioned himself where he could see the two women reflected in the window behind him. She spoke softly, but his ears were sharp.

'Father Nash is here, Lady Joan. With the young woman, Helen. She seems to be injured. He asks if we can look after her for the night.'

Nick spun around. 'Helen? Helen Oddfellow? But she's been kidnapped! Where is she?'

The secretary looked pained. 'Father Nash says he has telephoned the police, and they will come to take a statement from her tomorrow. But she needs somewhere to stay tonight, Lady Joan. I thought I could make up the blue bedroom?'

'I want to see her,' said Nick. 'She called me when it happened. And I can't believe the police don't want to interview her tonight.'

'Quiet!' Lady Joan threw the word at him as she might address a servant. 'Miss Elms, bring them here at once.'

Chapter 43

Nick gasped in horror as a fat white man in a dog collar pushed a wheelchair through the door. Helen's face was swollen and bruised. She was wrapped in blankets, her head lolling, eyes unfocused. Her feet were swathed in bandages, and gauze dressings marked her neck.

'We found her wandering across the golf course, very confused and distressed,' he said. 'She has lots of scratches and other minor injuries. My doctor gave her something to calm her down and help with the pain.'

'Helen!' He knelt by the chair, took her hand and tried to get her to look at him. Her eyes were vacant. He looked again at the priest. There was something familiar about him. 'What the hell have you done to her? She's been kidnapped. She needs to talk to the police. She should be under police guard, for God's sake.'

The man looked down at him with a puzzled frown. 'I've alerted the authorities. Helen is under the care of my personal physician. He administered a mild sedative. She was quite hysterical when we found her.'

Lady Joan nodded to the secretary, whose smooth face registered distress. 'Take her, Miss Elms. Make her comfortable.

269

I shall wish to speak to her tomorrow.' The woman took the chair from the priest and wheeled Helen away. Nick made to follow.

'Stay here.' Lady Joan held out a hand. 'Father Nash, this young man is a friend of Miss Oddfellow. He works for a newspaper. He says Miss Oddfellow had found Richard's notebook. Was it with her when you found her?'

He shook his head, looking sorrowful. Nick remembered where he'd seen him before. He was the TV priest, the one who wanted a stop to immigration, who thought Islam was a threat to Britain. The sort of bloke who talked about Christian values but inspired Gary Paxton and his mob to go and kick in a few Asians down at the mosque. Nick bristled with dislike.

'She had nothing, I'm afraid. I'll ask the groundsman tomorrow to look out for anything abandoned on the golf course.' The man was looking at Nick with renewed interest. 'Which newspaper do you work for?'

Nick longed for the day when he could reply with the name of a national newspaper, something to make them stop patronising him. 'The *South London Courier.*'

The man smiled. 'You're a bit outside your patch. I have great respect for the local press. You do such a marvellous job at serving the community.'

'We do the same job as any other newspaper,' he replied. 'Only we have to stick around after the big stories move on. Which means we have to get it right.' He pulled out his notebook. 'Can I have your name, please? I'll be including it in my story. Can you tell me again where you found Helen, and what time?'

The man raised his eyebrows, then repeated the details, as

if humouring him. Nick could see Lady Joan glowering over his shoulder. 'Thanks. I need to make a call.'

Outside the door, he set off in pursuit of the secretary. The blue room, she'd said. It could be anywhere in this vast place, but he supposed the bedrooms would be upstairs. He headed up the first staircase he came to and walked down the corridor, but most of the doors were locked. At the end of the corridor he heard a noise and turned the corner to see the woman struggling to get the wheelchair up another flight of stairs.

'Here, let me help.' He ran to her aid. Between them, they carried the dead weight, made even more unwieldy by the chair, to the landing. Nick straightened up, sweating.

'Wow. No lift?'

She shook her head. 'Listed building. No mod cons. Thanks.' She was breathing heavily. 'Can you hang on a bit? I might need help.'

At the other end of the corridor, she unlocked a dark, wood-panelled door to a large, square room painted duck-egg blue with dust sheets over the furniture. Together they pulled them off, exposing the sort of highly polished, carved furniture you only saw in museums or National Trust houses. It didn't look particularly comfortable. The woman made up the bed with sheets and blankets from a trunk, turning back the covers. He crouched before Helen, seeing her eyes trying to hold focus.

'Don't worry,' he told her. 'I'll look after you. I'm calling DCI Greenley, just as soon as we've made you comfortable.'

Together, they lifted her inert body and placed it gently on the bed. They stood and watched, listening to Helen's shallow breathing. The secretary's brow was creased with concern.

'She should be in hospital,' said Nick.

She nodded, biting her lower lip. 'I don't like it. But Lady

Joan won't go against what Father Nash says.'

'Bollocks to it,' he said, pulling out his mobile phone. 'I'm going to get a second opinion.'

Colin's squawk of indignation at being woken could be heard across the room, but he agreed to come out. Nick felt a flush of relief. 'My brother's a doctor. He works in accident and emergency,' he told the woman. 'He'll know what to do.'

The woman nodded, her anxious frown lifting for a moment. 'Thank heavens for that. I'm Charlotte, by the way.'

'Nick.' They shook hands awkwardly across Helen's bed. 'Stay with her, will you, Charlotte? I need to ring the office. And I think I should talk to the police. Just to make sure they really have had the message.'

He sat at the top of the stairs and made his calls. DCI Greenley seemed resigned when he told her where he was. She confirmed they'd had a call about Helen's reappearance.

'Then why the hell aren't you here?'

'Because we were told that she was safe and well, being looked after, and that medical advice was that she would not be able to speak until tomorrow. Is that not the case?'

'She's practically unconscious. And she has cuts and bruises all over her. She's being looked after, but I don't know how safe she is. Paxton is still out there, isn't he? Or have you caught him?'

'We're still looking for him. Things are busy.' She sighed. 'OK, I'll tell the local force to send someone round to keep an eye on the house. But there's no point us trying to talk to her if she's unconscious, is there?'

He rang off, dissatisfied. How come he felt more responsible than anyone else for Helen's wellbeing? He called the office on the off-chance someone was still there. Meena answered and he brought her up to date with the latest. She squeaked in excitement. 'You get all the luck. I'll tell the boss.'

'What else is happening?' he asked. 'How come you're still at work at this time on a Saturday night?'

'I've been at the hospital. Anjoy's family wanted to see me. I was just writing up my notes. Then I saw the records of Paxton's security firm had come through from Companies House. I thought it might turn something up.' She yawned.

'Sounds thrilling. Why don't you go home, get your head down?'

'Go screw yourself.' She hung up on him. He grinned.

He heard footsteps tapping up the stairs, looked over the bannister and saw the priest on his way up. He withdrew to a dark doorway and watched him go past, towards the room where Helen lay.

'May I just have a quick peek?' he asked Charlotte. 'I would so like to be sure she is sleeping peacefully before I go home.' She stood at the door and watched while the man went inside. Nick felt a powerful urge to go and drag him out again.

'Thank you so much. I will drop in tomorrow, as soon as I can. But I can see you're taking perfect care of her, Miss Elms.' The man withdrew down the stairs. Something about the look of satisfaction on his face gave Nick the absolute creeps.

Chapter 44

'You're right – she's been given something pretty heavy-duty,' said Colin. He lowered Helen's eyelid and put away the pen light. 'I can't tell what without lab analysis of her urine. But my bet would be on one of the benzodiazepines. She may have some memory loss.'

'Shit. So she might not be able to say what's happened to her?'

Colin looked thunderous. 'Right. Except I can see what's happened to her. She's been tortured, Nick. Tell that to the effing police, if they don't think there's any reason for them to get their arses over here. She has cigarette burns over her neck and chest. She's been tied up – you can see the weals around her wrists and ankles.'

Nick heard a gasp and turned to see Charlotte Elms, face white, swaying on her feet.

'Woah, let's get you into a chair.' He felt pretty sick himself. Torture was something that happened in other countries, something you might see in a gangster film or hear about on the news. He remembered what the *Lighthouse* journalist had told him about Paxton's reputation in the army in Afghanistan. They'd not been able to prove anything, he'd said. Well, they could damn well prove it this time.

'I want to know which poxy doctor gave her those benzos and didn't think she needed to be seen immediately by a police surgeon. I'm going to get the bastard struck off,' said Colin.

'It was Father Nash's doctor,' said Charlotte, faintly. 'I'm sure he was just trying to help.' She didn't look sure, thought Nick. She looked sick, like a woman who'd just found dodgy photos on her husband's phone.

'Do you know the man? Give me his number. I want to talk to him.' Nick had rarely seen his brother so angry, which was saying something. 'And I need to call out the police surgeon. I'll stay with her until she wakes up.' He paced the room. 'Would you be alright to sit with me?' he asked Charlotte. 'She might freak out if she wakes up and there's no one she recognises with her.'

Leaving Colin to reorganise the household, Nick wandered downstairs to the library, where Lady Joan was quizzing the copper sent over as security for Helen. She'd got it into her head that he was there because of the burglary and was demanding to know what progress they had made. He slumped into an armchair in front of the fire, realising suddenly how tired he was. Images of burning cigarettes danced before his closed eyes, Gary Paxton's brutal face behind them, as he slipped into sleep.

* * *

Paxton hunkered down beneath the branches of a spreading yew tree, one arm around the dog. The fallen needles from the tree softened the ground and the dog's solid body provided some warmth. The operation had blown up in his face. All he could do was keep his head, make his retreat and regroup his forces. Tiredness was making him stupid; it was time to get some sleep. There was nothing more he could do tonight.

The girl had got away. He'd seen no trace of her along the path or in the empty village streets. Police sirens had sent him scrambling down into a ditch beside the roadway, from where he'd watched the car turn down the drive to Cobham Hall. Did that mean she'd made it to the house? He'd retreated to the woods, then hiked cross-country to the outskirts of Rochester. He'd walked through a deserted industrial estate and onto a patch of waste ground beside the Medway river. Across the water he could see the square tower of Rochester Castle, floodlit like a toy fort, and the silhouette of the cathedral's squat spire. A few clumps of trees provided cover. Empty beer cans, plastic bags and tins of industrial solvent suggested he wasn't the only one who found refuge here. He sighed. The place spoke of people seeking oblivion, a complete absence of hope. For a while, he'd thought he could be the one to bring back purpose, hope, to places like this. But this operation had finished him, for now at least.

If Helen Oddfellow had been picked up by the police, the area around the mausoleum would be swarming with search teams. They'd find the dog van, which was registered in his name. He was screwed.

He needed to get away, out of the country. He couldn't do that without money, and the client was the only one who could provide him with that. He'd have a few hours' kip, then cross the river by the old bridge before it was properly light. He closed his eyes, tried to sleep. But the plans still made and unmade themselves in his head. From Rochester he could get a train to Dover, then a ferry. Except he had no passport, and even if he had his own, he ran the risk that it'd be flagged and he'd be picked up at passport control. Shit. Could his boys get him one? Or else he'd have to do the reverse of all the illegals trying to slip into Britain and smuggle himself out in a car or a lorry. A fishing boat, perhaps? If he had enough money, he could pay someone to take him over in a private yacht. The irony of a native-born Englishman having to resort to the sort of tactics that Somalians and Syrians used in Calais was not lost on him.

His phone vibrated in his pocket. It was the client.

'Lady Joan's letter. Did you have it stolen?' The voice was abrupt. 'I gave you no such instructions.'

'What? No, I've been dealing with this crap all day. Look, it's all gone wrong. We need to do some damage limitation. I need money and a passport.'

There was a short pause. 'The burglary at Cobham Hall. Nothing to do with you or your boys?'

'Nothing. I swear. I didn't know there'd been a burglary.' Paxton remembered seeing the police car heading to the hall, blue lights flashing. Maybe it had nothing to do with Helen Oddfellow after all. Maybe they'd not found her. He thought of the last time he'd seen her, tied by her ankles. She couldn't have got far.

'Has there been anything on the news? About the woman, I mean. Has she turned up anywhere?'

'I've heard nothing. Listen to me, Gary. I can't be seen with you. You realise that? I will help you if I can. But you must destroy all records of our alliance. After tomorrow, you must disappear.'

'Understood.' Paxton answered with a heavy heart. He was on his own now. He shrugged. He'd been there before. However desperate the situation, there was always a way out.

277

'Keep out of sight tonight. I'll meet you in the morning.' He gave Paxton detailed instructions for how to find him, then rang off. Paxton was impressed with his grasp of the situation. He pulled up his hood and closed his eyes. The dog was asleep, its breathing guttural. He wondered what he should do with it. It would be too difficult to smuggle it out of the country. He'd have to get rid of it, he supposed. Pity. It was a good dog, this one. He'd keep it until tomorrow, at least. Maybe as far as Dover. He leaned back against the tree trunk and tried again to sleep.

Chapter 45

Helen held her breath till her ears popped and a stream of bubbles escaped from her nose. She'd run the bath as hot as she could bear it, recklessly tipping in half a bottle of Lady Joan's English Fern bath oil. She surfaced and looked down at her body, bright pink from the water. The burns on her neck and chest hurt like hell. Nick's doctor brother, Colin, had warned her to keep the dressings out of the water, but she wanted to be submerged completely, as if she could scald away the experiences of the past two days.

She'd surfaced, groggy from a deep sleep, to Charlotte's worried face. A police surgeon was waiting to examine her. The man had been kind as he recorded and photographed her injuries. She'd told him all she could remember of what had happened. It had taken on the quality of an exhausting but surreal nightmare, layer upon layer of strange new trials. All she could remember clearly was the endless walk through the woods, then Father Nash comforting her and telling her it would be alright. Nothing from then until she awoke.

When the police surgeon had gone, Colin had given her painkillers. She'd slept again. When she awoke, she'd realised how filthy she was.

The enamel tub was long, narrow and deep, containing her perfectly. She usually had to sit in baths with her knees up to her chin, but here she could stretch out. She examined the cuts around her wrists with a detached curiosity. Everything was sore, but the pain felt cleansing, bearable. She'd found a spare toothbrush in the cupboard and brushed until her gums bled. She was surprised how much better she felt, although her head still ached.

She had a sudden desire for a gin and tonic, bracingly strong with plenty of ice and lemon. She wondered what would happen if she rang the bell beside the bath and asked someone to bring her one, perch it between the taps, pearled with condensation. The craving made her think of Crispin, alone in his hospital bed. She'd not been able to take him his teeth, she remembered. He must be wondering what had happened to her. What would he think if he could see her now, reclining in Lady Joan's bathroom?

She pulled the plug and let the water drain, then rose and took a blue-and-white-striped towel from the rail. She dried off, wincing at its rough texture on her damaged skin. Lady Joan apparently didn't believe in the modern luxury of the fluffy white towel. Glancing around, she saw a quilted paisley dressing gown hanging at the back of the door. It was too short, and tight around the armpits, but it would do.

Downstairs, she found Colin, Nick and Lady Joan tucking into bacon and eggs in the dining room. They seemed to be getting on quite well, she saw with surprise. She had only the vaguest idea of what she was doing at Cobham Hall and why the reporter and his brother were there. It all seemed a continuation of the strange dream world that she had entered. She decided to go with it.

'Good morning.' She helped herself to the breakfast dishes laid out on the sideboard.

'You're up!' said Nick. 'How are you feeling?'

'Hungry.' She piled mushrooms, bacon and tomatoes onto her plate. 'Fried bread. Fantastic. I haven't had that for years.'

'You might want to take it easy,' warned Colin. 'The sedative's still in your system. Don't make yourself sick.'

But she didn't feel nauseous. She felt ravenous and thirsty. She poured herself an enormous cup of tea and began to eat. She was aware of Lady Joan's hostile gaze. *Too bad*, she thought. *You ruined the last meal I had here; you're not going to intimidate me off my food this time.*

'You found Richard's notebook.' The words were an accusation, not a question.

Helen glanced up from her plate and nodded, her mouth still full of fried bread.

'Where is it now?'

She chewed, swallowed and wiped her mouth. 'I don't know. The man who kidnapped me took it.'

Lady Joan rose to her feet and placed her hands on the table. She leaned over until her beaked nose was a foot away from Helen's face.

'Then you must find it. It's all we have.'

Helen frowned. 'But you have the letter. The original, that we found in the library.'

The woman sat down again, heavily, and looked away.

'It was stolen,' explained Nick. 'They had a break-in last night. Someone took the letter and Lady Joan's diamond brooch from the safe in her dressing room.'

Helen put down her knife and fork. The food lost its savour. The letter had kept her going through her long ordeal. Her deduction that the doodle of the moon and the waves referred to Raleigh's poem had stayed with her. They'd had the coded message and no key to decipher it. Now she had the key, but no message. She pushed her plate away.

A brisk knock on the door and Charlotte Elms entered, Father Nash close behind her.

'Ah, so the invalid is awake! Helen, my dear. How are you feeling today? I do hope you are somewhat recovered.'

She summoned a smile. 'Much better, thank you. I'm being well looked after.'

'So I see.' His eyes went to Colin, still in his doctor's scrubs, who stared back implacably. He wasn't going to introduce himself, Helen saw.

'I have spoken to the golf club. They have asked the groundsman to search the course this morning and the woodland at the perimeter. If Richard's notebook is there, we will find it.'

Helen frowned. 'But it won't be, Father Nash. The man who abducted me took it. The same man who killed Richard.'

He came to sit beside her and took her hand. 'Let us pray that it will be found, nonetheless. And that whoever was responsible for Richard's death is found too and brought to justice. You've been under a huge strain, Helen, and you've been so strong. But you don't need to do it all on your own. The Lord will guide you. And I will help you in any way that I can.'

'If it is found,' said Lady Joan, her voice shrill, 'it will belong to me. I was employing Richard. His research notes are my property.'

Helen jumped to her feet. 'He left it for me. He wrote in it, specifically saying it was for me. And I'm the only one who can tell you how to decode it, anyway. So you'll bloody well have to let me have it.'

She stopped, breathless. She realised she'd been shouting. Everyone was staring at her. Lady Joan looked like she'd just had her face slapped.

'Young woman, you are a guest in my house,' she said, imperiously. 'You are eating my food. You are even, I note, wearing my dressing gown. You will not speak to me in that way. I will decide with whom Richard's research is shared. As I recall, he did not wish to share his findings with anyone.'

Helen looked around the room. Colin and Nick were transfixed, as if watching the television. Charlotte Elms hovered by the doorway, biting her lip. Lady Joan glared at her, the lift of her chin reminding her suddenly of Richard, with all his stubborn self-confidence. She felt a sudden pang of pity for the old woman, trying so hard to bend others to her will. She must be unable to relax, even for a moment. But Helen had been through the fire. She lowered her voice and returned to her seat.

'Lady Joan, I know you were fond of Richard,' she said. 'He was fond of you too. He wanted so much to help you solve this mystery. But he asked me to help him. And if you are to have a hope of finding Marlowe's missing play, you need my help now. I think I have the key to decipher the coded message. At the moment, you don't even have the message.'

She smiled at Lady Joan's disgruntled face. 'Richard showed me the work he'd begun on your grandfather's papers. I can go through them again, see what else I can find. There's all the other work we'd done too on the Henslowe papers and the letters at Corpus Christi. If anyone can get there, I can.'

She reached for a piece of toast and buttered it. *I've lost the man I was falling in love with. I've been kidnapped, tortured, humiliated. There is literally nothing you can do to me that is worse than what I've already been through.* She felt, for the moment, invincible.

Chapter 46

The silence held. Eventually Lady Joan waved the others away. 'Go. Leave us alone.'

'I must take my leave, Lady Joan. I have to be at Rochester Cathedral for the morning service.' Father Nash threw Helen an encouraging smile. 'But I will return. As I have said before, I will do anything I can to help you with this work.'

Nick and Colin followed, silently. Charlotte Elms pulled the door closed behind them.

'I was fond of Richard,' Lady Joan began, her voice cracked. 'I had hoped this work would lead to better things for him. He deserved... he deserved better.' She looked directly at Helen. *Better than me?* Helen wondered.

'Miss Oddfellow, if you are to work on this subject, in this house, it will be as my employee. Miss Elms will see to the details and offer you reasonable terms. But on the understanding that the results of the research will belong to me. Do you accept?'

Helen had not been expecting the offer. An additional income would be helpful, goodness knows. But it would involve a transfer of loyalty that she was unsure she could accept. She thought for a moment. Since leaving her teaching job, she'd enjoyed the freedom of working independently. Her contract with Capital Walks allowed her to choose the number of tours she undertook, and the rest of her time was her own. She didn't fancy a role as a tame historian, forever being summoned at Her Ladyship's pleasure.

'I will work for you as a freelance researcher. I will report the results of the research firstly to you, and of course you will own any papers I discover in Cobham Hall. But I want the freedom to work with anyone I think can help me. And I want to be able to publish the results independently, as I see fit.'

Lady Joan looked at her in exasperation. 'You are very sure of yourself for someone without any kind of academic credentials.'

'I am an MA, Lady Joan. Like Christopher Marlowe. And I'll have a doctorate within the next two years.'

'Like Doctor Faustus.' The woman's voice was tart.

Helen smiled. 'Except I don't want to sell my soul.'

The older woman raised an eyebrow. 'Does that make me the devil?' She barked her odd laugh and slapped the table. 'Right, Miss Oddfellow. I accept your bargain. When do you want to start? Straight away, or shall we have a cup of coffee first?'

She had won. She would have the work and resources she wanted, on her own terms. 'I think I'll take my coffee in the office, if that suits you? But there is one more thing. I don't have any clothes, and your dressing gown doesn't fit me very well. I don't suppose anyone has a pair of jeans I could borrow?'

The old woman looked at her meditatively for a moment, as if seeing someone else. 'Come,' she said. 'I think we can do better than that.'

* * *

Helen stood in wonder before an open wardrobe hung with a dozen Savile Row suits: grey Prince of Wales check, linen the colour of bone, black dinner jackets with satin lapels. Silk knitted ties in yellow and baby blue and bow ties in black and claret hung from the back of the door. A chest of drawers revealed neatly pressed silk squares and socks, jewelled tie studs and cufflinks. Silver hairbrushes, cologne bottles and a shaving kit were laid out on the ebony dressing table.

'My late brother's dressing room,' said Lady Joan, her voice brusque. 'I believe you are about the same height.' She retreated and closed the door.

Your brother the murderer. A not-unpleasant thrill ran through Helen. He must have been quite the dandy. The room appeared to have been kept as it had been when he left on his final journey to South America, ready for his return. The dressing table was dust-free, the silver untarnished.

She ran her fingers over fine Egyptian cotton and heavy crêpe de Chine. She pulled on a cornflower-blue shirt, enjoying the smooth weight of the fabric against her skin, then tied a silk square around her neck to hide the gauze dressings. She thought again of Crispin. He'd be a kid in a sweet shop here. In the wardrobe, she found a slim-cut navy suit, the trousers the perfect length for her long legs, and a yellow cashmere sweater with a flutter of moth holes around the wrists. She turned to the full-length mirror, an angular affair from the art deco era, and caught her breath. Jay Gatsby never looked more suave.

She sat at the dressing table, attempting to remove the tangles from her still-damp hair with a soft bristle brush. She gathered it tightly in her fist, twisting the rope of hair at the nape of her neck, remembering how her abductor had done the same. She took the silver scissors from the tray and began to cut, the sound like snipped silk. She placed the hank of hair in the wastepaper basket and shook her head free. Her locks hung around her chin, a rough bob shape like an untidy schoolgirl. She frowned and picked up the scissors again, shearing the hair away from the nape of her neck and snipping it short over the ears, close to her head. She dipped into one of the porcelain pots of unguents on the dressing table and smoothed her cropped locks back from her face.

She stared at her unfamiliar reflection. Whatever she looked like, she thought, she did not resemble the dishevelled, cowed victim of the night before. She looked serious, austere, even a little frightening. She could begin again, the long and painstaking work ahead.

Slowly, she descended the stairs in the elegant clothes of John Brooke, heir to Cobham Hall. She felt a sense of entitlement, as if his aristocratic confidence had imparted itself through his wardrobe. Lady Joan stood at the bottom of the staircase, her face frozen.

'You have a look of him,' she said. 'Miss Elms, please show Miss Oddfellow to the study. Make sure she has everything she needs.'

* * *

Nick sat astride his motorbike and checked his phone. He had one message from Meena.

'Give us a call. Something weird in Paxton's accounts.' She'd sent the message late last night, after he'd fallen asleep before the fire in the Cobham Hall library. He still ached from sleeping in the armchair, his neck stiff and shoulders cramped. Rolling his head around his shoulders, he called her number.

'What?' Her voice sounded scratchy, like she'd just woken up.

'You texted me. You told me to call.'

'That was last night, innit.'

He grinned. She tried to keep up her posh act for work, but slipped into street talk when she was tired.

'You got anything for me? I'm heading back home for a shower and a kip. Then I might go into the office.'

There was a pause. 'You haven't heard, then.'

'What? Are you OK?'

'Nah, man.' He realised her voice sounded weird because she'd been crying. He'd never known her to cry before, even on the toughest news stories.

'Anjoy's passed away. And Amir's been arrested. It all kicked off last night, Nick. The boss wants you back here.'

'Shit. What happened?'

'They turned off the life support last night. After I'd been to the hospital to see them.' She paused and blew her nose, noisily. 'Then Amir and his mates went round to Paxton's flat. They poured petrol through the letterbox and torched the place. The woman upstairs had to be rescued from the back window.'

'Oh, fuck.'

'Yeah. And all the neighbours saw Amir do it. His parents are in bits. Can you imagine?'

'Was that bloke Steve there?' Nick remembered the idiot saying they would take things into their own hands.

'Mohammed? Oh, yeah, you'll love this. The police found all sorts at his flat. They're calling it bomb-making equipment. There were loads of national press at the mosque this morning, asking if it's true he was a member.'

'I'm on my way back,' said Nick, grabbing his helmet. *The poor family*. And the imam at the mosque, with his dreams of a free school and community harmony. 'I'll be half an hour.' He checked his watch, then remembered.

'What did you text me about last night, though? Paxton's accounts?'

'What? Oh, yeah.' He heard shuffling papers. 'Hold on. Secure Solutions. He had a bunch of clients, small stuff, until about two months ago. Then he dropped most of them. Started working for one organisation exclusively. Looks like they kept him on a retainer. Thirty grand last month.'

'Yeah?' Could be interesting, he supposed. Follow the money, wasn't that what they said? 'What organisation?'

'That bunch of Christian nutters, run by some vicar. Goes on TV and tells everyone me and my lot are taking over the country.'

'Christianity in Crisis? Father Nash?' Nick almost dropped the phone.

'That's the one. I suppose they get death threats and stuff.'

'Bloody hell.' Nick looked down the drive, where the man's sleek navy Jaguar had disappeared twenty minutes ago. 'He was the one who found Helen. And he was here this morning, getting all cosy with her. Creepy. God, and if he's paying Paxton ...'

He thought quickly. 'I'm going to talk to him. He said he

was going to Rochester Cathedral, for a church service.'

'But the boss said ...'

'I know. But I'm not far from Rochester. I'll grab him after the service, then head straight back to the office. I'll be there by twelve, absolute latest. See you soon.'

He pulled on his motorbike helmet, revved the bike and pulled away from Cobham Hall in a spatter of gravel.

Chapter 47

The room looked exactly the same as when she'd last been here with Richard. The filing cabinets, the extravagantly painted wallpaper, the Chinese rug and the electric heater. Even the buff folders, piled on the desk. She wondered where on earth to begin.

She remembered Richard telling her the system: one drawer of the filing cabinet for household accounts, another for documents from Raleigh's trial and a third for those amassed by Lady Joan's grandfather, Albert. Papers which included information about Thomas Becket, she remembered. Maybe that's where she should start.

She began to sort through the Becket folder. There were newspaper clippings and scientific papers, letters from history journals and grainy old photographs, annotated in Albert's beautiful copperplate handwriting. For an hour, Helen lost herself in the story, the theories that had come and gone about the saint's remains. There had been a flurry of interest in the early years of the twentieth century, when a skeleton had been exhumed from the crypt of Canterbury Cathedral, discovered almost directly beneath the Trinity Chapel that had housed Becket's shrine. Albert had actually attended the exhumation, she saw with surprise. The length of the bones, the cracked skull – all spoke with promise that this was indeed the body of the saint,' he wrote. He sent an account to the letters page of *The Times* in support of the theory that these were Becket's bones.

Argument raged for months, without any satisfactory conclusion. Sir Albert's own letters indicated that he had moved from hope to scepticism. His tantalising conclusion, in another letter to *The Times*, was: 'I am reliably informed that these cannot be the bones of Saint Thomas, for the very good reason that his relics are no longer in Canterbury Cathedral.' Helen could find no explanatory note about his reliable informant.

She remembered the look on Lady Joan's face when she had first mentioned Becket. No wonder the name had meant something to her. Her grandfather had been almost as obsessed as Richard about finding their true location. Again, she wondered why. What had the old man known? She thought of the portrait in Lady Joan's sitting room, the man in the turban with a smile lurking at the corners of his eyes.

She leafed through the rest of his papers. He'd had an eclectic mind, it seemed, his enthusiasms diverse and surprising. One section of his folio was devoted to Sufi love poetry, another to the history of the Mughal empire in India and a third to photographs of the Alhambra Palace in Granada. He'd clearly had the Victorian interest in the exotic. Helen closed the drawer, dizzied by his wide-ranging interests.

She turned with relief to the household accounts, thinking of the payment in Henslowe's account book to Thomas Lawes, the master of Eastbridge. People's desire to keep track of their finances could tell you all sorts of things. She searched through the folders, looking for relevant dates. She opened a folder marked 1500 to 1700 and lifted out the bulky sheaf of paper.

Sorting through, she found a photocopy annotated with Richard's familiar, neat handwriting. She traced his words with her thumb, feeling the indent of his pen on the paper, comforted by this scrap of his presence. The document was a record of household expenses from the mid- to late-sixteenth century, a catalogue of payments to builders and glaziers, workmen and suppliers of stone and timber. This must relate to the period when the Elizabethan wings of the house were built, she realised. She scrolled through the lists of figures. She could do with a coffee, she thought, yawning. Numbers were not really her strong point.

Then she saw it, part way down the fourth page: 'Tho. Walsingham, 200 marks to relieve him from the Fleet, 3rd May 1590.' Richard had circled the name, inking a question mark beside it. Her heart started to thump. She could have told Richard who that was. Thomas Walsingham, gentleman, of Scadbury Manor in Kent. Cousin of Queen Elizabeth's spy-master, Sir Francis Walsingham. More to the point, he had been the friend, patron and quite possibly the lover of Christopher Marlowe, poet and playwright. Marlowe had been staying with him at the moated manor house when officers arrived to arrest him days before his murder. What she didn't know was why Lord Cobham had paid £200 to get him out of the notorious Fleet debtors' prison.

Thank heavens for the internet, she thought, searching online for information about any putative relationship between the Walsinghams and the Cobhams. She began with the obvious: they were neighbours. Barely twenty miles separated Cobham Hall from the Walsingham property.

Unlike Cobham, little remained standing of Scadbury Manor. Helen had visited the previous year, from a desire to see where Marlowe had spent the last weeks of his life. It had been a melancholy place, broken buildings overrun with ivy.

Thomas Walsingham was a few years older than Henry Brooke, the heir to Cobham Hall. He was a third son, always in need of money and without expectations of inheriting the family estate, socially inferior to the Brookes, with their wealth and favour with the Queen. As a young man he had earned his living as a courier for his cousin Francis, taking letters to and from France at a time of tension between the countries. There was a strong suspicion that this was when he had become acquainted with Christopher Marlowe, then a Cambridge student also crossing the channel on the Queen's business.

This period gave the first link between the Walsingham and Cobham families. As she cross-referenced swiftly between different online archives, Helen found that Walsingham had worked in France with Ambassador Cobham, the younger brother of Lord Cobham and the Elizabethan court's man in Paris. The men had worked together on an ultimately unsuccessful attempt to arrange a marriage between the Duke of Anjou and Queen Elizabeth. Letters in the archives showed Thomas Walsingham had been in financial difficulties. Ambassador Cobham had written to Francis Walsingham to ask for an increased allowance for the young man. Perhaps this period had brought the neighbouring families together and encouraged Thomas to look to the Cobhams for help, Helen thought.

Thomas had inherited Scadbury unexpectedly in 1590, after the deaths of two elder brothers. Before he could release any money from the inheritance, his debts caught up with him. He was arrested and detained in the Fleet. Checking dates, Helen saw that his cousin and primary source of income, spy-master Francis, had died earlier the same year. Where could Thomas turn for help while the legal process ground on?

She stretched out her legs, comfortable in her borrowed trousers, and ran her hands through her cropped hair. The account book made clear that Lord Cobham had paid Thomas Walsingham's debts, allowing his young neighbour to establish himself as a respectable member of the gentry at Scadbury Manor. Three years later, he'd entertained his friend, the raffish playwright Christopher Marlowe, in his newly acquired home.

She leaned back in the chair. If Marlowe had been working on the missing play in 1593, it was reasonable to think he would have had it with him at Scadbury.

She rested her hand on Richard's transcript of the Cobham accounts and tried to think as he had done. The playwright, unable to work in the theatre because of the plague, retires to rural Kent as the guest of his newly wealthy patron. He is writing *Hero and Leander*, which will be dedicated to Walsingham, re-telling one of the great classical love affairs. Helen adored the poem, alive with sensual imagery and teasing descriptions of seduction. The verses in which Leander swam the Hellespont river to be with his love contained some of the most startlingly frank celebrations of masculine beauty ever written. If this had been intended as a tribute to his patron, it hinted at a relationship of great intimacy.

But the idyll at Scadbury is interrupted by guards at the

gate, demanding that Marlowe accompany them to court to answer charges of atheism and blasphemy. He hurries away, leaving his half-finished manuscripts behind, with a promise to return as soon as he's sorted out this latest problem. Walsingham sees his recent hard-won respectability threatened by scandal. Even worse was the threat of guilt by association. The playwright Thomas Kyd, who had shared lodgings with Marlowe in London, had been imprisoned just days earlier after supposedly atheist writings had been found in his room. Under torture, he had blamed Marlowe for the presence of these papers, leading to the arrest at Scadbury. Walsingham must have feared that he could be next.

Helen scribbled notes. Kyd had sworn that the incriminating papers, shuffled in with his own, had belonged to Marlowe. Walsingham would surely have searched Marlowe's rooms at Scadbury, on the alert for anything that could have incriminated him if the Queen's men came looking. And then ... and then he'd have found the Canterbury play.

So, she thought, Walsingham discovers that Marlowe has abandoned the love poem dedicated to him and started work on a new play, set in his home town of Canterbury. A play about the life of Thomas Becket, the controversial figure declared by the Queen's father, Henry VIII, to be not a saint but a traitor. Worse, the play seems to suggest that the body of Thomas Becket was not destroyed as demanded by the monarch, but hidden by the monks. While a panicky Walsingham tries to decide what to do with the manuscript, word reaches him that his friend has been murdered in a brawl in Deptford. Within days, the playwright is being denounced, his reputation traduced, and his former associates abandon him.

The obvious thing is to destroy the play. But Walsingham is a scholar, a literary man, and this is the last work of his friend, possibly his lover. And what if the authorities already know about the play and take his destruction of it as an act of guilt? What to do with this literary hot potato?

His father, older brothers and influential uncle are all dead. Perhaps he turns to his saviour of three years previously, the man who'd rescued him from the Fleet prison. If anyone would know what to do with Marlowe's seditious play, it would be Lord Cobham. There was also the friendship between Lord Cobham's son and Walter Raleigh. Maybe he hoped the manuscript would make its way to Raleigh to be staged or preserved as Elizabeth's favourite saw fit. Either way, Walsingham sends the manuscript to Cobham Hall, then retreats with sadness but relief into respectability.

She laid down her pen. It was all conjecture, of course. She smiled, remembering Richard's words to her in this same room: 'All conjecture. You're learning.' There was nothing in the record to confirm it, but then nothing to contradict it either. It was plausible, it fitted with the known facts and relationships. It was another potential link in the chain. If there was a play, it could have travelled from Scadbury Park to Cobham Hall. But what happened to it next? Raleigh's note suggested that 'poor merlin's Canterbury booke' had survived to reach the next Lord Cobham, son of the man who had rescued Walsingham from prison. Where was it now?

There was a tap on the door. It was Charlotte Elms with a very welcome pot of coffee. Helen was relieved to see two decent-sized mugs on the tray rather than the tiny delicate cups she worried about breaking.

'Fantastic. Thanks so much.' She took a great gulp of the

hot liquid, feeling the caffeine chasing away the remnants of her headache, her synapses starting to crackle back to life. Charlotte closed the door and poured the second mug for herself.

'I wanted to talk to you,' she said.

'Go ahead.'

The woman took a padded envelope from the tray. 'This arrived ten minutes ago. The groundsman from the golf course brought it round to the kitchens. He said he found it this morning on his rounds. I should give it to Lady Joan, really. But I thought I'd show you first.'

Helen slowly drew out the black, leather-bound notebook from the envelope. She felt light-headed, her heart quickening. She turned to the inside front cover and saw Richard's words to her.

'It's the missing notebook?'

She nodded, emotion welling in her throat. She read over his last words, their urgent tone. 'Someone's following me. This is for you. With love.'

'I thought so. Helen, it doesn't make sense. I mean, I'm glad it's been found. But you said the man who abducted you stole it. So why was it on the golf course?'

'I don't know. It shouldn't have been. Unless ...' She tried to think of a plausible explanation. 'Unless he dropped it when he was looking for me?' Charlotte's sceptical face matched her own. 'I know. Not very good, is it?'

She turned back to the book, read again Richard's precious words. 'Maybe it doesn't matter. Anyway, it doesn't help us that much. I tore out the page with the coded message on it. I tried to hide it from him, but he found it.'

'Look in the flap on the back cover.'

Helen looked. A folded piece of paper. It was the page she'd torn from the notebook. The message was still clear, a string of seemingly random consonants and vowels marching across the page. She turned it over and saw the square of letters that Crispin had written out for her in his faint pencil marks. A rush of excitement flooded her.

'That's it! Charlotte, you realise what this means? I can decode it now.' She grabbed a pad of paper from the desk and started writing out a fair copy of the Vigenère alphabet grid.

'That's brilliant.' Charlotte's voice was still troubled. 'But doesn't that make it even stranger? I mean, you've just been delivered exactly what you need to decode the message, neatly parcelled up, shortly after telling us all that you had the key.'

She put her pen down and tried to focus on what Charlotte meant. 'You think this is a forgery? I'm pretty sure it's not.'

'No. I think it's much too convenient, though. I mean, why were they looking on the golf course?'

'Well, Father Nash asked them to.'

'Yes.'

Charlotte's tone changed. Helen looked up. Her face was neutral, but a line bisected her forehead. Her eyes met Helen's for a second, then swivelled away.

'I know you like him, Helen. I do too. But he worries me. He's been putting a lot of pressure on Lady Joan. She gives him money, you know, for that campaign group he runs. A lot of money. He came to break the news about Richard yesterday morning. She was so upset. Well, we all were, of course.'

Helen looked down, feeling the weight of his death once more on her chest.

'But afterwards he tried to get her to show him Richard's

research notes. I heard him. It wasn't fair. Much too soon to bother her with it. She said no, Richard hadn't wanted him to see his notes. But he wouldn't let it drop.' Charlotte's voice was raw with an emotion she didn't usually display.

Helen rubbed the back of her neck. 'He rescued me. Last night, when they found me on the golf course. And he's always been nice to me.'

'I know. Maybe I'm wrong. But Richard didn't want Father Nash to see his research, did he? And nor did Charles Fairfax.'

'No. Well, maybe Charles Fairfax didn't want anyone to see it,' said Helen. 'I'm not sure I trust that man, for all that he was Richard's friend.'

Charlotte bit her lip and walked to the window. 'It's difficult,' she admitted.

Helen drained her coffee. The tattered piece of paper tugged at her attention. Her morning's work had strengthened her conviction that there was a missing play to be found. She wanted to get on with it. She had a vague memory from the night before, Father Nash telling her that she had to find her purpose in life. If she had a purpose now, this was it.

'Well, look. Father Nash is at his service, isn't he? He won't be back till later. I'm not showing him anything yet. There can't be any harm in me just having a go at this now. I might not even be right, after all. Let me try.'

Chapter 48

N ick entered Rochester Cathedral among a throng of smart elderly white people and well-scrubbed families, feeling conspicuous in his bike leathers. He'd never been in a Protestant church before. He half expected the greeters at the cathedral door to turn him away like nightclub bouncers. He nodded warily at the kind-eyed lady who handed him a hymn book.

'Are you here for the service?' she asked. Nick decided to join them, locate Father Nash and confront him. There were ushers everywhere, though. He'd have to pick his moment if he didn't want to get slung out.

He checked around for the form, not wanting to draw further attention to himself. He didn't think Protestants crossed themselves, but was surprised to see a few bending their knee and making a quick sign of the cross before they took their seats. He sat towards the back, half-obscured by a hefty pillar. He thought cathedrals were meant to be uplifting, but this one felt heavy and dark. His mother would be outraged if she could see him.

His only previous experience with cathedrals was Liverpool's ultra-modern Catholic cathedral, where he'd been confirmed. He remembered feeling as if he was in a spaceship materialising on the top of the hill, filled with multi-coloured light. All this gloomy grey stone was cold and alien. He craned his neck, trying to locate Father Nash in the dim recesses of the cathedral.

It had been years since he last went to church. *Forgive me, Father, it's been bloody ages since my last confession.* But there were no confessional boxes here, no whisperings of sins or penance. As a boy, he'd made up lurid stories to impart to the man in the little dark box. His real sins had seemed too boring. Still, he couldn't really see the point of church without confession.

He tried to say a prayer for Anjoy. Would he mind being prayed for in a Christian church? he wondered. The cathedral was filling up. The congregation was being shepherded towards the front rows by the ushers. He could see he'd annoyed the chief usher, a sandy-haired man in a blazer, by sitting at the back. He had the expression of a school teacher who had no time for unruly pupils. Nick's natural habitat had always been the back row.

The gloom intensified as the doors behind him were closed. The congregation shuffled to its feet and the organ, which had been wheezing away in the background, began to thunder. A line of white-robed men, followed by a procession of red-robed boys, made its way down the centre of the nave. Pure voices soared upwards. Nick strained to see the men's faces, but he didn't spot Father Nash among them. Damn. Could he have misunderstood?

He was soon fully engaged in standing, sitting, kneeling, sitting and standing again, as the well-drilled congregation went through its paces. He got a breather when the sermon began and a priest decked out in green-and-gold robes spoke

303

in cut-glass tones about what Jesus might have thought about food banks. He wondered what he should do when they got to the Mass itself. He could hardly take communion in a Protestant church.

The ushers began their work, inviting the congregation up to the altar rail a row at a time. One or two people remained in their seats, Nick noticed, heads bowed. He slipped to his knees as the ushers worked their way to the back of the church. Either side of him, people rose to their feet.

He looked up, his view of the altar now clear of the people in front of him. He breathed again. Father Nash was at the altar rail, one of three priests holding chalices, offering people a sip of wine, wiping the rim with a white napkin. Nick wrinkled his nose. Grubby practice. At his church at home, they'd had individual little glasses of wine – far more hygienic.

He watched the man and wondered. He looked so ordinary with his round face and kindly smile. He moved smoothly, with practised grace, from one person to the next. Nick didn't like what he'd heard of the man's politics. But it was a big step from a belief that Christians were being persecuted to hanging out with the likes of Gary Paxton. Was it possible that this could be a coincidence? That he'd simply needed security and picked him out of the phone book? Nash's sudden appearance with Helen last night had seemed odd at the time. Now it seemed positively incriminating. Helen had been drugged; her memory had been affected. Had she really escaped from the mausoleum on her own? Or had he simply collected her from Paxton then told her a load of lies to gain her trust?

People streamed back into the pews surrounding him, and the head priest at the front launched into a lengthy prayer, for which they all knelt. A bit more to-ing and fro-ing, then they were on their feet again, being blessed. The organ thundered to life for a final hymn and the procession started back up the aisle. *Finally*, thought Nick, impatient to collar the priest.

Father Nash was in the second rank of white robes, wafting an incense-burner. Nick's mother wouldn't believe it. This was more over the top than a Catholic service. He tried to dodge behind the pillar but was too slow. He saw the man clock him, a quick look of surprise, then his eyes moved on. *Shit*. If he wanted to grab him, he'd need to move fast.

Apologising to the lustily singing family to his right, Nick squeezed past, earning himself disapproving looks. He walked swiftly up the side aisle and out the door, where a surprised-looking priest shook his hand and thanked him for attending. Nick pumped the man's hand, eyes scanning the cathedral close. 'Is Father Nash still around?' he asked.

'Ah, you're looking for our television star,' said the man. 'I believe he has another appointment, but you might catch him. He's just getting into his car.' He pointed. Nick sprinted across the green, ignoring 'keep off the grass' signs.

'Father Nash! Can I have a quick word?'

He had pulled his cassock over his head and emerged from the snowy-white linen. 'Hello, Nick. What are you doing here? Is everything alright at the hall?'

Nick dug out his notebook. 'I have a few questions for you. About Christianity in Crisis and its links to a character called Gary Paxton.'

Nash's face barely flickered. 'I don't think I know anyone of that name.'

'Yes, you do. You employ his firm, Secure Solutions. You have done for two months. I've seen the records.' Nick found people were more likely to admit to something if you told them you already knew, even if you hadn't actually seen the evidence yourself.

Nash frowned as if racking his memory. 'Secure Solutions. I don't remember the name. But perhaps that is the company, if you say so. I began employing a firm after I started getting death threats. They installed an alarm system in my home. I'm afraid I don't remember all their employees, though. I meet so many people in the course of my work.' He smiled, such an open and innocent smile that Nick found himself smiling back. 'You must find it equally difficult in your profession, I suppose?'

Nick got a grip. 'I think I'd remember if I'd paid them thirty grand for a burglar alarm. Father Nash, as I'm sure you know, Gary Paxton is a suspect in the abduction of Helen Oddfellow. That's a bit of a coincidence, isn't it?'

Father Nash frowned. 'Come with me. I need to show you something. I'm very worried about Helen.'

Surprised, Nick followed as the priest led him around the cathedral. 'Where are we going?'

'I have an office in the crypt.'

Nick trotted to keep up as Father Nash hurried down a set of narrow steps that led through a small arched doorway.

'You haven't answered my question. Why are you employing a man who is suspected of having kidnapped and tortured Helen?'

'Through here. Nick, I think we need to question whether this so-called abduction actually took place. Helen is in a very fragile psychological state.'

The steps were stone, worn shallow with footsteps over the centuries. The crypt had low, vaulted ceilings supported by a forest of round stone pillars, stretching away into the distance. *You could get lost down here*, thought Nick. He was starting to feel uneasy.

'When we found her wandering on the golf course, she was making all sorts of wild claims. She seemed to me to be undergoing a psychotic episode, possibly self-harming. She said you'd been stalking her.'

'What? That's rubbish.'

'I know. I fear the murder of Richard Watson may have been too traumatic for her. That's why I think we should be very careful how we treat Helen's accusations.' He put his hand on Nick's arm and propelled him deeper into the crypt, away from the windows that illuminated the cavernous space. 'I want you to see what she wrote while we were waiting for my doctor. This way.'

Nash pulled back a green curtain and unlocked a heavy wooden door, then stepped back as if waiting for Nick to enter first. The room beyond was in darkness. Uncertain, Nick turned to look at the priest. Nash shoved him into the room. Nick stumbled on the uneven stone flags. As he staggered, the priest gave him another shove. He fell onto his hands and knees.

'Hey! What are you doing?'

A match flared, then a candle gleamed into life. They were in a little chapel. On the green-draped altar stood a big silver cross flanked with candles. The priest stood over him. He picked up one of the hefty-looking candlesticks and held the flame close to Nick's face.

'Do not stand in the way of God's will,' he said. His voice was calm, his tone reasonable. But his eyes blazed in the candlelight. As Nick struggled to get to his feet, Nash blew

307

out the flame. Something crashed into Nick's cheekbone. His head flew back, crumping into the stone wall behind him, and he slid to the floor.

He opened his eyes to complete darkness. He was slumped against a wall and his head hurt. Cautiously, he put his hand to the back of his head and brought his fingers away sticky with blood. The blow had reopened the wound he'd picked up at the mosque protest. He found the tender spot on his cheek where Nash had coshed him with the candlestick.

Father Nash. Danger, his fogged brain insisted. The man was involved in Helen's kidnap, and he was the only one who knew. He pulled out his phone and tried to call the police to warn them. No signal. *Of course*, he thought, cursing. The crypt was underground, buried beneath thick stone. He scrambled to his feet and almost keeled over with the pain from his head. Sweating, he leaned against the wall, hands on his knees, breath harsh in his ears. It was the only sound, he realised. He'd heard nothing since they descended to the crypt. Yet overhead, presumably, hundreds of people had trooped out of the cathedral to the blaring of the organ. Not a whisper had reached the little chapel.

He had to get out. Using the blue light from the phone, he scanned the room. A white-draped altar, one candlestick missing, the other candle extinguished. The wooden door, black with age and studded with iron nails. He fumbled for the handle, knowing already. He turned it, pushed as hard as he could, set his shoulder to it with a shout of frustration. He was locked in. He hammered on the door for a minute longer, then slumped to the floor. Now what?

'Oi, mate?'

Nick yelled with shock. The voice was close by, somewhere

308

in the chapel. 'What? Who … where are you?'

'Dunno. I'm tied up. I can't see anything.'

Nick pulled aside the altar drapery. A figure, ankles and wrists bound with cord, lay under the table. He dropped to his knees and shone the light into the man's face. It was bruised and bloodied, and the eyes looked out at him in desperate relief. It was Gary Paxton.

Chapter 49

Paxton's head hurt and he felt sick. He wanted some water. His shoulders ached and he couldn't move his arms or legs. The floor was hard and cold.

The last thing he could remember was making his way to Rochester Cathedral, as agreed, to meet the client. He'd walked across the stone bridge in the cold dawn. He'd removed the dog's lead, but it trotted obediently at his heels until they reached the cathedral. He'd patted its head and slipped through the wooden door into the crypt where Father Nash was waiting.

He remembered nothing more. And now here he was, trussed up like a Christmas turkey in the dark. He could hear something, though. Someone banging around, swearing to himself.

'Oi, mate?' he called.

A curtain was pulled back and he could see a face peering at him through the gloom, illuminated by the feeble light of a mobile phone. Short dreadlocks and a goofy expression on his face. It was the reporter from the local paper. He was staring at him in shock.

'Alright, mate?' he said. 'Give us a hand here, will you? I can't move.'

The reporter made no reply, but sat back on his heels.

'Come on, mate. My arms are killing me. It's Gary. Don't you recognise me?'

The kid's expression had turned to one of intense dislike. 'I'm not your mate,' he said.

'It's Nick, isn't it? How did you get in? Is the door still locked?' No answer. He tried again. 'Alright, so I know you don't agree with me. But I thought we had a deal? You help me, I'll help you. Look, there's a lighter in my pocket. Why don't you untie me, then we can light it up? Once we can see, we can work out how to get out of here.'

The kid grabbed him with both hands and rolled him roughly out from under the table, turning him over with his foot. 'Where?' he demanded.

Before Paxton could protest, he stuffed his hand down his jeans pocket and dug it out himself. Cheeky black bastard. If he could get his hands free, he'd kill the little shit. No one treated Gary Paxton like that.

Candlelight filled the room. Nick gazed at him steadily with dark eyes, glinting with something that could be hatred. Paxton's senses sparked on full alert. The man was dangerous.

Nick turned the lighter over in his hands. 'Do you have any ciggies on you, then?'

Paxton nodded, his mouth dry. What did he know? 'Back pocket. Good idea. Why don't we both have a smoke, calm us down?' He winced but said nothing as the reporter pulled out the half-empty fag packet and lit one up.

The kid brought his face close, holding the cigarette. He took a drag, blew the smoke into his eyes. 'Are these the ones you used on Helen?'

Oh, Christ, thought Paxton. *He's seen the girl.*

311

* * *

Nick drew the unfamiliar fumes into his lungs. He'd smoked cigarettes a few times when he was younger, never really liked them. His mum had been a nurse and was fanatically anti-smoking. Some of his mates smoked skunk, but he didn't like the way it made you lazy and left your head full of cotton wool. He watched the smoke rise, blew gently on the end of the cigarette until it glowed. He could feel the nicotine coursing through his bloodstream, his heart pumping harder. He felt cold, detached, powerful. Slowly, he turned back to Paxton.

'Shall we see how you like being on the receiving end?'

The man's eyes flashed with panic. 'I don't know what you're talking about.'

'I think you do.'

As if watching from a distance, Nick saw himself touch the cigarette gently onto the man's forearm, the soft skin inside the elbow. Paxton's scream tore the air, harsh as a saw ripping flesh. Nick ground the burning tip on the stone floor and chucked it into the corner.

'If you're going to dish it out, you should be able to take it,' he said. His voice shook. He felt sweat on his forehead and wiped it away. He shot a look at the man's face, distorted with pain, pressed against the stone floor. *God*. He took a deep breath, reminded himself of what Paxton had done to Helen. It didn't help as much as it should have. *Doesn't matter*, he told himself. *You're a reporter. Find out what's going on.*

'Who paid you to kidnap Helen?' he asked.

The man stayed silent, his jaws clamped together. Nick reached for the cigarette packet and lit another. The taste made him want to throw up. Paxton watched as he blew gently on the glowing tip. There was fear in his eyes. He could not do it again, but Paxton didn't know that.

'Same person who tied me up.' The man's words came grudgingly.

'Well, you don't owe him anything then, do you? Who was it? Father Nash?'

The man rolled towards him. 'Untie me. Then we can talk properly.'

Nick thought that would be a seriously bad idea. 'Talk first. Everything. Richard Watson's murder. Helen's kidnap. Tell me what a bloke like you gets out of being the hired muscle for Father Nash and his merry gang of religious nutters.'

'I'm not hired muscle. We're a team.' His voice was obstinate.

'Look, Gary, he's knocked you out, tied you up and locked you in the crypt. Unless this is all some very cunning plan that you were in on from the start, I'd suggest your team has dissolved. He's dumped you. What's to stop you dumping on him?'

He saw calculation in the man's eyes and contempt beneath it. Paxton had been in the army, he reminded himself, and had a reputation for mistreatment of prisoners. He knew all the tricks, and he wasn't going to do anything he didn't want to. If he talked, either he had a reason to do so, or he didn't think it mattered any more. Nick wasn't sure which possibility alarmed him most.

The man started talking. He'd met Father Nash the previous year, when the security company he worked for at the time sent him to install security cameras and intruder alarms at his house.

'We talked about stuff. He'd been getting death threats from Muslims, people who realised he was onto them. He said he could use someone like me, with my vision.' He'd lent Paxton money to set up his own firm, employed him as a security consultant.

'Father Nash is a very clever man. Knows the Quran and the Bible and all that. He can see what's happening to this country. When he tells you that the West is vulnerable to Islam, you take notice. Unless you want to live under Sharia law.'

Nick sighed. 'You really swallowed all that shit? Less than five percent of people in the UK are Muslim. And do you think they want to live in a fundamentalist religious state? That's why half of them came here, you idiot. To live somewhere that you can just get on with your life. Peacefully, like Anjoy Uddin. He died last night. I don't suppose you knew that.'

The man shrugged. 'I told you, nothing to do with me. But don't come running to me when your mum can't walk down the road without a hijab on.'

'I won't do that, Gary. Anyway, she likes wearing head-scarves. It makes her feel like the Queen.'

Paxton stared at him, then spat. 'Think what you like. You'll see.'

'You haven't answered my question.' Nick often found himself so caught up in winning the argument that he forgot what he'd originally intended to find out. 'Richard Watson. Helen Oddfellow. What have they got to do with any of this? You might as well tell me. You're stuffed anyway. Cough up now and Nash goes down with you.'

It had started with surveillance, Paxton said. Father Nash

had learnt that Richard Watson was working for Lady Joan, one of his most important financial backers.

'Watson was hostile to our vision. Father Nash was worried he'd begun to influence her against Christianity in Crisis. He wanted to know more about the research they were doing, but Watson refused to tell him. So I made a few suggestions. My team kept an eye on them: where they went and what they did.'

'Helen said that Richard was mugged by some arsehole who punched him and nicked his bag,' said Nick. 'Was that your lot?'

Paxton shrugged. 'Sometimes you have to use unconventional methods. We knew they'd made a discovery. We had to find out what it was.'

Unconventional methods like murder and torture, thought Nick. He felt sick, realising that he'd himself succumbed to the same temptation, had inflicted pain to get answers. Paxton was in full flow now, justifications pouring out of him.

'And there was another thing. Lady Joan's getting on. She'd promised to leave her estate to Nash's organisation. I mean, she's stinking rich. Rolling in it. That sort of money could make all the difference. And suddenly she's fawning all over this historian bloke. We did some digging.

'Watson was adopted as a baby through a church-run agency. Father Nash got hold of the records. Earlier that same year, Lady Joan spent six months in a nursing home in the country, supposedly having a nervous breakdown.'

Nick couldn't imagine Lady Joan having a nervous breakdown. She was the sort of woman who gave nervous breakdowns to other people. Then again, he found it quite hard to imagine her having a baby.

'You're saying Richard Watson was her son?' His mind boggled at the possibility. Someone, back in the 1970s, admittedly, when everyone was doing it with everyone else, had had sex with Lady Joan. He supposed there were a lot of drugs around at the time.

'That's what Father Nash said. He worried she planned to leave the whole estate to him. And then there was this business about the missing play they were trying to find. Father Nash said it was important, that it could make a difference to the cause. And Richard Watson blocked any attempts to work with him. He had to go.'

Nick remembered the phone in his back pocket. It didn't have a signal, but the voice recorder would work. He got up and leaned on the altar table, where Paxton couldn't see him.

'Go on. Tell me what happened.' He pulled out the phone, set the recorder and left it running on the altar.

'Alright. So Father Nash arranged with me to pick them up from the hall, pretend to be a taxi driver. He gave Watson my number, said it was a local firm. He wanted to know what they talked about on the way home. Something must've happened during the dinner, though. I got a message. He said Richard had important information in his notebook, and I was to get it at all costs. I knew what I had to do.'

'You stabbed him.'

'I tried to get the notebook off him. He resisted.'

'But he didn't have the notebook on him.'

Paxton shook his head. 'No. So I reckoned he'd given it to the girl. We searched her flat that night. Then I picked her up the next day.'

Nick was silent. He sat down with his back to the door,

drew his knees up to his chin and closed his eyes as Paxton's self-justifications poured out. He didn't want to know about Helen's treatment at his hands. He certainly didn't want to hear him cloak the act in bureaucratic military speak as 'enhanced interrogation'. His eyes were drawn back to the angry red mark on Paxton's arm. He'd done that, had allowed his anger to push him into unforgivable cruelty. His mum would be ashamed of him. He felt disgust, both for the pathetic creature before him and for himself.

And Helen, at the hall, with that creep Father Nash hanging around her. He thought of the man sneaking into her bedroom last night and shivered. He needed to get out of here. Unsuccessfully, he searched the chapel for a key. He untied Paxton's feet, and together they put their shoulders to the door. It didn't budge.

Nick wondered how long it would be until someone needed to use the little chapel. Days? Weeks, even? There was nothing to eat, nothing to drink. The candle had burned halfway down. It would make sense, he realised, to put it out for a while, save it until they needed it. He shivered. He really didn't want to sit in the dark.

Chapter 50

Helen redrew the Vigenère square's alphabetical grid, then highlighted the lines that began with the corresponding letters of the key word: Cynthia. She carefully copied the long string of letters from the torn-out page: D G B E X Z B T Z G J B H R E H W T M F V P V T Z K I F W P I D W O T N R I M W S T M G A L U A K V M E H M M A K V J E B K O E. Then she went to the line of the alphabet beginning with the letter C, holding the edge of a page as a ruler. Reading across to the first letter of the coded message, she noted down the corresponding letter on the grid: B. Quickly she moved to the next letter, which deciphered as I. The next letter was O, followed by L. Biol. Biology, she wondered? Did that word even exist in the sixteenth century? She thought not, even among the scholars and proto-scientists of Raleigh's group. Was it Latin, perhaps, or Greek? Richard would have known.

The next letter stopped her short: Q. She frowned, checked it again. Definitely Q. With foreboding, she turned to the next letter, and the next. She sat back and looked at her work. B I O L Q I R. It looked like a bad hand at Scrabble. The energy that had sustained her, the hope that she could do this even without Richard, started to drain away. The key was producing nothing but nonsense.

She stared at the computer screen, her mind as blank as the empty search box. Had she remembered it wrong? A quick search confirmed that she'd been right about the portrait of Raleigh with the hidden symbol of the waves and the moon. She found a list of his poems and scrolled down. Finally, she found it. *The Ocean to Cynthia*. Except it was spelt in two ways in different versions, according to the website. On first publication, it was *The Ocean to Scinthia*.

Pushing aside the mouse, she turned back to the pad of paper and began again, using the new keyword: Scinthia. L, E and T. Then R, E, S and T again. *Let rest*. It was working, she thought. Her heart started to gallop. She worked fast and fluently, barely pausing until all sixty-four letters had been decoded. When she was done, she stared at the words that had formed themselves on the page. It had bloody worked. She gave a little gasp of laughter. She wrote the letters out again, grouped them into words and sentences. The first person, perhaps, to have done this since Lord Cobham in 1603.

'Let rest the book where Scinthia's diadem lay. Beware the master of Eastbridge.'

Work through it logically, she told herself, trying to organise her darting thoughts. The book had to be the play, the Canterbury book referred to in the uncoded portion of the letter. Scinthia's diadem must be Elizabeth's crown. Raleigh was telling Cobham to hide the play where Elizabeth laid her crown. She frowned. Where would Elizabeth's crown have been kept? She tried to remember whether Tudor kings and queens had kept their jewels where they were now, in the Tower of London. She remembered Lady Joan's scorn at her suggestion that her grandfather's 'infinite riches' were hidden in a jewel safe. Maybe she was being too literal. Raleigh's Scinthia was a goddess, not someone who had to remember to lock away her crown at night. Did it simply mean where her crowned head rested? In her palace or bedchamber? She scribbled it down as a possibility.

The second part of the message seemed clearer. Beware the master of Eastbridge. Well, she knew who he was. Doctor Thomas Lawes, the man who recommended students for the Parker scholarships at Cambridge, and who the theatre manager Henslowe had paid. The man, perhaps, who had taught Christopher Marlowe at Eastbridge school.

They'd made a list of all the things that needed checking out, she remembered. She opened the filing cabinet, rifled through until she found the big pad of paper she'd scribbled on. There it was.

'Payment to Thos. Lawes in Henslowe's diary, 1593.' She remembered Richard suggesting they should visit Eastbridge together. It had been a sunny suggestion, a pleasant excursion for two scholars with a shared interest. Now the place was imbued with menace.

Helen turned back to the computer and looked up the masters of Eastbridge Hospital. Dr Lawes had served as master for twenty-five years, but had died in 1595. Damn, she thought, so he couldn't have been the master that Walter Raleigh had warned Lord Cobham about in 1603. After Lawes, the hospital had two masters in two years, perhaps reflecting the toll taken by the plague. Then in 1597, Dr John Boys, Dean of Canterbury Cathedral, was elected and served until 1625. This must be the man.

Boys was almost Marlowe's mirror image, she thought,

reading about his life. He'd been the dutiful student who took the path set out for him. A few years younger than the playwright, he had also travelled from the King's School to Corpus Christi College in 1587, around the time that Marlowe graduated. Helen remembered the name – he was one of the Canterbury students recommended for a scholarship by Thomas Lawes. Boys and Marlowe might well have known each other. The year Marlowe died, Boys became a priest with a country living. A few years later, he was appointed master of Eastbridge, an appointment made by the repressive Archbishop Whitgift. He gained a number of increasingly important church appointments, preached and wrote widely on scriptural matters. Finally, he was appointed Dean of Canterbury Cathedral by James I. An obedient churchman who had followed the career intended for Parker scholars and been well-rewarded for it. Yet, according to Raleigh, someone to be wary of.

She grabbed the notepad again. Two masters of Eastbridge Hospital, both students at Marlowe's college in Cambridge. The earlier master might possibly have been young Marlowe's school teacher. Then, ten years later, he was in receipt of money from the playhouse that bankrolled Marlowe. The later master, Marlowe's near contemporary, was invoked as an enemy at the time when Raleigh and Cobham were trying to hide a lost Marlowe play. The sum of money in the payment to Lawes, she remembered, was roughly the amount that Henslowe had advanced his authors for a play. Could Marlowe's teacher have written a play himself?

She thought back to Henslowe's diary and read over her note of his exact words. 'Doctor Tho. Lawes at Canterbye, £6 for the archbishop,' she read. She suddenly saw the payment reversed. It was not clear in the diary whether the money was paid out or received. She'd assumed it was an outgoing payment, because it had been grouped with the money paid to license plays. But what if Thomas Lawes had paid Henslowe – had recompensed him, in fact, for the money Henslowe had already paid out to Christopher Marlowe as an advance? Was it a payment to ensure that Henslowe's theatre would not try to stage Marlowe's play? Perhaps the master of Eastbridge had bought Henslowe's silence.

The reversal made sense, she thought. For some reason, Eastbridge Hospital wanted the Canterbury play, and any gossip about it, suppressed. Then, a decade on, a later master of Eastbridge was involved in another attempt to discredit or destroy those who had a surviving copy of the manuscript.

What was a small, charitable hospital doing muddled up with London theatre and the lives of Elizabeth's favourites? Helen's head had begun to ache again. But she felt she had the pieces now; it was simply a question of fitting them together properly. If only Richard was beside her, ready to hold the shards of discovery up to the light, turn them one way and another until the whole kaleidoscope was revealed. His knowledge of Reformation Canterbury, and the fate of the pilgrim hospitals, might have solved the mystery at a stroke. She foresaw days of work in ecclesiastical archives, tracing the hospital's history to make sense of what she had found. And when she visited Eastbridge, it would be alone. Unless, of course, Father Nash came with her. She thought again of what Charlotte had said. Yet she'd had nothing from the man but kindness and courtesy. She might not see eye to eye with him on politics, but he stood up for what he believed. She respected that.

She turned again to the first part of the message. *Let rest the book where Scinthia's diadem lay.* Where Elizabeth rested her crowned head. In one of her palaces? Elizabeth had died earlier that year. Perhaps that's what Raleigh had meant – Elizabeth's grave. She was buried in Westminster Abbey, in the family's chapel. But the sense of it wasn't right. Raleigh had written 'where Scinthia's diadem lay', not where it lies now. Where her body had lain in state, perhaps? She checked online. After her death, Elizabeth had lain in state at Whitehall Palace, most of which had been destroyed by fire in the seventeenth century.

The great hall at the palace would have been an appropriate place for the play. It had been the site of many theatrical entertainments during Elizabethan times. Yet the hall was a public space that changed like a stage set, bare behind its tapestries and paintings. Helen couldn't imagine how you would hide something there, especially if you wanted to retrieve it later. Also, she wasn't ready to accept that the missing play had been consumed by fire. There must be a better answer, somewhere on a more domestic scale. Somewhere that Lord Cobham would have had easy access to.

Of course … She remembered her first visit to the hall, her excitement as the car drew up outside. She'd been a fool. Her heart began to beat faster. She made her way down the corridor to the library. Lady Joan was alone, seated before the fire with a book on her lap. She shot Helen a sharp look. 'You've found something. Tell me, quickly.'

'Elizabeth I visited Cobham Hall, didn't she?'

'She did. Twice.' Lady Joan looked almost affronted to be asked. 'It nearly bankrupted us. We had to build a whole new

323

suite of rooms for her.'

Helen smiled. 'Lady Joan, can you show me where she slept?'

Chapter 51

The Queen's Bedroom was a large, square chamber with a high ceiling, icing-white with plaster unicorns, lions and crowns picked out in gold paint. The walls were hung with primrose yellow silk. In the middle of the room stood an impressive canopied bed, hung with somewhat tattered green velvet, richly patterned and sprouting tassels.

'The bed is original,' said Lady Joan. 'Fortunately, our predecessors preserved some of the house's more valuable assets.'

Matching green velvet curtains hung at the tall windows. Between them was a fine portrait of Queen Elizabeth herself, magnificently stiff in gold-and-white brocade, holding a feather fan. To her excitement, Helen saw the painting included her crown, set to one side with her sceptre. *Where Scinthia's diadem lay …*

'Not the original, alas,' said Lady Joan. 'That went to the National Portrait Gallery when my father died. It's a very good copy, though.'

Where to begin? The chamber was sparsely furnished: just the bed, an impressive chest at its foot and a couple of side tables and Chinese vases, clearly much later in period. Helen found herself wishing that Nick was there, quick and limber.

Her body ached so much she wanted to sit down all the time. The thought of scrambling around and pulling up floorboards was exhausting. Yet she was determined to do this. She wanted to have something to show Father Nash when he returned from Rochester. It would be good to have an ally again, someone who would be as excited as she was by the discoveries she made.

Helen knelt on the rug before the big chest, which was upholstered in green leather and dozens of brass studs. 'What about this? Is it from Elizabeth's time?'

'It is.' Lady Joan, creaking a little, got to her knees next to her and opened the lid. 'It's empty. I have looked in here before, you know.'

Helen ran her hands around the hefty wooden box and tapped its surfaces. She wasn't entirely sure what she expected to find. Hidden catches, she supposed, hollow secret compartments. The chest seemed solid enough. She smoothed her fingers over the worn leather. No suspicious edges or thickness concealed beneath.

'What now?' Lady Joan's voice dropped an octave. 'Shall I look under the bed?'

Between them, they scanned the chamber. Under the bed, between the bed and the mattress, sneezing in the dust of the velvet canopy that hung over it. Behind the portrait of Elizabeth, inside the Georgian side tables and Chinese vases, never mind that they were later additions to the room. They pulled the bed away from the wall so Helen could check behind it.

'I suppose it could be hidden in the walls.' She looked apprehensively at the yellow silk wallpaper, decidedly un-Elizabethan in style. 'When was it decorated like this?'

Lady Joan snorted. 'Some time in the eighteenth century, I believe. It was originally linen-fold oak panelling, like the dining hall. Hung with tapestries, of course. We had them made in Flanders, hunting scenes of Diana and Actaeon. They're now in a museum in Brussels.'

'I guess they would have found anything hidden at the time they removed the panelling,' said Helen, wearily. 'The manuscript might have been thrown away, no one realising what it was.' She thought of the records downstairs, the cabinets full of accounts and inventories that Richard had begun to put into order. Maybe she should revisit the eighteenth-century household records to see if there was any note made of a manuscript being found at the time of the redecoration. It might even be there somewhere, bundled away unnoticed. She felt tired at the thought of it. It was an enormous task. Perhaps Father Nash would help her.

She paced around the room. 'What else? What have we missed? You said the family built a whole suite of rooms for Elizabeth's visit.'

Lady Joan led the way back through the door they had entered. 'The antechamber. But it's been completely stripped.' The room had the same striped yellow silk wallpaper, an elegant little alabaster mantelpiece and a quantity of portraits of wistful-looking Georgian ladies with elaborate frocks and powdered hair. As Lady Joan had warned, nothing remained from the Elizabethan period.

'OK, forget this one.' Helen was getting impatient. Had she been wrong? Surely not. If Raleigh had told Lord Cobham to hide the manuscript where Elizabeth's diadem lay, and Elizabeth had slept at Cobham Hall in her own suite of rooms, this must have been what he meant. 'Is there a dressing room?

Somewhere Elizabeth would have kept her clothes and jewels when she went to bed for the night?' She was aware that she'd reverted to her original thought: the literal laying down of the crown.

'The withdrawing room. I wonder … come with me, young woman.' Lady Joan broke out a rare smile. She looked almost mischievous, her grey eyes glinting with humour.

In a small chamber off the bedroom stood a large, square box, upholstered in green velvet and studded with brass in the same style as the chest in the bedroom. Lady Joan looked at Helen enquiringly. 'Any guesses?' She shook her head.

Lady Joan lifted the lid and set it back against the wall. The lid revealed a round, padded velvet seat with a hole in the middle. It was the very latest in Elizabethan modern conveniences – a close stool, or portable toilet.

Where Scinthia's diadem lay. A grubby joke between courtiers at Elizabeth's expense. Helen laughed. 'The en-suite,' she said.

'The what?'

'Never mind. Amazing. I've never seen an original one before, much less one used by such an illustrious …' She paused, not wanting to give offence. 'An illustrious visitor,' she continued, firmly. 'This was from the same period, when Queen Elizabeth stayed at Cobham Hall?'

The old woman nodded. 'The first visit, in 1559, the year after her accession. Everything had to be perfect. As you can see.'

Helen knelt before the close stool and opened the door at the front of the box. Beneath the padded seat would have stood a chamber pot, to be emptied by one of Elizabeth's most intimate ladies-in-waiting. The box was empty. Tentatively, she pressed the floor. The wood gave a little. She reached around the seams, pressing her fingers into the corners. She sat back on her heels, wondering. It would be sacrilegious to damage such an impressive artefact. But the thinness of the wood on the base was suspicious. Was it a false floor?

'Lady Joan, would you mind if we turned it over? Very carefully, of course.'

The woman was as eager as she was. Together they lifted the heavy box and placed it on its side. The velvet upholstery on the base showed a brighter green, from all the years hidden from the light. Helen tilted the box towards her, laying a hand against the cloth. Something inside sagged against her hand. It was heavy and flat. Her breath stopped in her throat.

The older woman snatched her hand away. 'What is it? What have you found?' She felt for herself, then before Helen could react, she snagged the material with her diamond ring and tore it across. Ignoring Helen's cry of protest, she reached inside.

Chapter 52

The two women sat on the floor, beside the upturned close stool, and stared at the bundle of papers. Helen's hands trembled. For a moment she thought she might faint. Was this really it?

It was tied with a ribbon of black leather, the pages curled inward. The paper was long and narrow, covered in faded brown ink. On her hands and knees, she leaned over it and tried to focus on the letters. Secretary hand, she saw with some dismay – harder to read than Raleigh's elegant italic. Was this Marlowe's own handwriting? Examples were so rare – only one undisputed example of his signature had been found – that it might not even be possible to identify the writing with certainty.

It certainly looked like a play. The top page was laid out like a play script, names to the left with lines of verse running to the right of them. She tried to focus on the words at the top.

'What does it say? I can't read the writing,' said Lady Joan. She perched her reading glasses on her nose and reached for the papers.

'Don't!' Helen couldn't bear to see the manuscript manhandled. 'Please, Lady Joan. It shouldn't be touched. It's very fragile. I should call the British Library and ask them to come and help.' She had not thought beyond finding the play, she realised. Indeed, until it tumbled from the close stool, she had not really, in her heart of hearts, believed she would find it. Had she even been sure it existed? She felt as if she had been playing a game. A deadly game with fatal consequences. But now the manuscript lay before her, and she was almost too frightened to read it.

'Fine. You call them. I'll read it,' said the woman, scooping it up. Helen walked alongside her, fretting, as she took the manuscript down the stairs to the library and laid it on her rosewood desk. She reached for a pair of scissors from the pen set on the elegantly scrolled desktop and made to cut the leather binding. Helen took them from her.

'No. Let me.' Firmly, she put the scissors aside and eased the leather band down the pages. It was powdery and soft. The pages retained their inward curl. She smoothed them with the back of her hands, placed Lady Joan's blotter over them to hold them flat. She took a pencil and paper and focused on the top line, setting out the letters that she could decipher.

'*The true historie of the traytor thomas becket.*' She stared at the words in surprise. She realised she had been expecting Marlowe to make Becket the hero of his play – that it would be dangerous precisely because it celebrated the rebellion of the archbishop against the power of the throne. Yet that wasn't how Marlowe worked. She thought of *The Massacre at Paris, Doctor Faustus, Edward II.* Each of them took as their central character a villain, someone whose downfall the audience watched with fascinated glee, seduced into sympathy with the devil. His portrayal of Thomas Becket would follow the same pattern.

331

'It's as we thought,' she told Lady Joan, who was not waiting patiently. 'A play about Becket. The true history of the traitor Thomas Becket.'

'Traitor?' Lady Joan sounded outraged.

'Typical Marlowe.' She smiled at the woman. 'Listen, it's going to take me ages to decipher this. Can I stay here while I do so? I really should inform the British Library, of course. But it belongs to you, to your family. They can't remove it without your permission. They would simply be here as advisers.'

She sat back, resting her hands lightly on the desk. Months, years of scholarship lay ahead. And she would be the first person to read this play since – since who? Walter Raleigh, perhaps. The tenth Lord Cobham. Perhaps she would edit the first published edition of the play, work with theatrical scholars on the first-ever staging. She shook her head in wonder, tears filling her eyes. The world premiere of a Christopher Marlowe play, staged four centuries after it was written. She remembered the cautious, dry scholarship she'd expended on her doctorate, thought of her desiccated and scornful tutor. This was the greatest discovery that would be made in her lifetime – and she had been the one to make it. For a moment, the pain of Richard's loss penetrated her excitement. If only he'd been here to share the moment with her.

'Father Nash is here again,' said Charlotte, from the doorway. 'Shall I show him in?'

Helen turned a bright smile to her. 'Oh, I think so. Don't you, Lady Joan?'

It was the older woman's turn to look uncertain. 'Perhaps … should we put this aside for a moment? Richard …'

'I can take it,' said Charlotte, moving swiftly to their side.

Helen put a hand protectively over the document. 'No. I think he deserves to see this.' Lady Joan shrugged and waved her hand. Charlotte bit her lip. Helen dropped her eyes, not wanting to meet the woman's gaze.

The man bustled into the room, his round face shining with bonhomie. He stopped short when he saw Helen, who rose with a swelling of triumph in her breast.

'You've cut your hair,' he said, his voice abrupt.

'What? Oh, yes. I was fed up with it,' she said. He was staring at her borrowed clothes. Helen felt his disapproval chill the excitement of her find.

'A woman who cuts off her hair ...' he murmured.

'Father Nash, we've found it,' she said. She smiled at him. He gazed back in puzzlement, and for a moment it was as if she had mistaken him for someone else, had accidentally hailed a stranger at a railway station. Then her words seemed to penetrate his brain.

'What! Helen, how marvellous. You clever thing.' He spun around to the desk. 'This is it? Where did you find it?'

She explained, laughing at the audacity of the man who decided that Elizabeth I's lavatory was the best place to hide Marlowe's last play. Scinthia's diadem, indeed. She decided not to explain what Raleigh might have meant by that. 'Look. As we thought, it's about Thomas Becket. I've just started to decipher the text. It'll take a while, I'm afraid. But we have the title.'

He looked at the words she'd transcribed. 'The *traytor*?' he asked, a tremor in his usually even voice. 'Why does he call him a traitor?'

Helen began to explain. 'That's what Henry VIII called him,

333

so it would be politic of Marlowe to use the same terms. But if I know Marlowe, he'll make him into the most compelling character in the play. Like in the *Massacre*, where the Duke of Guise is portrayed as a terrible villain, but the audience find themselves totally on his side by the end.'

Nash sat down, looking as if he had been personally insulted. 'This is not what I expected,' he said. 'What does it say about the grave? Richard said it would tell us where Becket is buried.'

Helen had almost forgotten about that. It seemed of secondary importance, given the immensity of finding a missing Marlowe play, quite possibly in his own handwriting.

'Well, we certainly hope so,' she said. 'That was Richard's theory, anyway. But I'll have to decipher the rest of the play to find out. There's a lot of work here.' She indicated the stack of papers.

'How long?' His eyes had the same type of greed she'd seen in Lady Joan, she realised: a focus on the end result with little interest in how that end was achieved. A flicker of doubt stirred. Was this why Richard had not wanted him involved? She thought of how Richard would have revelled in the task ahead, the step-by-step discovery of an untouched masterpiece.

'I don't know,' she said, her voice flat. 'Weeks, I expect.' She saw impatience in his eyes, matched by Lady Joan's. All of a sudden, Helen felt very alone.

Chapter 53

Helen was holed up in the office, just her and Marlowe's play. Despite her initial fears, she was getting the hang of the handwriting. She could make a decent guess at enough of the words to get the sense of it, although she would need to go back and make a slow, painstaking transcript later. Her progress through the document was faster than expected. For now, she preferred to keep that quiet.

Was the play really by Marlowe? She had read nothing that made her discount that possibility. The lines had his swelling rhythm, insistent as breakers rolling in from the ocean. She recognised Marlowe's use of rhetoric, the way he piled up images, phrase upon gorgeous phrase.

The play began the night before Becket's ordination as Archbishop of Canterbury, at the high point of his triumphant career. After a bit of scene-setting with various monks and bishops, the character was left alone to soliloquise about how he would use his position to exert power over the King and to enrich himself.

Marlowe's Becket listed the church's treasures in a litany that could have been lifted from *The Jew of Malta*. In a rhapsodic passage, he described the priceless volumes in the library, including Canterbury's 'ancient testament of Augustine'. Saint Augustine's Gospel, she thought with a thrill. Archbishop Parker had given the book to Corpus Christi just a few years before Marlowe had been a scholar there. Perhaps he'd seen it, been dazzled by its beauty and antiquity, as Helen and Richard had been.

The Becket character went on to explain how he would feign religious fervour to win support, but that he believed faith was for the common herd, not for men of destiny like himself. Religion, the character said, was 'naught but a bugbear to keep men in awe'. Helen's eyes widened. The same phrase, that Marlowe thought religion a 'bugbear' invented 'to keep men in awe', was used against him when he was accused of atheism in the last weeks of his life. Had his accuser seen the script, or even heard Marlowe read the speech aloud? She imagined him at the centre of a rowdy group in a tavern, knocking back wine and declaiming lines from his new play. Laughter from most of his audience – but one of them noting his dangerous words, reporting them back to the authorities.

She read on. Marlowe's Becket was a Machiavellian troublemaker. He was intent on building a power base in the church to rival the barons, who mocked Becket for his low birth. He planned revenge on those who had scorned him and sent a hooded monk to murder one of the barons, assuring the man that he would be safe from the law, as churchmen were subject only to ecclesiastical courts.

Helen turned the pages. The archbishop clashed with King Henry, who was somewhat improbably depicted as a champion of the poor against the avaricious church. Becket's flight overseas was not in fear of his own safety, but to incite an invasion of England by the King of France, backed by the Pope. It was his treachery, not that of Henry II, that undermined the King's attempts at reconciliation. The play was, in short, a hatchet job on Becket's reputation.

There was a tap on the door.

'Lady Joan wants to know if you'll join us for lunch.' It was Father Nash, back to his usual smiley self. She hesitated.

'Would you rather have it here? I can tell her you don't want to be interrupted.'

'That would be kind.'

The priest closed the door and perched on the edge of the desk. 'I'm sorry I was impatient earlier. I think it's wonderful, the work you've done to discover this manuscript. How are you getting on? Do you really think it's by Marlowe?'

She grinned. 'I do. Of course, it's entirely possible that it's a very clever fake. But it feels like Marlowe to me. The language, the themes. It's thrilling.'

'How exciting.' He walked to the window, gazed out at the topiary monsters marching across the lawns.

'You know, Helen, faith comes to us at strange times. I can remember when it happened to me. I was in Canterbury Cathedral, believe it or not, at the spot where Thomas Becket was martyred. I was eleven years old, and miserable – a bullied, fat schoolboy with no friends. I walked in, and I couldn't believe it. I'd never been in such a beautiful building in my life. It was a school trip – we lived just ten miles away, but my parents would never have thought to take me.'

He turned to face her and she saw his face was shining. 'That visit changed my life. Saint Thomas's story of courage and defiance inspired me to become a Christian. I felt like I'd been handed a sword and given a cause to fight for. I've been fighting ever since.'

Helen felt embarrassed. She wasn't good at talking about personal faith. 'That's a very moving story,' she began. She wondered if she should warn him that the play might not show him a version of Thomas Becket that he liked.

He sat next to her, took her hands and leaned forward, his eyes intense. 'Isn't it? And just think how we could move people if we could show them the actual body of Thomas Becket, as the church did in the Middle Ages. Imagine – it could prompt a re-awakening of Christianity across the country. The people of England, reminded of what it means to be English. It would be a crusade, a pilgrimage. We would rebuild Saint Thomas's golden shrine in Canterbury, place the saint back where he was meant to be, at the heart of the Church in England.'

Awkwardly, she tried to withdraw her hands. The man was possessed by his vision.

'And you would be beside me, Helen, leading that crusade. This is your true purpose. With your help, I will discover the lost relics. And with God's help, we can awaken the faith of this country. I know how many silent Christians there are. They write to me. They join my campaign. They are in every parish, on every council, every school's board of governors. We've been silent so long, but this discovery will be a clarion call. The trumpet will sound!'

'I'm not sure I'd be much good at that sort of thing, Father Nash. If I had a true purpose, I think it was to discover this play.' No wonder Richard had been cautious about the man. His religious fervour seemed more like mania. She didn't dare to tell him that she had no religious faith herself.

'Your purpose is to find the burial place of Thomas Becket,' he said. 'And I know you will. I believe you have been touched by God.'

She said nothing.

'Now,' he said, his tone light again, 'how far have you got?'

Chapter 54

She fobbed him off, telling him she'd barely deciphered the opening scene. She didn't feel equal to explaining that Marlowe had drawn Becket as an atheist, a traitor and a chancer. She worked on, typing a quick transcript into a computer file, full of question marks and gaps. She scribbled phrases of particular interest in Richard's notebook. Somehow it felt right to use his notebook to complete their work.

Twenty minutes later she took a tray from a red-cheeked woman in an apron. Hungry, she attacked the plate of roast chicken. As she chewed, she wondered again why the play had been suppressed. It seemed calculated to appeal to Elizabeth, showing the perfidy of the Catholic Church against a saintly monarch.

The church, of course, might not have seen it that way. While it might suit the state to portray Archbishop Becket as a power-hungry charlatan, the play would not necessarily be to the taste of those elements of the church still loyal to Catholicism. The religious rupture, after all, had come very recently. She thought back to Raleigh's letter to Lord Cobham. He had warned him about the master of Eastbridge Hospital. Not about the new King's courtiers or statesmen, but the old church foundation. It was Eastbridge – the hospital founded to accommodate Saint Thomas Becket's pilgrims – that had sought to suppress the play. And the masters of Eastbridge were strongly linked to Canterbury Cathedral.

If Eastbridge had wanted to suppress Marlowe's play in 1603, she thought, would it still want to do the same today? She remembered, as if from years ago, Richard telling her that the Eastbridge Hospital foundation was still in operation.

She opened a web browser and looked up the address. It was open to the public, she saw, except when the chapel was in use for services. She made a note of the address and wondered, a little uneasily, whether she could ask Father Nash to drive her there.

She read on. The next scene, she saw with a slight sinking of the heart, was a comic interlude. Marlowe's comedy, like Shakespeare's, had not worn well. The scene pitted a not-particularly-funny French monk at the monastery where Becket was in exile against a Jewish money-lender and a Turk, described by Marlowe as a 'black devil'. *Oh, Lord*, thought Helen. The medieval equivalent of an Englishman, Irishman and Scotsman walking into a racist joke.

The money-lender was insisting that the monk pay him the money he owed or be thrown into prison. The Turk tempted him, telling him that as an 'infidel', the Christian law had no reach over him and he could not be imprisoned. The monk threw up his hands and declared he would 'turn Turk' to escape his debts, whereupon the Jewish money-lender forgave him the money, because he would not be responsible for the monk's apostasy. The scene ended with the Turk declaring that the Christian monk was the most culpable of them all, as he was prepared to deny his faith for money.

341

Helen yawned. A fairly standard swipe against the Catholic Church, although it was interesting that Marlowe showed the Jew behaving in a more Christian way than the others. It was certainly a shift from the notoriously anti-Semitic *The Jew of Malta*. As far as she knew, it was the only example in a Marlowe play of a Christian threatening to convert to Islam.

How long, in reality, would it take to read to the end of the play? She counted the pages. Another day, at least. She paused, her eyes still on the final page. Then she did something she thoroughly disapproved of. She started to read, impatient to see how Marlowe had ended his play – if, indeed, he *had* finished it.

He had; the last page was part of an epilogue, a dialogue between monks after Becket's death. She turned back a couple of pages to read Becket's last scene.

To her fascination, she saw that Marlowe had not dramatised the final coup de grâce of his execution, even though his martyrdom was the single most depicted event of his life. Instead, the play ended with Becket alone in the cathedral, the furious knights beating at the doors. In a closing monologue reminiscent of the last scene of *Doctor Faustus*, Becket tried to prepare for his impending death. The speech veered from defiance to terror. He imagined his turbulent life 'snuffed by the cutler's edge', then spoke with bravado of 'the welcome sleep that eases us from day'.

The hairs rose on Helen's neck. Carefully, she transcribed the next line. 'But in that sleep of death, what dreams may come?' She stared at it, astonished. William Shakespeare's masterpiece, the tragedy *Hamlet*, was thought to date from around 1600. This play, if it was by Marlowe, could have been written no later than May 1593. And yet the plays contained the same line. Had Shakespeare seen a copy of Marlowe's last play? Had he been inspired by it to create perhaps his greatest soliloquy, Hamlet's meditation on death? That was the question. Hands shaking a little, she read on.

She came to four lines that made little sense to her. Frowning, she jotted them into Richard's notebook. There was a reference to Cynthia, which she supposed was a nod to Queen Elizabeth, and to the 'Turkish Alcoran'. The 'Alcoran', she remembered from *Tamburlaine the Great*, was how Marlowe and other Elizabethan dramatists referred to the Quran.

She read the words over again, puzzled. Marlowe seemed to be showing Becket reading from the Quran. Did copies of the Islamic text even exist in England at the time of Thomas Becket, she wondered. What was Marlowe suggesting?

The soliloquy ended with Becket's plea for 'one hour more of life' as the knights rushed through the door, swords aloft. Helen sat very still, absorbing the impact of what she had read. Whatever the merits of the rest of the play, that final scene stood with Marlowe's finest work. With a shudder, she realised that Marlowe had written those words, had imagined what it must be to face violent death, mere weeks before he too would die at the point of a dagger. She wondered again how it had been for him. A desperate desire for one hour more? A defiant expectation of nothing but sleep? Or the terror of hell that paralysed Faustus, who knew it was more than a fable? His final play now spoke for him, as it must have spoken to his friends and colleagues, even to the upcoming playwright of the day, the glove-maker's son from Warwickshire. Death and how we bear it, she thought. The constant fear that haunts humanity through the ages.

Her eyes went to the epilogue. She realised with some

surprise that Marlowe had jumped forward five hundred years, to the time of the Reformation. The lines were a dialogue between two monks, described in the text as Old Friar and Young Friar. They discussed the approach of the King's commissioners, with orders to destroy Becket's shrine. Old Friar contended that 'bones are but dust, revere them as we may'. Young Friar replied that 'these relics of our saint deserve our care'. He continued:

'Let's rest his bones where pilgrims paused before
Where Henry penance did and alms bestow'd
Our English poet cleped the place ful well
And there the mauncipel began his tale.'

Helen rubbed her tired eyes. More riddles, she thought, wearily. This, however, must be the prize that Richard had been seeking: the clue that would uncover the final resting place of Thomas Becket. Compared to the rest of the play, the lines were mere doggerel. And yet this would be all that Lady Joan and Father Nash wanted. Perhaps she should just hand it over, let them make sense of it. She wanted to be left in peace with the rest of the play, the delicate task of a full transcription and edition. She'd already spotted a host of textual similarities to other Marlowe plays, not to mention the line from Hamlet. This was her treasure: a living manuscript. Let them have the dusty bones.

She transcribed the lines from the epilogue into the notebook. As she did so, the first line caught her attention. *Where pilgrims paused.* Eastbridge Hospital, she thought, began life as a hostel for pilgrims to Becket's grave. Eastbridge, which had fought to suppress the play. Was it as simple as that? Was Becket's body hidden in the old hospital? Thoughtfully, she stashed the notebook inside her borrowed jacket pocket.

Time to find out.

She gathered the fragile papers together on the desk and slipped them inside a plastic folder. The manuscript should be in a safe, of course. Or, better still, in a controlled environment in the British Library or the National Archives. She smiled. She liked being the only person in the world to have it in their hands.

* * *

She tried to look nonchalant as she walked into the parlour. Lady Joan was pacing up and down by the windows. Father Nash sat in an armchair by the fire, tapping messages into his mobile phone. Both looked up with avaricious eyes as she entered the room.

'Well?' demanded Lady Joan. 'What does it say?'

'I've read the first scene,' said Helen. 'In my opinion, this could well be a Marlowe play. The use of language, his imagery and the structure are consistent with what we know of his work.'

'The first scene? How long is this play? Why is it taking you so long? When do you expect to get results?' Lady Joan fired questions at her so fast that she couldn't interject to answer.

She smiled. 'It's your property, Lady Joan. As I said before, you can employ me as a freelance researcher on this project, or you can work on it yourself.' She tried not to show her nerves. She was fairly confident that no one without specialist training and experience of sixteenth-century documents could read the text. Yet she could not bear the thought of being told her services were no longer required.

The woman turned her back and stared out of the window.

'Other researchers are available, you know,' she said.

'It's very exciting, Helen,' said Father Nash. 'It's thrilling to think that we might actually be close to uncovering his resting place.'

'It certainly is. And when I've finished the transcript, I hope you will enjoy the play as a different take on his life from a very specific point in English history.' She smiled, tried to sound casual. 'Is Charlotte about? I wanted to ask her something about the computer.'

'She's in the library, dealing with my correspondence,' said Lady Joan. 'Please don't disturb her more than is necessary. Remember you are both working on my time.'

She followed Helen to the door and stepped outside. Surprised, Helen saw uncertainty in her face, almost nervousness.

'Don't tell Father Nash anything further about the play,' she said. 'I'm going to send him away. Richard didn't want him to know about this. My grandfather …'

She checked through the half-open doorway and dropped her voice yet lower. 'There may be reasons why Father Nash should not know, if what my grandfather once told me was correct.'

Helen sighed. More puzzles, more complications. 'What did your grandfather tell you, Lady Joan?'

The woman shook her head. 'Another time. Carry on with your work. Leave Father Nash to me.'

Helen trotted down the hall to find Charlotte. The sun streamed through the library windows.

'Hi. I don't suppose I could ask you for a lift? I rather need a trip into Canterbury.'

The woman looked up, her eyes tired. 'Why not? I'm about finished.' She packed away the papers. Helen caught a glimpse of legal documentation. Charlotte seemed to be reading over Lady Joan's will.

'Is Father Nash still here?' she asked. 'I need to speak to Lady Joan privately. I do wish he'd go home.'

Chapter 55

The man at the desk inside the ancient stone gateway was charm itself, with his smart suit and persistent smile. She listened politely as he gave her a potted history of Eastbridge Hospital.

'The chapel is closed to visitors this afternoon, although of course we are delighted to welcome anyone who would like to join the evensong service,' he concluded.

'That's the room that was once the school?' she asked. 'I'd like that. Who will be there?'

'All the residents. The master will join us, and of course the vicar comes down from Saint Nicholas to take the service. It starts at five o'clock. Would you like to visit the undercroft and the refectory?'

Helen descended to the undercroft, which was cool as a cave and smelled of damp limestone. The low, vaulted ceiling danced with points of light, reflected into the room from the river outside the windows. She cupped her hand against the diamond panes of glass and looked out. The hospital was actually built on the bridge, she realised. Water flowed beneath her, the building's feet bathed in the shallow river.

She sat on a step within an alcove and leaned back against the stone. This was where the pilgrims had slept. The undercroft had absorbed centuries of sleep as men and women stretched their bones on rushes laid on the floor, easing muscles that had walked or ridden for days. If travellers told tales of their pilgrimages, it was these walls that heard them. Her imagination sketched in rows of people, propped on their elbows, telling of the party of bandits that robbed them on Blackheath or the wild boar that menaced them in the forest of Blean. Swapping stories about cheating landlords in Faversham, generous farmers in Sittingbourne and, of course, their fellow pilgrims on the road to Canterbury. The holy blissful martyr for to seek.

But was she right to seek him here, in the place where the pilgrims rested? She pulled the notebook from her pocket and read again. *Let's rest his bones where pilgrims paused before, where Henry penance did and alms bestow'd.* Had Henry II bestowed alms on the hospital? She knew he had walked barefoot into Canterbury, where the monks of the cathedral whipped him before he spent the night praying at Becket's tomb. *Our English poet cleped the place full well.* The only English poet she could think of associated with Canterbury – apart from Marlowe himself, of course – was Geoffrey Chaucer, poet of *The Canterbury Tales*. Had he written about Eastbridge? And then there was the final line. *There the mauncipel began his tale.* She didn't even know what a mauncipel was. But perhaps he was one of Chaucer's pilgrims. She wished she knew the epic poem better. She'd studied the prologue, and some of the better-known Tales, but had never read the work in its entirety.

Glancing around, she saw a print of an illustration of the Tales, framed and hung on the wall of the undercroft. There was the Wife of Bath, in her scarlet stockings, and the simpering Prioress. The fat Cook, falling off his horse, and the courtly Knight in his armour, carrying his crusader flag. She frowned, looking for a man who might be a mauncipel. Whatever that was.

The light dimmed. Helen turned to see a figure silhouetted in the doorway, blocking the light from the street outside. Was it the man from the welcome desk? She shaded her eyes and tried to make him out. He was shorter and held himself very still. He closed the heavy wooden door and walked down the stairs.

'Who's there?' he asked, his voice nervous, peering at her from behind his thick, round spectacles. *My God*, thought Helen. It was Charles Fairfax, Richard's former friend. From his expression, he had failed to recognise her in her masculine clothing with her hair cut short.

'I'm a visitor,' she said, keeping her voice low. 'And you?'

He had stopped on the last step, as if reluctant to cede any advantage. 'I'm the master of Eastbridge Hospital,' he said.

She gasped. 'What! You?' She put out a hand to the wall to steady herself. It was as if the final piece of the puzzle had slipped into place.

His face changed, a frown creasing his forehead. 'Good grief. Is that... Helen? I didn't recognise you. I thought...'

She took a step back. Charles, who was supposed to be Richard's friend, was the present-day master of Eastbridge. The last man to have seen Richard alive. This neat, precise man, head of the organisation that had suppressed Marlowe's play down the ages. She imagined him lifting a telephone, like a Bond villain, and ordering Richard's death. Deciding that he knew too much, had got too close to the truth.

Rage swelled inside her. This horrible little man, posturing on the steps, ordering murder like other people ordered coffee.

'You thought I was being tortured by one of your thugs? I suppose you did.' She glanced around, looking for a way to evade him. 'But as you can see, I'm alive and well. And the police know exactly where I am,' she added, wishing to goodness it was true.

He raised his eyebrows and continued down the steps. 'I thought you were at Cobham Hall. It was on the news that you had disappeared and then been found. I was worried you had come to harm. Helen, I'm glad to see you. I wanted to talk to you about Richard. About the work you had begun together.'

She folded her arms. 'Good. I have some questions for you. But if you come any closer, I will scream the place down.'

He stopped. 'I won't hurt you. I don't know why you think I would—' he began.

She interrupted. 'Firstly, I want to know why the master of Eastbridge Hospital paid Philip Henslowe not to stage Marlowe's play, *The True History of the Traytor Thomas Becket*, in 1593. I'd like to know why, ten years later, Walter Raleigh warned Lord Cobham to beware of the master of Eastbridge when he advised him to hide his copy of the play at Cobham Hall. And I'd like to know why the current master of Eastbridge had a historian murdered because he was on the brink of discovering it, just last week. Perhaps we can start with that one.'

Fairfax had gone very white. He stepped back until he tripped on the bottom step. He sank to the ground and sat on the stone ledge. 'You've found it,' he said. His voice was flat. Behind his glasses, his eyes were unreadable. 'Where was it?'

351

'I'm asking the questions. Why did you have Richard killed?'

'I didn't. Of course I didn't. I would never harm Richard. I tried to warn him. I tried to warn both of you.'

'You tried to warn us. Then, when we told you to mind your own business, Richard was murdered and I was kidnapped by the man you set on us.'

'You are mistaken.' His voice remained calm.

She remembered the infamous letter written by one of Marlowe's enemies at the time of his death. 'All men in Christianity ought to endeavour that the mouth of so dangerous a member may be stopp'd.' Was that it? Had Richard really been too dangerous to be left alive?

'He thought you were his friend!' She hurled the words at him, powered by outrage. 'He trusted you and you had him killed. I saw his body, you know. Saw him lying in a pool of his own blood on the floor of a Deptford pub. He turned to you for help and you betrayed him. I hope you rot in hell.'

'Helen …' He was on his feet. He looked towards the door, but it remained shut.

She could not stop herself now. She strode over to him and pulled aside her scarf. 'Look at this, Mr Fairfax. These are the cigarette burns your man inflicted on me. Ugly, aren't they?' He flinched away. 'I think you should be able to look, don't you? Given that you paid for them.'

'You've got it all wrong. I don't know who kidnapped you or who killed Richard. I wish I did.' He reached for her arm.

'Don't touch me. I'm leaving now. I'm calling the police. Murderer.' She clenched her fists, ready to strike him to the ground if he tried to stop her.

Chapter 56

C harles Fairfax covered his face in his hands. As she watched, he closed in on himself, bending forward as if in great pain. He sank to his knees and pressed his forehead to the stone flags. He began to rock backwards and forward, emitting a high-pitched noise. She watched, uncertain. What was this?

He was crying, she realised. Sobs that seemed to be coming from his gut, heaving out of his body, shaking his whole frame. She crouched beside him, waiting. Whether this was guilt, grief or a combination of the two, she didn't doubt the authenticity of the emotion. The pain came from the same well of anguish as her own.

'It's my fault.' His voice was almost inaudible, his hands covering his face. 'It's all my fault.'

He raised his head, his face wet with tears. 'I blame myself. But I promise you, I did not make this happen. It is dangerous. If I'd known it was him...' He gave way to another fit of weeping.

'What do you mean?' She felt she was getting close to the truth.

'The missing letters in the Dulwich archive. They told me someone had asked about them, and about a Canterbury play.

But I thought… I thought it would be someone else. So I didn't know until that night, at Cobham Hall.' She watched him narrowly.

'Why is it dangerous? Why did Richard need to be warned?'

He brought his gulping sobs under control, sat on the ground with his arms around his knees. She noticed that his shoes were scuffed, his shirt crumpled. He didn't seem to have shaved for several days.

'It's always been dangerous,' he said, with a sigh. 'Christopher Marlowe knew that. Some secrets are best left undiscovered. If he had not threatened to make it public, to endanger the resting place…' He trailed off. Did he mean Marlowe, Helen wondered, or Richard? Perhaps both.

'You know.' It was not a question.

He nodded. His eyes were full of despair and exhaustion.

'Is he buried here?' she asked. 'Where pilgrims paused?'

The man lifted his head. There was a broken sort of smile on his face. 'You have not yet understood. That may be as well.'

'I will find out.' The words jumped from her mouth and she shivered. Richard's insistence that he would discover the truth had been his death warrant. 'I want to understand,' she said, more softly.

'Helen, I think Richard was very dear to you,' he said, his voice low. 'As he was to me. He needed protecting. From his own imagination, his own brilliance. His own persistence.'

She waited.

'I tried to protect him. He consulted the Lambeth archive frequently when he was researching his doctorate. His mind was so sharp, and he could make these leaps of understanding. I could see the way his research was going. I was worried about what he might turn up, so I offered him the job at Lambeth Palace. I thought I could direct his energies into a more profitable channel.'

His face had taken on a sort of radiance, his eyes shining with the memories. 'We worked closely together for four years. They were the happiest of my life. It was like working with quicksilver, the way his mind flowed. We collaborated on a history of the King James Bible. It would have been the best thing I ever published.'

He paused for a moment, as if reluctant to move on from the happy times. 'You know he was married? Ruth. Sweet girl. And their daughter. He was so proud of her. I was Madeleine's godfather. They – *we* – spent a lot of time together.'

'I was with him when the message came about the accident. In the months that followed, I tried to keep him from despair. I failed. It was the most dreadful time for all of us who cared about him. I thought we had lost him for good. But he fought his way back, with God's help. I was able to put a little work his way. I was so happy to see his recovery.' His voice trembled. 'That night at Cobham, in the library. The Raleigh letter – we thought Sir Albert had destroyed it. To see you and Richard unearth it was the most appalling shock.'

'We?'

'Eastbridge.'

'What is Eastbridge? Today, I mean.'

'Eastbridge Hospital is what it has always been. A religious foundation devoted to charitable service under the protection of Saint Thomas Becket. The members of the foundation carry on that tradition of service. The masters have the added burden of caring for Saint Thomas's resting place and protecting it from harm. We swear to do this when we accept our office.'

She pressed on. 'The Raleigh letter. Stolen from Lady Joan's safe with her diamond brooch.'

'Lady Joan's brooch is misplaced, not stolen. She will find it, soon enough, in her dressing table. The letter, regrettably, will not be found. We have ensured we have a sympathiser at Cobham Hall for some years now. It was felt necessary, after Sir Albert's death.'

'A sympathiser... Charlotte?' Helen was startled. She thought of the woman's quiet patience, her kindness and unruffled air. The way she allowed Lady Joan to bully her, seeming not to take offence at any slight. And yet she had helped Helen. Charles lowered his eyes and said nothing.

'Sir Albert...' She thought again of Lady Joan's words. 'What did he know? Lady Joan knows something. But she wouldn't tell me what.'

Charles shook his head. 'He came close. He never found the play. But he was privy to certain information from one of my predecessors. He agreed to keep certain confidences. I understand that he was a very fine man with a wide-ranging curiosity about the world. Much like Richard.'

How much further would he go? she wondered. Did he know who had killed Richard? Did Charlotte know? Had they tried to protect him from the foundation? She weighed her next question.

'Was it so terrible, the idea of us finding the missing play? Did Richard really need to be stopped in that brutal way?'

He stared at her, shocked. 'We had nothing to do with his death. No one at Eastbridge would have a man killed. Those days are long gone.'

She noted the implication. 'But in the past?'

'Another country.' He sighed. 'People were less scrupulous in the sixteenth century. Even churchmen. They were violent times.'

She needed to know. 'Marlowe. Killed by his own dagger because of his play. Who told Eastbridge he was writing it?'

To her surprise, he laughed: a soft chuckle that was almost affectionate. 'Marlowe himself. He went to see his old school teacher to talk to him about what he knew. The teacher told Master Lawes. Thomas Lawes had always liked the boy. He had even arranged for his scholarship to Corpus Christi. But the agent we sent to Scadbury Manor said the play went too far. He was a reckless boy. We arranged for his arrest.'

'And for the reckless boy to get his reckoning at Deptford,' said Helen, sorrowful. 'Your agent, Walsingham's man, Ingram Frizer?' She plucked his name from her memory. Frizer had been a low-life informer in the secret service until the day he was arrested for the murder of Christopher Marlowe. Acquitted with indecent haste, he later became Walsingham's most trusted servant and lived out his days in respectability.

'What about Cobham and Raleigh? Sentenced to death on trumped-up treason charges ten years later. What had they done?'

'Ah. It was a desperate attempt to curry favour with the King. Their positions at court were precarious after Elizabeth's death. They attempted to arrange a presentation of Marlowe's play at court, thinking it would please James. We could not allow that to happen. The treason charge was the idea of Master Boys. They needed to be discredited so that no one would believe them if they did talk. The threat of execution was enough to silence Cobham. Where did he hide the play, out of interest? We were never able to find it.'

She hesitated. Yet he had told her almost all she wanted to know. 'Elizabeth I's close stool,' she said.

He stared, open-mouthed, then began to laugh. 'How Richard would have enjoyed that!' he said.

She smiled, then joined his laughter. Tears started into her eyes. Before she knew it, she was weeping. All the jokes she would never now share with Richard. All the discoveries she would make without him. The glimpse of a future together, the possibility of deeper happiness, brutally curtailed. She pressed her fists into her chest. 'It hurts,' she said.

He patted her shoulder, tentative. 'I know, Helen,' he whispered. 'God knows, I know.'

Chapter 57

'Look, you might as well untie me. I've got cramp. My arm's gone numb.'

Nick stared into the darkness. Paxton had been on like this for ages now, wheedling to be untied. He was mired in guilt about what he'd done to the man.

'Oh, come on, mate. I told you everything, didn't I? I need a piss. I'm going to wet myself.'

Nick, feeling bad about it, had already had to urinate in the corner of the chapel. He could hear desperation in the man's voice. He'd tortured him. No point in humiliating him further. Neither of them was going anywhere until someone found them.

'Sit still.' He lit the candle and placed it on the ground.

The knots around Paxton's wrists were tied tightly. Nick picked away at the cord, easing the knots loose inch by inch. He shook the last knot free and turned away to give the man some privacy.

One meaty hand closed over his face, fingers gouging for his nose, his eyes. An arm wrapped around his neck, across his windpipe, cutting off his shout. He flailed as the man kicked his feet out from under him and he crashed to the ground. Immediately, Paxton was on top of him, sitting on his chest, hands gripping his hair. Nick felt his head yanked forward, then an explosion of pain as it was driven back into the stone floor.

'You black bastard!' the man yelled, face puce with fury. 'No one treats me like that. I'm going to kill you, you fucking half-breed.'

Nick thought he might throw up with the pain. But if he didn't fight back, Paxton would do it again. One or two more of those blows to the head could kill him. He didn't want to end his life with some racist oaf sitting on his chest.

Wrenching his right arm out from under Paxton's knee, he swung a desperate punch at the side of his head, aiming for the ear. It barely connected, but it distracted the man for a second. Paxton let go of his hair and grabbed his wrist, twisting it backwards until Nick screamed. He felt muscles and tendons being wrenched apart, and finally a sharp snap as a bone gave way. Paxton released it with a shout of laughter. Nick saw his hand hanging at a weird angle. *Shit*, he thought, through a fuzz of pain. *My writing hand.*

Paxton shifted back and knelt upright. Nick was soaked in sweat, dizzy. He needed to move. His limbs were heavy, dragging him down. He felt a powerful urge to close his eyes and slip into the dark. But he forced himself to stay conscious. What was the man doing? He was fiddling with his jeans, a smirk on his face. Seconds later, a warm stream of urine was pouring down on Nick's chest, soaking his T-shirt and splashing into his face. The foul smell invaded his nostrils.

Channelling all his disgust, Nick brought up his knee, hard, catching the man cleanly in the testicles.

Paxton roared, doubling over with pain. Nick wriggled out from underneath his weight. With his good hand, he pulled the green cloth from the altar and threw it over Paxton. He grabbed the candlestick and stood warily, waiting for the man to move. With one useless hand, he needed every advantage he could get.

There was silence for a moment. Nick could hear his ragged breath, his blood pounding in his head. The lump under the green tablecloth was still. Nick had a sudden flash of a childhood memory, Colin hidden under a blanket, pretending to be a sea monster. His own squeals of delighted terror. Slowly, the figure straightened up and pulled the cloth from his head. His eyes were murderous. Nick trembled, ready to swing the candlestick. Paxton took a step towards him. Nick swung and the candle extinguished. In the darkness, Paxton swatted it away and charged.

Nick was flattened against the chapel wall, the breath knocked out of him. In the darkness, Paxton grasped his neck, pinning him against the wall with one big hand. He struggled to release the grip, but soon the man had captured his remaining useful hand.

'No messing about,' he said, his voice close in his ear. 'You are dead meat.'

He began to press harder against Nick's windpipe. He gagged, unable to breathe in. His chest started to hurt and his head was filled with static. *Forgive me, Father, for I have sinned…* The familiar words ran through his head in a panicky gabble. The pain in his head and wrist started to fade.

Chapter 58

A rush of light and noise. The vice around his neck released and he dropped to the floor. There was shouting, a scramble of impressions. Someone had hold of him, hands gripped his shoulders. He could not move, could not breathe or see.

'Is he alive?' asked a girl's voice. *Meena*, he thought, with a rush of relief. *Thank God. Hers or mine.*

'He will be,' said a woman, her tone grim. He felt himself laid flat, hands pressed down firmly on his chest. He gasped and opened his eyes. Above him, he could see the fuzzy outline of DCI Greenley looking angry.

'Good. Well done, Nick. Stay with us.'

'Paxton,' he croaked, his throat hurting.

She nodded. 'I know. Don't worry. We'll get him.'

He turned his head to look for Meena and winced as his wound made contact with the floor.

The policewoman felt gently for the wound, pressed a handkerchief against it to staunch the blood and rested his head in her lap. It felt weird, like she'd turned into his mum or something. 'My hand,' he said. It hurt like hell. He cradled it against his chest.

'Keep it still. The ambulance will be here soon, then we can get you some pain relief.'

'Nick, you scared the shit out of me.' Meena leaned into his sightline, her orange headscarf glowing like some kind of halo. Her big brown eyes were fierce. Why did everyone seem angry with him? he wondered. 'I've been trying to ring you all afternoon. You smell like a public toilet, by the way.'

There'd been trouble with the mosque, Nick remembered fuzzily. He was supposed to have gone straight back to the office.

'What's going on?' he asked DCI Greenley. 'Why are you here?'

'Your colleague was very insistent. Said you wouldn't miss out on a story. She called me when she found your bike outside. We've searched the whole cathedral. I'm supposedly off duty after a somewhat lively day.'

A third figure loomed above her. Nick didn't recognise the man at first. He had a sandy-coloured moustache and stood upright as a soldier. Then he remembered. The chief usher from the service that morning – the one who had been cross with him for sitting at the back. He had a bunch of keys in his hand.

'I've called 999,' he said. 'The ambulance and police are on their way. I should go up to let them in. But I'm worried about the other chap.'

DCI Greenley sighed. 'He'll be long gone, I suppose. But we can cordon off the surrounding streets.'

'Well, that's the thing,' said the man. 'He won't be able to get out. He could be anywhere in the cathedral, but all the exterior doors are locked. I was just closing up, when you arrived. And I locked the main entrance before we set off.'

'Shit,' said Meena. 'We're locked in with him?'

The man nodded. 'Perhaps if I open some of the doors? I expect he wants to get away.'

Nick forced the words out. 'Catch the bastard,' he told DCI Greenley.

She gave a grim smile. 'We need to stay together. I don't want a hostage situation,' she said. 'Nick, if we help you, can you walk?'

Between them, DCI Greenley and the man hoisted Nick to his feet. They made their way to a set of stairs, expecting Paxton to leap out from behind every pillar. At the foot of the stairs, they halted.

'I should check it out,' said DCI Greenley, looking up into the gloom.

'You stay with Nick,' said Meena. Before anyone could stop her, she scampered up the stairs in her big white trainers. Nick held his breath.

'All clear,' she called. They followed into the cathedral nave and gently set him down on a row of chairs.

'Hold on, Nick. Won't be long now.'

Meena shrieked. Paxton had her head twisted under his arm, her feet barely touching the ground. She clawed at the hand clamped over her mouth.

'Listen up,' shouted Paxton. 'You. What's your name?'

'Let go of her,' called DCI Greenley. Nick saw the man twist Meena's head again. Her eyes were pleading, her neck at the furthest extent of its flexibility. Another turn ...

'I said, what's your name?' He pointed to the usher.

'I'm Alexander Foulkes. I'm the cathedral warden. Please let her go.'

'You do what I tell you, and I'll let her go. Right, Alex. Keys. You walk over there, open that door, then come back over here and turn away. The rest of you turn away now. Is that simple enough?'

'Do it,' said DCI Greenley.

The warden nodded and clicked through his bunch of keys. The policewoman turned her back. Reluctantly, Nick looked away. The warden's footsteps rang across the stone. They heard the lock click and a door open. A shaft of light painted the floor.

'Right,' said Paxton. 'We're going for a walk, sweetheart.'

Nick heard them stumble across the floor and out of the doorway. He turned his head in time to see him release Meena's neck. She straightened up and faced him. Then she spat in his face.

'No!' shouted DCI Greenley.

Paxton punched her full in the mouth, Meena's lip exploding in a mess of blood and teeth. She staggered backwards, tripped over the edge of the lawn and crashed down on the grass. Paxton ran for the perimeter wall and started to climb.

DCI Greenley was shouting into her radio, gesturing for the warden to unlock the main doors to the cathedral. He ran up the aisle. Sirens sounded loud from the street.

'He's going to get away,' shouted Nick, dragging himself to his feet. In the doorway, the policewoman grabbed his arm. 'He won't get far.'

Meena rolled over, blood smeared across her face. She staggered upright, sprinted across the grass and grabbed Paxton's ankle. He lost his grip on the wall, came crashing down on top of her.

'Oh, shit,' breathed DCI Greenley, starting forward. Nick was ahead of her, a cathedral chair in his good hand. As the man turned on Meena, his face ferocious, Nick raised it with

365

his last ounce of energy and brought it down on Paxton's head. He collapsed to his knees.

The little garden was suddenly full of people. The warden was back with four police officers. 'That one,' he said, pointing at Paxton. 'Assault. Grievous bodily harm. Goodness knows what else.'

Two policemen were quickly on top of Paxton. One fixed the handcuffs while the other held him by the shoulders and rattled through his rights. They hauled him to his feet and led him away.

DCI Greenley knelt beside Nick. 'The ambulance is right outside. The paramedics will be here in a second as soon as we've secured the scene and got Paxton in the van. You're safe now.'

'Meena?' He raised his head.

'I'm OK,' she said. Her voice was shaky. He reached out and took her hand. After a moment, she squeezed it.

'You're a bloody star.' He remembered something. 'Shit. The priest. Did you tell her?'

He scrambled onto his elbows. DCI Greenley nodded. 'Meena told me about the links to Father Nash's organisation. We'll look into it.'

'But he was the one who locked me in with Gary Paxton. And he was at Cobham Hall earlier with Helen and Lady Joan. He's the one behind it all. Paxton told me as much.'

The woman's face changed. She pulled out her mobile phone and called a number. She paced to the end of the garden and spoke for a moment. When she turned back, her eyes were wide.

'I have to go. There's been a report of a fire at Cobham Hall. The brigade are on their way. We don't know whether there's anyone still inside.'

Nick struggled to his knees. 'Take me with you. Please.'

'Absolutely not.'

'We're witnesses. You have to look after us, don't you?'

She gave him a weary look. 'Back of the car. And stay there.'

Chapter 59

'What will you do with the play?' Charles Fairfax's voice was steady.

Helen considered the question, staring down at the stone flags. 'It stands with Marlowe's other work,' she said. 'It's incredibly rich. And I think some copies must have circulated before it was suppressed. Shakespeare seems to have read it. There's a line that appears in *Hamlet*. It's – I can't tell you how important it is. I want to study it, to work on the first published edition.' The thought of the play, the work still to be done, sustained her.

'Of course.' His voice was sad. 'I wish you every success.'

She turned to look at him. His shoulders had sagged forward. His face was propped in his hands, the network of lines around his eyes making him look much older. The icy control he had kept over his feelings had gone. He looked as if he'd defrosted, his mortality asserting itself as his emotions broke through. He had struggled so long to keep everything under control: to protect both his secret and his friend. His whole bearing spoke of his failure.

'Charles, I still don't understand. Why does it matter so much, now, that Becket's burial place should be kept secret? I mean, his body could come back to Canterbury Cathedral, couldn't it? No one is going to object to that, surely?'

He stared at the ground. 'It is not so simple. One day, perhaps, it might be possible. But I don't think that day has come.'

'But why—' she began.

'Please.' He drew his hand across his eyes. 'Believe me, Helen. There are some things I cannot tell you.'

They sat a moment in silence.

'The epilogue is the weakest part of the play.' Her voice was slow, as if reluctant to admit the possibility that now seemed to open before her. 'It has the feel of something quickly dashed off. The play stands alone without it.' She paused. 'The epilogue seems to be the part that leads to the burial site.' She reached into her pocket and pulled out the transcript she had made before leaving Cobham.

He read it quickly, as if he'd seen the words before. He nodded briskly.

'You've read the play?' she asked. 'Is there another copy somewhere?'

'No. But Eastbridge has a transcript of these words. Nothing more.'

She considered this. 'Do you understand what it means?' she asked. 'Does it lead to the hidden burial place?'

He dipped his head in acknowledgement.

'I should like to know. Now that I am so close to what Richard wanted to find out.'

He stood and walked to the windows. 'Helen, I cannot tell you. I am sworn to keep the secret. But you are very close. After... after what happened to Richard, I will not stand in your way. Tell me what you need to complete your task.'

She thought for a moment. Our English poet; where

369

pilgrims paused; the mauncipel's tale.

'I need a copy of *The Canterbury Tales*,' she said.

He led her upstairs to the whitewashed chapel. It was plain and peaceful. Above her head, dark beams ribbed the ceiling like timbers from an upturned boat. The unadorned wooden pews made it easy to imagine the place as a school room, perhaps one that had contained the irrepressible energy of the boy Christopher Marlowe, learning his letters. Charles motioned her to a seat while he unlocked a cupboard at the back of the room. Moments later, he put a copy of the *Complete Chaucer* into her hands.

'Evensong will begin in three quarters of an hour,' he said. 'You will be undisturbed for half an hour at least.' He withdrew, quietly closing the door.

He had made no demands, Helen noticed. She had expected him to strike the bargain that she had half-suggested: that she make no mention of the epilogue when she prepare her edition of the play. It would be easy to do. To lose the last pages of the manuscript, to finish the play with Becket's cry as the swordsmen broke through the door. It would be better, dramatically. It would allow the bones of Thomas Becket to continue to rest in peace, wherever the monks had buried him, four centuries ago. But it would be dishonest.

She turned to the volume in her hands. Had Marlowe first read Chaucer's *Canterbury Tales* in this very room? she wondered. She leafed through to the general prologue, which she would now hear forever in Richard's voice. It introduced the pilgrims, one by one, as they set off from Southwark's Tabard Inn on their journey to Canterbury. Was there a mauncipel among them?

She found him at the end of the general prologue: 'A gentil

mauncipel was ther of a temple.' A maunciple, or manciple
as it was in modern spelling, she read in the notes, was the
officer who bought provisions for an inn of court, college
or monastery: in this case, probably London's Temple Inn.
The mauncipel in the Tales was financially shrewd, always
coming ahead in his accounts and making money out of his
clients. He would be one of the last characters to tell his story,
speaking as the pilgrims approached Canterbury, she read.

With a prickle of excitement, she turned the pages to the
prologue before his tale.

'Wot ye not where there stont a little toun
Which that cleped is Bob-up-and-down
Under the Ble, in Canterbury way?'

A little town under the Ble? Her eyes darted to the notes
underneath the text. 'The little town is generally agreed to be
Harbledown, a village on the outskirts of Canterbury in the
forest of Blean,' she read. She noted with a thrill the use of
the archaic word 'cleped', meaning named. 'Our English poet
cleped the place full well' Marlowe had written. The notes
explained that Chaucer's 'Bob-up-and-down' referred to the
steep hills on which the village was built. Marlowe, Helen
thought, would have known the topography of Canterbury
and its surrounding villages intimately.

She read on. The verse continued with a scene of robust
medieval clowning. The pilgrims paused in the little town for
the cook to tell his tale, but the man was too drunk to speak
clearly and fell off his horse, at which point the mauncipel
took over. *Where pilgrims paused. There the mauncipel began his
tale.* Everything in Marlowe's epilogue fitted. Harbledown,
she felt sure, was the place that Marlowe had meant.

But where to look in Harbledown? She read over her

transcript of Marlowe's verse. Only one line was unexplained: *where Henry penance did and alms bestow'd.* A church, perhaps, or an almshouse? She took the volume of Chaucer and replaced it in the cupboard at the back of the chapel, incongruous among the hymn books and orders of service. It was a quarter to five; soon the members of the foundation would arrive for their service. She slipped out of the door and down the stairs to the street.

Outside, the sun still shone. She squinted in the bright light, feeling it warm the bare nape of her neck as she strolled up the high street in the direction of the cathedral, losing herself in the tourist crowd. No one knew where she was. Charlotte had gone home after dropping her by the West Gate of the city. She was properly alone for the first time since they'd found her on the golf course. She relaxed into the feeling, the freedom of anonymity. She wondered briefly whether the police had caught the man who kidnapped her. The policeman who interviewed her at Cobham had told her that they would search the area, set up road blocks.

But she felt a million miles away from the girl she had been last night. Her elegant, masculine clothes gave her confidence. She felt unencumbered, her steps light as she walked towards the great cathedral, its pale stone rising in majesty above the rooftops of the surrounding streets.

Beside the gate house she saw what she had been looking for. The cathedral shop, doing a roaring trade in replica medieval pilgrim badges, mugs, T-shirts and postcards. She stepped inside, jostled by groups of foreign visitors, and reflected that little had changed in eight hundred years. Canterbury was still making a good living from the pilgrims who came to see where its archbishop had been martyred.

She headed for the books section. There were guidebooks, biographies, books about Christianity, and archaeological guides to the cathedral. She browsed among the stacks, looking for local history. Turning her head, she jumped, thinking she had seen Father Nash's familiar face in the crowd. Yet when she looked again, she realised it was his photograph: a poster announcing that he would be signing copies of his soon-to-be-published memoir at the shop. She pushed aside her little grab of guilt. She wondered if her absence from Cobham Hall had been noticed. She was free to come and go as she pleased, she reminded herself, without asking permission from anyone. Although it might have been courteous to tell them when she left.

Eventually, she found something tucked away on a high shelf that looked promising. It was a modest pamphlet published by a local history society, with black-and-white photographs. *The Almshouses and Religious Foundations of Canterbury.* She wondered whether they sold many copies. She went straight to the index and looked up the village. 'Harbledown, the hospital of Saint Nicholas,' she read. The man at the welcome desk at Eastbridge had talked of the vicar coming down from Saint Nicholas, she remembered. Quickly, she turned the pages. There was a blurred photograph of a long, sloped tile roof, above a lawn.

'Saint Nicholas Church and Leper Hospital was established in the eleventh century by Archbishop Lanfranc,' said the text. 'In 1172, King Henry II prayed in the church before walking barefoot to Canterbury to do penance for the murder of Thomas Becket, Archbishop of Canterbury. The King made a bequest to St Nicholas' of twenty silver marks a year.' This was the one.

'Since the dreaded scourge of leprosy died out in the fourteenth century, the establishment has provided shelter to the elderly and poor of the parish as almshouses. It is under the same jurisdiction as Eastbridge Hospital in Canterbury High Street,' the book continued.

She closed the book and set it down. The monks of Canterbury Cathedral had found a fitting place to hide the relics of their beloved saint. And the twin foundations of Eastbridge and Harbledown had worked together to keep him safe down the centuries. Marlowe's epilogue was unmistakable to anyone who knew Canterbury well. She had no doubt that Richard would have deciphered it in seconds. Whoever had the play had the secret. No wonder Eastbridge had wanted it suppressed.

She picked up a guidebook to Canterbury and its environs and looked up Harbledown on the map. The village was less than two miles from the city centre. She traced a route back through the city streets to the West Gate, along the riverside walk and then across to the main London-bound road. It would not take long.

Outside, she returned past Eastbridge Hospital, hearing the sound of music from the chapel windows upstairs. Inside, she supposed, Charles would be at prayer, celebrating evensong. Knowing that she possessed the secret that he had tried so hard to keep hidden. And wondering, as she herself wondered, what she would do with it.

Absorbed in thought, she did not see the man who stood in the doorway of the shop opposite watching her. He had blood on his shoes.

Chapter 60

The police car drew up outside the hall. Plumes of black smoke rose from the building, drifting from the lower windows. The air was acrid, the taste bitter in Nick's mouth.

'Stay here,' said DCI Greenley, jumping from the car. 'I mean it.' She ran across the gravel drive.

He looked at Meena. 'Come on,' she said, undoing his seatbelt. She'd fixed his hand in a sling around his neck. 'Lean on me if you need to.'

His legs felt unreliable, divorced from the rest of his body. But he struggled out of the car and they followed the policewoman around the building.

She was heading for the green door with the broken window pane. The boot room, he remembered, where Lady Joan had threatened him with her shotgun. As DCI Greenley reached it, a woman stumbled out, her face blackened with smoke. She fell to her hands and knees on the gravel and vomited.

'Helen!' he yelled. But already Nick could see it wasn't her.

Charlotte Elms looked up, tears streaking grubby tracks through the soot. Her cream blouse was stained with what looked like blood. She wiped her mouth with the back of her hand. Nick knelt on the ground next to her.

'She's dead,' she gasped and began to cough. She spat a mouthful of black liquid.

'Helen?' Cold despair ran through him. They'd come too late. If only he'd managed somehow to get out earlier, if only he'd not followed that bastard priest down to the crypt.

She shook her head. 'Lady Joan. She's been shot. It's all...' She gestured to her face. 'It's all gone.'

DCI Greenley, face grim, took Charlotte's shoulder. 'Who is in the building?' she asked, urgently. Fire engines were crunching over the gravel now, four of them with lights flashing.

'Only Lady Joan. I took Helen to Canterbury. And Father Nash has gone.'

'Staff?'

'I was the last to leave. The kitchen staff had gone home. I don't know why I came back, really. Something was bothering me. I'd been talking to Lady Joan about changing her will. I wanted to see if she was alright.'

While they talked, Meena edged closer to the doorway. Nick saw her reel away, hand clasped over her mouth.

'Keep away from there,' yelled the policewoman. 'Live crime scene. I mean it. No one goes in there. Do you hear me?'

She strode over to the fire crews, approaching over the lawns with hoses dragging behind them.

Meena sat back down beside Charlotte, her lips pale. 'Did you find her like that?'

Charlotte nodded. 'I parked round the side. Father Nash's car was still there. I walked round the back way. I don't know why. Like I said, I felt anxious.'

She wiped a hand across her eyes, leaving streaks of dirt.

'I heard shouting, and someone screamed. Then there was a shot. I ran to the boot room. I knew that's where the guns were kept, of course. I thought maybe there had been an accident. Lady Joan likes to get the guns out and clean them herself.'

She swallowed. 'She was alone, next to the gun. I tried CPR, but it was hopeless. Blood all over the place. Other stuff… brains I suppose. Up the walls. I rang 999. Then I smelled burning.'

Charlotte had ventured into the hall to see where the fire was coming from. 'It was just a smell, like burnt toast. I was worried that Father Nash was still in there. I shouted for him, went to the library where I last saw him. But then I opened the office door and the smoke poured out.'

She rubbed her eyes. 'The play, Nick. Helen found the play. After you left this morning. She was working on it in the office. Father Nash was angry because of what it said about Thomas Becket. He must have started the fire – to destroy it. I saw him, then, through the window. He was driving off in his car.'

'What?' Meena was on her feet. 'The play they were looking for, this Marlowe play? It's still in that building?'

Smoke was pouring from the windows now, billowing in thick clouds. Nick could feel the heat on his face. Charlotte Elms nodded, her face wretched.

'I did what I could. I got a couple of jugs of water and chucked them in. But the fire had taken hold by then.' She paused. 'All I could think of was that lovely Chinese wallpaper blistering off the walls.'

'Where is it?'

'Meena, no.' Nick managed to get the words out. 'Don't be

a dick.'

Charlotte got to her feet. 'The window was open. We could take a look. It's round this way.'

Bloody hell. Nick struggled along with them. Why were all the women he met determined to get themselves killed? It made a change from the men who wanted to kill him, he supposed. They came to a garden crowded with weird creatures carved out of bushes. Smoke swirled around them, giving the whole scene an air of nightmare. The fire was roaring now, the twisted brick chimney stacks shooting out flames. Nick began to worry that the whole hall would collapse.

'This one,' said Charlotte. They stood under the window. Grey smoke poured over the sill like water.

'This is stupid,' he shouted. 'Meena, for God's sake.' She had pulled her headscarf around her mouth and nose and was dragging a stone bench over to the window. Before he knew it, she'd scrambled into the room.

'You're bloody mad,' he yelled after her.

He stood on the bench and peered into the gloom. He couldn't see anything in there. His hand was hurting, his head was hurting, and now his eyes and throat were stinging with the smoke. He could hardly hear anything beyond the fire's roar.

Pulling the fabric from his sling across his nose, he sat on the window sill and swung his legs in.

'Meena!' He couldn't see her. He dropped to the floor and inched forward on his knees, groping his way with his one good hand. It was hot, and the smoke made him want to throw up. *Keep going forward*, he told himself. *Don't get disorientated.*

His hand touched something. A denim-clad leg, which

immediately kicked back. He pulled. Something scrabbled around in the smoke, then her face loomed up at him, eyes streaming. 'I couldn't find my way back.' She started to cough.

'Come with me. Hang onto my shirt.'

There was a rumbling overhead, and something shattered on the floor next to him. 'Christ! Are you OK?'

She loomed into his sight again, a cut across her face. 'Bloody chandelier,' she shouted. 'Get us out of here, Nick.'

He crawled backwards, feeling his way. It took longer than he remembered. For a sickening moment, he thought they were lost. He started coughing, felt the burning air sear deep into his lungs. He stopped, tears streaming from his eyes. Which way?

He felt a draught of cool air away to the left of him.

The open window. With his good arm, he pushed Meena up to the sill and watched her tumble from it. Finally, he dragged himself up. He sat for a second, looking back into the room. He couldn't even see the desk. There was no chance of getting to it, never mind rescuing any papers that might be on it. Another rumbling. Hastily, he swung his leg over the window frame. This time the crash brought down the whole ceiling, plaster and slats of burning wood sending a shower of sparks and dust out of the window, blinding him as he rolled to the ground.

Chapter 61

Helen stood at the lychgate, catching her breath from the walk up the steep hill into Harbledown. Birdsong sounded in the trees. A smooth stretch of green lawn, punctuated with cheerful daffodils, clothed the slope up to the church. Facing the church, a row of low, flint-built almshouses basked in the mellow evening sun, like something out of Tolkien's Shire. An elderly gentleman had set a picnic chair outside his front door and was reading a newspaper. A woman knelt before a little garden, easing new plants into the earth with her trowel. It looked like paradise. Helen was reluctant to intrude.

She gazed at the church looming above them. It had the quiet dignity of extreme old age. The building was simple: a high gable and a square tower built of flint and limestone. How many pilgrims had stopped at the church, given alms to the lepers and said one last prayer, before turning their steps east to the glory of Canterbury Cathedral?

The newspaper-reading man turned a page and saw her standing in the gateway. 'Can I help you?' he called, struggling out of his picnic chair.

Helen hurried over. 'Please don't get up. I was just wondering if I could see inside the church.'

The man sat back. He wore a neatly pressed shirt and tie, his jacket hanging on the back of the chair. His gaze was mild, but Helen had the feeling he was taking in everything about her, from her roughly cropped hair to her elegant calfskin brogues.

'Where have you come from?' he asked.

'I walked up from Canterbury.' He raised an eyebrow, as if waiting for something else. She thought for a minute. 'From Eastbridge Hospital? I spoke to the master.'

'Ah.' He folded the newspaper and placed it on the ground. 'She's come,' he called to the gardening lady. The woman straightened up and smiled at Helen, bright blue eyes below a blunt fringe of white hair. She dug into her basket of gardening tools and pulled out an enormous iron key.

'Good for you,' she said, with an impish smile. 'We don't get many pilgrims, nowadays. The master said you might find us.'

They walked slowly up the slope. The woman fitted the key to the iron-studded door. Helen reached out and pushed against the sun-warmed timber. Stepping over the threshold into the cool stone interior, she felt the deep peace ripple with their entry, then settle, absorbing their quiet presence.

The church was simple and lovely. Thick flint walls were rendered in creamy plaster with limestone pillars punctuating the uneven red tiles of the floor. At the altar, wall paintings in faded reds and blues emerged like ghosts from the walls. Traces of blue flowers wound around one window. Two figures in red robes stood sentry either side, giving a hint of how colourful the church must have looked hundreds of years ago before the Puritans stripped England's churches of their icons.

Had Richard already been here? Helen wondered. Perhaps he had visited the church as part of his survey of Canterbury's ecclesiastical history. She imagined him striding around, expounding on the imagery of the paintings. The blue flowers – Canterbury bells, she thought, with a sudden smile of recognition. Campanula, the flower of Thomas Becket. Everything connected down the centuries.

She circled the church while the woman waited silently at the door. She came at last to a small side chapel. Saint Thomas' chapel, with a red martyr's lamp hanging above the altar. A big Turkish rug lay before the altar rail. Helen paused, took in the implications. This, surely, was Thomas Becket's final resting place, hidden in plain sight to those who knew. She drew back the carpet.

Beneath, a long slab of stone. Incised upon it, two symbols. As one might expect, a cross, worn shallow over the centuries. At the head of the cross, a crescent moon, pointing upwards.

She turned to the old woman. 'Here?'

The woman nodded, a smile breaking across her lined face.

Helen sat before the stone, musing. The woman came and sat next to her.

'The crescent moon?' Helen asked.

'A very ancient symbol,' she said. 'With many meanings.'

Helen pulled out her notebook and found her transcript of Becket's final speech. 'This confused me. It's from the Marlowe play – Becket's final speech. What does it mean?'

The woman took the book, her eyes sparkling. 'How exciting. I've dreamed of finding this, you know. Sir Albert spent years trying to break the code.' She read the words aloud. Her voice was warm, as lively as her face.

'What says my sacred Alcoran of death?

That none shall die but of Mahomet's will.
As Cynthia's pride declines, so Becket sees
The crescent rise high in the firmament.'

She turned her bright eyes on Helen. 'What do you think it means?'

Helen shrugged. 'It sounds like Becket consulting a copy of the Quran. But that makes no sense.'

'Doesn't it?'

Helen saw that impish smile again.

'Saint Thomas Becket spent five years in France, exiled from England. It was an interesting time for European Christendom. Half of Spain was under Muslim rule. The second crusade had just failed, the Catholic Church was split between two popes and the Cathars were gaining support for their supposed heresy in the Languedoc. All the old certainties were being questioned.'

Who are you? Helen wanted to ask. How do you know all this?

The woman patted her hand and answered as if she had heard Helen's thoughts. 'I was married to the last master of Eastbridge. Since his death, I have been here, living in the almshouses. Reading, thinking, learning. Like the monks from Cluny Abbey, who made the first Latin translation of the Quran in the twelfth century, fifteen years before Becket arrived in France. And the European scholars who travelled to Cordoba and Constantinople to make Latin translations of Arab texts.

'Becket became a great student of devotional texts during his time at Pontigny Abbey, but he was sometimes criticised for not concentrating enough on Christian works. Read John of Salisbury's letters to Becket.'

She turned again to the book. 'None shall die but of Mahomet's will. Well, the Quran says that no one shall die unless Allah wills it. This muddles the prophet with Allah. But the general idea is correct. What about Cynthia?'

Helen thought again of the little drawing of the crescent moon, which had given her the code word to decipher Raleigh's secret message.

'Walter Raleigh wrote a poem which addresses Queen Elizabeth as Cynthia, goddess of the moon. As the moon wanes, it becomes a crescent.'

'True. But a crescent moon is also a sign of Islam and has been associated with that faith since the Crusades. It was a double symbol for Raleigh and his circle. It could suggest Elizabeth's power was waning and the Ottoman Empire was on the rise. But this is Saint Thomas Becket speaking. So perhaps it means the Islamic faith is supplanting the fractured Christian world of the twelfth century.'

Helen shook her head. 'Are you saying that Saint Thomas Becket converted to Islam? In reality, I mean, not just in the play?'

The woman held Helen's eyes, her face kind. 'Well, he was buried with a copy of the Quran in his hands. The monks found it when they moved his body. I believe that Saint Thomas Becket was only one early convert in the church. There were many others. Look at the work of the monk Herbert of Bosham, one of Becket's closest friends, and the way he wrote about the Psalms. His history of Saint Thomas is kept at Corpus Christi College, you know.'

'Marlowe's college,' said Helen.

'Indeed. And with many close links to Eastbridge Hospital. The manuscript is badly damaged. You may well ask what happened to the pages of Herbert's text that were destroyed, and what they could have told us.'

Helen traced the words in her notebook again. 'Marlowe knew this. And was ready to tell the world. No wonder there were people who wanted to keep it quiet.' She thought of what this discovery might do to someone like Father Nash, whose entire life was inspired by Becket's example of defiant Christianity.

'My dear child, Thomas Becket didn't come back to England to make peace with Henry. He came back to convert England to Islam.' The woman's blue eyes held hers, their expression mild. Despite her words, Helen thought she had rarely met anyone who seemed more sane.

'Eastbridge knew this and kept the knowledge secret. Sir Albert knew and kept his own counsel. And now you know too,' she said. 'I'll leave you to think about what to do with that knowledge.' Quietly, she walked out of the church.

Helen stared at the stone slab before her with its double symbol. Was it a tacit acknowledgement of Becket's conversion? Crowds had lined the streets of Kent to welcome the saint's return from exile. Would they have followed him had he declared himself a Muslim? An alternative English history shimmered at the edges of her imagination, one in which Norman cathedrals converted to mosques, the towers of England's parish churches became minarets, bells ringing out across the green fields and villages were replaced by the call to prayer. Christianity, she reminded herself, had also been a Middle Eastern import, brought to England from Palestine by Romans and Celts. Only with the passing of time had it come to seem like the natural order of things.

She thought of the monks in Henry VIII's time, uncovering

the coffin of their beloved saint to preserve his relics. What did they think when they found the Quran in the coffin? Was it a shock to them, or did they already know? Whatever their private thoughts, they brought him here, perhaps at night, for a hasty reburial ahead of the arrival of the King's men in Canterbury. She knelt on the cold stone and traced the lines of the crescent moon. Which stonemason had inscribed it, and had he known the significance of his commission? Who had ordered this symbol to be placed here? The lines were deep and sure, worn as the cross was worn. The two symbols had been carved by the same hand at the same time. With a pang, she wondered whether Richard had ever seen this gravestone. She hoped he had, even if he had not known its significance.

Helen lit a candle, adding it to the array of little flames burning below the red lamp. For Richard, who set her on the path that brought her here. The flame flickered, then settled to a steady glow.

Carefully, she replaced the rug. She imagined for a moment this tranquil haven invaded by news cameras and workmen, the stone slab lifted, the bones sifted and photographed, carbon-dated. The discovery of a centuries-old copy of the Quran, possibly the first to enter Britain. A huge, divisive argument about reburial in Canterbury Cathedral and whether the saint was truly Christian. She touched her hand to the transcript of Marlowe's epilogue in her jacket pocket. It was in her power, she thought. She could let the chapel keep its own secrets.

She rose and walked again to the main altar to say a last farewell to the church. She heard the latch lifting and the creak of a heavy door. The woman with the key, she supposed.

Time up.

'I'm just coming,' she called.

'Helen.'

She turned quickly to see Father Francis Nash walking down the central aisle towards her.

Chapter 62

His round face was pink with exertion above his black cassock, rivulets of sweat escaping from his chestnut curls and onto his forehead. His smile was absent; instead, his plump lower lip jutted like an angry child.

How had he found her? Her thoughts darted to the manuscript she'd left at Cobham Hall. Had he somehow managed to read it, decipher the epilogue and follow the clues here? If so, the decision was out of her hands. Father Nash would not let the bones rest in peace.

'Hello. This is a surprise,' she said.

'Where is it?'

'Where is what?' she retorted, stupidly.

'You lied to me, Helen. You deliberately lied to divert me from God's work.'

She stared. His tone was light, as if his accusations were merely small talk.

'I... what do you mean? I haven't lied. I haven't said anything.' She could hear her voice rising in pitch as her throat tightened. Her face flushed hot, betraying her own feelings of guilt. Had he seen the computer file with her partial transcript of the play? Or was he talking about her trip into Canterbury without him?

'You set out to deceive me. You claimed to have read no more than the first scene of the play, yet you had read it all. Hadn't you?'

'Well, I skimmed through…'

'Stop. Don't make it worse. You conspired against me, you and the Elms woman. And Lady Joan connived with your lies. You obstructed the work of God, and that is a grave sin.'

He was close to her now, so close she could feel the heat pouring off him. Startled, she saw what looked like blood stains on his white cuffs under his cassock. She backed away. He shot out a hand and grasped her wrist, pulling her close.

'Do you know what comes of sin, Helen? The wages of sin?'

What madness had possessed the man?

'Death. For the wages of sin is death, for you and all the legions of she-devils and whores, deceivers and liars, undermining the work of the Lord.' He dropped his voice, pressing his hot cheek against hers. She shuddered at the touch of his oily skin. She could smell rank sweat, the copper tang of dried blood.

'I trusted you. I had plans for you. I would have raised you up, given you a place by my side. But you betrayed me. You were Richard's whore. I should have destroyed you along with him.'

She stared at him. 'You? You killed Richard?'

He ignored her question. 'You will not speak. You will not use your manipulating lies. You know the sacred resting place. You were with Charles Fairfax at Eastbridge. I saw you there. Fairfax knows too. I will deal with him as the Lord dealt with the sinners of Sodom. But now you will take me to the place where Saint Thomas is buried.'

The contrast between his mild tone and the madness of his

words frightened Helen more than if he'd shouted and raved. Was it possible that the charming, media-friendly priest was responsible for Richard's murder? She thought of the stone slab under the rug in the chapel with its tell-tale symbols. If the man looked around the church, he would find it. Could she distract him from it, at least for now? If there was one last thing she could do for Richard, it was to keep the secret from his killer.

'Father Nash,' she said, trying to control the tremor in her voice, 'you have blood on your shirt cuffs. Are you hurt?'

He looked at the bloodstains as if for the first time. He wrinkled his nose. 'It's not mine.' He raised his eyes to hers and she saw they were glazed, as if he barely saw what was around him. 'An accident,' he said. 'It doesn't matter.'

An accident. *Dear God, whose blood had he spilt now?* She wondered if she could break free of his grip and get to the church door before him. She could call for the woman to help, lock him in, call the police…

'Do not think anyone will help you.' His hand was suddenly at her throat, caressing the silk scarf that hid her burns. She flinched as he pulled the fabric tight around her wounds.

'Lady Joan can't protect you any more, Helen. She killed herself, like she killed that boy. Her brother isn't going to take the blame this time.'

'Father Nash…' Helen was bewildered. What on earth did the man mean?

His face was convulsed with disgust. 'An impure woman coupling with a sodomite. How could any good have come from that unholy union? And still she tried to protect her bastard, to keep me away from his precious work. I tried, you know. You were there, weren't you, Helen? If she and

Richard had agreed to help me, to let me work with them, they would still be alive today.'

'What do you mean, Father Nash? Is Lady Joan dead?' She tried to back away, glancing again at the blood on his shirt sleeves.

'She paid the price of being an obstacle to God's will. As Richard did. As you will, if you try to distract me again. Take me to the place.'

Helen struggled to make sense of the flood of words. But she knew one thing: she would not give up the saint's resting place.

She was filled with cold determination. This man thought her deceitful; she would prove it. She would promise him everything he wanted, then watch him fool himself.

'The wall paintings,' she said. He turned to look at the figures decorating the niches behind the altar. He led her there by her scarf, like a dog on a lead.

'Look at the flowers. Campanula. The bell flower, or Canterbury bells. Symbols of Thomas Becket.' She tried to sound as if she knew what she was talking about.

'Are you playing games again?'

'Did you read the epilogue?' She took a gamble that he would not have deciphered it fully. 'The line about the bells sounding out around his resting place?'

'Show me the words.' He pulled the final page of the manuscript from his pocket, creased and damaged at the edges. Helen stared in dismay.

'Father Nash, this is a precious document. It shouldn't be carried around like that. Where is the rest of the play?'

His smile was cruel. 'It was filth. I did what one should do with blasphemy. I burned it.'

'No!' She stared at him in horror. He didn't mean it, surely. 'You can't have done. You're making it up.' His smile was maddening. Why hadn't she insisted on calling the British Library and had it taken into safekeeping at once? Her own pride, her greed at having the play to herself, had stopped her.

'I kept the important part,' he said. 'The Lord bid me to take the fruit and throw away the stone.' He twisted the scarf again. 'Now, what were you saying about the bells?'

Helen was so angry she could barely think. This man, this stupid, evil man. First he took Richard, then Marlowe's play. Despite her grief, she felt the loss of the play as almost more of an outrage. To deprive humanity of such a masterpiece forever. It was an act of profound evil. And his smug assertion that he had kept the important part, the trivial verses of the epilogue. She could not conceive of a mind that could miss the enormous aesthetic achievement of a Marlowe play simply because he didn't agree with its message. She wanted to show him how stupid, how wrong he had been.

'If you've read it, you'll know about Becket's conversion,' she said, impetuously. 'How he became a Muslim in his exile and returned to bring Islam to Britain. Is that the truth you want to uncover?'

He stared at her in horror, then turned again to the manuscript in his hand. 'It's a lie. This whole filthy play, a tissue of lies.'

She shrugged. 'If you believe that, then you've nothing to fear, have you? Marlowe says that Becket was buried with a copy of the Quran, but if you think he was lying, there's nothing to worry about. Shall we go and look?'

She turned her head cautiously, still tethered by the scarf.

His face was congested with blood, the flesh swollen and slicked with sweat. His eyes were small, almost lost. They peered out at her, filled with a desperate, child-like longing. He'd destroyed her world. Now she took a vindictive pleasure in bringing down his most treasured beliefs.

'Show me.' His voice trembled.

She took a deep breath. Despite her words, she did not want to expose the saint's funeral slab to Nash's destructive impulses. She tried to pick up the thread of what she'd been saying about the wall paintings. The bells. She looked towards the bell tower at the corner of the church, where a wooden staircase led upwards. Her eye was caught by a sign at the bottom of the stairs, warning that they were dangerous and should not be used.

'The bell tower. They hid his bones in the tower, surrounded by the sound of Canterbury bells,' she improvised. A tentative plan had begun to form in her mind. Could she trap him up there and call the police?

'Look, that's the entrance to the bell-ringers' loft. They want to stop people going up there. Why would they do that? What are they hiding? Let's find out if Becket really is holding a copy of the Quran.'

With Nash still gripping the scarf tightly, they moved towards the stairs. At their foot, he turned her to face him. Helen was assailed by a memory of the classroom, of a fat, bullied boy she had taught. She shivered. The boy had finally snapped and plunged a sharpened pencil right through the hand of his chief tormentor.

'If you are deceiving me again, Helen, you will find no mercy. Not in this world or the next.'

'I'm trying to help you,' she told him. 'Trust me.' Somewhere in his lonely heart, she thought, he wanted to believe her.

'Go on then. You first.'

She put a foot on the bottom step and grasped the hand rail. The dark wood was worn by age and riddled with woodworm. Here and there it had been patched up where someone had filled in missing stair treads and reinforced the rail. But the whole structure felt precarious. Slowly, she began to ascend. The staircase led to a wooden hatch in the ceiling. She stopped and pushed.

'It's stuck, or locked,' she called. He was close behind her, straining impatiently to see.

If she took him by surprise, she realised, she could kick him off the stairs. She imagined how he would fly backwards, scrabbling into the air, breaking his neck as he landed on the tiled floor.

'Let me see.'

She stared at him. Could she do it? This man would have no compunction in killing her as soon as she was of no further use. He had murdered Richard, destroyed the only copy of Marlowe's last play. Would the world not be better without him? Her hand tightened on the rail.

She could not do it, despite her anger, her loathing for what he had done. She did not want him to live, but she could not take his life. With an upwelling of nausea, she blinked her thoughts away and turned to the hatch. She heaved, braced against the stair rail. It shifted an inch, then stuck again.

'I think it's coming. I felt it move,' she told him.

He pushed up the stairs, jostling her aside, and put his shoulder to the wooden boards. With a shout he crashed against them, bursting the hatch open. He lost his footing on the slippery old steps and began to slide.

'Help me!' he screamed.

She grabbed the priest's robes, digging her fingers into the cotton. The loose cassock went over his head before catching under his arms and arresting his fall. His weight pulled her down and she felt the bannister shift. With one hand, she grabbed at the open hatchway into the loft to steady herself. But the whole wooden structure began to creak and move beneath her feet.

'Father Nash, get down! The staircase is collapsing.'

He was on his hands and knees, pulling the black cassock off and dropping it into the void. His white shirt was flecked with blood. He began to climb. The wooden treads started to come away from the wall.

'Get down now!' She grasped the edges of the hatch and hauled herself inside. He was still crawling upward when the bannister came loose and crashed into the nave. The stair treads twisted sideways with nothing to hold them in place. Nash reached up, his hand almost within her grasp. She saw the desperation in his face. And she hesitated, a second too long.

Screaming, the priest fell into the nave with dark timbers crashing about him. Wooden beams hit the tiled floor with a thunderous clatter, bouncing into the pews. The scream stopped as he hit the ground. Timbers piled up on his body until all Helen could see was one leg, sticking out from the heap of debris.

She watched in silence, lying on the floor of the bell-ringers' loft. Was he dead? She felt the echo of the long second when he reached out his hand and she watched him fall. It would live within her, a heartbeat when she chose to let him die.

And yet he might not be dead. She had a chance to do

395

something, to call for help. She sat back up, looked around the dim and dusty loft. There was one narrow, tall window, glazed with small panes of leaded glass. Across one wall were a line of ropes – the bell ropes, she realised, leading up from the bell pulls now on the ground floor. She seized one and pulled it down as hard as she could. For a second, nothing happened. Then a loud clanging began, discordant and deafening above her head.

She ran to the hatchway and lay down, looking into the church. A moment later, the door opened. It was the white-haired old lady.

'My goodness!' She hurried over to the heap of wood, then called to someone out of sight. 'It's him. Francis Nash.'

The old man walked slowly across the church. He moved a piece of wood from Nash's face. 'Dead.'

He gazed around the church. 'Young lady! Where are you? Are you alright?'

She leaned through the hatch. 'I'm up here.'

'Are you hurt?'

'No,' she said. 'I'm fine. I'm – I'm sorry.'

But she wasn't really, she thought. She was not sorry at all.

Chapter 63

The Gilt Hall, sparkling in white and gold, had escaped the fire that all but destroyed the west wing of Cobham Hall. It was packed with people from Lady Joan's funeral in smart dark suits and dignified frocks. They squawked like parakeets, avid for a look around the hall and a gossip about what had really happened to Lady Joan. Most of the village had turned out, along with anxious-looking company employees, no doubt worrying about what would happen to Brooke Estates now that Lady Joan was dead.

Nick stood in a corner, his arm still in a sling, wondering who to talk to first. He'd walked down from the church with Helen, who stood silently beside him. The service had been given by a somewhat overwhelmed curate who was clearly short of nice things to say about Lady Joan. Father Nash had yet to be replaced by a permanent vicar. Nick's latest scoop was that the Archbishop of Canterbury had demanded an inquiry into the affairs of the diocese as alarming news emerged about the links between Nash's Christianity in Crisis and the hoodlums of the English Martyrs Brigade.

Nick had spent time in the village before the funeral getting chatty with the bar staff in the three pubs and the shop. He'd decided he quite liked the countryside. People tended to be friendlier than in the suburbs, once they got over the shock of seeing a non-white face. Opinion was divided about Lady Joan's death. Those who had seen her waving shotguns about before were adamant she'd shot herself, by accident or design. Others blamed 'that mad priest' who had started the fire.

According to Nick's sources, the blood on Nash's shirt showed he'd been there when the fatal gunshot was fired. The gun carried fingerprints from both Nash and Lady Joan, making it difficult to be sure who had pulled the trigger. But Nick knew who he blamed and said as much in his newspaper articles. There was no libelling the dead, after all.

As far as they could tell, Nash had found Helen's computer file with her partial transcript of the play and worked out from her browser history that she had gone to Eastbridge Hospital. At Eastbridge, he'd spoken to Charles Fairfax, who was adamant he had told him nothing about Helen's destination. But CCTV footage from Canterbury High Street showed that Nash had simply followed Helen to Harbledown.

Helen's account of what happened in the church leading up to his fatal fall was not particularly coherent. Nor had she told Nick why she'd gone to the church, although he was hoping she would crack eventually. There would be an inquest, of course, into the priest's death. Maybe he would learn more then.

Nick could see Meena working the room, chatting away to the bishop as if they were old mates. He caught glimpses of Charlotte Elms, back to her usual glossy self, making introductions and smoothing over arguments. He thought of the last time he'd seen her, covered in soot as they ran for the trees when the west wing of the hall collapsed. As the three of them had lain on the grass, watching the inferno,

Meena had pulled a bundle of charred paper from under her sweatshirt. The manuscript of the missing Marlowe play, or what remained of it.

The play was badly damaged, but not irretrievable. With Helen's notes, the British Library had hopes that a decent reconstruction of the text would be possible. The discovery and near-destruction of the missing Marlowe play had the academic world and the more serious end of the newspapers in a frenzy of excitement.

Lady Joan's will had been the next surprise. In an amendment written just after Christmas, she'd left everything – the hall and all its contents, her majority shareholding in Brooke Estates – to Richard Watson, who she described as 'my natural son'.

The scandal had delighted the press and Nick had found himself much in demand as a source of information about both Lady Joan and the Watson murder. He'd also found himself acting as an unofficial spokesman and protector for Helen, who'd been under media siege for weeks. He'd teased her once about how, if she'd married Richard, she could now be the mistress of Cobham Hall. But her distress had been such that he wished he'd never made the joke.

Things had moved fast for Nick. The full story would have to wait until after Paxton's trial for Richard's murder and for abducting and torturing Helen. Nick's recording of Paxton's confession while they were trapped together in the crypt would form an important part of the prosecution case. However, Nick had been able to file tantalising stories packed with inside detail about the deaths of Lady Joan and Francis Nash, the links between the church and the far right and the drama of how he and Meena saved the rediscovered play.

The *South London Courier* had scooped the national press time after time. The nationals had come knocking and Nick was considering a number of tempting offers.

'I should be interviewing people,' he said to Helen, not budging. 'Jesus, though. Will you look at them all? They've not enjoyed themselves this much for years.'

They stood in silence, fanned by the breeze from the French doors. It was the hottest day of the summer so far. Nick glanced at Helen's severe profile. Her face no longer had the impulsive, open smile that he remembered from his first interview with her, when she'd taken him on her tour of Deptford's historic waterfront. She'd kept her hair short. It was brushed back from her face, accentuating her sharp cheekbones and straight nose. He thought she had lost weight. She wore a plain white shirt tucked into black trousers that made her legs look endlessly long.

It was hard to believe that this reserved, silent woman was the same girl who had shinned down a drainpipe, jumped on his motorbike and dragged him off to graveyards to hunt for hidden messages.

She'd moved back into her Greenwich flat and spent a lot of time with Crispin, now home from hospital but very frail. She had recently re-started her tourist walks around Bankside. Her notoriety as the woman who discovered Marlowe's last play meant they were always sold out. The rest of the time she worked with the conservation team at the British Library, trying to piece together the lost text from the damaged manuscript.

He spotted the caterers coming in from the kitchens with trays of canapés. Food. Food was always good. Maybe he could get Helen to eat something.

'Back in a sec.' He weaved his way through the crowd, leaving her with her thoughts.

Chapter 64

Helen gazed up at the gilt cherubs and musical instruments that decorated the walls and ceilings. No one seemed to know what would happen to Cobham Hall now. Representatives from the National Trust hovered eagerly. She could see the man from the trust, deep in conversation with the Brooke family solicitor. With Richard dead and no descendant, the situation was unclear. There was talk of the hall becoming a hotel or conference centre.

She tried to imagine Richard living here, arriving home with his satchel of papers over his shoulder, working in the library or striding around the park. He'd have brought life to the place, vigour and purpose.

Charles Fairfax had told her that Richard had applied to trace his birth mother a year previously as part of his struggle to come to terms with the death of his family. It had been Charles's idea to recommend Richard to Lady Joan as a researcher. He'd thought it would allow them to get to know each other before he told her about their relationship. There had been no father's name on the birth certificate, but Crispin was adamant that it must have been her brother's lover, the handsome Kenneth Lloyd. She'd told no one of Nash's insinuation that Lady Joan, and not her brother, had shot Lloyd dead.

She thought of Richard's easy manner with Lady Joan, the way he teased her and her awkward affection for him. With a little shock she realised that – without telling her that's what he was doing – he'd taken her home to meet his mother. She remembered Lady Joan's words. 'He deserved better.' Her mouth twisted. She refused even to contemplate what might have been her own place at the hall. The thought of living in that vast, chilly edifice did not appeal.

The din in the room was incredible. Helen spotted Sarah Greenley, the policewoman, standing stiffly by the door with a cup of coffee. She had last seen her at Richard's funeral a month ago. What a contrast that had been. Just Helen, Charles, Charlotte, the warden from St Christopher's Hostel and the policewoman, gathered at a soulless municipal crematorium. And two elderly strangers, shrunken and anonymous, who Helen had been shocked to discover were Richard's adoptive parents. They'd lost touch with him in recent years, the woman told her sadly, pain in her eyes. After the accident. Helen had taken her phone number, promised to go and visit.

The Christian service had left Helen feeling bleak, certain that the words were hollow. There would be no joyful reunion in the afterlife. Death did come as the end.

Helen had been back once to the church at Harbledown. The old lady had let her in, wordlessly, and left her alone. She had lit candles for Richard and Lady Joan. After a moment, she'd added one for Father Nash. She sat for a long time in Saint Thomas' chapel, glad that its secret had not been revealed. Father Nash's appalling death had brought enough notoriety to this peaceful and ancient place. Let

Saint Thomas and his secrets rest quietly. The play's epilogue, which Nash had in his jacket pocket at the time of his death, had disappeared. Helen suspected the old lady and Charles had something to do with that.

'Here. Get that down you.' Nick returned, balancing a plate loaded with vol au vents, quiche and sausage rolls. 'I don't think much of this wake. Where's the whisky?'

'Thanks.' She took it, but did not eat. He was always trying to look after her. Spending time with him was like warming yourself at a fire. She was still frozen, stiff with mourning. Nick was all life, youth and future. He seemed like a different generation.

She saw how Nick's eyes followed the young Asian reporter, Meena, around the room. The girl's respectable black hijab was sprinkled with silver stars, shimmering as she walked. Helen liked her very much, her verve and bravery. And she'd risked her life to rescue the Marlowe manuscript from the Cobham Hall fire. Helen felt guilty about keeping the play's secret from her. What would it mean to her, she wondered, to know that England's saint was possibly its first Muslim convert? Perhaps she would tell her a little of what she'd discovered, without betraying Becket's resting place.

Sarah Greenley crossed the room.

'Nick, we need to go over your statement,' she told him without preamble. 'Can you come in tomorrow?' He shrugged and agreed, then disappeared into the crowd to do his interviews. He wasn't a fan of the policewoman. Helen rather liked her; the brusqueness reminded her of Lady Joan.

'Trouble?' she asked.

The woman examined her short, neat fingernails. 'Complications. As always. Paxton wants to press charges for assault against Nick.'

'What? That's crazy.' Helen had visited Nick in hospital while his head wounds and broken wrist were being tended to. He'd needed two operations on the wrist and it had only recently come out of the cast.

'Paxton says he was tied up for some of the time they were locked in that chapel together. He has a scar on his arm from a cigarette burn. He claims Nick did it.'

Helen was silent. She knew she should jump to his defence, exclaim that he would never have done any such thing. But she couldn't. Nick had ruthlessness in him and she knew how fear and anger could bring out cruel impulses.

'Just one?' she asked, mindful of the necklace of scars around her own throat.

'Just one.'

'Good.'

They looked at Nick's back as he hustled his way into the conversation between the lawyer and the National Trust man.

'Will he be charged?' asked Helen.

'I doubt it. But it will come up in court. Paxton could claim the confession he made was under duress. It might detract from the overall case.'

Helen was dreading the court appearance, the day when she would have to tell a room full of strangers about her day and night at Paxton's mercy. 'Is there a date for the trial yet?'

'Not yet. It'll come soon enough. Your liaison officer will tell you. Which reminds me. She says you're refusing to see the counsellor.'

Helen turned her head away, irritated. 'Why does everyone keep worrying about me? I'm perfectly alright. I'm not going to crack up.'

The policewoman looked incredibly awkward as she put out a hand to pat Helen's arm. 'Post-traumatic stress. Happens to lots of people who've been through less than you. Why not meet the counsellor, see how you get on?'

Helen smiled but said nothing. She had her own way of dealing with things, and talking to a professionally sympathetic stranger was not going to be one of them. She felt restless, standing around making small talk. It was time to get out.

'I'm going for a walk. Can you tell Nick and Charlotte I've gone? I'll make my own way home.'

Moments later, she was striding across the smooth lawns, heading for the woodland and the high ground beyond. The tension eased from her shoulders as she lengthened her stride. Her face softened. She only felt truly relaxed while on the move these days, the steady rhythm calming her thoughts. At night, she lay awake replaying Nash's dreadful fall, his scream loud in her ears. Guilt choked her attempts to sleep. She frequently rose, dressed and strode into the night, walking into an exhausted dawn.

During the day, she had the all-absorbing consolation of work. Her reconstruction of the text was partly memorial, partly from her own notes, but mainly from the fragments of paper that had escaped the blaze. It was almost a collaboration, she felt, a joint production between herself and the dead playwright. When she was alone with Marlowe's words, she felt his fierce wit working through her, whispering suggestions in her ear. She was careful to keep this sensation to herself, wary of undermining her academic credentials.

Her supervisor, at first dismissive and incredulous about the new play, had finally agreed that this work could form the new basis for her doctorate. He was nominally supervising the work and had agreed to be joint author on the paper she planned to publish later this year on the discovery of the text. She felt his caution as a constraint, but perhaps a necessary one. She tried not to imagine how different the experience would have been had she been writing this with Richard.

The process of reconstructing Marlowe's work had ignited a desire to write for herself. She found now that words and phrases emerged while she walked, arranging themselves with the beat of her feet. They came from dark places, from the plague pits and burial grounds housing the countless millions of Londoners who had come and gone before her, who had trudged over the same ground.

London seemed to her a vast mausoleum, built ever higher above the remains of earlier generations. Not just their bodies but their pottery, jewels, clay pipes, shards of glass. The foundations of their buildings and the bones of animals they'd eaten, the delicate skeletons of rats that had fed on their waste. All trampled down, decade by decade, flattened by Londoners' feet. Layers of history over the centuries.

Helen found the words were revealing themselves as poems as she chipped away at them, turning them this way and that, cleaning off the dust. They felt too fragile to commit to paper just yet, but they were there, every time she walked, emerging from the London clay.

She passed through the shade of the tall beech trees, her cheeks warm now and a slight smile on her lips. In her head rang words that felt durable, phrases that would last. They would be dark poems, tales of the city that the city might not care to hear. They were there, waiting to be written. She walked on, London-bound.

Epilogue

B rother Matthew covered his ears with his hands. The noise in the school room had reached an unacceptable level. Dragging his mind back to his duties, he rose to his feet and took the willow wand from the hook on the wall.

'I'll beat the next boy who speaks out of turn.' He strained his voice, cracked now with age, to be heard above the hubbub.

The boys broke off their quarrel and returned to their seats. Some of them grinned openly and winked at their fellows. He sighed. Discipline had never come easily to him, and he could not remember the last time he had chastised one of his charges. Mostly, his unspoken agreement with them held. The boys would keep their conduct within modest bounds, and he would make his school room a refuge from the rough treatment they met outside of these walls.

Fifteen heads bent over their slates. They were the sons of the town's tradesmen and would soon be busy helping their fathers to butcher beasts, bake bread or forge iron. Before they left his care, he would be sure they had their letters, and could reckon their accounts. Some – his gaze fell on one head of chestnut curls, copying from his primer with a suspiciously industrious air – were capable of far more. Sharp as a lancet, and well deserving of a place at the King's School. His eyes lingered for a moment on the boy's handsome face.

The message that had arrived at Eastbridge that afternoon had come as a shock. The waif who delivered it had a frightened, half-starved look, and had not waited for payment or reply. Matthew wondered who had sent him. Archbishop Parker, perhaps, wanting to keep his distance? The situation was urgent and delicate: a visit from Queen Elizabeth, who would stop at Harbledown on her progress to Canterbury Cathedral. The Queen wished to view the church and give alms to the poor, as her predecessors had done. But the work in the chapel in St Nicholas' church was incomplete and the contents of the grave almost an open secret among the inmates of the almshouses. He needed to warn them, tell them to complete the work with all haste, remove the martyr's lamp and – above all – to cover the tombstone before the week was out.

Eastbridge had not thought any urgency in completing the work that had been set in train so many decades ago. The church had been chosen for its humble location: a poor parish just outside the city, unlikely to come to notice. Forty years ago, thought Matthew, feeling every one of them in his bones. He'd been the same age as his charges were now, fourteen or fifteen, a novice with the Christchurch monks. He had prayed at Saint Thomas' shrine the night the message came that the Royal Commissioners were on the road to Canterbury. And not just the commissioners, but Thomas Cromwell himself, the old sinner. Come to ensure the jewels all found their way to the King's treasury – or to his own brass-bound coffers, if you believed the rumours.

Prior Goldwell had led them in prayer through the night. As a boy, Matthew had found it hard to stay still during lengthy vigils, but that night he had prayed fiercely, like a soldier might pray before battle. He had pledged himself to protect the holy martyr's sacred body. The rest was mere baubles and glitter. Let them take it and be damned.

But what baubles. Matthew remembered how the candles' flames had glinted off the golden canopy, studded with rubies and beryl that glowed in the flickering light.

The next morning Prior Goldwell had appointed him messenger, riding hard with secret letters. He had been glad to be given the task, which better suited an ardent boy than watching and praying with the older monks. With the monastery's gold seal in hand, he'd travelled the Pilgrim's Way to Winchester, where Saint Swithun's shrine was also threatened. From Winchester, he rode to London itself, a bewildering morass of people and buildings. He had met with messengers from as far north as York and Durham. The monks of Durham had a plan to protect their beloved Saint Cuthbert. They would remove the saint's body and replace it with another skeleton until such time as the danger had passed. The news had flown home to Canterbury, where the Christchurch monks had adopted the plan as their own.

He'd been there, the night they uncovered the saint's body. And found, clasped in the bony hands, the holy book. Not, as he had expected, the sacred testament of Christ. A little book, bound in vellum, crawling with foreign script that bore no relation to Christian language. Instead of a cross, the cover was decorated with a crescent moon.

He'd looked up to Prior Goldwell, fearful. 'Is it magic? Heathen necromancy?'

The old man had taken the book in his hands, his rheumy eyes overflowing. 'No, son.' He'd turned it in his hands, examined the heathen text. 'I had heard stories... but I thought they were just rumours. To discredit our blessed saint.'

The book, the prior explained, was the Alcoran, testament of the Mahometan faith professed by the Turks and Moors. It must be very ancient, he'd said, from the time when Christian knights rode out to liberate Jerusalem. 'They say that the faith is, in many ways, not so different from our own. That the Moors revere our Lord Jesus Christ and worship one Almighty God, as we do. Perhaps Saint Thomas wished to reconcile our faiths, to heal the divisions of the wars.'

The prior had ordered that the book be reburied with the saint's body in St Nicholas' church. 'We do not know what was in his heart,' he'd told the monks. 'But we see what was in his hands. We trust in him, and in the Lord, to carry out his will.' The good old man had spoken to the stonemason at Harbledown, and the tombstone placed above the grave was adorned with not just the cross of the crucifixion, but the Turk's symbol of the crescent moon.

Matthew had not seen the shrine again. By the time the commissioners arrived, he was back on the road. He remembered the thrill of galloping horses, the fear that he'd be stopped by the King's men and searched, his letters discovered. He'd felt a driving sense of purpose, that he was working as God's instrument on earth. And he remembered the sickening sights, the destruction of so much beauty in God's houses. Cart-loads of treasure dragged away, statues of the Virgin and the saints pulled down and smashed. Bonfires of painted panels, the saints' sweet faces shrivelling and blackening in the flames.

After the destruction of the shrine, Matthew had been allowed to join the new foundation, although Prior Goldwell and many of the older monks were thrown onto the streets. The temporary reburial of Saint Thomas Becket settled into a lasting solution as King Edward succeeded King Henry and Queen Mary succeeded him. Horror compounded horror, the bonfires of icons succeeded by worse outrages. He remembered the first time he'd seen men and women burned for their faith, the stench of roasting flesh and the ragged screams. Like many a professed man of God, he had toiled quietly and avoided notice. His reward, this place as Eastbridge's school master, suited him well. He was not proud of his silence. And yet he had survived, been spared the fire, the noose, the sickness that had carried off so many townsfolk during those turbulent years.

All for what? For today, perhaps. Saint Thomas needed him again. He drew out paper and ink and began to write. Master Lawes was out of town, on a visit to the university at Cambridge to speak to his former college about scholarships for Canterbury boys. In his absence, Matthew had charge of the Eastbridge coffers. He wrote swiftly, authorising the brothers at Harbledown to pay whatever was necessary to complete the work in the chapel, cover the tombstone, and to ensure the silence of the workmen. He picked up the big golden seal and thought for a moment. They would need the seal itself to guarantee the payments. He needed a trustworthy messenger, one with faster legs than his own, who would not be suspected or stopped on his way.

Through the window came the sound of the cathedral bells tolling the hour. The boys rose, clattering their stools on the bare boards of the school room floor.

'Wait,' called Father Matthew. He sought for the chestnut-curled lad with the bold stare and the quick wit. He was tussling with his neighbour. 'Come here, boy. I have a commission for you.'

He bounced up to the desk. 'I'm willing, sir. What will you pay me?'

Matthew raised his eyebrows. 'Take this letter and seal to the priest at Saint Nicholas in Harbledown. Go by the West Gate, quickly, so you can be back before sun down. Your service will not go unrewarded, I promise you. Master Lawes shall hear of it, and Archbishop Parker.'

The boy's face took on a faraway look. 'Is it true that Master Lawes plans to send boys to the university?' The lad didn't miss a thing.

'He hopes to be able to do so, yes. Good boys who work hard and obey their masters.'

The lad grinned and put the letter and seal into his shirt. 'Trust me, Father Matthew,' he said, and darted away.

The old man crossed himself as he walked slowly around the little school room, making sure that the floor was clear of apple cores and walnut shells. Only when he got back to his desk did he realise that he had forgotten to seal the letter before he handed it over. He went to the window, but young Kit Marlowe had disappeared into the busy Canterbury street.

Notes

The historical background to *Unlawful Things*, including the trial of Walter Raleigh and Henry Cobham, the death of Christopher Marlowe and the destruction of Thomas Becket's shrine in Canterbury, are based on real events. I have however played fast and loose with history, inventing my own versions.

Notably, Cobham Hall is now a private school. It is not inhabited by the Lords of Cobham who replaced the Brooke family in the 17th century. Eastbridge Hospital does not have any secret knowledge about the whereabouts of the remains of Thomas Becket, and certainly did not arrange for the murder of Christopher Marlowe.

There is sadly no evidence that Christopher Marlowe ever wrote a play about Thomas Becket, or that Becket's body survived the destruction of his shrine at the hands of Henry VIII's commissioners.

Many of the settings for *Unlawful Things* are real, however, and can be visited. Why not take Helen's tour of Shakespeare and Marlowe's London? Subscribers to my mailing list receive a free hand-drawn annotated map, with exclusive photographs and information about the historical sites on Helen's Southwark tour, as well as updates on news and special offers. Sign up at www.annasayburnlane.com.

If you enjoyed this book, please consider writing a review and help other people to discover Unlawful Things.

Acknowledgements

Thanks to all who helped with my research for *Unlawful Things*, including Dulwich College Archive, the British Library and the National Archives. Thank you to my writing group for your unfailing support. Thank you to my English teachers, who introduced me to Marlowe, Chaucer and Shakespeare. Above all, thank you to my lovely Philip, for everything.

Bibliography

I read a lot while researching *Unlawful Things*. Here are some of my inspirations and sources. None of them should be held responsible for anything I may have got wrong.

- Jerry Brotton, *This Orient Isle: Elizabethan England and the Islamic World*
- John Cooper, *The Queen's Agent: Francis Walsingham at the Court of Elizabeth I*
- Charles Nicholl, *The Reckoning: The Murder of Christopher Marlowe*
- David Riggs, *The World of Christopher Marlowe*
- Simon Singh, *The Code Book: The Secret History of Codes and Code-breaking*

- Esme Wingfield-Stratford, *The Lords of Cobham Hall*

I referred to the following editions of Chaucer and Marlowe:
- Geoffrey Chaucer, *The Canterbury Tales*. Wordsworth Poetry Library 2002
- Christopher Marlowe, *The Complete Plays*. Penguin Classics 2003
- Christopher Marlowe, *The Complete Poems and Translations*. Penguin Classics 2007

About the Author

Anna Sayburn Lane is a writer, editor and journalist. She lives in south London. *Unlawful Things* is her first novel.

You can connect with me on:
- 🌐 http:www.annasayburnlane.com
- 🐦 https://twitter.com/BloomsburyBlue
- 📘 https://www.facebook.com/annasayburnlane

Subscribe to my newsletter:
- ✉ http://eepurl.com/dyUtmX